PENGUIN BOOKS

JOURNEY TO ITHACA

Anita Desai was born in Mussorie, India, and was educated in Delhi. Her published works include short stories, children's books, and nine novels. Two of her novels, *Clear Light of Day* (1980) and *In Custody* (1984), were short-listed for England's celebrated Booker Prize. *In Custody* has recently been made into a full-length feature film by Merchant Ivory Productions.

Anita Desai teaches in the writing program at MIT and lives in Cambridge, Massachusetts.

Journey
to Ithaca

Anita Desai

PENGUIN BOOKS

PENGUIN BOOKS
Published by the Penguin Group
Penguin Books USA Inc., 375 Hudson Street, New York, New York 10014, U.S.A.
Penguin Books Ltd, 27 Wrights Lane, London W8 5TZ, England
Penguin Books Australia Ltd, Ringwood, Victoria, Australia
Penguin Books Canada Ltd, 10 Alcorn Avenue, Toronto, Ontario, Canada M4V 3B2
Penguin Books (N.Z.) Ltd, 182–190 Wairau Road, Auckland 10, New Zealand

Penguin Books Ltd, Registered Offices: Harmondsworth, Middlesex, England

First published in Great Britain by William Heinemann Ltd., 1995
First published in the United States of America by Alfred A. Knopf, Inc. 1995
Reprinted by arrangement with Alfred A. Knopf, Inc.
Published in Penguin Books 1996

3   5   7   9   10   8   6   4   2

Grateful acknowledgment is made to the following for permission
to reprint previously published material:

Farrar, Straus & Giroux, Inc.: Excerpts from *The Journey to the East* by Hermann Hesse, translated by
Hilda Rosner, copyright © 1956 by Hermann Hesse; "Death" from *Poet in New York* by Federico
García Lorca, translated by Greg Simon and Steven F. White, translation copyright © 1988 by the
Estate of Federico García Lorca and Greg Simon and Steven F. White.
Reprinted by permission of Farrar, Straus & Giroux, Inc.

Harcourt Brace & Company: "Ithaca" from *The Complete Poems of Cavafy* by C. P. Cavafy, translated by
Rae Dalven, copyright © 1961 and copyright renewed 1989 by Rae Dalven.
Reprinted by permission of Harcourt Brace & Company.

Milan Kundera: Excerpt from *Immortality* by Milan Kundera.
Reprinted by permission of Milan Kundera.

THE LIBRARY OF CONGRESS HAS CATALOGUED THE KNOPF EDITION AS FOLLOWS:
Desai, Anita, [date]
Journey to Ithaca/Anita Desai.—1st ed.
p.   cm.
ISBN 0-679-43900-5 (hc.)
ISBN 0 14 02.5818 3 (pbk.)
I. Title.
PR9499.3.D465J68   1995
823—dc20   95–841

Printed in the United States of America
Set in Bembo

For Kiran, Tani, Arjun and Rahul

Then pray that the journey is long.
That the summer mornings are many,
that you will enter ports seen for the first time
with such pleasure, with such joy!
Stop at Phoenician markets
and purchase fine merchandise,
mother-of-pearl and corals, amber and ebony,
and pleasurable perfumes of all kinds,
buy as many pleasurable perfumes as you can;
visit hosts of Egyptian cities,
to learn and learn from those who have knowledge.

Always keep Ithaca fixed in your mind.
To arrive there is your ultimate goal.
But do not hurry the voyage at all.
It is better to let it last for long years;
and even to anchor at the isle when you are old,
rich with all you have gained on the way,
not expecting that Ithaca will offer you riches.

Ithaca has given you a beautiful voyage.
Without her you would never have taken the road.
But she has nothing to give you now.

And if you have found her poor, Ithaca has not defrauded
you.
With such great wisdom you have gained, with so much
experience
you must surely have understood by then what Ithacas
mean.

     C.P. Cavafy, *Ithaca* (translated by Rae Dalven)

. . . things exist in their essence even before they are
materially realized and named.

     Milan Kundera, *Immortality*

Journey to Ithaca

❖Prologue❖

She was taken up the stairs to the upper floor and shown into the room where he lay on an iron cot, clothed only in pyjamas and the upper half of his body emaciated and moist with perspiration. Sophie thought he must be dying.

To begin with she bent over the cot and over him, then she sat on its edge and held his hand in hers, and although his eyes were open and looked in her direction, she could not tell if he recognised her.

'Matteo, Matteo,' she said again and again, her voice harsh with despair and accusation.

He would not speak her name in return but she thought he saw her from the way he clutched at her hand. Then he closed his eyes and tears of distress slipped from beneath his lids.

Later she set about making the room hers as well; she had a rucksack and she pulled out some clothes and a limp grey towel. In search of water, she found at the end of a corridor a communal washroom where she was able to bathe in luke-warm water from a tap. Squatting to soap herself, she remembered how she had first learnt to bathe from a bucket under a tap, so awkwardly. She remembered the ways of bathing publicly – the techniques of efficiency and modesty – and used them again. Everything came back, without her trying.

At one point in the afternoon, when the flies dizzily knocking against the closed window and the heat accumulating under the ceiling of the room made staying awake almost impossible, a male nurse in dark green clothing brought a tall steel glass of tea and a plate of biscuits, small sweet biscuits of the kind one buys cheap in the bazaar. She devoured them, for Matteo was still asleep, only occasionally twitching if he felt a fly crawl upon him. She saw that his skin was scarred with boils and drew back her lip in a hiss of horror. When she brushed the biscuit crumbs off herself a swarm of ants immediately arrived as if out of the dark cement of the floor to carry them away.

Later that evening when the harsh afternoon light was gone and it was possible to open the windows to the veranda where the air was cooler and the light darker, a doctor came to see Matteo, placed a dark square hand on his forehead with a large ring set with a square red stone just at the temple, felt his pulse with his other hand and made some notes on a paper clipped to a board.

As he turned to go, she ran after him. 'Doctor,' she cried hoarsely, and he stopped at once and listened politely to her questions and spoke reassuringly. It took her a minute or two to accustom herself to his accent which belonged, stubbornly, to his own tongue, not the English he spoke. He said he had seen, and cured, worse cases, that Matteo would recover if he was nursed carefully and that her coming would greatly help the process, that there was no reason to fear a relapse or further deterioration if care was taken. She looked hard to see if she could detect a lie but he seemed straightforward if a little anxious to get away.

'He came from the ashram?' he asked finally, in the Indian way making a declarative sentence sound interrogative.

Sophie noticed in that non-professional moment that his teeth were stained red with betel-juice. She nodded and turned away: the sight always sickened her slightly. She turned back, stopping at the veranda balustrade to look down into the central courtyard with its grassy square, its few palm trees, its benches on which families sat waiting or picnicking, the circular drive on which they descended from bicycle

2

rickshaws and cars and tongas, and the big gates at the end opening onto a city road with its bus stop, its fruit barrows, its kiosks for soda water and cigarettes in bundles. She went back to the room, passing on the way other rooms to which doors and windows stood open now so that she could look in and see, without wanting to, patients lying or sitting on the edge of their beds in green cotton shifts, and families huddled around them in attitudes concerned, solicitous, tired or bored. It might have been an old, shabby hotel, only the strong smells of disinfectant and medication gave it away for what it was.

As if to prove the doctor's prognosis, Matteo had propped himself up on his grimy grey pillow when she returned. He looked at her with an expression she recognised: humble, pleading, begging to be understood. It had always irritated her.

'So, Matteo,' she said, more drily than she had meant. 'If the Mother is ill, it seems the devotees must fall ill too. Is she some pharaoh to take you all to the tomb with her?' She could say such things and people listened: she was a big, strong woman, square-shouldered; she wore her hair cut short and her eyes were a level grey. 'If you stay, you will kill yourself.'

He twitched a little and scratched at his arm. 'I fell ill,' he whined. 'One can fall ill, Sophie – one can fall ill anywhere.'

'Oh yes,' she mocked, 'with hepatitis. Yes, anywhere,' she said sarcastically. 'In Europe. At home on the lake, I suppose.'

'If not this, then something else,' he said with a sudden show of spirit. But he looked beaten, his shoulders began to sink against the pillow. The whine entered his voice again as he complained, 'You left me. I was alone.'

'Oh, I left you, was that it?' She could not repress the anger. 'And did you want me? Did you even notice if I stayed or left?'

He lifted his hand as if to ward off her anger, then dropped it to his forehead and kept it clasped there – she thought theatrically.

'All you wanted was the Mother,' she reminded him passionately. 'You told me that. You said you needed the Mother – not me, not the children.'

He made a small sound like a sob. She had to remind herself he had been very ill and was very weak. She made herself lift a glass of sweet lime juice the nurse had left on the table and hold it to his lips. 'Drink,' she told him sternly, but she knew she would have to be stern with herself too. She must not tire him by talking, or distress him by her accusations till he had recovered. Till then, she would have to be more patient, more tolerant, as if he were a child, not a man.

Late at night, when the other patients slept, Sophie ran her fingers through his hair, spreading it out on the flat pillow, to soothe him. He lay still and let her comb his hair over and over, with her fingers. When he seemed entirely at peace, possibly even asleep, she leant closer to him and murmured, 'When you are well, Matteo, we will leave.'

She should have been prepared but she was startled by the jerk he gave, stiffening his neck and twisting his head away from her touch. She had thought only a healthy person could react so strongly. She had overestimated his weakness, and compliance, not for the first time.

'You will leave, Sophie,' he hissed fiercely, 'but not I,' and he covered his eyes with his arm. Now she could see only his mouth in the dim light from the veranda, very pale and trembling, with a growth of beard around it like a brush, or thorns.

'Why, Matteo, why?' she begged very softly, keeping her hand near his cheek, on the pillow. 'Why can we not be together again, at home with the children?'

He did not trouble to answer her. He shook his head very slightly, as if he were shaking off a fly that bothered him. The gesture said plainly: they did not count, they were what he had left behind.

⌒

'Isabel! Isabel!' A short pause and then, again, 'Isabel! Isabel!'

The child looks up at the insistence of the voice, reluctantly surrendering her occupation of watering a bed of pinks. She forgets to lift up the watering can as well and it continues to spout, onto her shoe. She stands in her white pinafore, holding the dripping can, and lifts her face up to the open window where her grandmother stands, full of rebuke.

'Isabel, don't get yourself wet!'

Now Isabel remembers to right the watering can but it is too late – her shoe is wet, her sock is soaking. She looks down at them in dismay, and lets the watering can drop onto the gravel. There it lies, under the glint of waxy magnolia leaves. The bed of pinks has been half watered, and half is white with dust. Their clove-like fragrance, too, is partly released by the watering can and partly obliterated by the dust.

'Isabel! Where is Giacomo? Have you seen Giacomo?' Grandmother persists in pursuing her.

'I'll go and look for him, Nonna,' Isabel responds. She walks down the gravelled path, away from the house. The whole garden stretches, falls away, retrieves itself on another level, and another. Giacomo might be anywhere. She can wander in search of him down a pergola of wistaria, past an urn at the end of it that holds marble pineapples and marble grapes, around box-edged beds of artemisia and rosemary, into the empty hothouse where the sun thrums upon the dust-filmed glass and rouses invisible crickets to audible ecstasy. Beyond it is the compost heap, a territory fiercely guarded by the gardener. So Isabel turns back and climbs flight after flight of stairs to the upper terrace where, on the gravel beneath the camellia tree, her grandfather sits on a canvas chair, his face covered by a newspaper and a bottle of mineral water and a glass beside him, while Giacomo, on a stool, sits stitching, on a square of cardboard, a sunflower in bright yellow wool.

He stops stitching when he sees her approach and says immediately, 'You've wet your shoe, Isabel.'

'I know,' she says miserably. She has been squelching up and down the garden in that wetness. She sits on the edge of another canvas chair, too large for her, hazardously.

Grandfather lifts the newspaper from his head and looks at

her with eyes so pale they do not seem properly equipped for sight. 'You have wet your shoe, Isabel?' he asks.

She is tired of it suddenly – the wet shoe, the accusation, the guilt. She pulls it off her foot, and then the sock, and flings them down on the gravel. For good measure she pulls off the other sock and shoe as well. Her feet emerge, plump and brightly pink. She kicks them up and down in the air, hilariously. The cold air on her feet tingles and refreshes.

'Nonna will see,' Giacomo warns her.

'Nonna will be angry,' Grandfather agrees.

But Isabel has slipped off the canvas chair and is running over the gravel. It cuts into her feet painfully but the pain is exhilarating. She likes it much better than the sock and shoe, dry or wet.

When Grandmother comes down to join the group under the camellias, Isabel has already climbed the grassy slope that rises to the top of the hill where the stones of a ruined folly lie under a clump of pine trees. She is flapping her white pinafore with her hands, trying to catch two butterflies – one white, one yellow, like the primulas in the grass. Grandmother does not notice; she has forgotten that she wanted Giacomo. Instead, she is holding out a letter to Grandfather, one of those soggy, limp Indian aerogrammes that look as if they have travelled a long and difficult way over the Indian plains and across the oceans.

Giacomo has noticed; he wants to ask, 'Is it from Mama?' but stops himself because it is unnecessary. Instead, he stares steadfastly at the letter, watching as it passes to his grandfather's long, dry fingers. As he had hoped, Grandfather complains, 'I haven't my spectacles with me. Read it, Livia.' Grandmother gives a meaning look at Giacomo and he drops his gaze, embarrassed to be present. But he does not get up and follow Isabel: he will stay and hear what he can.

'Is it from Mama?' he asks after all, unable to stop.

'Of course,' she replies. 'Who else will write from that benighted country? Your father?'

Giacomo picks at the wool stitching on the cardboard

square, considering taking it up as a safe alternative to Grandmother's temper when aroused by news from his parents. But she snaps at him, 'Sewing again, like a girl. Is that for you to do, or should it be for Isabel?' and he guiltily puts it down. She does not notice, she is holding the letter under Grandfather's nose accusingly and he thinks it wiser to escape after all. Slipping off the stool, he slides away sideways. Once around the geranium pots and over the gravel, he makes a run for it up the slope of the hill, towards Isabel who has vanished into its higher reaches. Down below Grandmother is shouting, 'Now it is a round-the-world trip she is going on! How long will her parents indulge her? Eh? They have only to stop sending them money and those two will come home straight away. But whatever she wants, she is given. Isn't it time for them to grow up and take responsibility? Eh?' The rest Giacomo knows by heart already.

He finds Isabel behind the tumbled stones of the folly, sitting under a cluster of pines beside the stone basin of water in a clump of rushes from which a trickle falls by way of a dolphin's mouth into a narrow stream. He had known he would find her there: for Isabel the basin is an ocean, and the two aged goldfish that live concealed beneath the waterweeds, a fleet of whales. He has never been able to prove to her her naiveté.

'I saw the heron by the pond below,' he tells her threateningly: something in her placid contentment stirs in him the desire to wreck it.

'No, you didn't,' she replies stoutly.

'I did. It's looking for your goldfish, you know.'

'But it won't find them,' she says, still more spiritedly, although with an effort. 'They hide.'

'The heron's eye is sharper than you know.'

'Not like mine,' she says, putting her hands around her eyes to make binoculars through which she peers at him.

'Much better than yours,' he tells her. 'Much, much better.' But he is arguing aimlessly, only for the sake of not saying what he needs to say. Suddenly he forgets why he is arguing with her, and sits down on the grass beside her. 'I think Nonna wants us to leave,' he says miserably.

She turns on him. 'No, she doesn't. She won't. She won't let us go to Mama and Papa.'

'I know she won't. But she doesn't like us *here*.'

Isabel is quiet, separating two ideas and then putting them together again: Grandmother does not want them to go to their parents, and Grandmother does not want them here. 'Then where can we go?' she asks, not knowing a third place for themselves.

Giacomo can't say. He knows about herons, about goldfish, about cross-stitch, but not about themselves. He tears up tufts of grass which come away easily from the damp earth by the trickling water. Primulas and hepaticas come away with it; he is managing considerable havoc, however miniature the scale.

So Isabel pulls herself together. She sets her jaw and it gives her an elderly look (she looks, in fact, not unlike her grandmother). 'We can run away,' she says hoarsely, speaking the words she has heard in fairytales, testing them for their possibilities.

Giacomo looks at her from under his heavy brows. He would like to believe her.

Isabel sees she has him in her hold. She crosses her legs nonchalantly. 'We can pack some clothes in a tablecloth,' she says, 'and steal bread and cheese from the kitchen. And run away at night, after they go to bed. You can unlock the door, Giacomo.'

He nods, yes. He wants to believe, but it is for what comes after that he looks to her in appeal.

She sees his look and reaches out her hand. At first it just lies on his knee, damp and not very clean. When she feels it trembling a little, she begins to pat and stroke it as Grandmother does the dough when she is making bread. Like bread, it rises and grows larger. Giacomo feels its weight; his whole leg aches for her stroke, her touch. The ache travels up to his groin, where it is a pain, a throb. With a small sigh, he lies down against her side, burrows into her lap, snuffling like a

8

puppy, breathing in her damp, female smell. His face in her lap, he nuzzles her, breathing her, and she puts her hands on either side of his head, pulling him in, closer. 'Down,' she mumbles, 'down *here*, Giacomo.'

They make programme cards with stiff pieces of yellow paper they have cut out and pasted over with butterflies from one of Grandfather's books in the library. Their skill in spelling is too rudimentary to give the audience any idea of what to expect.

What they see, when they settle onto the dining chairs the children have dragged into a row, is Giacomo in velvet shorts kneeling before a gilt Buddha he has brought out of the marble fireplace where it stands amongst potted plants in the summer when they do not light fires. He kneels and bows and prays in a low mumble while from behind the curtain which is a tablecloth draped low over the edge of the dining table, Isabel's voice hisses directions. In response to them, he picks up the bell with which Grandmother summons the maid at meals, and rings and rings.

Instead of the maid – who is standing in the doorway, giggling so hard that every now and then she snorts inadvertently and has to cover her mouth with her hands – it is Isabel who appears with a flourish of a peacock feather fan. As she prances around, the audience discovers that she is quite naked except for the maid's apron that she has tied around her neck and that falls to her feet in starched folds of muslin. While Grandmother and the maid gasp and Grandfather blinks his eyes almost audibly behind his spectacles, Isabel begins to dance. Giacomo, remembering his role, dives under the tablecloth and frenziedly cranks up the gramophone. The music that issues from it, rustily but loudly, is *Anitra's Dance* from *Peer Gynt*. To its exotic and vaguely eastern rhythm, Isabel gyrates and gestures theatrically, revealing her bare bottom to muffled shrieks from the maid and a harsh intake of breath from the grandmother. She has just come to a standstill and raised her arms and opened her fists to let fall handfuls of geranium petals on Giacomo – who has resumed his kneeling

9

posture before the Buddha – when Grandmother rises to her feet with a great thump and shouts, 'Stop! Stop at *once*. Isabel, go to your room. At *once*!' Her voice is like a rent torn through a dress. The child falters, gathering the gauze of her apron about her. Giacomo turns around to study the effect of their performance on the audience. He had warned Isabel but she had not listened. 'Mama lets us dress up and dance,' she had said, but Grandmother is approaching her with an outstretched hand, preparing to smack the shameless bottom. When the smack descends, it is Giacomo who howls. While Isabel goes red and silent, he wails, 'We're only acting a play, Nonna, about India.'

'A fine play!' she turns upon him. 'A fine play!' The look in her eyes is not only terrifying for Giacomo but terrified. 'This is what your father and mother brought you up to do, is it?'

This is so unfair – it seems years since he lived with his parents, years and years – he begins to snivel.

Isabel, her hands over her smarting bottom, backs away, blazing. 'I'll write and tell Mama what you did. I'll tell Papa.'

Grandmother watches Isabel as she lifts her cup with both hands and drinks deeply, leaving behind a moustache of chocolate on her upper lip. For some reason, she refrains from passing Isabel a napkin to wipe it off; instead, she pushes a plate of pastries across the table to her and watches while the child chooses gravely and after deep deliberation.

Isabel knows she is being given a bribe to make up for Giacomo's departure that morning. What Grandmother does not realise is that it is too early for sorrow or loneliness to have set in; half an hour ago Isabel was standing on the gravel driveway by the magnolia tree, waving as her brother was driven away to his aunt's home in Milan, and now already she was being given hot chocolate, pastries and a pink ice in a black glass goblet: they add up to a pressure, a weight that sits on her belly – too rich, too sweet. She burps uncomfortably.

Grandmother smiles faintly, pretending not to mind. She sits upright at the table under the single palm tree in its circle of paintbox-coloured primulas. She is wearing a hat that has been smart in its time: now its grey flannel brim and its pheasant's feather look a bit pathetic. Isabel might even feel a little sorry for her but what she cannot bear is the long thin fur that is lying on her shoulders and hangs down on either side, limply, so dreadfully dead.

When Isabel has chosen her pastry and is nibbling at its crust, Grandmother relaxes and leans back in the sun that gilds the cream-coloured walls of the Hotel Metropole and the small glassy waves of the lake before them.

'Giacomo will soon settle down,' she says, as much to herself as to Isabel. 'I know it – he is not rebellious like your father.'

'Papa?' Isabel halts the inroad she is making into the soft almond paste that fills her pastry, and waits, listening.

'Matteo could not stand the school from the first day to the last,' Grandmother continues, almost proudly. 'He couldn't take orders from the teachers. They could not make him do his lessons or sing or play football, it didn't matter what they did to him.'

'What did they do?' Isabel asks in a stifled voice. She feels the hot chocolate and the almond paste come together in her throat and rise in protest.

'Oh, they complained to his uncle and sent notes. Maybe gave him a smack on his knuckles now and then, nothing more,' Grandmother says, gaily almost, aware of the effect she is having on the child. 'In those days that was not so uncommon. But Matteo could not take it at all. Now Giacomo is different.'

Isabel is not at all sure. She gulps at the thought of Giacomo being threatened or intimidated. She knows he is not brave.

Her silence makes Grandmother forget her presence. She talks on, less guardedly. 'The football was the worst. Matteo would not play. He would get knocked down and trampled and he would not get up and play,' she recalls. 'His uncle minded that most – *his* sons were all such first-class players.' She taps her tiny cup of espresso with a small spoon; it rings out clearly, with a melancholy air. She looks at Isabel, remembering her. 'Now Giacomo will be happy there, playing football with the other boys. He had no one to play with here.'

'He had me,' Isabel reminds her bitterly. She is breaking the pastry crust into crumbs on the plate, and has lost all her appetite.

'A boy needs company of his own kind. He will have that in Milan, in his aunt's house and at school,' Grandmother explains. 'For your father, we got a tutor when he came back from school, and that was not good. It was not a good idea. I would not want that for Giacomo.'

'Why?' asks Isabel.

But Grandmother has opened her purse, she is taking out coins, paying the bill. Isabel follows her to the car and climbs in beside her. The chauffeur starts it and they begin to climb up the hill to the villa. Isabel watches the view of the lake with its fringe of flowering oleanders and the white façade of the hotels fall away below them, then turns to ask, 'Why won't you have a tutor for Giacomo, too, Nonna?'

Grandmother gives her an irritated look very far from the look reserved for the hotel and the waiter and the guests sipping coffee and eating ices at tables in the sun. She fidgets with the fox fur – it is too warm for it. 'Because it would not be a good idea,' she repeats.

'Did the tutor smack Papa?'

'No, no, he did not beat him at all,' Grandmother snaps and looks out of the window as the car sweeps past the wrought-iron gates of a neighbour's villa with a view of a bank of pink camellias. More thoughtfully, she murmurs, 'He was a Booda – a Boodi – what's it called?'

'A Booda?' Isabel's eyes grow dark and grave. 'Like the one in the fireplace?'

'Oh, something eastern and foolish,' Grandmother cries, thoroughly irritated by now. 'They have them in the east.'

'In India?'

'Don't ask me,' Grandmother snaps. What made her take

12

the child out for a chocolate? What a mistake all this fussing and spoiling is; much better have done a spot of gardening instead. 'I know nothing about India.'

'I was born there,' Isabel reminds her accusingly, and suddenly tears well up in her eyes. She dips her face down so Grandmother will not see. She tries to keep the sniffling to herself and yet the tears run, she has no idea whether for Giacomo or for her disregarded birth or the nausea which is a result of eating too much cake and chocolate. Searching in her pocket for a handkerchief, she finds a button she had meant to give to Giacomo as a keepsake, a brass button with a greenish dragon on it. Now the howls break from her unrestrained, and the button falls to her lap.

'That is the button from my sewing box,' Grandmother cries, snatching it up. 'Where did you find it? Why are you crying? Do stop, Isabel.'

Early in the mornings now Isabel creeps into her grand-mother's room when she knows Nonna will be sitting up in bed with the cup of coffee the maid has brought her on a small tray painted with golden grapes and silver birds. Her feet chilled by the marble squares of the floor, she jumps into the bed and snuggles against Nonna's flannel sides. 'Oh Isabel,' Grandmother gives a sharp cry, 'you are so *cold*.' Then she pulls the quilt up to the child's chin and says severely, 'You must get warm.'

Isabel's toes curl up; she lies against the pillows, feeling herself surrounded by warmth and softness. The light that comes in at the french windows that open onto the balcony is still pale, almost silvery. This has become her time for talking about Giacomo. Now that he is away in Milan, living in his aunt's house and going to school there, she feels the urge to recreate him through speech, and since that has its limitations she stretches the attempt with questions regarding their father, who had once done much the same. She realises she has a double prey and stalks them carefully, prowling along in search of secrets.

To begin with, Matteo cannot be separated and made to stand clear of all the uneven surfaces, the subtle colourings and the shadowy interweavings that construct the house and their family. He dwells in them, a part of the pattern of the Chinese silk screens in the bedrooms, no more than a grey and white moth's wings brushing across the ivory silks, and the merest shadow in the tapestries in the hall, thickly woven forests of blue in which birds hang suspended in silence and apples redden sunlessly. He hides from Nonna, and from Isabel, in the rushes of the lake in the great tapestry that hangs over the table in the hall, together with a stag that has been driven into its waters by baying hounds while the huntsman blows his horn to summon the hunter with the knife for the kill.

Frightened out of hiding, Matteo leaps up into the chandeliers like a small monkey, and hangs there, no more than a velvet tassel, of olive or mahogany silk, or a spray of bronze ivy or mistletoe or leaves of crystal that catch the light and separate it into fragments of ice.

If Isabel tiptoes in to find him, if she catches at a corner of the tapestry and shakes it or pushes a brocade-upholstered chair out of a dusty corner or draws a forbidden book off a shelf in the library, Matteo flees, as thirty years previously he had fled from his mother. The garden has even greater possibilities for hiding for one so skilled. Isabel knows it well but Matteo knows it better. In the pergola of orange and lemon trees, he hides under the leaves while her eyes are drawn to the bright globes of fruit. He does not hide in the fountain where water spouts from the dolphin's mouth but under the lily pads, with the frogs and their floating threads of spawn. In the hothouse he sits with the crickets under the upturned flowerpots, silent while they sing. The terraces fall further and further down the hill till they come to the red brick wall that separates the garden from the village. In that brick wall there is a wooden door. It is kept locked and Isabel does not have the key.

● ● ●

Everywhere Mama followed him and found him. Matteo did not know that he had left tracks, spoor that she could spy: the moth-wing silk patterns blurred, the tapestries disturbed – the startled eye of a parrot on the pomegranate tree, the stag's head turned in a direction other than the baying of hounds – and the chandeliers faintly tinkling, or merely jarred, with so minute a sound that no one heard but Mama. Then, in triumph, she cried, 'There you are!' Matteo stood frozen, and did not know if he was glad she had come to put an end to his flight, or if it meant a defeat and he was captured. So he locked one leg around the other, put his finger in his mouth, and looked uncertain. 'What is wrong, child?' she cried, and seeing him start, lamented, 'Child, child, what will we do with you?' She had her ways of catching and holding him: the doctor brought in to look down his throat and peer into his ears with a minute torch-light, cups of warm milk and woollen stockings, beef stews and soups, cold baths and dips in the lake. These were like nets and traps with which she held him but she could hardly be unaware how he squirmed. 'Who would believe you are a child of this house, that this house belongs to you?' she cried in vexation as he struggled.

Only when she did not try so hard did he come to a standstill. Then, to her own astonishment and joy, she would find she had him in her hands. In bed with one of his frequent colds, he sat up against the pillows and she did her sewing on a chair beside him. It was his pleasure to have her sewing box open across the quilt on his knees, and to lift off its lid – the satin-wood intricately inlaid with a pattern of vine leaves, and at its centre an oval of ivory painted with the picture of a lady clinging to a shadowy tree on which a peacock sat trailing its golden tail down the branches onto her shoulders, where it mingled with her open golden hair. Inside, the box was as fascinating as outside for it consisted of trays that could be lifted off each other, and each was divided into a series of compartments – one for needles and thimbles, another for reels of thread in every shade of colour, a third for a plump velvet pincushion and a long slithering tape measure, and more than one for a glorious collection of buttons that Matteo never tired of sorting into groups across the silk coverlet. There was one he never placed in any group but kept always separate – a brass button carved with a green dragon that seemed too splendid to put in with the lesser ones of shell and wood. His eyes streaming, his nose snuffling, his chest rasping with a cough, and shivering in an icy fit of fever, he would play with these objects with such silent concentration, no one could guess what they represented for him. Mama would start to tell him the story of Bluebeard or Cinderella but would become aware that he was not listening and fall silent, sighing as she stitched a lace collar or mended a stocking, only now and then reminding him to pull her shawl over his shoulders, and seeing to it that he did so, hitching up the faded ivory wool with its pale blue stripes, so old that it felt like silk to the touch, or aged skin.

If his sister Caroline came in to fetch the dress with the lace collar or the mended stocking, and saw him, she would cry, 'Oh, you look like a grandmother sitting in that shawl with the sewing box!' and burst out laughing. 'Doesn't he, Mama, doesn't he?'

He would look up at her, shrug, sniff, and say nothing. He had nothing to say to either her or Mama. His entire presence seemed made up of his silence.

When Caroline left for the convent school in Milan, Matteo stood at the chest of drawers in her room and looked at himself in the misty, silvered mirror that hung above it in a copper frame, green with verdigris. He opened the drawers one by one and found each had something left behind in it – a small satin sachet, a brooch of jet and crystal, a flat box of powder. Picking up a piece of limp velvet, he dipped it in the pink powder and raised it to his nose, close enough to breathe it in: it smelt equally of violets and perspiration, the one sickly and the other stale. Suppressing a shudder of revulsion, he rubbed it onto his face with the velvet pad, spreading it gently and thoughtfully. When it grew too thin, he dipped the pad in again and raised another layer of the perfumed, tickling powder. Then he rummaged around and found a smaller, round, flat box that contained a blue paste. This he rubbed onto his eyelids with his finger. He found a thick black pencil and drew circles around his eyes, very slowly and carefully so as not to stab his eyes with its point. He had never seen Caroline, or his mother, do this but he had seen the carnival masks in the shops in the village with their eyelids coloured blue and outlined for dramatic effect. He even found a sequin in the crack of one drawer, dug it out with a fingernail and, with a small dab of spit, stuck it to his cheek, below an eye, exactly like Pierrot's. At last he came across a tube containing a stub of plum-red paste, and with this he was painting his mouth when Mama walked in and let out a scream so loud that it seemed to rip the mirror from the wall so that his face slid out of it, an exotic painted lily sliding into disgraced oblivion.

So then Matteo too was sent to school. With a box that had broad leather straps to keep it closed on the pile of white shirts and grey shorts. His uncle would keep him at home in Turin and send him to school along with his own sons: that would be best. Matteo too had to be driven, like Caroline a little earlier, down from the villa and around the lake, the chauffeur braking sharply whenever he saw another vehicle coming so that Matteo was shaken and sick by the time they reached the plain.

In Turin the severe angles of the architecture revealed themselves to him like lessons in a geometry book: he had seen nothing like that in his landscape of villa, village, hills, lake. The school was a theorem set within a larger theorem. Matteo, raised on curves, rotundities and irregular lines, felt himself chilled by so much mathematical beauty, defeated by its logic. He put his hand out to the chauffeur in a moment of need. Vittorio knew better what should be done: he gave the boy a slight push and reminded him of who he was and what he was to do – go up the stairs and greet his uncle and Father Giustino, who stood waiting together in the villa by the river.

The sense of mathematical mystery proved prophetic. Matteo could understand nothing. He rubbed and rubbed at the pencil markings in his book till everything was a grey blur but could come to no solution; none that was accurate. If he was in any doubt about that, he was soon provided by certainty: the angry, slashing lines made across the page by Father Giustino's pen and the zeros furiously scrawled in the margins.

Failure followed him up and down the long corridors of the school. In the choir, Matteo learnt that he could not sing. At home he had bellowed out the hymns in San Giacomo along with Caroline and his mother and no one had told him that the sounds he made were not singing. Now he was told. It baffled him, like the geometry and the algebra.

Matteo had always played by himself. Now he was put into a team and saw that he was expected to play with, and for, the team, not himself. But he did not know how to do that. He watched the other boys from the corners of his eyes and tried to pick up clues but they always proved wrong. He kicked the ball away from the goal, tackled a boy on his own team, not an opponent, whereupon there was a great roar and the captain walloped him across the shoulders, catching his ear with a fist, painfully, and he sprawled in the mud in agony, then felt them trampling over him as they streamed away in another direction. When he got to his knees, he saw them all racing back, towards him, and so – the greatest disgrace of all – he turned his back and ran for his life. No boy ever forgave him for that. Matteo had to be taught a lesson and they set to with a will.

Matteo told no one – not in his letters to Mama and not to Papa when he came to visit. These were not things one could confess. He hid his scars from his uncle, and when he caught a glimpse of himself in a mirror or a windowpane after the lights were lit at night, his swollen eyes and flattened nose, blue and purple and bronze, seemed to him so grotesque that he looked away. He tried to keep clear of others and to run if anyone came towards him. He ran down the corridors and around the playing fields. On Sundays he ran out into the country, at first along the sides of the dusty motor roads and then along the stone walls separating fields from vineyards. He ran for hours, aching, his muscles functioning like pistons. He looked a rough boy, his hair caked with dust, the muscles hardening with exercise, brushing past people, running and running.

It was Mama who caught him when he came back to the villa for the holidays and held him at arm's length and stared. With a gasp of, 'Matteo, my child!' she folded him in her arms. He struggled away, offended by her pity. He found the villa with its velvet hangings and tapestries and brocades stifling. He thought the mountains hemmed him in and shut off the view. He was anxious to run, but she held him by his arms and screamed for Papa to come and see.

Papa came and made him lift up his face and stretch out his hands for examination. Papa did not touch him – his face was pinched with dislike – Matteo could not tell of what. Then Papa made that clear by snapping, 'What is all the fuss about? The boy has been playing football; he is learning to be a man. Is this something to howl about?'

Matteo gazed at him. Papa's face seemed to him entirely round, entirely pink – the skin smooth and glistening, the eyes pale and the hair and eyebrows bleached and colourless. Unlike Mama's anguished, enraged face with its flush and dishevelled hair. He stared at both of them and felt they repelled him equally. It seemed painful that they should be related.

He looked away, sulking. He would tell them nothing about the school or his uncle's household. His answers to their questions were sullen and monosyllabic. He would eat none of the meat and gravy and pastries Mama tried to force on him; he insisted he wanted only bread and water, that was all.

'Perverse!' Mama exclaimed. 'Unnatural! I call this un-natural.'

Matteo gave her a cool look; he said something she was to remember later. He said, 'You don't know what natural means, Mama.'

It made her gasp. It made her determined to get him away from Turin and the school. She set to work diligently, on her husband. Like a bird with a long beak that knocks, knocks, knocks on the dead wood till the insect emerges and she can have it, she worked to defeat him and have her way.

As a result of her strategies, Papa withdrew him from the school – souring his relations with his brother into the bargain, since it was taken as a criticism of his guardianship – and engaged an English tutor who would prepare Matteo for examinations at home. She had her triumph. If Matteo's face registered dismay and apprehension, that was part of her reward.

They were seated at the wooden table out by the camellia tree, drinking cups of afternoon coffee, when they heard the gate open with a long groan, as it always did, followed by a sudden clank as it swung back on its hinges. They could hear the porter turn the key in the lock, and exchanged looks with each other but remained silent, watchful.

Eventually the visitor came in sight. He was still far below them and they saw only the top of his head, the light brown hair in long curls under a straw hat as he walked slowly up the zig-zagging path that curved whitely up the hillside. They saw him disappear behind some silvery, rustling olive trees, then emerge on the flight of stone steps laid through the thick grass, the blue irises and the brown ground orchids. Then he vanished behind a hedge of box and it was a while before they saw him come out onto the flagstone path between the cypress trees and the beds of pinks. He paused by the fountain and the family leant forward to see if he would sit down beside it to rest – he seemed slow and tired – or if he would wash his face and drink from it, unaware of their watching. But he merely stood with his hands on his hips, gazing at the mossed basin of the fountain and the cold drops trickling into it. When he made a move it was to reach into his pocket and draw out a book which he began to read, seemingly unconscious of their presence, standing there in the blue shade of a cypress within the sound of falling water, a pale blue sweater tied carelessly around his waist by its arms.

Matteo, who watched most intently of all, let out his breath as if in relief. 'He is reading,' he sighed.

'Reading,' said his mother, much more tartly, 'while we are all here, waiting.'

'At least we have learnt he can read,' said Papa.

For some reason this made Matteo leap to his feet, clutching at his head in a wild gesture that the young man so far below seemed to sense for he looked up and saw all the faces peering at him from over the wistaria that wound along the wooden railing. Matteo lifted his hand to wave and slowly, serenely, the young man waved back.

When at last he joined them at the wooden table under the camellias and Mama went in for a fresh pot of coffee and the jug of water he had requested, he laid the book on the table and Matteo craned forward to read the title: *The Journey to the East* by Hermann Hesse. Matteo was confused – what was it, a geography text?

'You can borrow it if you like,' the tutor said, smiling.

Papa bellowed, 'Is it in English? The boy must read English. English is what you must read with him.'

'I will, and we will read it together,' the young man lightly replied, and took a cream horn from the plate on the table and bit into it without any self-consciousness. Over its ridged crust he gave the watching Matteo a cream-flecked smile.

From the beginning Mama could see the lessons were not going as she had planned. What, she asked herself, peering out from between the curtains at the window, was going on on the hillside where Matteo and Fabian were walking with an open book, it was true, but running downhill at times and at others uphill to the ruin under the pines, throwing back their heads to shout to each other like two madmen? She could not of course hear what they were reading or reciting and, if she had, the verses would have made no sense to her.

21

'Is it that from some bright sphere
We part with friends we meet with here,
Or do we see the future pass
Across the present's dusky glass?

'Or what is it that makes us seem
To pick up fragments of a dream
Part of which comes true, and part
Beats and trembles in the heart?'

Matteo read the words slowly and hesitantly but when he saw Fabian beaming at him in encouragement and delight, his voice strengthened and lifted.

'The One remains; the many change and pass,
Heaven's light forever shines, earth's shadows fly:
Life like a dome of many-coloured glass
Stains the white radiance of Eternity,
Until death tramples it to fragments.'

When he looked to Fabian for explication, his forehead creased with puzzlement, Fabian lifted up his arms and shouted the lines:

'. . . Die
If thou wouldst be with that which thou dost seek!
Follow where all is fled!'

and both burst into shrill laughter and ran downhill into the wind, leaving Mama at the window, aghast.

Fabian was given permission, when he requested it, to take Matteo in the boat across the lake to Varenna. The day was so still, the boat scarcely moved. They lay in it, bemused by the sun, and Fabian dutifully read from the guide book how the pink and ochre and terracotta houses that clung like the cells of a honeycomb to the looming limestone crags of the mountain had been built by the refugees who fled from the Isola Comacina when their city was razed by the armies of Como in the twelfth century; how the castle had been built on top of the mountain by Queen Theodolinda, wife of the Lombard King Authari, in the sixth century; how, during the Renaissance, it had been one of the principal strongholds of the Fief of the Riviera; and how the church of pink and yellow marble they would visit contained frescoes from the fourteenth century . . .

But when they reached the shore and, leaving the boat, set off on foot, the steep and stony path leading up through the beechwoods to the cliffs defeated them quickly. Laughing, they fell back, allowed their determination to dissipate, and neither visited the castle nor even entered the church, but wandered through the narrow lanes where the rose-pink and ochre houses had their green and grey and blue shutters closed to the sun and black and white cats dozed beside pots of geraniums, down to the gardens of the Villa Monastero. Here they paced the avenues of dark cypresses and palms till they came to a low stone wall spread with wistaria and, sitting by the edge of the lake where the water washed and washed the pebbles, Fabian read to Matteo from *The Journey to the East*.

It was my destiny to join in a great experience. Having had the good fortune to belong to the League, I was permitted to be a participant in a unique journey. What wonder it had at the time! How radiant and comet-like it seemed, and how quickly it had been forgotten and allowed to fall into disrepute. For this reason, I have attempted a short description of this fabulous journey, a journey the like of which had not been attempted since the days of Hugo and mad Roland . . .

Late in the afternoon, with the sun now invisible behind a heavy silver haze that was reflected dully by the lake so that it had turned to molten silver in which the surrounding hills floated without any substance, mirages of blue, mauve and purple, Fabian was still reading, in a voice that grew softer and lower.

Brother H. was led to despair in his test, and despair is the result of each earnest attempt . . . to go through life with virtue, justice and understanding and to fulfil their requirements. Children live on one side of despair, the awakened on the other . . .

The light was gone from the silver lake, now dull and tarnished, when Fabian stuck the book back into his pocket and said, 'Matteo, we must go. They'll be sending out a search party for us,' and they ran past the dark villa with its row of curious domes lining the flat rooftop, and all the way to the docks and their boat. While Fabian readied the sails, his face clenched with tension, Matteo murmured to himself, ' "Children live on one side of despair, the awakened on the other . . ." '

When they returned, Mama stood in the driveway, tearing a hydrangea flower to bits in her hands. She said nothing but gave Matteo a quick and bitter look, then went in to order dinner. Matteo looked at the clock in the hall – were they so late?

At dinner he left it to Fabian to describe their expedition and said nothing himself, eating so little that Mama became angry and demanded to know how it was possible that sailing across the lake had done nothing to improve his appetite. At this, he looked at her, sighed, 'I'm tired, Mama,' and was given permission to go to bed. As he passed Fabian's chair, his tutor slipped him the copy of the book, all crumpled and crushed, so that he might be able to stay up and read it to the end.

Inside the figures I saw something moving, slowly, extremely slowly, in the same way that a snake moves which has fallen asleep. Something was taken place there, something like a very slow, smooth but continuous flowing or melting; indeed, something melted or poured across from my image to that of Leo's. I perceived that my image was in the process of adding to and flowing into Leo's, nourishing and strengthening it. It seemed that, in time, all the substance from one image would flow into the other and only one would remain: Leo. He must grow, I must disappear.

Matteo fell asleep with the image in his mind of the two figures 'transparent and that one could look inside as one can look through the glass of a bottle or vase', and within them something that could be a stream or else a snake, magically illuminated, flowing from one to the other till both were filled, filled with the dark of sleep.

24

A week later Mama walked down the hill to the boat dock and came upon the two of them seated in the boat which was moored by a ring in the wall, going nowhere, their knees touching as they read to each other from Fabian's book of poetry.

> 'Oh Rose thou art sick (read Matteo).
> The invisible worm,
> That flies in the night
> In the howling storm:
>
> 'Has found out thy bed
> of crimson joy:
> And his dark secret love
> Does thy love destroy.'

They were not aware of her listening, looming, and went on to declaim:

> 'Never pain to tell thy love
> Love that never told can be
> For the gentle wind does move
> Silently, invisibly'

when she broke in: 'Matt-e-o!'

He looked up, startled, and she called, more sharply, 'Come here, Matteo!'

Fabian gave him a little smile – encouraging, sympathetic – and Matteo climbed up out of the boat and went up the water-washed steps to her, sullen with resentment. She said to him, 'I call and call and you do not come.'

'I heard you and I came. What is the matter?'

'Nothing is the matter, but I want you to come to the house. Uncle Filippo is coming to see you.'

'Uncle Filippo? To see me?' Matteo asked in apprehension, but followed her dutifully. He glanced back to see if Fabian had stayed in the boat but it was so far below the wall, he could not see the boat or his tutor. His mother, turning back, caught the look of chagrin on his face.

To Matteo's surprise, Uncle Filippo appeared to have come

to the house to invite him to visit Como with him, offering him a tour of the family silk factory 'seeing that you are not at school now'. It was not at all what Matteo wished to see or do, but the look on his parents' faces made it clear that there was no question of declining.

When he told Fabian he would have to go, Fabian gave a small twist of a smile that Matteo interpreted as sad. 'I will be back by night,' he said quickly. 'I'll see if I can find another Hesse in the bookshop in Como.' Fabian nodded.

When Matteo returned, Fabian had left, leaving no note behind for him, no message.

Mama shrugged. 'He had to leave quickly. The telegram said he was wanted urgently – he had no time to write you a note. He said to say goodbye.'

Fabian did, however, send Matteo a gift. A few days after his departure, a parcel arrived at the villa. When Matteo heard of it, it had already been opened by Mama and she was standing at the hall table, her feet amongst the brown paper wrapping, reading with an expression of total incredulity, from Hesse's *Siddhartha*:

'She drew him to her with her eyes. He put his face against her, placed his lips against hers which were like a freshly cut fig. Kamala kissed him deeply, and to Siddhartha's great astonishment he felt how much she taught him, how clever she was, how she mastered him, repulsed him, lured him, and how after this long kiss, a long series of other kisses, all different, awaited him . . .'

Catching Matteo by his collar, the book in her other hand, she marched into Papa's room, shouting, 'Will you come and look? Will you see what this Englishman of yours has sent your son to read? Will you kindly take a look and see if it is fit to place in the hands of a schoolboy? This is the reading, the study the two of them were up to – this! I knew it. I told you, I knew it.'

Matteo was running once again. They could not stop him – he

26

would not stay in the house or garden, he would climb the walls or over the gate if they locked it, and run and run as if all he wanted was to place a distance between them and himself, a distance he drew out to greater and greater lengths with each run.

No one was able to hold, or to pursue him. The boat was lifted out of the dock and locked away but Matteo did not ask for it. The family sent the porter to the man at the ferry to ask that he sell no tickets to the young Matteo. The old man snorted in the porter's face. 'Tell those high and mighty folk on the hill to keep their noses out of my business. I sell tickets, I run the ferry, not they, and if the boy's got money to pay, he can ride the ferry, who's to stop him?' and he rolled the butt of tobacco across his lower lip and spat out a fleck of it with such disdain that the messenger fell silent and did not pursue the matter. What was more, he became the butt of jokes in the bar where unfortunately the man from the ferry too went to drink in the evenings and told everyone of the arrogance of the folk on the hill and his pithy response to it.

People saw Matteo fleeing like a hare through the white dust of the oleander-lined promenade by the lake, round the corner by the lido and the gardens of the Villa Melzi, or – in the other direction – through the lanes of Pescallo out onto the wide grassy swath from the Villa Giulia to Loppia, pausing to get his breath in the cobblestoned square of Guggiate where he stared up at the fresco of San Andrea bowed under the weight of the cross on the whitewashed wall of the church, and then, with a scatter of stones under his heels, swinging uphill and out of sight. No one saw him as he climbed above the hamlets of Perlo and Brogna and the isolated, windswept farmyards with their scraggy chickens, their barking dogs, manure heaps and lines of washing, into the beech woods where the wind rustled in the leaves and the stream over the stones. No one was there to see where he flung himself on his knees in the damp leaves or clung to the tree trunks, beating his head fiercely against them and crying, 'Dove sei? Dove sei? Where are you?'

He no longer heeded the dinner bell or mealtimes. When Fabian had been there, he had made a pretence of eating meals for the pleasure of his tutor's company, but that was gone now. He would eat nothing, he told them, but bread, and that he could eat by himself at any time, preferably in hunks out of his pocket. His mother would scream about disease and illness resulting from such a diet and threaten him with visits from the doctor, but he was adamant: most people in the world lived on just such a diet, and he wanted no more – in fact, he would prefer less.

He grew painfully thin and haggard and still seemed to wish to reduce further his contact with the family and household and all its rites. He no longer slept in his bed but stretched himself on a worn rug on the floor. Once the maid came to open the front door in the pale milky mist of early morning and found him asleep in front of it. She told the cook, 'Just like a tomcat who wants to escape from the house and go on the tiles.'

He stayed away even at night, slept in silent abbeys or in ruined chapels on a pew with a book he had brought to read in the flickering light of votive candles. A woman coming in to clean and tidy before a service might come upon him and rouse him; then he would go and sit in the pale sun with his sandalled feet in the dried grasses, his breath coming out in clouds in the cold air and looking out over the lake with the eyes of a man who is planning a long voyage.

But when he emerged at last from what Mama called 'that phase', he appeared calm, gentle, detached – no longer defiant and no longer impelled to fight. It was arranged for him to take lessons in Latin and history from old Father Pirrone, who had retired from most parish duties, and in addition to study mathematics and logic with the sister of the village school-teacher; she was crippled, bound to a wheelchair, and could not go out to work. Between them, they filled the gaps in Matteo's education; they made up a patchwork, not very exacting, in some parts even pleasing. In any event, they found it desirable not to put him to any test: this satisfied all parties. Anyone watching Matteo go downhill through the thin drizzle or the lake mist with a satchel of books to Father Pirrone's rooms behind the high walls of San Giorgio, or up the narrow walled lanes to the schoolteacher's small house in Aureggio, would not have thought him a reluctant student. The truth was he did not care at all what he did. When Papa spoke of his future in banking in Turin or the silk business in Como with his uncle Filippo – he was fortunate, he was born to both, Papa pointed out – Matteo looked at him with the faintest smile as at something so absurd it merited no more than that – a smile. If he had taken it seriously, he might have struggled but he gave no grounds for complaint.

In the event, it was Mama who released him.

When Papa announced he needed to meet a German banker who was visiting Bellagio and staying at the Hotel de la Grande Bretagne for Easter, Mama arranged for him to come to lunch, with his wife and daughter. Caroline, on finding out the guest list, preferred to go out and play tennis with her friends. Since it was a dazzling spring day of liquid summery light that poured from blue sky to blue lake, lunch was served outdoors under the camellia trees, looking onto the slope of the hill where pear and cherry trees bloomed like bouquets amidst the quiet grey olive trees. The banker did not take off his dark glasses once, the glare was too much for his northern eyes – 'One might be beside the Mediterranean here,' he marvelled – and his wife scarcely stopped exclaiming, 'Ah, the camellias! How lovely! Look, Sophie. Look, Klaus – the camellias!' Papa seemed to find it difficult to discuss business in these circumstances, the light and the camellias were too powerful a distraction. Mama had gone to great trouble over the lunch but was disappointed by their lack of attention to it: was the lasagna too drowned in its béchamel sauce? Were the little grilled fishes too bony? The salad of fresh spring herbs too exotic for her guests' taste? No one seemed to do more than pick at the dishes.

Except for Sophie. She alone was totally unaffected by the surroundings and the company. She was said to be a journalist, to have contributed articles to German journals, but did not refer to them at all. Sitting up at table, knees together, elbows lowered, she concentrated on the dishes before her. Matteo was transfixed: such concentration, he had not seen its like. Mama noticed him staring from under his brows and was irritated. The girl's hair was cut as short as a boy's and she was dressed like one too, in blue jeans, of which Mama disapproved, and clearly nothing on under her loose, faded cotton shirt. She had taken so much trouble over the lunch, could her guests not take the trouble to dress appropriately? It was of course for the mother to point that out but she, silly woman, waved her pudgy pink hands about and cried yet again, 'Ah, the camellias! Do you see, Sophie? Do you see, Klaus? How lovely, lovely, lovely.'

It was Matteo who interrupted, quite uncharacteristically. No sooner had Sophie put down her knife and fork than he asked if she would like to walk uphill to see the folly. Mama felt a pang and cried out, 'So soon after eating? Is that wise?' and looked at the other mother for support only to find the lady lifting a waxy pink and white camellia to her nose and sipping, as it were, the non-existent fragrance with her eyes closed. Neither Matteo nor Sophie bothered to answer Mama's cry which hung in the air till it fell soundlessly to the table for lack of support, which Matteo and Sophie took as permission to leave, and walked away, their big sports shoes crunching on the gravel and emphasising their solidarity against the others.

When Papa determinedly roused himself from the Sunday torpor into which he was sinking and remembered to ask the questions he needed to put to the banker regarding international finance and a possible career for Matteo in banking, unfortunately at that very moment the banker closed his eyes behind the dark glasses and let sleep overcome him. Mama smiled tightly over the camellia extended to her by a plump pink hand and watched the two walking slowly up the gravelled path that led between the wistaria, coiled with its clusters of tight grey buds around the wooden rail, and the hillside where hepaticas and primulas bloomed in the grass, then disappearing behind the stones of the ruined folly at the top of the hill.

In that summer of 1975, Sophie and Matteo, having first married to pacify their tearful and lamenting parents, left for India, dressed in identical blue jeans and T-shirts and sports shoes, carrying identical rucksacks on their backs, as did so many of their generation in Europe. Only Sophie still wore her hair very short and Matteo was growing his long. They left on foot. In Matteo's pocket was the copy Fabian had left him of Hesse's *The Journey to the East*.

৵Chapter One৴

Smoking a cigarette while she leaned over the balustrade in the veranda, Sophie watched darkness fall in the courtyard, its square, the driveway, the city outside the gates. Crows were settling into the trees, cawing with that piercing intensity peculiar to evening. Lights were going on in the kiosks and shops out on the streets and smoke was rising from the coal dust and cowdung fires everywhere. Rickshaws and cars wheeled around and drove out.

She stubbed out the cigarette, let it fall into the drain, and went back to the room. Matteo was sitting up in bed, writing in his diary. She sat down on the upright chair and watched him.

'When will we leave, Matteo?' she asked sharply, out of a wish to interrupt more than anything else, and break into his privacy, his maddening privacy. 'Must we wait till the Mother's death?'

He looked at her sorrowfully, not closing his book or putting down his pen. 'You are free to leave when you like, Sophie,' he said, trying to sound cool and controlled. She hated it when he made this effort to seem controlled.

'I know,' she replied. 'I know I am free. But you? What I want to know about is you. Are *you* free?'

'I am free, Sophie,' he said in the same infuriating tone. 'But I am waiting – for a sign. I have always waited for signs. And then followed them.' He shifted his legs in their threadbare pyjamas: they were still pathetically thin and weak. 'I must follow the signs. There is a design.'

She threw back her head, rolling her eyes at the ceiling. 'A design? You mean, your destiny?' It made her laugh. 'Your great and glorious destiny? Look, just look – how glorious!' She swept her arm to indicate the sick room, its enamel pan, its steel furniture, its metal tumbler of water and tray for pills, and the patients slowly shuffling down the veranda outside the door.

He closed his diary and held his head in his hands. Moments passed and then he looked at her again. 'You are trying to tell me I have failed. You are trying to tell me that this scene –' and he too gestured at the sick room and its trappings – 'is a scene of failure. I am not claiming it is glorious, Sophie, or that it is what I want. But it is not what you think it is.'

'Oh, it is not a hospital room? And you are not sick? And *I* am mad, the crazy one who imagines it all?' Sophie tapped her head with a finger, hard.

'It is not what you think it is,' he repeated, biting his lip. Then he stammered, 'If you read a little bit, Sophie, you would see . . . I will tell you what I read in the *Katha Upanishad*.

' "There is the path of joy and the path of pleasure. The two paths lie in front of one. Pondering on them, the wise one chooses the path of joy; the fool takes the path of pleasure." '

There was a silence. Both sat listening to the sounds of the hospital outside the room: the patients shuffling, the nurses clicking past in their quick shoes, the crows giving the last caws before dark. The room was murky: someone needed to switch on a light but no one did.

Sophie's lips felt dry, and she spoke through those dry lips, hoarsely. 'I can't understand what you mean. The path of pleasure, the path of joy. To me, they are the same, they are not separate. But I see that you are saying I am the fool, the one who takes the path of pleasure, and that you are the wise one. Yes, the wise one who takes the path of joy. This is where it has brought you, and you tell me it is the wise choice?'

'Yes, Sophie, yes!'

'Then you are the fool, not I,' she snapped and got up to switch on the light abruptly.

It was true, though: from the beginning it had been as though there were a design, a pattern, to their wanderings. At every turn they seemed to be shown signs, given directions, drawn further, taken deeper. Of that Matteo was convinced, and he never ceased to try and convince the scoffing Sophie.

'Was meeting Pierre Eduard a sign?'

'Meeting Pierre Eduard was most certainly a sign, and Mr Pandey also,' he assured her.

She covered her face with her hands and laughed. 'Mr Pandey! You make me laugh, Matteo.' She tapped her head with a finger. 'And Pierre Eduard, that madman!'

~

They had been sitting in the restaurant below their hotel room, drinking tepid lemonade and looking out onto the street where a man was spreading his merchandise – rubber slippers, small mirrors, plastic buckets – on the pavement by the bus stop, placing them strategically so passengers would stumble on them as they got off the buses, when a fellow inhabitant whom they had befriended at the Hotel Monaco dropped onto the bench beside them and mopped his flushed face with the cotton scarf he wore across his shoulders. He called loudly for *chai* and, while he waited for the cook to bring it from the sooty corner at the back where the kettle was kept going day and night, he told them, 'While you two were sitting here, so lazy, I have been out, searching. And do you know what I found?'

'We will try to guess, Pierre Eduard,' Matteo said languidly, mocking his activity and excitement. 'An elephant?'

'A maharaja?' Sophie volunteered.

'Elephants, maharajas – my God, you two, is that what

35

India is to you?' Pierre Eduard rolled his eyes. 'When will people from the West free themselves from Hollywood? Can you think of nothing that is not concrete, material, an entertainment?'

'Oh, please,' Sophie protested, and Matteo said, 'Why can we not have Hollywood dreams in the Hotel Monaco in Bombay?'

The tea arrived, in a tin mug, and spilt across the table. Instantly flies settled where it spilt for it was sticky with sugar. Pierre Eduard swept them away with his fist. 'No, but seriously, you two, you must break out of this – '

'Yes? And go where? Tell us, please, we are waiting.'

'And find the India that lies outside. Shall I tell you what I have just seen on the beach, this morning?'

'Film stars!'

'Dolphins!'

'A yogi who lay in the sand with his head buried underneath it. Completely. I checked. For forty minutes. And people did nothing – stood and watched, he could have been dead. They threw a few coins on the sand and went away. I talked to a man – his name was Mr Pandey – who told me it is the study of yoga that makes such a thing possible. I waited for forty minutes and then he rose. He was alive. That is what I saw, I promise. A few paces further, an old sage. Ancient, with a white beard. Please do not laugh. He read from the *Gita* – Mr Pandey told me it was the *Gita* – and people sat by and listened to him. Oh, his voice was like the ocean. You should have heard!'

'Perhaps he was the Sage of the Sea,' Matteo laughed, 'the Ancient Mariner. Did he lament the albatross?'

'What?' Pierre Eduard put down his mug. 'He was a sage, expounding a holy book, not natural history. Please tell me, on what beach in the West will you meet such a one, or hear such a thing? I tell you, it is the spiritual experience for which you must search in India, nothing less.'

'Oh, please,' groaned Sophie again, 'what is spiritual about sticking one's head into the sand? Is an ostrich holy, Pierre Eduard?'

Nevertheless, for lack of anything else to do, and for the sake of getting out of the Hotel Monaco, which was admittedly neither relaxing nor exciting but merely squalid, one evening they let Pierre Eduard's newfound friend, Mr Pandey, take them to visit a saint. Pierre Eduard was busily collecting saints as earlier travellers had collected gold, spices or shawls.

The saint lived in a suburb at the other end of Bombay and they had to take a train. At the station they nearly lost Pierre Eduard in the crowds: he was small and had taken to wearing Indian clothes, pyjamas and slippers. Pressed forward by the people behind them and somehow lifted up through the door in spite of the crowd that was escaping from it with equal ferocity, they found themselves, to their surprise, in the same compartment as Pierre Eduard: he had been propelled into it ahead of them. There seemed no question of sitting down, there was no seat visible, but several women tugged at Sophie's clothes and dragged her into a space they made for her between, or on, their knees. Matteo and Pierre Eduard stood over her, protectively, but actually they would not have been able to move a finger in that solid human mass of which they had become a part.

As they had entered, so they were extruded from the train – like an excrescence – onto the platform of a suburban railway station. Here they were met by Pierre Eduard's friend, a small man in white trousers and a blue bush-shirt.

'Oh, you have come, you have come,' he beamed at them welcomingly, and at once turned and led them up the road which was lined with warehouses and bins and barrels where cattle stood munching the straw and cardboard of packing cases, and then down lanes where the commerce of that area was being carried out even at that late hour – bales of cloth, canvas and rubber sheeting spilling out of the small shops that hung out over open drains. The merchants' families lived on the upper floors and cheerfully emptied their garbage out of their windows into the lanes. Although it was evening, it was oppressively hot, the air bottled in by the high buildings and the life that boiled inside them.

Sophie, limping, plucked at Matteo's sleeve and complained, 'I can't go on,' but just then Pierre Eduard's friend stopped at a staircase that led up from the side of a cigarette and soda water stall to the top of a building at the end of the lane. There was a blue door on the uppermost landing, hung with marigold garlands, and Mr Pandey stopped to take off his sandals, gesturing to them to do the same. Leaving their rubber slippers amongst dozens of others on the landing, they followed him in barefoot.

There, in a surprisingly large room painted a bright pink, under a tube of blue fluorescent light and a framed oleograph of a god with a snake around his neck and a crescent moon in his matted locks, there sat an elderly woman in a purple cotton sari with a green border, her greying hair open on her stooping shoulders. She was surrounded by a throng of men and women all seated crosslegged on the white sheets spread across the floor and they were all silent. In some embarrassment, Sophie and Matteo lowered themselves to the floor, keeping close to the wall at the back so they could lean against it, not having much confidence in their ability to sit crosslegged for long. The silence continued, and it had the effect of making them very conscious of the sounds other than speech – the breathing, the snuffling, the very frequent burping and eructating, as well as the shouts and automobile horns and amplified music in the lane below. Equally intrusive and clamorous of attention were the smells – of people, of perspiration, of hair oil, of food being fried in hot oil and stirred with spices in kitchens all around them, as well as the shoes and slippers they had left outside, and of course the city itself, thick and cloudy and oppressive.

Then, when the silence and its components had gathered into a pressure they would not be able to bear any longer, the grey-haired woman in front of them lifted her arms and held them out. Since it was the first movement she had made, they were transfixed and watched her slowly bring her hands together and rub her palms against each other as if she were washing them, or crushing something invisible.

'Ahh,' cried the people in the front row, and 'Ahh,' the cry was taken up by others so that their 'Ahhs' rippled through the room and lapped against Sophie and Matteo, who strained to see the reason for their wonder. They could see nothing that had not been there before but gradually became aware that instead of the conflicting, noisy and obstreperous odours that had earlier filled the room, there was now a sweet scent of flowers – tuberoses, spider lilies, jasmine and roses – swirling almost visibly through the brightly lit pink room. Sophie craned to see what was the source of the perfume, and what was it that made people exclaim in wonder and shake their heads in amazement. Pierre Eduard cried, 'Miraculous! Miraculous!' and his friend wagged his head and smiled as if to say, 'See, did I not tell you?' Matteo said nothing.

So they had come to see a performance of magic tricks, Sophie thought, sinking back on her heels in disappointment. She watched as the elderly woman lowered her hands almost to her knees, then changed the movement and waved them over a brass tray, heaped with fruit and small brass ritual objects, that stood on the floor in front of her. As she did so, the brass objects revealed themselves to be lamps: small flames flickered up from them.

The people called out louder still in wonder. The woman rose, slowly, lifting the tray in her hands, and walked away into the room beyond. Through the open door they could see her carrying it across to what seemed to be an altar in a niche in the wall for it contained a brass idol, an oleograph of a goddess, some incense and a book bound in red cloth. With her back to the people in the pink room, she began to revolve the tray slowly around these several objects and as she did so some people who had been seated in the darkness of the unlit room struck up on the drums they held on their laps and loudly clanged their cymbals. With this introduction of music into the ceremony, everyone's feelings of praise seemed released and, throwing back their heads and clapping their hands, they sang:

'Glory to Shiva,
   Glory to the Mother.
The light of Shiva
Shines from the Mother.
   Glory, Glory, Glory!'

Pierre Eduard would not go to sleep. He sat at the table in the restaurant and kept shaking his head in wonder at what he had witnessed.

'But Pierre Eduard,' Sophie protested, 'I have seen tricks like that at parties and magic shows. When I was a child, my parents would engage magicians to entertain us. What is so —' she was going to say 'magical' but stopped to search for a more critical word.

Pierre Eduard's face became contorted with anger. 'But did *she* do it for money? As entertainment? Didn't you see *why* she did it? For the glory of God! As a form of worship!'

Sophie shrugged and lit a cigarette. 'So what's the difference?'

Pierre Eduard began to tear his hair at her cynicism but Matteo, who had been silent so far, said suddenly, 'The difference is what Pierre Eduard said – not of how she did it, but why she did it.'

Sophie took the cigarette out of her mouth and regarded him with surprise. She said, 'All right then, she did it for-the-glory-of-God. Can't she find a better way of worshipping him than with party tricks?'

Pierre Eduard flung himself forward and beat at the table with his fists. The waiter, wiping glasses at the counter, stared. Sophie blew streams of smoke through her nostrils and smiled.

'Can there not be many ways, more than one way – the Christian way – to glorify God?' he raged. 'Hers is to create belief in people, through her powers. Is that wrong?'

Sophie looked at him in the throes of his ardent belief and wonder. She smoked her cigarette down to a stub and then crushed it in a saucer. 'Depends on what she gets them to believe,' she said. 'What if all it is is that God can do party

40

tricks?' She got up. 'I'm going to bed. That train ride nearly killed me. I won't go again.'

Pierre Eduard let out a groan. Matteo scratched at his flea bites reflectively.

That was what Sophie suspected most – Matteo's reflectiveness. She kept a sharp and suspicious eye on him, especially when Mr Pandey came to visit them.

Swinging his leg energetically up and down under the table in the restaurant, Mr Pandey enthused. 'She is great, the Perfume Saint, no?' Up and down, up and down swung his leg. 'I can show you others, many others like her – saints, great souls, siddhis. Our country is full of such people who have found enlightenment. I will take you to see others if you like.'

Matteo too, as if hypnotised, swung his leg – up, down, up, down – although more slowly, in wide pyjamas. He had given up wearing Western dress – he was dressed now in wide pyjamas and a cotton vest bought from a pavement stall, already tattered and faded from the original red to a mottled salmon pink. Cautiously, he asked, 'Are they here, nearby?'

'Here only,' Mr Pandey assured him, sweeping his arm to include the sooty, sulphurous air inside the stifling restaurant. 'Here, everywhere. Come, I will show you.'

Sophie protested, 'We were going to the beach today.'

'Chowpatty beach? Very good, very good,' Mr Pandey pounded his leg furiously in the air. 'At Chowpatty beach itself there are saints.'

While Sophie walked determinedly in the surf that crept over the sand to wash over her feet, and tried to derive vicarious pleasure from watching a family of Bombay women and children walking into the waves with their saris and frocks tucked up at their waists, screaming when a wave lifted to dash itself at them and leave them drenched, she saw from the corner of her eye Matteo following Mr Pandey from one live sideshow to another: a begger with no limbs who sat on a wooden cart and held out a can for alms between his teeth; a man who was painting a picture of his favoured saint on the sand in powdered chalk – bright yellows and pinks and violets; a woman who wore a string of wooden beads around her neck and held another in her hand, and lectured to a reverential crowd.

Coming out of the waves, her skirt, wet with sand, dragging at her ankles, she caught up with them and told Matteo, 'You look like a woman in an Italian market, shopping for vegetables.'

'Very good,' laughed Mr Pandey who had overheard, 'but it is fish he is buying, madam, fish.'

Another time she did have Matteo to herself by the sea. They walked along the Worli seaface, bending over as the wind struck at them, laughing when the waves climbed so high over the seawall that they towered, briefly, glittering over their heads, and then washed over the street to the delighted shrieks of the other walkers.

'Monsoon is coming!' they heard children scream. 'Monsoon is coming!'

'When?' Sophie asked, screwing up her eyes at the livid sky, the heavy leaden light of afternoon. 'I don't see it, do you?'

'Sophie, Sophie,' Matteo said, putting an arm over her shoulders and shaking her, 'will you believe only what you see?'

The monsoon did come, that very night, and they climbed up onto the flat roof to feel it pouring down while the city went collectively mad. Cars were stalled in the streets, horns honking; urchins splashed through the floods and bargained with the drivers over the price of pushing them out; drains clogged and overflowed, shoes floated away in the gutters, and people waded across the streets holding onto useless umbrellas that had been battered into shreds. Thunder boomed and ricocheted off the walls and lightning flashed out at sea, over and over. Sophie and Matteo were not alone on the roof – all the other inhabitants of Hotel Monaco were celebrating by leaping up and down, hugging each other, throwing their arms up and letting the rain wash over them. No matter how filthy it might all have been, that night the water seemed a blessing coming after the heat of the long summer days, cleansing and refreshing.

In their room, after stripping off their soaked clothes, Sophie and Matteo made love for the first time since they had come to the hotel. Laying his hand on her shoulder and curling her damp hair about his finger, Matteo said, 'It's like being children again, isn't it?'

'I thought you hated your childhood,' Sophie said. The dampness of the hard cement floor was beginning to penetrate her, bleakly. 'Or have you come here to have another?' she asked suddenly.

Matteo lifted himself onto an elbow and lowered his face right into hers. 'The past is over, Sophie,' he said, 'over, over, over – not to be repeated. Don't repeat it.' He pressed his finger on her lip, hard.

The roof of the Hotel Monaco had soon taken as much rain as it could hold. Saturated, it could not shelter them from the monsoon much longer. Everywhere in their room damp patches were creeping across the walls, the ceiling and the floor, and turning green with mildew. Sophie set out mugs and basins and tumblers to catch the worst drips, but they overflowed quickly. The clothes she washed hung about limply on the line in the humid air.

Pierre Eduard had fever and lay in bed: his body ached till he groaned, and Sophie had to bite her tongue in order to be patient and gentle and bring him flasks of tea from the restaurant downstairs. Mr Pandey came to see them and said, 'Very damp, very bad here – how much are you paying?' When they unwillingly revealed to him how much, in their innocence, they paid, he told them, 'I can get you rooms in an ashram. Nice ashram, nice rooms, very cheap.' Sophie glared: she had begun to think him a sinister *deus ex machina* in their lives. Of course Matteo and Pierre Eduard took him as a divine sign.

'Who *is* he?' she cried angrily, throwing damp clothes into her rucksack. 'Why does he keep coming here? What does he want?' She swept her toilet articles off shelves and ledges, making them fall to the floor.

Matteo, who was on his feet again, picked them up for her. 'He is helping us,' he said.

'You call it help?' Sophie could already visualise the ashram in which they were to be trapped: a place just like the Hotel Monaco only filled not by tourists with guide books but tourists with holy scriptures – the ones Mr Pandey and Pierre Eduard called 'devotees'. This whole country, she reflected, was populated with devotees; the gods could not have enough: now they recruited them from abroad as well.

She was very nearly right, although not entirely. They made their way through the city, tense with expectation – sometimes on a bus, sometimes on the train, then in a rickshaw and finally on foot, arriving at the ashram tired and silent. It consisted of three or four floors of small rooms in straight rows off long verandas in a rainstreaked building that stood in a yard filled with overflowing drains and floating debris behind an unfinished temple building of unpainted grey concrete, fitted up with a loudspeaker system and iron-barred doors behind which the deities lived in dim lamplight. On the veranda balustrade all the crows in Bombay seemed to have gathered to huddle, shaking their bedraggled feathers and letting out caws of complaint at the season and their fate.

Matteo followed Sophie up a steep flight of stairs to one of the small rooms off the veranda. 'Cheer up,' he said, remembering one of Fabian's phrases. 'It will be better tomorrow.'

She lifted the rucksack off her back and hurled it to the floor.

It did not stop raining all of July and all of August. Sophie had been trying to keep a diary and plan articles she might write for a German magazine, but now found herself doing little else but hanging their wet clothes and belongings on a string across the room to dry and running out onto the veranda to drive

44

away the crows that maddened her with their cries from before sunrise to after sunset. The others who lived along the veranda – and Sophie had been wrong about them, none were foreign tourists, they were all Indian families and Indian pilgrims – laughed to see her dart out screaming and waving her arms. The crows hopped off the ledge, flapped about in the rain like clowns miming for an audience, then drifted back and settled down on the ledge again, shaking their feathers and giving extra loud caws of indignation and outrage.

For meals they all went down to the dining hall on the ground floor, a long, bare room spread with mats on which steel trays were arranged in rows. Everyone settled down in front of the trays and the devotees who were on kitchen duty came out with pails of rice and dal and vegetable curries and ladled out large, soupy helpings. Sophie found it a ridiculous arrangement to sit and eat at one level. She found herself bending over double and hanging over her tray in order to get the food to her mouth with her fingers, and the others who sat beside her and opposite her watched and giggled and laughed outright to see the food slip from her fingers and spatter across her knees. One small boy who sat between his parents, large and rotund and dressed in crisp fresh clothes and shining gold jewellery, said in careful English he must have learnt in school, 'See, she is eating like-a-crow.' Sophie's face reddened.

She was no more adept at bathing which also had to be done in public, communally. Standing at one of the taps, she found herself amongst a row of women, none of whom had undressed. All bathed under the taps in their saris, then somehow managed to remove the wet clothes from under the dry ones, with no flash of nudity in between. Sophie watched and observed but could never see how it was done, and decided it could not be if the clothes were jeans or a dress. She tried baring only one portion of her torso at a time but found everyone staring and heard a mocking voice say, 'See, she does not know how-to-take-a-bath.' Sophie would gladly have emptied a bucket of water over the speaker's head but saw there was little point since the speaker was already drenched.

The ashram rules had to be observed by all inmates but Sophie refused to rise at dawn with Matteo and go down to the temple for the morning hymns: the loudspeakers blared them out for everyone for miles around to hear them anyway, she said. She did follow him downstairs in the evenings out of desperation at having been indoors all day. The head swami, who was Mr Pandey's guru, was not present – he was abroad, lecturing – and it was a bevy of junior swamis who ran the place and officiated at prayers and held discourses. They were energetic, active young men who flapped around in faded pink robes and worn rubber slippers, and the atmosphere was rather like a boarding school where the monitors had taken over in the absence of the teachers. The discipline was haphazard and erratic, but could be severe.

The evening sessions were always crowded because not only the ashram dwellers attended but visitors from the neighbourhood. Some of the families who came brought along sick relatives, others physically or mentally handicapped ones and those considered 'possessed', who seemed to Sophie to be in the throes of epileptic fits; she stared at them with unconcealed horror. 'Why don't they take them to hospitals for treatment? All they get here are prayers and hymns,' she said. 'That *is* the treatment,' Mr Pandey explained to her serenely. 'It has very soothing influence.'

Every place in the meeting hall was taken up and the air thick with the odours of perspiring humanity in an atmosphere already heavy with incense, marigold garlands and lamp oil. Drums banged, cymbals clanged, voices rose and rose till they reached shrieking point, then broke into pieces and scattered like glass shards.

Sophie held her hands to her ears. 'Can't we go there at some other time when it is quiet?' she complained to Matteo. 'I thought you said you wanted to meditate.'

'One must learn to meditate anywhere, at any time, Sophie. What is important at these assemblies is the *satsang* itself – the company of the truthful – being with others who have the same thoughts, the same belief.'

'Oh, is that what it is? I thought it was body odour.'

He gave her a hurt look. 'You make no effort, Sophie.'

'To like the smell of truth? No,' she agreed. 'I'd like to smell something really sinful – a beefsteak, a Martini, perhaps. Or at least chocolates, strawberries.'

Pierre Eduard had been sitting very quietly in the cross-legged position he had learnt to assume. Now he let out such a groan of desire, both Sophie and Matteo had to laugh.

That evening they went to a hotel in Juhu for a meal. They did not get Martinis or beefsteaks but they sat under a coconut tree by a swimming pool and ate fried fish and chips, omelettes and chips and chicken sandwiches and chips. They drank feni out of coconut shells and watched Indian boys and girls in limp wool swimming suits chase each other in and out of the pool and throw themselves into the water with loud thwacks. They went to the cinema and watched Kabir Bedi in *Sandokan* and laughed so loudly that some in the audience turned to stare and reprimand them. Linking arms, they sang as they walked back to the ashram down roads already dark and deserted where film posters loomed into the dirty city sky so that doe-eyed heroines with pink breasts showing through gossamer clothing and moustachioed villains with guns at their hips and wine glasses in their hands were illuminated in the smoky dark and saints with golden haloes floated upon lavender clouds above them. It made it possible to ignore the garbage and mud through which they made their uncertain way.

Yet when Matteo came to her in the night, she fought him off fiercely. 'I can't – I can't here, in this zoo. I want to go away. I want us to be by ourselves.'

'By ourselves.' Matteo withdrew in distress. 'By ourselves we'll never come to know India.'

'Why not? I want to go to Goa and eat shrimp. I want to go to Kashmir and live on a houseboat. And lie in the sun and shampoo my hair and eat omelettes all day.'

Matteo was disgusted. 'That isn't India.'

'What is?'

'What is? We must search for what it is.'

She got up and pulled a sarong off the line to wrap around herself. 'I suppose you think the ashram is India – the loudspeakers at dawn and the crows and everyone eating off the floor.'

'No,' Matteo contradicted her, 'it is not here in the ashram. We have to leave.'

She stopped tucking the ends of the sarong about her and waited expectantly for more but what he added was, 'I have heard that many are leaving to go on a pilgrimage. To a shrine outside the city. I asked them, and they will take us along.'

Four o'clock in the morning, the sky like a basin of dirty dishwater, the city sunk in listless, tepid murk. The ashramites with their bundles and baskets – some containing offerings to the deity of the shrine, some pots and pans, others stores of cereals to be eaten on the way – set off in the darkness for the bus depot not far away. It was deserted except for the guard in the kiosk by the gate and a few sleeping cleaners stretched out on concrete benches. One woke and showed them which bus had been hired for their journey and they struggled onto it with their belongings, making a din that sounded all the more raucous for the silence around them in that harshly lit but deserted depot with its ancient, grime-streaked buses and pools of oil spread upon the tarmac.

Their early enterprise seemed to stir up the city and by the time they were on the move shutters were being lifted from shop fronts with a great clatter, queues beginning to line up at milk booths, handcarts loaded with vegetables trundling towards the markets and the families that slept stretched out on the pavements rising and performing their ablutions at public water pumps. The office-going traffic started to grind bitterly through the streets. The bus crawled, the heat and airlessness within it accumulated. Matteo and Sophie slept, slumped on each other's shoulders in exhaustion, while babies leaked puddles across the floor, chickens cackled in baskets of straw, and some of the passengers managed to gossip, argue and even play drums and sing in order to remind everyone of the high purpose of their journey.

It was noon before they had left behind them the cotton mills and warehouses and workers' shanties and emerged into the straggling outskirts of the city where dwellings made of battered tins and plastic sheeting stood by pools of city sludge and effluents, and palm and drumstick trees made smudges of green upon a landscape otherwise uniformly grey. Finally even these shanty towns dwindled and ran out in flat fields of mud that stretched as far as the horizon. Here, unexpectedly, the bus drew to a halt and they were ordered off.

Sophie woke unwillingly to the heat and glare of the empty, desolate fields. She stood there in the mud, her face an angry red from sleep. Matteo scratched himself in his tattered pink vest: he was infested with bugs, or convinced that he was – the effect was the same. They watched dully the excitement of others tearing around and collecting the baggage that was being flung down from the roof of the bus by the driver's attendant with destructive energy. Everyone rooted out their separate belongings, lifted their bags onto their heads and determinedly set off behind a band of swamis who supported a small palanquin by bamboo poles slung across their shoulders. The palanquin, a frilly object of red velvet, bore a pair of silver slippers. Pierre Eduard informed them that they represented the saint who had travelled on foot to the shrine where he obtained enlightenment; they were now to replicate his journey. The devotees were shouting themselves hoarse with enthusiasm. Sophie had no idea how so many had emerged from the bus: they made up a sizeable procession. Some carried orange pennants on bamboo flagpoles and these were the most vocal of all.

'Now we must walk,' Matteo told Sophie bleakly.

She stood rooted in the mud in disbelief when a group of ragged urchins came shouting out of nowhere, followed by a pack of pai dogs that barked frenziedly, whether out of excitement or ferocity it was hard to tell. The three foreigners seemed to be the focus of their attention, possibly of an attack. Sophie decided they could not stay: she lifted her rucksack onto her back and set off.

There was sometimes a slippery track to walk on, between the sharp, rustling grass that grew in the ditches, and sometimes only a mudbank between two flooded fields on which they had somehow to balance themselves, getting splashed and spattered if they slipped. The walking required all their attention. They could not lift their eyes and scan the scenery to see if anything loomed on the horizon. The pilgrims who had been chanting, with such enthusiasm:

'Hari, Hari, come to me,
Hari, Hari, I pine for thee'

slowed their tempo, even fell silent at times till someone roused them with a hymn that had a brisker pace or a song to cheer them:

'The crow is cawing,
What is it telling?
Good news, bad news,
What is it bringing?'

The wits amongst them shouted out answers that made the others laugh.

The sun, polished like brass by the rains, beat down on them with the stridency of metal. Occasionally a lingering monsoon cloud puffed up out of nowhere and obscured it, casting a shadow on the huge empty stretch of land, then moved on and let the sun drum on their heads and backs again. Still, gradually they felt it lessen; they found the perspiration dripping instead of pouring down their bodies. The muddy track turned into a wider stretch of road and when they did look up they found, as if by a miracle, a village standing in a grove of mango trees. Outside it, a group of women in bright Maharashtrian saris of blue and purple, with flowers in their hair, stood with brass trays in their hands with rice, coconuts and ritual lamps with which to pay homage to the saint approaching in the palanquin.

Sophie and Matteo held back as the palanquin was carried into an open space in front of a small pink temple and set down in the centre, where people rushed out of their houses to greet it. They realised now what they had hardly dared to hope – that they were to rest here. Everyone was lifting their bags and bundles off their heads, groaning with relief. Sophie sank down on her haunches, her head in her hands, too tired to speak, and was ashamed to see the other women – some much older than her, others with babies clinging to them – already bustling about, unpacking their pots and pans, sending their children off to collect twigs and brush, lighting fires, fetching buckets of water from a well, getting the cooking going.

Sophie sat as if sunstruck in that haze of dust and wood-smoke, watching the cauldrons bubble, the steam rise. By the well the men were washing, turning the dust to slush around them. When darkness fell and the fires flared like torches, providing the only light, the food was ready and the pilgrims sat down to eat, the younger and stronger amongst them hurrying up and down to serve the others on squares of banana leaf. Sophie saw that there were two distinct groups of eaters, with the low brick wall of a ruined or unfinished yard to separate them: one group had washed and changed into clean clothes, the others still wore their soiled, dusty garments. She knew enough to realise that it was caste that separated the groups and Matteo and Pierre Eduard agreed that it might be so.

Not having helped to cook the meal, Sophie did not expect to share it. Moreover, she was so bone tired, it was not food she wanted. She took some peanuts out of her cloth sling bag and was sitting on one end of the brick wall, shelling and eating the nuts, when she found herself being beckoned by the women in the everyday clothes. They patted the ground, spread out a banana leaf for her and were clearly inviting her to eat along with the men who were eating in the first shift, Matteo and Pierre Eduard looking sheepish amongst them. Evidently their lack of caste was not being held against her, and she was even being raised to the status of an honorary man. She did not know if she should feel pleased about that but suddenly discovered she was hungry after all, ravenously so; she even picked up and ate the green chillies placed alongside the hills of rice and dal on the leaf. When her mouth went up in flames and she turned scarlet and tears ran down her cheeks, they laughed and offered remedies – rice balls, or bits of banana, they urged. Sophie, who had become inured to a mixture of contempt and curiosity from the Indians she had met at ashrams, found the pilgrims extended neither or, if they did, it was so generously mixed with the irrefutable claims of hospitality that it did not show. Pierre Eduard told her later that on a pilgrimage extremely good behaviour was expected of all. That might have been what the children who were quarrelling or spilling their food were being told in scolding tones by their mothers; it might have been what so quickly drew apart two men when an argument flared up in anger. Sophie found herself nodding, smiling out of politeness if not genuine goodwill; she had turned into a pilgrim herself – although only in her behaviour, she qualified.

Matteo, as he walked past to go and wash, stopped and put his hand on her knee, caressed it. 'Better?' he asked.

The women, watching, began to giggle behind their hands and Pierre Eduard hissed, 'You are not supposed to *touch*, you know.'

Sophie flushed. 'If not, how do all *those* come about?' she snapped angrily, pointing to the children who were rolling on the ground or tearing around like puppies. As if they understood, the women giggled harder, and Matteo hung his head in embarrassment for her, for both of them, and disappeared.

It was all so wearing, and it seemed hours before she was able to roll herself up in her sarong and stretch out on the ground to sleep. She thought she would fall asleep instantly and remain asleep until the trumpets raised her but, for all her weariness, it proved impossible. She was too acutely aware of all the others wrapped in their white sheets and stretched out beside her, their breathing, their twitching in a collective unrest. Some seemed to go on and on talking in a low monotone, or else praying. Her lack of the language excluded her even when she was physically in such close contact that they could touch, even smell each other, sharing the same stretch of earth for a bed. The pai dogs that barked in the village and in other villages, plaintively or aggressively, pleadingly or even conversationally, as though addressing each other over great distances in the dark, were more comprehensible to her: she listened to their dialogues with greater understanding and sympathy. Once she was certain she heard a pack of jackals howling, as eerily as wolves, and this roused the dogs to a frenzy: she felt their fear in her own veins. It was nearly dawn before they fell silent, and Sophie had watched the stars turn in the sky, shift their positions according to mysterious mappings and diagrams, and was trying to think of them as pilgrims too, on a journey or a search which would end, it seemed, in the light of dawn when she woke, or was woken, by the wail of pipes, the beating of drums and cymbals.

As she stumbled towards the well to wash, she saw others were already streaming towards the palanquin, going up to bow to the silver slippers held out to them on a tray by the priest who had fresh prayer marks drawn across his forehead, while hymns were being sung with the special clarity and intensity given to them by a new day. Sophie felt very much the outcaste again as she stood throwing tumblers of water over herself and slunk off into the fields to find herself a private place in some rushes. Overhead, on telegraph wires, grass-green bee-eaters sat teetering, then launched themselves into the brilliant air to swoop after insects. A herd of buffaloes was driven out to graze, rustling through the grasses; the herdsboy bringing up the rear chewed upon a stem and turned his head to look at her with curiosity. She scrambled to her feet and returned to eat some bread from the night before and drink a tumbler of tea given her, and even smoked a cigarette furtively behind a hut while the women conducted a great wash of clothes and pots and pans by the well, feeling both guilty and grateful to be excluded. Determinedly, she ignored the looks that Matteo and Pierre threw at her.

Then they were on the road again, their number greatly increased by fresh groups of devotees from the villages around as well as a few bullock carts. To her relief, she was able to load her rucksack into a cart; some of the older women and younger children were even allowed to ride in them. Orange pennants fluttered everywhere, and there were men in red and blue turbans to add to the river of colour that flowed along the dusty road between fields of black earth and groves of mango and coconut trees under a sky alternately sunlit and blue and thunderously grey. Sophie found her feet, sore and blistered as they were, falling into the rhythm of the songs that were being sung, 'Gyanadeva, Gyanadeva . . .'

Occasionally a bus or a truck ploughed through the dust, forcing the pilgrims onto the banks on either side, and then passengers leant out of the windows to stare at them, some with curiosity, some with admiration, even crying out, 'Jai jai Rama!' and 'Jai jai Hari!' which the pilgrims answered full-throatedly.

Of course the vibrancy of the early morning could not last. The day was as hot as the last and Sophie was exhausted by the time camp was struck, the washing that had been done earlier spread out on bushes and grasses to dry, fires lit and last night's food warmed up. There was to be no rest, however: they soon rose to go on.

Sophie found herself falling back, behind Matteo and Pierre Eduard who were marching easily and well today. She was left behind with the women, slowed by their various burdens. One of them, although young, was so pale as to look ashen. She did not sing or talk but breathed heavily as she walked for she was carrying a child on her hip. The child looked old enough to walk but was clearly too weak to do so; his head lolled on the woman's shoulder as if he were asleep, or unconscious.

When they sat down on the roadside, by a field of sugarcane, to rest, Sophie asked her, 'Is he sick?' The woman of course did not understand but spoke a few sentences and a young man who stood listening explained to Sophie, 'She has eight children. Seven are dead. This one only is living. She is going to the shrine to ask the saint to spare him. But he has fallen ill. There is no doctor or medicine. She will pray for him at the shrine.'

Sophie stared at the woman's thin, narrow face and sunken eyes under the fold of the sari she wore over her head. How could she bring her only child out on this arduous march and take such a risk? she wanted to know. But already the woman was lifting up the child and they were on the road again, marching as the others sang, 'Tukaram, Tukaram . . .'

Later they paused at a roadside stall that sold cigarettes and soda water, and Sophie bought an orange drink and held it out to the woman, indicating that she should give it to her child to drink but the woman turned her head away. Sophie was angry enough to throw down the bottle; she was sure it was her lack of caste that made the woman refuse. Later she saw the young man fetch an earthen tumbler of tea and watched as they tried to dribble it into the boy's mouth. Thinking he might be the father or a relative, she said sharply, 'She should not have come.' He replied 'What can she do? If you have nothing else, you must have faith in God.' He threw the tumbler down in the dust and added, 'If this boy dies, she cannot go back to her husband. His family will blame her.' Then he picked up an orange pennant and marched ahead, disappearing into the crowd around the palanquin, all singing:

'Hari, Hari,
Bliss in my heart,
Hari . . .'

Sophie lost sight of the woman too. More people joined them, the *dindi* grew larger and larger and straggled through a landscape that was changing from muddy slush to the drier earth of a plateau where veins of black rock ran through the grassland and the air seemed drier even though clouds crouched on the horizon, waiting for a current of air on which to rise. Low hills bulged out of the earth, and eagles wheeled above them, wings outspread, circling slowly as if keeping a vigilant eye on the people crawling ant-like beneath them.

Yet another hill rose, on its peak another small pink temple like so many others they had passed. But now the *dindi* halted and Sophie saw it could not proceed – in front of them, at the foot of the hill, in a square field, crowds had assembled and a fair was in full swing. There were ferris wheels rotating in the air, with excruciating squeals, a loudspeaker was blaring music, a man with a bioscope was charging a few *paise* for the chance to peer into it, magicians squatted with their packs of cards and their cages of fortune-telling birds in front of them, and everywhere stalls were set up with goods for sale – heaps of onions and potatoes, hills of chilli powder and turmeric, glass bangles, mirrors, plastic buckets, bolts of printed cloth and toys of pith and paper dyed a lurid pink or violet. The crowds milling in the field were from other villages and towns, who had arrived earlier and already clambered up the hill for a *darshan* of the saint enshrined in the temple.

Matteo appeared at Sophie's side and clutched her arm. 'We are there, Sophie!' he cried, with such emotion in his eyes and on his face that she stared, bewildered. As far as she was concerned, they had arrived nowhere.

She did not try to follow the others up the hill to the temple which seemed too small and insignificant to be the goal of their long journey. She sank down on a flat bit of rock to smoke a cigarette and watched the crowds swarming up the hillside in a cloud of dust tinged saffron by the sun which was setting over the horizon, a great globe of pale light, before the darkness of another night fell. She was disturbed to find herself dis-appointed at the anti-climax of arrival, even reluctant to have their journey end.

Eventually she became aware that while everyone else had surged forward and upwards, there was one other person who had stayed back, not moving. Of course it was the woman with the child; she had placed him on a fold of her sari spread on the ground, and he was terribly still. The woman was not looking at him or at anyone; she held her head in her hands and stared at the ground.

Sophie got to her feet. She knew she ought to go to the woman and see to the child, but she could not move. She whimpered 'Matteo! Pierre Eduard!' finding that she was afraid to look at death.

The rain began to fall again that night.

'Matteo,' Sophie said, 'what are we doing here, Matteo?'

The policeman they had called to see to the dead child had offered them a space to sleep on the veranda of the police station, now locked and dark at the edge of the field. Sophie could not sleep or even lie down. She sat with her arms around her knees looking at the rain that dripped off the roof and splashed onto the edge of the veranda. The fair seemed to have been quenched by the rain, washed away by it, leaving no sign.

Matteo lay with his limbs spread out, wanting only to sleep. Why would she not lie down quietly and let him sleep? He groaned, 'What do you want, Sophie?'

'I want to know why we are here.'

'I told you – to find India, to understand India, and the mystery that is at the heart of India.'

'I have found it. At its heart is a dead child. A dead child, Matteo!'

'Don't shout, Sophie, I can hear,' he hissed. 'And why is it the dead child? Why not the temple? Or the people climbing up the hill, singing when they reach their god? Why not their journey, our journey?'

'Because at the end of that journey is a dead child,' she repeated.

Matteo covered his ears with his hands. 'Don't people die elsewhere?' he cried. 'Haven't children ever died in your own country?'

'Then why,' she breathed, lowering her knees and coming closer to him, 'couldn't we stay in our own country? To die there?'

'I told you, because here it is possible to understand the mystery. Over there it is not.'

'*Why* not?'

'Over there people don't even know there is a mystery. No one thinks about it. Here they do. There are people – great sages – to guide you. I need such a person.'

'And I?' she put her hand to her chest. 'Don't I need you? Don't you need me?'

He gave a groan. Now he had to sit up. He had to put his arm around her. He had to give in. Sighing, he promised to take her to Goa after the rains were over. To help her to go to sleep, he gave her a cigarette, one of a bundle he had been given by a sadhu he had run into at the fair. He lit it for her and while she smoked, sat breathing in its deep, pervasive aroma. Sometimes he held out his hand to take it from her so he could smoke too. Instead of sleeping, or talking, they sat on the veranda, looking out into the dark and the rain, while they smoked.

Perhaps that was why the last clear memory Sophie retained of that early time in India was of the woman squatting on the ground with her head in her hands, looking away from the dead child on a square of her sari on the ground, and of herself and Matteo smoking on the veranda while it rained in the dark.

After that all her memories became blurred, she could not make sense of what they had done, what had happened to them, where or when or how. The diary she had tried to write fell apart and disappeared without anyone noticing. The pilgrimage through India became suffused with the rich and aromatic haze of marijuana; it clung to her and became her clothing. It penetrated her and became her being.

Goa. She saw very little of Matteo there, or very little that she remembered. He vanished, or receded, like Pierre Eduard, and she found herself with Marc, with Gustave and Francis. The sand was warm as a bed, they burrowed into it like puppies, and slept. The sea caught them up, tossed them up on glassy green waves, then flung them back on shore. On their knees, they scrambled out, drenched, as far as the dry sand, and lay stretched out there, laughing. All night the palm tree leaves glistened and shivered, and Marc, who had a guitar, played the sad laments of fado that he had learnt from a Goan musician in a bar. Once someone hurled a bottle at him and cut a gash into his temple. He had sunk to the ground, holding the wound and crying, 'You have killed music. You have killed poetry. Call the police, call the police.' Sophie held her sarong to the cut, letting his blood soak into the patterned cloth. Then she walked into the sea and washed it clean.

Sometimes she cried herself. When her head throbbed and she was so giddy that she could not walk as far as the bushes for privacy, and seemed to be lying in a spreading pool of her own excrement, she cried quite shamefully. Peggy appeared and said, 'Come along now, there's a good girl,' and lifted her head so she could drink coconut water which was said to be a cure for diarrhoea.

Peggy disappeared, having found a buyer for the van in which she had driven to India through Iran, Afghanistan and Pakistan, so she could buy an airline ticket and fly home for Christmas.

All over India, in those years, ragged white mendicants in loose pyjamas and bandanas milled around ashrams and sadhus and yogis to the mirth and disbelief of Indians who composed a song for them and sang it everywhere, over loudspeakers, in markets and streets, on trains and buses:

> 'Take a puff, take a puff,
> Feel yourself disappear.
> Hare Krishna, hare Rama,
> Hare Krishna, hare Rama.'

In places like Goa they formed whole communities by themselves and scarcely ventured beyond them. By day they milled around the open markets that they set up on the sands under the coconut palms where they picked over each other's rucksacks, mirror-embroidered Rajasthani blouses, turquoise and coral jewellery from Tibet, incense sticks from Pondicherry, and the less visible contraband of drugs that had to be concealed from the vigilant Goan police. By night they gathered in bars where the feni was cheap, and drank till they needed to sleep and crawled away to their huts along the beach or the houses they rented in the villages to share between them.

Everyone had a story to tell. Stories swarmed, stories multiplied and proliferated. Sophie was uncertain which story belonged to whom: they droned in her ears like flies or mosquitoes and she listened, smiling, in the haze of smoke in which she lived as in a net.

Henri had just returned from the great fair on the banks of the river in Allahabad, the Kumbh Mela that all of them aspired to visit. 'Oh, it was *fantastique!'* he cried, quite aware of his enhanced status. *'Mer-veill-eux!* All day roaming in the sands, having *darshan* of the saints who had come, and hearing the discourses of the great sadhus – not from books, not from lecture notes, but from memory, from inspiration! Everyone dressed in the sacred colours. And the singing, all of us singing together. Eating together, spending our days in that holy atmosphere, *fan-tas-tique!'*

Andrea, sitting and plaiting Shula's hair into tiny braids entwined with coloured threads, told them, 'I went to a mela, too – not the Kumbh; this was in the South, on some other river, I have forgotten which one. There were hundreds, millions of people there too. Not one latrine in sight, of course. I got up in the dark and went down to the river bank before anyone else got there, being a modest sort of person, as you know. And I was sitting there when it started to get light – the way it does before the sun actually rises – and what do you think?' she giggled. 'Right next to me, all around me, everywhere, on every square foot of the river bank, there were people squatting with their water pots, to get things done before daylight! And when the sun came up, there we all were in the river together, washing our bottoms. Oh, yes, *fantastique!'* she mocked, flipping the tight little braids about in her hands expertly.

60

Henri glowered at her, then continued as if she had not interrupted. 'It was the sadhus I met at the Kumbh who were truly amazing. One brought with him his pet lioness. It is true! En-tire-ly harmless – he had fed her on rice and milk since she was a cub. He had even taught her to growl the sacred syllable: *Aum*!'

Gustave said that was not so impressive as what he had seen in a forest through which he had travelled, and where he had come across a yogi who meditated in the most remote and dangerous region. 'Tigers prowled around there but he paid them no attention – and he had no weapon, of course, with which to defend himself. One day he was deep in meditation when a tiger came right up to him to take a sniff at this strange human being and see if he was for eating. The yogi didn't even open his eyes. And the tiger just went away, left him unhurt.'

Shula, her head all covered with stiff, whip-like braids now, sat crosslegged and warned, 'But you have to be careful, too. I knew this woman who came to India to learn these powers, you know. They told her if she travelled to a cave in the Himalayas and sat there and meditated day and night without sleep for five days, she would gain these psychic powers she wanted. She did that – she travelled to it, she went into the cave and stayed there, alone, for five days and nights. It was full of snakes and scorpions but she stayed there, man! Then she came out and walked down to the village to get a taxi to the city. As they were driving along, she suddenly said, "Stop!" She made the taxi driver stop and got out on the roadside. One second later the taxi exploded – boom! Like that. So she had a sign, see, of the powers she had got in the cave. And she was very happy. When she got to the city, she checked into a hotel for the night. She was flying home next day. But when the manager came to call her the next morning in time to get to the airport, what do you think? She was lying there, dead. At the autopsy, they found the main artery to the heart had been severed, and one portion of the heart was entirely missing.'

This drove others to recount yet more experiences they had had, or had heard of others having, and of still more

61

remarkable people that they had met in ashrams and temples they had visited with all the zeal, Sophie thought, of shoppers in a market. She herself only half-listened, and when one of them began to give a discourse on the philosphy of Sri Aurobindo or to explain the creed of the *Bhagavad Gita* as expounded by Yogi Paramahansa, she found herself dipping lower into the haze of marijuana: she preferred the comfort of ignorance.

When she came to and listened once again, she discovered that the admiration and awe they had expressed was somehow weakened: they were talking now of the spectacular diseases they had caught and suffered from in the course of their pilgrimages. Typhoid vied with hepatitis, cholera with eczema – 'And Alexandra, you remember Alexandra? Well, will you believe it, but she is suspected of having leprosy, and is in a home for lepers. Comes from living with what she called a Buddhist monk. Buddhist monk!' Their horror escalated into laughter. Still more improbable affairs and romances were brought up – did anyone know what had become of Francesca who had followed a Khampa trader she had met in the market-place in Kalimpong to Tibet and was said to be held prisoner there as a Western spy? Or of Phyllis who claimed she had been raped by a boatman on the lake in Kashmir?

But how could anyone take that seriously? Phyllis, they all laughed, who believed in her stories? Not really so improbable, Andrea reminded them, and they remembered how she too had been raped, here in Goa, not so far from where they were sitting.

'Ahh,' beamed Nanette, a mother of three who had left them and her husband after twenty years of cooking them dinners which she finally realised they liked better than they did her, 'what would my husband and sons say if they could see me sitting here with all you adventurers?' She smiled rapturously.

The mention of homes and families made them catch each other's eyes, smile. They knew what their families could never guess, shared what their families would never know. They passed the marijuana joints around in the warm spirit of camaraderie.

Yet in the morning Theo was weeping because he had been robbed of the last of his opium and he had no money to buy more till he reached the post office of his next port of call but had no way of getting there, and Andrea accused Nanette of wearing a bandana that belonged to her and managed to scratch her cheek in the attempt to retrieve it. Marc withdrew to the furthest edge of the compound with his guitar and sat there amongst the canna lilies and papaya trees, playing a melancholy tune, then vanished altogether, leaving behind his belongings which the others fell upon and began to distribute amongst themselves.

When Sophie saw this, she struggled to her feet to snatch back his things and keep them for him but found someone had stolen her shoes. For some reason, this upset her dreadfully. Cursing her erstwhile friends, she ran into the village to escape from them, seeing them now as fiends and monsters who had caught her in a trap from which she had to break free.

After wandering in the sun and dust without her shoes for what seemed days, Sophie found herself seated at a small wooden table, on a bench, in a tea stall in the bazaar, a bottle of lemonade in front of her. She was trying to drink the lemonade because her mouth felt as if it was filled with hot sand but she could not drink it because she was choking and each time she raised the bottle, she set it down again, vaguely aware of being watched and laughed at by others in the place. She stared down at the tabletop, and at her hands resting on it. How large they were, with blunt fingers, how misshapen and ugly, with twisted purplish veins standing out on the backs, and swollen knobs for wrists. She lifted them to her hair and her hair felt dry, in thick, dirty strands on her shoulders. She stared down at the front of her freckled chest and could not recognise it as hers: the colour was all wrong, and the texture. She plucked at the faded, discoloured cloth of her sarong with her lips pulled downwards in a frown. Then, pushing aside the

63

lemonade bottle so that it fell over and foamed across the table-top onto the floor, she saw her feet planted on the earthen floor amongst the cigarette butts and bottle tops – her large, filthy feet, the soles cracked, a nail torn off at the toe, the heels rough as pumice stone and blackened around the edges. Could these be her feet? Or had someone replaced hers with another's? She had to get rid of them, leave them behind and run. She began to shake with horror, struggled to get up and lurched towards the door, then started to stumble away from her feet. The shopkeeper stood in the doorway and yelled at her to pay for the lemonade. She waved her hands to show she had no money. India was full of such creatures then, such dregs of Western society – what was a decent shopkeeper to do? he lamented and the others commiserated with him.

Sophie, still attached to the monstrous feet, went stumbling through the dust outside and crying. She was crying for Matteo – where was he? Ought he not to be with her, take care of her? Where was he – Matteo?

Matteo was seated crosslegged on the bare floor of a room he had rented, the door closed and the shutters lowered. He had done with the travels, the crowds, the pilgrims, the talk, the drink, the smoke, the adventures. He had had them, too, had travelled and searched them out with the others, but neither seen nor experienced what the others did.

Bathing in a wide river along with other pilgrims on a flight of steps leading down from a temple on the sandbank, he had noticed them standing and pointing at an object swirling in the muddy water, shouting excitedly to each other, 'Baba-ji! Baba-ji!' Matteo too climbed out of the water and stood on the steps, shading his eyes with his hand against the glare, trying to see what the others saw. He thought it might be an alligator or giant turtle, but a man flapping his cotton dhoti in the wind to dry it, told him, 'That is the Baba-ji of the temple. Eighty years old and he can swim from one bank to the other even when the river is in flood. He can dive and stay underwater for one hour, two hours, then suddenly appear sitting on the waves in lotus position, floating like a flower. See, see – ' he threw out his hand and chuckled with pride as if he himself had arranged it all for Matteo to see. Matteo did his best, standing on the steps in his streaming clothes, to see what the others saw. But the sun was strong, the muddy water turbulent, and the dark object rolling over and over in the waves, appearing and disappearing by turns, might have been a log, a dolphin or a turtle. Yet the others standing there on the temple steps by the river cried out, 'Baba-ji ki jai! Baba-ji ki jai!'

In another town he visited a yogi who had not slept for twenty-five years. A group of pilgrims returning from the cave where he lived pointed the way to Matteo and he trudged up the dusty track to a scattering of rocks like debris left behind on the red earth. They formed eerie shapes, leaning against each other, worn down by wind and rain. The track wound round them to a cave where the yogi sat, as they had told him, on a deer skin, looking with a bored expression at the flat landscape and the pilgrims struggling across it in lines. Matteo stared into the face which was heavy-jowled and vacant. Without returning his look, the yogi stretched out his hand to point at the notes and coins scattered on the deer skin by the others who had been to see him. When he did so, Matteo noticed the glint of a gold watch strap on his wrist. Twisting his lips, he turned away: why did the yogi who did not need sleep need a watch to tell him the time?

In one particularly squalid little town where everyone seemed to him to be diseased or disabled, and more than normally poor, he ran into a sudden pandemonium of excitement and learnt that the police had caught a yogi who walked about naked and refused to clothe himself. They had locked him in the gaol house for the night so he would learn the rules, and the people crowded around the little concrete block in which he was being held. The next morning he was released, and Matteo saw him walk out as he himself stood at a tea stall, drinking a tumbler of tea in the grey morning light, and the yogi was still naked. Now the people who had been laughing and mocking him followed him with devoutness, seeming to salute his defiance and steadfastness. 'Sky-clad baba, sky-clad baba,' they called him and walked behind him in a procession through the market-place. All Matteo could see was a gaunt, naked man, his skin scorched black by the sun, and covered with a coating of dust and ash. A poor man ill-fed and undressed, but Matteo failed to see how that made him, amongst all the others who were also ill-fed and barely clad, a saint.

Returning to the beach, Matteo collected with the others to see a yogi whose face and name appeared on posters printed and displayed all over the town, declaring that he could summon clouds out of the sky and bring rain through his psychic force. Matteo stood on the sand, straining to see a cloud appear over the horizon. When it grew dark and the others cried out in amazement, Matteo alone insisted that it was night that fell, and not rain but spray that dashed against them.

In disgust, Theo said to him, 'You're blind, man, you do not see.'

'Tell me how to see.'

'Through faith,' Theo roared, shaking his mane like a lion. 'Through faith. "With faith," ' he quoted, ' "the blind man pierced the pearl, the fingerless put a thread through it, and the tongueless praised it." You need to learn, man, and meditate. Do you think you can acquire faith without working for it?'

Then, feeling himself alone in his lack of faith, Matteo began to keep to himself. He felt disabled, without the skills the others possessed, a kind of leper amongst them. So he rented a room for himself where he might be alone and meditate and concentrate upon his need for the extra faculty that he desired and required if he was to survive. He had begun to feel that if he could not have a vision of spiritual truth then he could not continue to live – not here, not as he had done.

It was then that Sophie came stumbling in, weeping, her feet bare and dirty and her hair dishevelled. Sighing, Matteo gave up the room to her, fetched her water to wash in, left her sleeping on his mat, and went out, blinded by the sun, to be by himself. At night, he still did not feel he could go back into her company – or anyone else's – and spent the night out on the beach, in a boat a fisherman had pulled up under the coconut palms.

It became impossible to return to the room, to the company of anyone. He wandered away to be alone and to be further away from everyone. He walked inland where the others did not go, and the landscape changed to one of mudflats and then tilled fields, sparser vegetation, everything flattened by the immense sky and the punishing sun. He remembered hearing some talk of a temple in this region; he could not remember which deity was worshipped there but he had been told a *darshan* of it was considered specially blessed. He would go and find it: in this country one was never far from a temple. In fact it surprised him when, scanning the horizon where a line of trees was scribbled across the sky, there was no temple spire or mosque's dome to be seen. He set himself to find one, if only to prove himself right in his belief in Indian religiosity. It led him on a longer walk than he had anticipated. Most of it was across flat fields, drying in the sun; the stubble cut his feet painfully, and he would have been glad of a cloud or the shade of a tree.

Eventually he came to a grove of banyan, mango and jackfruit trees. He wondered if the temple might be there: there was often one in the vicinity of a banyan. Besides, he could rest in its shade. Wiping his face on his bandana, he went towards it but could see no structure, however elementary, that could be taken for a temple. Long aerial roots trailed from the branches and parrots sat at the top, eating the small red fruit. He wished there were water, that he might have a drink. There was nothing. A koel, high up and invisible amongst the leaves, mocked his disappointment with its high-pitched, repetitive call. As he stood there, dejected and fatigued, he saw lodged in a crack of the great grey tree trunk, a stone, and wondered if it were carved into the shape of a deity, an idol. But it was simply a smooth, round stone that had found a niche in the tree; there was no red or yellow powder, no flowers or lamps to suggest it might be an object of worship. No, this was no temple – only a stone, and an abode for a stone.

He was about to turn and leave in search of a drink of water when the bamboos at the other end of the grove parted to reveal a path he had not noticed earlier, and on it an old man appeared, wearing a bit of cloth tied around his waist, his matted grey hair tied in a topknot above his head, holding a brass pot in his hand. His face was so crossed with wrinkles as to appear scarred and his eyes were small and seemed half closed.

The old man gave him scarcely a glance through those small lost eyes. He walked past Matteo to pluck some flowers from a bush nearby, then returned to the banyan tree. Matteo watched as he bent towards the stone lodged in the tree trunk, dribbled water from his brass pot over it, sprinkled it with flowers, murmuring what Matteo took to be prayers. Having done that, he hobbled away, sighing 'Aum, Aum,' to himself, and disappeared behind the bamboos from where he had come.

Now Matteo studied the stone again – was it carved after all, but so smoothed by time and touch as not to have appeared an idol to him? He stared and stared but it still seemed nothing but a smooth, round stone even if it was now consecrated with drops of holy water and some flower petals. Then, as he continued to gaze at it, he saw that what was perfectly balanced there in a cleft in the tree was not a stone at all but a circle, and it contained within it another circle, and another; that there was no beginning and no end to them; they were infinite; they were infinity. That circle was the universe itself, containing world within world, ring upon ring, sphere within sphere, and to his dazzled eyes they revolved within each other and yet remained perfectly static, maintaining a total balance and harmony that could only be divine. The stone glowed now, became brilliant in Matteo's eyes, refulgent with what was, he felt certain, divine light.

He let out a cry and heard the koel flutter out of the tree and sweep upwards into the sky.

Down the village road, with a great din of drums and trumpets that made the stray dogs get up out of the dust and howl and the villagers come to their doors to look out, a procession passed by, waving streamers and balloons in party colours of pink and purple and yellow. In its midst, six men in black suits carried upon their shoulders a small bier which they held tilted so all could see that it contained a small, wax doll-like girl child in a lace dress and a lace veil, her head upon a pink lace pillow and her hands folded over a velvet-bound prayer book laid upon her chest. She was surrounded by flowers. The women in the procession held flowers too, and prayer books, and shuffled slowly through the dust.

From the other direction came Matteo, stumbling along the road, blinking as if amazed by the sight he saw. Before anyone could stop him, he leapt in front of the procession and there began to dance, jumping and whirling, twisting and whirling, till Nanette and Francis seized him and dragged him out of the way of the mourners, some of whom were threatening to give him the beating of his life.

'The goddess!' he howled, thrashing around on his knees, 'the goddess is going to be married. Let me go – let me go to her wedding,' he screamed, but they dragged him through the dust, up the stairs and across the veranda to his room and locked him in, telling Sophie, 'Don't let him out till the funeral is over, or he'll get beaten up, d'you hear?'

Sophie watched him beat against the door and then lie sobbing on the mat. Pity stirred inside her. 'It was a doll, Matteo,' she said. 'Couldn't you see it was a doll?'

'A doll for you. To me, a goddess,' he responded with passion.

A few days after that, when she was sitting on the beach, they came and pulled her to her feet and hurried her to the tavern where Matteo was lying prostrate on the floor, heaving himself to his knees and falling again amongst the feet of the drinking customers.

'He thinks it's a temple,' Francis told her in disgust. 'What's gone wrong with him? You'd better do something, Sophie.'

Sophie walked up to him where he grovelled in the centre of the curious onlookers. Now she felt no pity for him. She merely found him ridiculous, an insect that had become disoriented and lost its bearings. Putting out her foot, she gave him a kick in the side. 'He's a fool,' she said.

Everyone fell silent, their expressions turning grave and disapproving. Francis dragged her out.

Then he nearly drowned himself in the sea where he had gone bathing at high tide, insisting it was the holy Ganga and that he had to bathe while the sun was in eclipse. They saw him disappear again and again under the high crested waves that leapt up to the sun, now at its noontime height and blazing, and finally a fisherman went in to catch him by his hair and drag him out onto the sand where he lay spewing sea-water in gasps.

Sophie was shaken when she saw him: he lay so limply on the wet sand, his head twisted to one side and the water gushing from him. She remembered him now as he had been, went down on her knees and wept, 'Matteo!'

The doctor in the small village dispensary to which they took him said to her, as she sat beside the narrow bed on which Matteo had been laid, 'Do you want him to die? Don't you think it is time to leave for your own country?' Although he had worked hard at pumping the water out of Matteo's lungs and reviving him so that he was now breathing evenly and recovering, the doctor's face was tense with dislike.

Sophie was ashamed and muttered something about tickets and travel. The doctor turned back to the counter where he had been dividing a bottle of powder into small paper spills that he dispensed through a hole in the wall to his patients queuing on the veranda outside. Francis, who had sat beside Sophie through Matteo's ordeal, muttered, 'Matteo doesn't need a doctor, he needs a guru.'

Although he had kept his voice low, the doctor heard him

and looked over his shoulder at them with disgust. Francis tried to explain: 'He has it bad; all that searching and meditating can drive you crazy if you haven't a guru to guide you.'

The doctor said nothing, simply went on folding his paper spills, but after Sophie and Francis left, he went back to check on Matteo's pulse. Matteo was awake, and the doctor said to him, 'So I hear you are searching for divine light.'

Matteo was too weak to deny, or to assent to his words. He lay motionless, his face pinched and pale.

'Divine light can kill,' the doctor went on. 'The gods are destructive in this country.'

It was not fair: Matteo could not protest, he was far too weak. Tears liquefied his eyes out of weakness and self-pity.

The doctor saw them and sat down on the chair by his bed, and lit himself a cigarette. He seemed to have contempt for Matteo and yet could not leave him alone. For a while he stared out of the open door at the veranda which was empty now, the last of the patients having left. The light on the road outside was dim, it was nearly evening. Suddenly the emptiness of the scene filled with a flock of crows that arrived out of the sky to hover over something in the ditch that had caught their alert eyes. They cawed in excitement.

'Why not try books instead?' the doctor asked. 'Study?' He continued to look enquiringly out into the road in the evening light as if he were addressing the crows there.

Matteo stirred on the thin mattress, wanting to reply.

The doctor glanced at him. 'You come to India and you do not even bother to learn about it. You think you can understand it without any study, that divine light is like a flash of lightning.' He drew upon his cigarette and then exhaled slowly. 'It is not a bad idea to acquire knowledge first. In books you can find a way – or a flash of light – that will show you how to deal with – with this – ' he gestured with a long graceful hand at the scene outside the door. What was struggling along in the ditch, he saw, was a dog, either maimed or sick, and the crows were bent upon its extinction.

He flung his cigarette out of the door at them and got up abruptly. 'Now I am going to leave you here for the night to rest. Please don't try to get up before morning.'

He went across to his work table and began to collect his belongings, then went towards the door. Before he left, he said, 'If I had not studied, I would be like that dog in the road. But I went to medical school; my parents saved all their money and sent me to medical school. It was very hard. I had no food sometimes, no money for clothes or books. The college was not good, too crowded. Somehow I passed the exams. I became a doctor.' His face was in the shadows and the room was nearly dark now but Matteo, staring at him, could see that it was for himself that he had contempt, and for his own life. 'I would have died to go to the West for studies,' he ended, before shutting the door.

Francis and Theo came to the railway station with Sophie and Matteo to put them on the train. On the way, Matteo fell upon his knees before a young girl carrying a basket of eggs to market, a broom for sale in a wayside shop, a lamppost outside the police station; when they hauled him to his feet and dragged him away, he pleaded, 'Don't you see? Are you all blind? The divine manifests itself in everything, everybody – '

'Yes, yes,' they agreed, and handed a slip of paper with an address to Sophie. 'Here it is, keep it safe – Matteo will only lose it. It is the address of the ashram that will take him in. The swami we met said it was the best place for anyone who really wants to learn.'

Matteo stood on the platform meekly, his hands folded before him. But suddenly he darted aside and rushed over to a magazine and book stall; he had seen something there that he wanted, amongst all the garish paperback books with their lurid titles of war and lust. It was the life of a saint, cheaply printed by an ashram press, and bore on its cover a photograph of her face, blurred beneath a white turban. *The Mother* was its title and Matteo clutched it so fiercely that the vendor became agitated, shouting, 'Hey, pay up.' Theo came to pay him and led Matteo away by his arm.

'My God, Sophie, you better watch him,' he said, and then helped them into the third-class compartment of the train to Bihar. Francis bought them packets of biscuits, paper bags of guavas and bananas, clay pots of tea, then stood with Theo waving to them from the platform.

As he felt the great iron wheels start up under him and begin to roll, Matteo got to his feet in alarm. His eyes looked wild with fear and his hands sought a way out through the crowds. Sophie caught and tugged the ends of his shirt violently to bring him back to the seat beside her.

'Listen, Matteo,' she hissed, 'you sit down now, and I will get you to your guru, hear?' It seemed to her that she must hand him over, hand over responsibility for him, and if this guru and the ashram in Bihar were willing to accept Matteo, then she must get him there. For this purpose she was willing to travel a thousand miles in the company of peasants who smelt powerfully of unwashed clothes, stale food, wood smoke and dust, merchants and their families who travelled with large baskets of food and pickles, beggars who could not afford to buy tickets and cowered under the benches or made themselves invisible in the latrines when the sweating and harassed conductors came to check. Resolutely she held on to her place on the bench and made sure that Matteo was not edged off his. Heads in their hands, they dozed through the sweltering day, and at night were wakeful and watched the powerful lights of wayside stations go by, lighting up scenes of coolies bowed under bales and crates of goods, shrouded figures stretched out to sleep, others patiently filling jars and pots at water pumps, and dogs scurrying amidst the debris, that might have been scenes from a nightmare, or pictures of hell. As they travelled relentlessly through the great dark plain that seemed to have no end, Sophie heard Matteo muttering to himself in horror. 'The light's gone – I can't see – I'm blind – '

'Fool,' Sophie said to him shortly. 'It is night and we are out on the land where there are no lights to see.'

Yet, when they arrived in the city, he rather than Sophie summoned up the resolve to make their way through the choked streets and bazaars to the ashram and face the disappointment of finding it was no secluded grove upon a river bank but a mass of concrete structures behind a high iron gate and walls topped with barbed wire in the heart of the city. He had the surly guard open the gates to them and led her into the courtyard that lay between the dark, drab buildings that made up the ashram. When they were taken down a long veranda littered with debris to a room with streaked and faded walls, dust-coated windows, shadeless light bulbs and an electric fan that did not work, Sophie sighed before lowering her rucksack to the ground and sinking onto it.

'Yes,' she said, 'I knew it would be like this.'

He made her come with him to the swami whose permission was required for their stay. The swami was sitting at a desk on an upholstered chair, his well-groomed appearance in striking contrast to the squalor outside his room. After Matteo had introduced himself, he said disapprovingly, 'Look at yourself. Look how you have come to hear the holy words spoken. Don't you know you should be clean and bathed and well clothed and in good health to receive them?' Matteo hung his head in apology and heard a titter from the younger swami who had brought him here and stood at the door, listening.

Sophie had not understood the words – she found the English spoken by Indians as incomprehensible as the native languages – but she heard the hostility in them and glared.

Later Matteo stormed at her, 'When did you last wash your clothes? Do you even have a piece of soap with you? Have you given up washing your hair?' She spat back 'Wash, what for? To go and sit with those beggars?' She refused to leave the room again but Matteo went out of the ashram gates to find a barber in the bazaar. He sat in a wooden kiosk hung with a single small mirror amongst many pictures of gods and goddesses all decorated with tinsel, had a sheet tied around his neck and then a shave and haircut from a small bald barber who whistled through his gold teeth as he flashed his knives and scissors and worked. Urchins gathered to watch and giggle and followed him back to the ashram gates. He bathed under an outdoor tap, trying to rid himself of the small bristling hairs that had fallen into his clothes, and remove the clinging stench of perfumed hair oil the barber had rubbed onto his head.

He was still damp and gleaming when he asked to be taken back to the swami. The younger man who was to lead him there asked, 'Don't you know, you must go to your guru with an offering?' Matteo returned to the bazaar and from a fruit barrow bought a bag of oranges, bananas, custard apples and cheekoos. Feeling dusty and hot again, he returned to the ashram and presented them to the swami. There was a drawer pulled half open in the desk and the swami made the briefest gesture in its direction. Matteo saw it was filled with Wills Goldflake cigarettes, fountain pens, a gold-plated lighter, and even currency in several different denominations. Matteo's offering was clearly despicable in comparison.

Nevertheless he was aware he had been accepted when he was given instructions regarding the rules and regulations of the ashram to which he would have to adhere. Everyone had to wake at four o'clock in the morning and come down for an hour of meditation in the long, colonnaded hall on the ground floor of the main building. They were given some time in which to bathe and dress, before returning to a public room for their breakfast of black tea and bowls of sprouted lentils. Then the lessons began for Matteo and he spent the day going from one teacher to another. He took a class in Sanskrit with a swami who had been a schoolteacher and was now too aged for work but still had a professionally fierce expression and held a wooden ruler in his hand as though it were an indispensable adjunct to the teacher's role. In the evening there were prayers around a shrine in the central courtyard and after that the head swami gave a discourse that was relayed over loudspeakers to every part of the ashram, interspersed with hymns that rang late into the night.

Sophie, who remained by herself in their room upstairs,

found herself kept awake by the loudspeakers although she was determined to take no part in Matteo's life any more. She had of course to go down for meals and baths but the others seemed to be aware of her angry resistance to the regulations and eyed her with animosity. She found that the foreign contingent in this ashram worked sternly and hard at their lessons to prove themselves equal to and perhaps superior to the Indian disciples, who clearly felt they had a natural right to all the ashram offered, and both groups were equally contemptuous of Sophie although they showed it in different ways. The foreign disciples became tight-lipped and silent when Sophie was present to show they did not approve of the loose-living, fun-loving flower children of Goa to whose company they knew she had once belonged, and were quick to point out any mistakes to her, while the Indian disciples were chiefly concerned that she knew her place when it came to such ritual activities as baths and meals. Collecting water at the hand pump in the bathing enclosure at the back of the buildings was a perpetual occasion for bickering: it seemed to Sophie that she was always being edged out of the queue and never came up to the front of it and was made to wait for what seemed hours to fill a bucket. Once she was holding only a drinking mug to be filled when the swami in front of her had a row of buckets and pots and jars lined up. 'Here, let me just fill my mug,' she said repeatedly but it was ignored, whereupon she lost her patience and held out the mug over his bucket to fill. The next minute she found he had seized the bucket and emptied it over her feet in outrage and was screaming hysterically that she had polluted the water. Even Matteo came to see what the row was about, the news of it spread all over.

Meals were served to the foreigners not in the dining hall with the Indian disciples but on the verandas outside and they were served on leaf plates that could be thrown away after a meal and were not re-used; in other words, there was no chance of the Hindu disciples being polluted. When Sophie understood this arrangement, she refused to eat in the veranda and went to sit on the steps behind the kitchen where a pack of stray dogs lived by licking the discarded leaf plates clean. She ate a bag of peanuts instead, cracking the shells between her teeth and spitting them out on the steps. Loud complaints were made and Matteo came to hiss, 'Sophie, please, do you mind! If you don't like it here, please remember I have to stay in order to study. Can't you behave?' She got to her feet, gathering her sarong about her, stared into his angry face as if she were about to reply, then turned and trailed away helplessly. The spirit to fight him required a strength she no longer had: it had dwindled away.

It was difficult to remember, let alone regain the spirit of adventure with which they had set out for India. To begin with the possibilities had seemed endless and fascinating: with the money from Sophie's parents they might have trekked in the Himalayas, lived as beachcombers in Goa or even as rajas in a palace for a while. Then how was it they were living in this filth and squalor, this meanness and hardship amongst people who despised them even as they exploited them? Sophie tried to retrace their steps, but the speed with which they had moved left her dazed and bewildered. Sitting on the steps, plucking at her sarong, scratching at her arms and legs, Sophie was baffled by what it had all come to, and the dark inexplicable gulf that now existed between them. Then she shook her head fiercely, her hair whipping around her face in angry denial of that gulf. They had come to India together, to share an adventure: they would go through it together, stay together, recover their unique and essential love. She pushed out her underlip and scowled to persuade herself of that, but the flies bothered her, the heat of the sun made her wilt and soon she was wondering if her strength had not already run out. Then she was ready to cry.

She kept out of the ashram as much as she could, shuffling down the city streets, trying to find a bench to sit on, or a tea stall in which she would not be harassed by the curious. She missed her friends in Goa and the beaches, but Matteo had brought her to a city where there were no tourist attractions, where the people all seemed as hard and driven as he himself was becoming in their company. Was it for this that they had come to India?

Looking out of a bus window – she had wandered further than she had meant to and was obliged to take a bus back to the ashram – an improbable signboard, hanging askew on a gatepost, caught her eye: *Zoological Gardens* it said, in rusty letters on a tin board, *Entrance Re. 1, adults, 50 p. children*. She could hardly believe the words but there was a ticket booth, a gate and a barrow with peanuts for sale – and then the bus trundled on through the traffic and she lost sight of it.

With some determination she made her way back to it, however, and discovered it was the back entrance to the municipal park, one portion of which had been fenced off as a zoo. After that, she went there almost daily, even when she had no money; she found ways of slipping through a gap in the hedge and throwing flirtatious smiles at the gardeners who noticed her unorthodox entry. To begin with, the relief of sitting under a shady tree quietly was enough to please her for hours on end but soon she fell into a routine of visiting the cages by turn: first the small brown rhesus monkeys who sat on their leafless tree in a concrete yard with expressions of total dejection on their wizened faces, then the cage of Himalayan mynahs and whistling thrushes that clung to the wire netting and shrieked, and even a hyena with a hunched back and bristling hair that seemed to have just emerged from its lair and its meal of bloodied flesh, it smelt so offensively. For all its slouching ugliness and malodour, Sophie found she preferred its company to that of the inmates of the ashram, its cringing, snarling defensiveness more compatible. But always she was drawn in the end to linger by the most beautiful beast of all, a black leopard. Still young, perhaps new to the zoo, it was not broken in, and paced in its small cage without ceasing, up and down, up and down, on restless silent paws, and only by the faintest twitch of its whiskers or a glint in its glassy green eyes betraying what churned in its unquiet heart. Sometimes it glanced at Sophie who stood there, holding onto the railings and admiring it, but mostly it pretended she was not there, that it was alone with no one to observe its humiliation.

As she did the round, she tried to get free and shake off the onlookers she always seemed to attract, just as the beasts in the cages attracted them: bands of children or, more often, of young men who seemed to have nowhere to go and nothing to do and to be endlessly in search of diversion. Mostly they achieved this by devising ways of infuriating Sophie, by loudly smacking their lips or making obscene gestures with long, supple fingers, or bursting into rollicking songs when they were within her earshot, of which some words were in English so she would understand:

> 'Lovely-si-madam,
> O lovely-si-madam,
> Come he-re, my de-urr –'

they yowled, maddening her. Or else they drew her attention by teasing the animals – poking sticks at the hyena and throwing lighted cigarette butts into the monkeys' cages. She scolded and cursed them but what made all reserve break in her was to see them torment the leopard, pelting it with gravel, throwing rocks into its cage or striking the cage with sticks till it snarled in protest and clambered up the bars in an effort to break out and demolish them.

Seeing that, Sophie lifted her sarong and came at them, screaming, even bending to scoop up pebbles to fling at them and make them retreat, although they continued to jeer and call out obscenities from behind the hibiscus bushes and canna lilies. Then she could only hope for a gardener to come to her rescue.

Why did she go there anyway? Why did she let this happen to her again and again? She wept with her head in her hands.

'We have to leave, Matteo,' she said at night, 'we have to.'

'No, we don't,' he protested. 'I have to stay and study. This is where I have come to learn – '

'Learn what, Matteo? To be like them?'

He stared at her and then said something extraordinary to her. 'It would be better than to be like you,' he observed coldly, and amended that a moment later to 'like us'.

'Why do you hate us so much?' she asked. 'What do you find so hateful that you must become someone else?'

He said nothing but he tried to avoid her and keep to the company of his teachers, barely acknowledging her presence when they met in public areas. He came to their room late at night, having sat up and listened to the swami's discourse downstairs while she lay on her strip of matting, shutting out the bright lights trained on the assembly outside by laying her arm across her eyes and wishing she could somehow shut off the sound. Occasionally at this hour he would make love to her and this he did with a new contempt, and a violence that was so unlike him, it shocked her. He would grasp her and manhandle her as if to hurt her and, in fact, when she cried out in pain or fear, he would let out a small laugh, exultant, as if he had achieved his end. Sometimes, if she felt strong enough, she struck at him and fought him but this made him more violent. Then he would leave her to go and sit against the wall, his face twisted with revulsion, or he would grab his roll of matting or a sheet and fling out of the room to go and sleep on the veranda.

His disgust infected her as if it were a disease. She came to loathe herself, scratching at the scabs and boils on her body with something more than physical revulsion. Nausea rose in her throat and she often lay on the ground, sick till she was drained. Once it came upon her when she was on the street, at the gate of the zoological gardens; a rickshaw driver picked her up and pedalled her back to the ashram, depositing her there and demanding payment from the sullen guard. A quiet Australian who spent most of his hours meditating alone behind the banana trees in the back garden, even removing his meals to the privacy of their shade, happened to see the fracas as he picked his way through the courtyard, and came to pay off the rickshaw driver and lead her into the ashram. She had never heard him speak before and could hardly believe it when she heard him say, 'You're ill, you need a doctor.'

No one had mentioned a doctor to her earlier, and she had not considered seeing one; it had gone out of her mind that anyone could help her, or might want to. 'Doctor?' she repeated foolishly.

'The ashram has a doctor, and a dispensary. You should go there.'

She laughed: the idea seemed so incongruous, something she had left behind in her past. But he evidently spoke to Matteo, or possibly to the doctor, and she found herself taken there and sat upon a stool beside the doctor's desk in a small gloomy cell where there was a bed with a rubber sheet, a glass cupboard filled with bottles of tiny pills, and even an enamel bowl. Throughout the examination she stared at the enamel bowl – its whiteness, its glaze – as if it were a remnant of the past that had curiously caught up with her here. She paid no attention to the doctor's probings or questioning and let Matteo lead her back to their room upstairs. At least, he tried to but she collapsed on the stairs, doubling over, and was very sick.

Unexpectedly, Matteo did not withdraw or push her away in disgust. He held her head and when she had finished, told her the doctor had said she was pregnant.

'I am?' she asked stupidly, shivering now because although her face was wet with perspiration, she felt icily cold.

Matteo took the corner of his shirt and wiped her face.

It did not help their situation at all. The news that she was pregnant made everyone shun her even more zealously. One of the women disciples was heard to say, during a meal, 'What do they think, that they can come here and live like animals in our ashram?' She was ladling out food from a pail and Sophie, hearing her, turned away without any. Some sniggered.

This attitude was made plain not only to Sophie but also to Matteo who had until now felt he was making progress and achieving the status of an exceptional student of Sanskrit and yoga. His Sanskrit teacher who had come to regard him as his star pupil and hold him up as an example to those like the Australian, Richard, who were slower and clumsier, now shouted, 'You are making no progress, no progress at all.' Matteo had just handed in a page of careful handwriting and read half a dozen verses without faltering, and looked at him in amazement.

It was not the first or only time that someone had fallen out of favour. The making and unmaking of favourites was a perpetual drama at the ashram. During Matteo's and Sophie's stay a particularly dedicated disciple had gone so far in his meditative practices that he had fallen into a trance from which he could not be roused. Another time he had had a violent seizure. Thereupon he was asked to leave and when he refused, weeping, 'Why are you so cruel to me? What have I done wrong?' his parents were summoned to fetch him away. Another disciple had been dismissed from the ashram because a servant girl was found to have become pregnant, it was rumoured by him. However, he was already back, forgiven, although the girl was no longer to be seen. Matteo found the man particularly revolting, with yellow eyes and a stubble beard. Did he himself resemble this bestial fellow? Is that how the others saw him now?

The Australian waited until the Sanskrit lesson was over and then, putting his books away carefully in a cloth bag, said quietly, not looking at Matteo, 'Why don't you go away for the summer? I know an ashram in the hills – well, not real mountains, but at the foot of them. Your wife will like it. It's different from here.'

'What d'you mean?'

'It's different,' Richard repeated. 'The head is a – is a – ' he stammered, for the first time revealing this flaw in his speech, 'a – a woman – '

Matteo stared.

'It's not – not – not like this – this place. She l-lets families stay. You can h-have a f-family there,' he finished, red-faced. Having done so, he retreated to the safety of his silence.

Matteo waited till he seemed composed and then asked him for the address. Richard did not attempt to utter it but wrote it out on a piece of paper. Handing it over, he brought himself to say some words that puzzled Matteo further. 'The m-mother,' he said, 'm-m-mother.'

But Matteo had no intention of following this well-meant piece of advice. He had sworn to be a disciple and it seemed only right that the disciple's life should be hard: humility and penance were lessons he set himself to learn. Of course he could not be blind to the thickening and darkening of the atmosphere in the ashram and finally realised that it was egoistic folly to imagine he and Sophie were at the centre of all the acrimony and censure. No, from the talk he heard in the dining hall and during baths, he learnt that far greater issues were being debated than the teaching of lessons to one more poor disciple.

There had always been much talk of various court cases in which the ashram was involved; some of the disciples – the Indian disciples – were lawyers who handled these cases for the swamis, so reports were frequently presented and freely discussed. Most of the cases had to do with property: it appeared the ashram owned extensive properties in the town and also outside it. Several of these were under dispute of one kind or another, and whenever one was brought to court, the atmosphere became quite charged.

Of course the disciples had little to do with these except observe their development although occasionally there was a celebration of a successful court case when the lawyers, or others involved, brought to the ashram special treats of rice pudding and fruit and distributed it amongst all the inmates. They would enjoy the treat even if they knew little of the reasons for it. Sometimes the lawyers would bring along their wives and daughters to serve the food. It was evidently considered a meritorious act. These women dressed in fine clothes and gold jewellery and hurried about with their heads covered, showing how aware they were of the privilege.

At this time a case came up that did directly involve them all. Matteo learnt that a house next to the ashram grounds, a three-storeyed stucco structure with a flat roof and deep verandas, had been left to the ashram by a devout disciple in his will at his death. His tenants had steadily ignored the eviction notice served them and continued to occupy it.

One morning when the disciples were having their breakfast of black tea and lentils in the veranda, one of the swamis came in at the gate and shouted out an excited account of what had happened in the night: a band of hooligans had attacked the house and looted it, throwing the furniture out into the street and driving out the occupants. Some of the younger swamis sprang up to go and have a look, others discussed the matter loudly and with many gesticulations, but there were some who fell silent and did not seem to know what to say. One who got up and began to shuffle away was heard to mutter 'Very bad, very bad. Head swami should not have given such orders. Not in accordance with *dharma*. Bad, bad.' He spoke in a low voice but those who were sitting on the steps as he passed by heard him and so learnt where the orders had come from.

Matteo was one of them. Like the others, he hung his head and considered the implications of what he had heard. Then he rose and slipped away, intending to fade away into the back garden till the furore had died down. He found his pyjama leg seized and grasped so fiercely that he nearly fell. It was Sophie who had been huddled against a pillar on the veranda, dull-eyed and sick but now looking like an animal about to spring.

'Sophie!' he exclaimed.

'You heard?' she hissed at him, dragging at his leg. 'Don't say you didn't, Matteo. Don't lie.'

'What – ' he began weakly, whereupon she raised her voice and began to scream. 'If we don't leave this place – if you don't leave today – I'll – I'll go to the police.' She was shaking her hair about her face, as if possessed. Others were staring. 'I'll tell the police what we heard. The police had better hear about this. I'll tell them if you won't – '

He had to bend and grasp her arms and shake her. 'We'll leave, we'll leave. Just be quiet. Stop screaming, Sophie.' When she showed no sign of calming down, he drew out the piece of paper Richard had given him and showed it to her, like a promise. 'We'll leave today. It's in the hills, Sophie, the hills.'

Sophie took it from him and stared at it, then flung it away, saying bitterly 'Another ashram!'

∿Chapter Two∾

Matteo was lying in bed again. When Sophie had gone to have a bath he had rolled up his belongings and slipped down to get a rickshaw to take him back to the ashram – or had tried to but had then collapsed and had to be carried back.

The doctor had to be fetched, nurses came scurrying. The day went by in the tense routine of a hospital crisis. Now he lay on his side, quite spent, with his knees drawn up and his hand under his chin.

Sophie, exhausted, sat on the upright chair beside the bed, drawing on her cigarette, and knew that he was awake. She did not mean to agitate him yet could not restrain herself from saying, 'It all comes of reading Hesse, that damned *The Journey to the East*, doesn't it? If it weren't for that book, you would not have thought of coming to India or of following this guru of yours to your death.'

He gave a small sigh. 'It was the book that opened my eyes,' he protested. 'Why do you say it leads me to my death when it is to my awakening I go?'

'Don't speak so, Matteo!' she cried, flinging away her cigarette. 'It will kill you if I don't get you away from here, I see that I must.'

For a while he did not say anything but when he spoke again it was in an even and reasonable voice. 'What is death?' he said. 'Do you remember that scene in *The Journey to the East* when the narrator sees the two figures by candlelight, one pouring himself into another?'

87

'And is that why you pour everything into her? What does that leave for me? For the children? Or for yourself? It has finished you –'

'What does the body matter? Or earthly life? What matters is – is the search. She takes me with her on her search.'

Sophie sat brooding, her hair hanging about her face. Then, sweeping it aside, she said defiantly, 'And what is it the two of you expect to find?' When she had no response from him, she went on, 'I read Hesse too, I can quote him also. Do you remember that scene in *Siddhartha* when Govinda says, "I will never cease seeking. That seems to be my destiny," and Siddhartha says to him, "Perhaps you seek too much . . . as a result of your seeking you cannot find." ' She saw Matteo go tense: he was listening, so she continued, slowly, trying to remember the words with accuracy. ' "When someone is seeking, it happens quite easily that he only sees what he is seeking; that he is unable to find anything, unable to absorb anything because he is only thinking of the thing he is seeking, because he has a goal, he is obsessed with his goal. Seeking means to have a goal, but finding means: to be free, to be receptive, to have no goal." '

Then she saw his face contorted with pain and became overcome with remorse. Touching his face with her fingertips she asked as gently as she could, 'What do you hope to find, Matteo?'

'I have found it, I *have*: what I never had before, what my life had been empty of – and now is not.'

'You believe that because you want to believe it,' Sophie snapped in spite of her better intentions. 'And what is this thing, this miracle, this unique being you believe in? Not what you imagine she is. You delude yourself, you know. Look again, Matteo, look again!'

Matteo entered the ashram alone. Sophie became so violently ill on the long train journey across the country from Bihar to the north, in the great heat of summer, that on their arrival she had to be lifted out and placed on a stretcher and taken directly to the city hospital. Matteo, hurrying to keep up with the stretcher so that he could hold her hand, found it cold. Her head lolled upon her shoulders and her eyes rolled in the dark sockets; she was no longer conscious.

When she did regain consciousness and begin to take in her surroundings – the white walls, the stained ceiling, an iron bed rail – the fierce stench of antiseptics told her where she was but it did not explain the chalky white face lowered over her, the pale blue eyes and the fine grey hair and the English voice saying, 'Feeling better, my dear?' She became confused; the sights and smells, the very air, limp and heavy with heat, were familiar enough, but the foreign voice and foreign face did not fit into the context. She reached out to touch whatever was real, and grasped a square, cool, clean hand. For some reason this made her cry, wordlessly, and the doctor – clearly she was that – patted her, saying, 'There, there, no need to cry, dear. You're going to be well soon, we'll see to that.'

Sophie found her voice: she let out a wail. 'Please, please, I want to go home,' she wept like a little girl. The more the doctor patted her and comforted her, the louder she wailed, 'Please, please, send me home – ' till the doctor said, 'There, you sound better already! That's a good, strong cry if ever I heard one,' and she seemed so pleased that Sophie stopped abruptly. 'Good girl, now just let me fix this oxygen mask on and give you a whiff – we've got to take care of the baby, too, you know,' the doctor clucked on, and Sophie gave herself up in helplessness. 'No need to look so frightened,' she was saying to Matteo now, 'she will be all right, and so will the baby.'

Matteo was gone when Sophie next looked about her but Dr Bishop came every few hours and whenever Sophie saw her come in, unvaryingly clean and cheerful and white, she broke into sobs and clutched at her hand abjectly and shamelessly, pleading again and again, 'Send me home.' As she grew stronger, her grip on the doctor's hand became fiercer but Dr Bishop would somehow extricate it and stroke Sophie's hair, saying soothingly, 'Yes, yes, get your strength back first and then we shall see about going home.'

Matteo would come to visit her, slouching into the ward with his eyes lowered – Sophie had been put into the maternity ward and everywhere women were lying half-clothed, some in the throes of childbirth, screaming, 'I am dying, I am dying!' and others sitting up and nursing their small, wizened babies at breasts that swelled out of their hospital shifts like great moons. He would seat himself gingerly on the metal stool beside her bed, still not looking up. Sophie found this irritating beyond endurance and grew impatient for him to leave, to be alone with her legitimate and sanctioned weakness and helplessness.

She clung to her weakness, using it to draw sympathy and gentleness from the nurses and, above all, from Dr Bishop. In her crumpled white coat and with her grey hair combed into a bun and her swollen feet bulging out of boat-shaped white shoes with neatly tied laces, the doctor seemed to her a saviour. When Dr Bishop placed her freckled hands on the edge of the bed and bent over her so that her stethoscope swung into Sophie's face, it was all Sophie could do not to let out a sob and snatch at her hand in the same abject manner as on the day she had arrived. She deliberately assumed a helpless air and made her voice smaller and weaker in order to have more of such nourishing attention, but Dr Bishop would place her fingers on Sophie's pulse which gave away the truth and say brightly, 'Getting stronger, I can see. All that's needed is plenty of rest and – ' lifting up her finger and wagging it at Sophie as at a little girl, '*no* smoking.' Sophie knew without being told that she referred to the smoking of marijuana; she had forbidden it strictly and Sophie, with her memories of the train journey on which she had nearly died, and the consciousness of the living creature inside her, set her jaw and nodded in total agreement. 'Good girl!' the doctor would exclaim and Sophie glowed. She began to devise ways of keeping the doctor by her for a few minutes longer. Since she could no longer feign illness, she would try to ask questions and establish a more personal relationship.

'And when will you go home, doctor?' she asked once with what she thought cunning. Dr Bishop misunderstood her and thought Sophie meant the mission house on the other side of the wall from the hospital, and said yes, breakfast would be waiting for her there, but Sophie insisted, 'No, no, your home, I mean your real home.' Dr Bishop continued to look puzzled but said, 'Oh, I see, you mean where I come from? Why, it's just the tiniest little village in Cornwall and I haven't been there in years. Not since my mother died and my brother moved into her house. Oh dear, I can't say when I'll go again. It's a tiny house and he has a wife and four children. They send me a big box at Christmas, every year, with enough old clothes for all the servants at the Mission house,' and it was that home that she began to talk of again.

Sophie interrupted. 'When did you come to India? When did you leave home?'

'The year I joined the Mission,' Dr Bishop told her. 'I heard the Lord call me to India and I came to serve Him and have never stopped being grateful for this chance to serve.'

'Here, in this hospital?'

'No, no, no,' Dr Bishop laughed and, growing expansive, began to tell Sophie about the Mission, its other centres, the schools and hospitals it ran, and the ones where she had 'served'. Sophie lay against the flat pillow and the limp mattress and listened to Dr Bishop rattle off the names of South Indian villages, Bengali cities and Oriya towns and felt as if she herself were setting off on another journey through them. She became dizzy and nausea overtook her. Dr Bishop seemed not to notice and went on and on till a nurse came running to call her and then said, 'I'll bring you a little book about the Mission, you can read it all for yourself,' and hurried away.

Sophie sighed and folded her hands over her stomach, she closed her eyes and felt herself being swallowed up by her state of pregnancy.

That night she dreamt she was squatting on a dark hillside and suddenly the baby came slithering out of her in a stream of blood. She picked it up and spread out her skirt and placed the infant upon it. It lay there in coils, its head buried within. As she touched it and tried to unwrap it, she found it was a snake, cold and limp, and drew back her hand in horror.

Leaving Sophie in the hospital in Dr Bishop's care, Matteo had gone out into the street and climbed into one of the brightly painted bicycle rickshaws lined up at the gate for custom. Setting his rucksack between his feet and mopping his face with the bandana he kept tied around his head, Matteo directed the driver to take him to the ashram.

The driver seemed to know the address and complained, 'Very far, sir,' and argued over the fare for a while, then mounted the bicycle for the long ride.

They pedalled through the city without Matteo's noticing much about it: it was Sophie's bloodless face and limp hand that remained in the foreground for him, and the city was, after all, exactly like all other cities: improbably pink and violet cinema posters looming into the gritty sky over the flat rooftops and their paraphernalia of washing lines and pigeon roosts, small shops for grain and soda water and printed cotton lined along the open drains, above them the dilapidated living quarters of the shopkeepers and their families, wet clothes hanging out of the windows, women standing in the cluttered balconies and combing out each other's hair while rickshaws, bicycles, trucks and bullock carts rolled past endlessly. Loudspeakers blared cinema music, a local politician passed by on a float, holding a megaphone to his mouth and haranguing the public while his supporters threw coloured leaflets that fluttered up and then fell to be trodden under in the mud and debris. Two trucks locked in combat hooted their horns while the drivers shouted abuse and refused to unblock the traffic; the rickshaw driver manoeuvred his vehicle around them and past them wearily.

Gradually the bazaar petered out into a string of petrol

pumps, small cheap hotels garishly painted pink and blue, and signboards, schools and dispensaries standing haphazardly in barren fields. There were dusty lantana bushes growing beside the ditches and spindly eucalyptus trees along the road. Now they passed flat-roofed villas sunk deep in disorderly gardens of guava and citrus trees, potted marigolds and vegetable vines. Behind them open fields of ploughed earth stretched as far as the low scrubby foothills. Beyond them, in the thick haze of summer dust, the merest outline of the distant mountains could barely be discerned. They seemed illusory, possibly a mirage. Yet, going towards them, even if at this tortuous pace through the deeply rutted and dusty road, Matteo felt something inside him that was not so different from hope, or at least curiosity. He had now been in India long enough and travelled its plains for sufficient distances to regard the sight of a mountain as an event, both physically and metaphorically significant.

Now the cycle rickshaw was ploughing through dust so thick and deep that the wheels threatened to become embedded. They had gone off the main road and were making their way between deep hedges of pink and yellow lantana, over stones and rocks and through scrub, all thrumming in the heat of noon and rasping with the fiddling and scraping of cicadas. The driver no longer sat on his bicycle seat but stood up to pedal with loud grunts that made Matteo look at him with concern, and hold onto the sides of the rickshaw as it swayed and jolted.

Unexpectedly, a high iron gate painted a vivid sky blue reared up out of the scrub under a rank of tall, ramrod-straight ashoka trees that were the first sign of human habitation. The driver grunted to a halt, slipped off his bicycle and sank onto his heels in exhaustion. Matteo, paying him with a roll of notes from his shirt pocket, heaved the rucksack onto his back and unlatched the gate – a curved circle of ironwork above it gave the name of the ashram – and entered.

'Wait for you, sir?' the driver called, and Matteo half turned to wave him away, then continued on his way.

• • •

It seemed deserted even if everywhere there were signs of habitation and cultivation as though a magic spell had fallen upon the place and removed the inhabitants and cultivators themselves. In every direction a narrow path lined with bricks that were freshly whitewashed led into groves of oleander and hibiscus bushes in flower and citrus and guava orchards bearing fragrant fruit; bougainvillaea gushed up out of the sandy earth in fountains of papery flowers – pink, orange, yellow, crimson and lilac. Birds called to each other from the dense shade of mango and lichee trees in ringing voices as if they watched over the garden and were there to interrogate intruders like Matteo.

He heard water being pumped out and splashing onto stone, lavishly. He heard laughter but still saw no people. Matteo felt the hairs on the back of his neck begin to bristle and he recognised the sensation as one he had had as a child when he had wandered through the embroidered landscapes of old tapestries and lost himself in their magic wilderness.

He walked slowly and cautiously past signs that lined the paths and dotted the gardens, carefully lettered and painted with flowers, bearing such legends as *Well Beginning is Half Done, Character is Spirituality* and *Respect the Elders*. He read them as he walked past, increasingly bewildered.

Eventually, having passed hedges of flowering jasmine, he came upon a settlement of low houses, some in the shade of immense trees and others blazing white in the glare of the sun. These severe barrack-like structures were somewhat softened in effect by verandas that ran along them and the flowers planted in beds around them. As he moved closer to them – still slowly, still cautiously – human beings at last revealed themselves to him, but in the postures and attitudes of forest creatures: a pretty young woman with a head of golden hair and dressed in a salmon pink sarong carried a pail of water down a path, smiling as she did so with mysterious complicity; several young people, similarly dressed, sat on the veranda steps and seemed to be reading aloud to each other but looked up and smiled in greeting; behind the house, small

94

children were running about in a game, their voices raised in excitement. Matteo found himself as amazed by it all as he had been on encountering embroidered figures in the old tapestries. What was more, he found he was no longer accustomed to friendliness: he found it difficult to believe in their smiles, and smile back.

Was this a place for serious study and meditation? Had Richard misled him, for Sophie's sake? The atmosphere was so sunlit, so calm, so lit with smiles that he could not believe it was true, and searching for hidden clues gave his face a wary look.

More prosaic signs appeared at the sides of the paths now and directed him to an office. It did not exactly look like one, its veranda filled with birds, its door surrounded by bougainvillaea and canna lilies, but when he entered it he saw he was not misled: immediately in front of him, high on the wall, hung enormous tinted photographs of Swami Prem Krishna and the Mother, both garlanded with tinsel and paper roses. Moreover, the Mother's was the same he had once found on a book cover in a railway station; he had it in his rucksack and could have taken it out to verify it but did not need to: this ashram was clearly the one they had founded. They were nothing less than royal in their stateliness and dignity. Underneath were glass bookcases in which their books were displayed with their names repeated on every cover and spine.

The secretary at the desk, a small grey woman with a tiny precise mouth, produced forms for Matteo to fill in, looked at his documents and then allotted him a room in a house called Welcome; it was where guests stayed for short periods, she said. Matteo felt a pang of uneasiness – Welcome, not Truth or Knowledge? But as he hesitated, a passing devotee, barefoot and humming, offered to show him the way.

Welcome was another long low building with a row of doors opening onto a veranda – a common arrangement in hostels of the type, Matteo knew, but distinguished by its fresh paint, its extreme neatness and cleanliness. Similarly, the room he was shown was as bare as he knew he should expect, but its floor was polished till it gleamed and its single window looked not upon any city squalor but onto hillside – rocky, reddish, scrubby and stretching out as far as the huge and radiant sky. The cicadas' song rose, at that moment, to its crescendo and at the same time the sun reached its dazzling zenith.

'Welcome!' smiled the devotee, and vanished.

Matteo waited for the crash to follow.

It did not come. The day played itself out like the cicadas' song that had risen out of the sunstruck landscape and now dissipated in the twilight that fell upon the ashram like a visual silence. But then bells rang, conches blew and lights came on; everyone came out of their lairs and hurried towards a central courtyard. Here, on open verandas, the devotees were fed in the usual ashram arrangement of the *pangat*, seated in rows and bending over their trays that were filled for them. In spite of his preoccupations, Matteo could not help noting the freshness of the food and the tastiness. Once that was out of the way, they collected on a large, flat patio outside, under an immense ficus tree. Music followed, on drums, harmoniums, cymbals and guitars, and devotional songs were sung. Matteo saw that most of the devotees were young, particularly the foreign ones, dressed in pink and some of them quite comely, but there were also older people, dressed in white, who sat crosslegged up in front, and these were chiefly Indians. The singing was led by a young man of great beauty who played the harmonium, tilted his face to the sky and poured out a song so filled with the ache of desire that Matteo felt he could hardly bear it.

Then silence fell and everyone appeared to shuffle and change places; the rows broke up and instead a circle seemed to form. The circle of course had no leader and there was no one at its centre. When Matteo heard a voice begin to speak, in low, reverberant tones, he looked to see who it was that spoke, but it was a while before he made out the speaker: a small, aged woman who sat crosslegged like the others, dressed in a deep crimson robe under which she seemed shrunken and somewhat hunched, with her large head sunk between her shoulders, her hair done up in a turban and her eyes heavy lidded, hooded. She was speaking very slowly and clearly, enunciating each word very precisely, almost as if it were a lesson in elocution, but it took Matteo some time to make out that she spoke in English, for her voice and accent sounded so Indian, in its pronunciation of *d*s and *t*s, its rolled *r*s and heavy emphasis on the first syllables. Her deeply wrinkled skin was also dark as an Indian's, and he took her to be one of the older, perhaps the oldest devotee. Certainly the woman bore no resemblance to the handsome and radiant woman in the photographs of the Mother. Yet it quickly became evident that she was a figure of authority: when she spoke, or fell silent, everyone waited in intense anticipation of her next word, her next gesture, and took it in with grave avidity.

Then words did begin to link themselves into sentences and Matteo found himself taking them in.

'My friends, why have you come today? Why do you come every evening to sit with this old woman? You think she is old so she must be wise and can give you wisdom?

'She can give you no wisdom at all! No Knowledge!

'Do you hear that? Do you?

'You only smile! Why? Now you laugh! Tell me, why do you laugh? What is it that makes you smile and laugh? Ah, I understand! When you sit here with me, you remember why you have come to live here, you feel again the purpose of your lives: to experience bliss. And you are smiling because you know that together we experience Bliss, experience Joy. We feel we are in the presence of the Master. Yes? You feel his light coming to you like the Light of the sun that has set over there but still sends out light. No longer hot, no longer blazing, but tender, loving, good. Yes? And in this light, we feel ourselves loved and we are filled with Bliss. Yes?

'It is not like going to church, eh? Not like going to the temple? We do not bring offerings with us, we do not take off

97

our shoes or put on hats. We come as we are. We know the Master does not care what we wear, how we sit, what we sing.

'This is no church, my friends, this is no temple or mosque or vihara. We have no religion. Religion? Like the black crows up in the tree, caw–caw–caw, scolding, scolding! But do they crow at us now? No, they are silent! We have silenced them! They know we do not listen to the black scolding voices of religion here. Religion makes one ashamed, makes one guilty, makes one fearful. The Master has told you not to feel guilty, not to feel ashamed, not to be afraid. Open your hearts to love and light and the joy of loving, he said, and so we turn our backs to religion – so, like this! – and we close our ears to the scolding – like this! – and instead we look at the sky, and the light . . .'

And although everyone's attention, including Matteo's, was so concentrated upon her, upon her extraordinary words and her commanding gestures, what was strange was that this did not preclude an attention to the outer world. What Matteo noticed – and Sophie would have been incredulous for she was convinced that Matteo noticed nothing – was that while she spoke crows had settled into the branches of the ficus tree, ruffling their feathers, but made no sound and that an invisible cricket that had earlier played a strident tune now merely whispered in the background, and that the light in the sky that had seemed to dwindle into darkness while they ate now flared up behind the tree and over the rooftop in an extravagant display that was heightened from pale yellow to intense gold, and pale pink to deep rose, before it was finally blotted out, suddenly, by an inky welling up of darkness. In a strange way it was the old woman's voice – not the words but the voice itself – that gave all these natural phenomena a wonderful significance. It was the music that heightens emotion, heightens mood, and becomes inseparable from it. So she, too, was inseparable from the evening light, the silhouettes of the great trees, the darkness, the stirring, breathing life within it, and the first star, and because of her they had now an intensity that they had never had before.

Matteo, in an effort to describe later, to Sophie, how it had been, could describe it only as an experience of unity, the unity of the spiritual with the physical, the dark with the light, the human with the natural. But Sophie was to grimace and Matteo to fall silent – his words were dead words, they failed to convey the quality of flowering, of the opening up of petals and the revealing of a great luminous bloom which was what he experienced that evening.

'No, we have no shrine, we have no god. People come to us from the town, from cities and countries all over the world, and ask: What do you believe in? You believe in *no* God? Oh, they are shocked!' she laughed, clapping her hands. Everyone laughed. 'Shocking, is it not?

'But are we unbelievers? No, we are not! Oh, we believe, we believe much more than even they believe. We know the Divine Force is not in some idol, not in the cross, not even in the book. We know the Divine Force is everywhere. Sitting here under this great tree, this old tree that has been here ever since we first came and was here much before that, don't we all feel its Power? Is it not a good Power – giving us shelter, giving us shade, providing those birds with roosts and berries, and so many insects with homes? Yes, yes, I just felt one here on my neck – it dropped onto my neck to remind me, you see, that it also exists . . .' She touched the back of her neck and everyone roared. 'And look up at the sky, those birds that are flying home, making their way to their nests before it is com-plete-ly dark. What power is it that makes them fly through the sky and cover so much space with such beauty and grace that you would also like to have? But it is they who have been given the Divine Power. They too possess it.

'Everywhere we turn, my friends, we come upon the Divine Power. Turn, turn – and everywhere you turn, please look, please touch, please see. Be open to the Divine, let it enter you. Let the Power of the tree and the bird and the Master flow into you. Feel it enter your body, flow up through your fingers, up into your arms to your shoulders and into your very centre. Feel it here on your chest and down here on your abdomen – ' she touched these parts to show them – 'feel it go through you like a glowing light. When it enters you, are you not transformed by it? Allow it to happen, allow this transformation to happen!

'Some of you tried to feel the transformation and did not feel it. Some of you are feeling a little sad. I see some of you are sitting there and feeling a little sad, a little tired. Now you look around, you smile quickly, you put your shoulders back – so! Why? Why are you ashamed of feeling sad, or tired? I will not come and whip you. Do you see a whip in my hand? I am stretching my hands to you, my friends, I am telling you: take from me, take my strength, take my love for you, hold my hand, let me help you. Why do you think I live here amongst you? Why did the Master call me and tell me to stay with you? I would have followed him but he said No, he wished me to stay with you and help you at times when you are a little tired, a little sad.

'Do not try to pretend you are not tired and you are not sad. Let yourself be tired, be sad. Allow yourself this feeling – it is not bad. The sadness will take you along a path that will lead you where you have not gone before. The tiredness will let you experience what you have not experienced in the day when you were strong and active. These feelings must be felt fully, with all your being. That is the only purpose of our existence here, to experience fully, to *be* fully, my friends!

'Yes, I am limping a little today. You saw me limping when I came. Now my leg is a little stiff and I have to keep it – so. It hurts – a little. Walking here, I stumbled. She is growing old, you thought. And that is true,' she laughed, 'but I know something else. That stone was *put* in my way to make me stumble. Oh yes. Now you look surprised: who would do such a thing? Who is it who wants Mother to stumble and hurt herself? You look at each other, you look at yourselves, you wonder.

'No, no need for that. An Evil One put that stone in the path, an Evil One made me walk into it. Has it not happened to you? Have you not been hurt sometimes, fallen ill, heard someone shout at you, or perhaps even hit you? Yes, there is Evil in this world. If there is God or not, I cannot say, but there is Evil, I know. We do not want to believe this beautiful world contains Evil but it is there. Every day it tries to break into the world and destroy what is beautiful and well and happy.

'So, please, watch for it. Be very careful. Take very great care, please, and whenever you see it – turn upon it and tell it, Shoo! Go away! Do not come near!' She made shooing motions of her hands, creating ripples of laughter in her audience. 'I will tell you a story. When I was very young, came here as a very young girl, full of ideas, full of dreams about gods, about temples and religion – I went to a temple. I said all the prayers, I went around every one of the idols, left them money, placed flowers – but I was not happy, and I was not blessed. Oh no, I was not. It was very dark, and even if there were lights, it was still dark. And I could see Evil – I could *feel* Evil. And from one corner of that temple, from behind a pillar, the Evil One stepped out and approached me. I could see it –oh it was so ugly! It said to me, whispering in a low, low voice – like this – Come with me. Together we will be strong. We will be friends and together we will go out and make fools of the people and laugh at them and grow rich.

'Did I listen to it?

'Well, I stood, listening, and then I made *such* a face – like this! – and I pushed, pushed, pushed with all my strength – oof! – I pushed till I had sent the Evil One back into the hole from which it had come. And I stamped, stamped, stamped on it to keep it down, down, down – with all my force, yes.

'But sometimes it comes out again. It tries to catch me. Puts a stone in my path to make me stumble. Then I remember it. Ah, I think, the Evil One! It is hiding, it is not gone. I know I must be alert. I must be careful, so-o-o careful . . .

'Now, my friends, I let you rest a little. I let you sit here after eating a good meal, and rest a little. You have worked all day. Cutting vegetables, watering the garden, looking after the chickens and the cows, building the new sheds – oh, this Mother, she thinks up a lot of work for you to do, does she not?

'Yes, it is hard work. If you write and tell your families what work you are doing in the Mother's ashram, they will ask: Why? Why are you building sheds and milking cows and growing vegetables for the Mother? You never do these things at home! You do not *need* to do these at home! Is that not what they say to you? Tell me!'

There was laughter, embarrassed.

'Well, let me tell you why. You are doing it for the Mother because one must work, one must make efforts to achieve *anything*. And what are you trying to achieve? To make a farm for the Mother? To feed the Mother?

'I will tell you, you do not need to feed the Mother, my friends. The Mother is happy to retire to a cave in the mountains and live on spring water and roots and berries. That is all I need. I do not need this estate you have made through your efforts.

'But yes, you *do* need to learn the life of a devotee, have the experience of being a devotee. And that cannot be done without an effort.

'Ask a musician how he trained and he will tell you – how he went to his guru, begged to be taken as a pupil, came to live in the guru's house so that for twenty-four hours a day he lived in the atmosphere created by the guru. He served his guru, even by cooking his food and sweeping his floor, everything. Then the guru agreed to give him a lesson, and he learnt. Through many years this *sadhna* carried on before he could call himself a musician and play music.

'This effort, this endeavour, this exercise, it is *sadhna*! If the artist performs this exercise, it is artistic. If the farmer performs it, it is agricultural. If the devout practise it, it is spiritual. And it all leads to Achievement!

'So, if you, the devotees of the Master, make these efforts

for the Master, you are performing a spiritual *sadhna*, yes? And if the farmer achieves a crop of corn, and the musician plays a di-vine raga, and the sculptor carves a perfect piece of sculpture, then the Master's devotees are achieving the spiritual e-quiv-a-lent, yes?

'And what was it you came to achieve? Eh? Tell me.'

No one breathed. The expectation of her next words was so great, it stretched itself so taut, it almost split when she spoke again:

'Bliss! Bliss now, bliss here, forever bliss!

'There is the ordinary world that most people experience in the ordinary way – that is, they touch, they taste, they see, but without being *aware* because it costs the greatest effort, my friends, to be aware, con-stant-ly aware, full-ly aware. So mostly we eat our meals, we wash our hands, we go to sleep.

'But if you are aware of what you are doing – every minute, with every breath – then this ordinary world takes on a vi-tal-ity, it is transformed. That vital world will feed you and nourish you and offer you experience such as you never dreamt you could have: you can drink just one cupful of water and find it will quench your thirst for a whole day even in the hottest summer; you will eat only a few grapes and these grapes will nourish your body for twenty-four hours and there will be no weakness, no hunger pangs; you will close your eyes for only a minute, or two minutes, and when you open them it will be as if you have slept for eight hours. Water has these in-cred-ible properties, and grapes, and sleep – but you must discover them, my friends, *discover* them! Do not think oh, I know what a cupful of water is, or a handful of grapes, or five minutes of sleep. I beg you, don't! Go a little further, and then a little further still – stretch and stretch the possibilities and you will find you make *such* discoveries.

'You don't believe me? Listen. Suppose you are going down the road. On the way you meet a beggar. Poor man, dressed in rags, hungry, his hand stretched out, like this. You feel in your pocket – have you money? A little, not too much? Yes, you take it out and you drop it in his hand and you go on your way. But have you really met this beggar on the road? Do you know that he is a pilgrim who has travelled the whole length and breadth of India, visited all the places of pilgrimage and paid his respects at every shrine, Hindu, Muslim and Buddhist? Do you know what his home was like that he left, how he turned away from his family and what they said? Do you know what experiences he had along the way that turned him into the ragged fellow you met on the road? What do you know about him?

'Anything? Nothing! Nothing!

'So, I tell you, you know nothing about a drink of water, or a bunch of grapes or the act of sleeping that you perform so well for so many hours every day and every night – you cannot know till you have made the effort to know its whole, its true and total meaning which is nothing less than divine.

'And think, if you can extend this exercise, what you can make of your entire life – the prison you are locked in, the cell in which you are chained, the murderers and beggars you meet. Think how they might be transformed, my friends, and how it might be for you to live in a world so transformed!

'How do I know this? How do I tell you this as if I know it? But it was so with me! Till I met the Master, the world was my gaol, I lived in a cell and the people I knew were criminals, murderers, they nearly finished me off. But when I entered the presence of the Master, these very things were transformed. He transformed them by teaching me what I try, try so hard to teach you.

'In whatever you do, all day long, remember the Master. Not his work, not his words, just the Master himself and his love for you. If you do that, I promise you that you will never be sad or hungry or in pain.

'You ask: is that all? Is that all I have to do?

'I want to tell you – stop struggling. The Master does not want you to struggle. Let the Master pick you up and carry you. You know the saint Ramakrishna said we should be like kittens – allow the Master to pick you up and carry you. Don't struggle, don't resist. The Master, the Mother – they are the mother cats, they will carry you, the kittens.

'Was Ramakrishna not de-light-ful?' she laughed.

'You will ask: who is this old woman who tells us these things about the Master?

'I will tell you. I am the one the Master left here on earth to show you the way into His Divine Presence. I can show you how to find his Light, and how to live with his Light.

'I am here to drive away Darkness and remove screens so that you may come directly to the Master and see his Light. I am here, my friends, to bring you the Light,' and she raised her arms above her head and her fingers were long and tapering and reached up to the tree and the stars that shone there.

At that moment, a peacock's call rang out, raucous and irreverent, and the old woman, throwing back her head to laugh, said, 'Listen, my *piyari mor* is telling me: be quiet, and let me sing.'

Everyone laughed. Then singing broke out. Someone started the hymn:

> 'Awake, O man, from thy deep sleep.
> Awake . . .'

and soon everyone was singing, some seated and swaying back and forth as they clapped to its rhythm, and others on their feet dancing with their eyes closed and their bodies swaying with ecstasy. The small old woman remained seated, cross-legged, her hands folded on her knees, watching with an enigmatic smile.

Afterwards everyone prostrated themselves before her, full length on the patio, touching their foreheads to the stone in total obeisance.

• • •

When Matteo rose and left, hazily aware that he must find his way back to his room in the house Welcome, he walked without knowing where he walked, and saw not the dark hedges or the paths or the other figures strolling back through the groves, but only the huge silhouette of the ficus tree with its silenced birds and the night sky over it and the small and wonderful being seated beneath it, her eyes that shone from even such a distance and the hands with the long tapering fingers which seemed to reach up and bring the immensity of the night sky down to them.

When he was in his room, he flung himself full length upon the floor, clenching his fists and shutting his eyes, trying only to retain those impressions, keep them from disappearing.

He felt that the only thing in his life that mattered was to retain those impressions.

His days seemed to pass motionlessly. They formed a great, sun-struck emptiness. He hovered in that vacuum, hardly breathing, hardly existing, waiting only for that hour when he could make his way to the patio again, seat himself and wait for the presence to manifest itself before him.

Only that moment mattered when she made her appearance. It always happened without him seeing it happen. Although he strained his eyes to catch the moment, it eluded him. Suddenly she was there, seated against cushions and bolsters, quiet, commanding, in complete authority, filled with the calm of her authority.

He became convinced that she was always there, only he did not see. He wept into his hands with frustration at his dullness, his blindness, and even cried out, 'Mother, where are you?'

Then, in the evening, the miracle occurred: she was there, he in the presence.

Of course Sophie had to be visited. Tearing himself away from the ashram, he made his way to the hospital in town as if it were a penance, and sat by her bed with a face of suffering while she lay – calmly, willingly, even contentedly – at the centre of the hospital world of beds, babies, food, bodies and their smells. To see her so was to have a vision of what the world was for the ordinary, the unblessed: a nightmare world of physicality.

It brought him a strong reminder of what his life had been before he had seen the Mother. He realised now why even the paradisaical surroundings of his home on the lakes had been for him empty and desperate, because no one had been there to show him that they were an expression of an eternal and essential truth. He remembered how as a boy he had torn through the landscape as if through a shining fabric, crying, '*Dove sei*? Where are you?' When he thought of how the question had been answered at last, he covered his face for emotion.

Sophie meanwhile was telling him, with a certain smugness, how Dr Bishop feared she might have a miscarriage if she were moved from the hospital and continued to live an itinerant life, and how important it was to stay here and rest – 'But you're not interested, you're not even listening.'

'I am, how can you say I'm not?' he replied hurriedly.

'Oh, I know that look, that face, I know it.'

When the doctor came in to examine Sophie and inform Matteo that they would have to keep Sophie at the hospital for observation a bit longer, he was afraid his face would reveal his relief and gratitude for the situation; he had only to glance at Sophie to see that it did.

When Sophie seemed stronger, and was sitting up in bed, knitting – one of the nurses had shown her how and Dr Bishop had approved of it as an excellent occupation and suggested she knit small blankets for the children of the poor in the non-paying patients' ward – Matteo tried to explain to her how the ashram he now lived in was run by a woman they called the Mother. He soon gave up, acutely aware of the inadequacy of words and his lack of skill with them. Yet he must have given away his passion for she said drily, 'And what is she, this Mother – a hypnotist, a magician? It sounds as if she gets up on a stage and hypnotises you all like some magician.'

He groaned, 'Must you have a scientific explanation? You remind me of the child who pulls a butterfly to bits so it can see what makes it fly.'

The extreme bitterness of his voice roused her. Tapping with her long needle – how he hated the knitting needles, the sight of her mindless activity – she said, 'Must we believe everything without any questioning? Are you afraid my questions will expose her?'

'Your questions do not expose her, they expose you – your, your pathetic –' he stammered.

'Stupidity?'

'Oh, call it what you like – it is your refusal to see and experience – '

'What?'

'What *I* see and experience!'

They stared at each other in hostility and incomprehension.

Then Matteo pleaded, 'If you allow yourself, Sophie, just to see her and be in her presence, she will make you well again, and the baby well, I am convinced.'

Sophie pursed her mouth and resumed her knitting. 'There is one thing that will make me well,' she said, 'and that's not having to see another damned ashram or mad guru.'

Any time spent away from the Mother, without her, was wasted time, empty time, dead time: he could not account for it, it did not pass, it stood like a block or an emptiness around him. That he could not do away with it filled him with such despair that he would lie helplessly on the bare floor of his room, or sit upon the veranda steps, dully, in a state of non-being.

Only during the *darshan*, in the Mother's presence, he and everything else came alive. Then *darshan* would be over and he would return to his room for the waiting to begin again. Was he to spend all his allotted time in an ante-room, waiting to be summoned?

No summons came, but one afternoon he rose from the floor and stood looking out of the single window at the wild rocky scrubland that lay behind the ashram when he saw, silhouetted against the sky, a band of devotees making their way over the rocks. The older ones walked in a cluster at the head, stately and slow, most of them in white, and the younger ones, in pink, bounded and leapt behind, cavorting like young goats over the stones and the dark sand. Seen against the yellow afternoon sky, they were like figures in an etching, or a tapestry. Matteo clutched at the windowsill, staring, somewhat surprised that a scene that did not contain her should have such vitality.

Then there was a slight halt, the devotees at the head stood aside to let one pass and lead the way up a narrow path between two rocks, and Matteo saw it was the Mother who led them. Again, she had manifested herself suddenly and wonderfully: she had been there all along, at the very centre.

Giving a shout of excitement – although perhaps it was someone on the hill who actually shouted – Matteo pulled on his sandals and ran out of the room, around the house to the back and then set off after them. He had never ventured out on the hills before and found them criss-crossed by an intricate network of paths between the scattered rocks. He was misled by them again and again, and although he could hear their voices in the distance, laughing, he was clumsy and agitated and lost his sense of direction many times, sometimes finding himself headed for a gully full of thorn bushes and at others faced by rocks too jagged to climb.

Eventually the slope of the hillside flattened out and from the level top he saw that on the other side of it there stretched an immense sandy riverbed with a narrow channel of water running through the centre of it, and beyond it bank upon bank of silvery plumes of pampas grass from which birds rose singing into the vast air.

The group was seated at the edge of the level hilltop under a twisted flame of the forest tree on which thin curved petals of brilliant orange spurted out of sooty pods. In its sparse shade the Mother sat upon a rock, a purple robe falling in folds about her and the air yellow gold around her, as always drawing it into her so that she was a figure of light and flame amongst the others. They were seated around her in the dust or on low flat rocks. As he stealthily came closer, not knowing how they would receive him, he saw that she was not giving a discourse; the devotees were holding out to her, by turns, some object they had picked up along the way – pebbles, berries, flowers – and she was holding each object in turn, fondling it and stroking it and building up a small parable around each.

'Ah, a feather! Look, a feather – white along the quill, then grey, then brown, and at the edge the grey and the brown merging to become black. But look how it is made – all these fine, fine filaments coming together, holding together with some in-vis-i-ble power to form a perfect feather that provides the bird with flight. Do you think we have in our own bodies something like that, something that is so purr-fect-ly made? Hard to tell, is it not? We are all covered with this ugly bag of skin –' she plucked at the backs of her hands with comical distaste. 'But my friends, I assure you, if you and I were anatomists and if we were to observe a dissection, we should see the parts of our body as perfectly constructed as this feather, and if we were only *aware* of that perfection, don't you think we would move, and behave differently in order to achieve what the birds achieve?'

She let the feather drop into her lap and now someone was offering a pebble to her. She rolled it about in the palm of her hand, lifted it to her cheek, saying, 'Mmm, mm' as if considering something she saw inside it, and she did not notice Matteo join the group and drop onto his heels beside the others so as to merge with them and not be noticed while he feasted his eyes on her and his ears on her voice. The scene was utterly extraordinary to him – she seated in purple robes beneath the orange-flowering tree, the air and sky saffron about her, and beyond her the vast riverbed, shimmering in the afternoon light, edged with the silver of the blowing pampas grass, and beyond it the watery grey-blue line of the horizon. It might have been called unreal, but why? Why not reality heightened and raised to a pitch he had not experienced before but was now revealed as what it might be and could be?

The magical hour went by so swiftly it might have been water flowing through the riverbed. The group was rising to its feet, dusting off its clothes, preparing to return to the ashram, and Matteo rose too. As they wound their way along the dusty path through the rocks, one of the older devotees at the front came back to Matteo and said, 'The Mother wishes to speak to you.' Everyone seemed to hear, everyone stared and there were expressions of surprise and curiosity. Matteo edged past them on the narrow path to the Mother's side. She continued to shuffle forwards in little, gliding steps, but when he came to her side, she gave him a sidelong smile with her large, mobile mouth and glanced at him in a way that made him feel totally exposed to her attention. The elderly devotee who had brought him forward murmured something in her ear.

'Ah, Mat–t–eo from It–a–ly,' she pronounced it as if trying out the names, just as she had turned over the pebble in her hands, regarding it from every side, scrutinising it. 'I once lived in Italy,' she murmured. 'So beautiful, so beautiful, but so sad, sad,' she went on. 'On the outside, rich and beautiful, but on the inside – death and the grave, death and the grave.' She seemed pensive. Then, putting out her hand and resting it lightly on his arm, she asked, 'Will you stay?'

Matteo stammered a reply; he wanted to give it with his entire being, his total assurance, and there were no words to convey so complete a commitment as he wished to make. She continued to shuffle forwards, her head hunched between her shoulders, keeping her hand on his arm for support in a graceful, girlish way. Matteo hardly knew how to live up to it; it seemed to belong to the age of knights and maidens and chivalry.

'And how,' she continued in a rather low and hoarse voice – entirely different from the voice that rang out with such thrilling clarity at the evening *darshan* – 'how did you come to us?'

Matteo found himself blurting out, 'I read *The Journey to the East*, Hesse's book.' It sounded insufficient, he ought to add something to that, he knew, but he could hardly unfold before her the saga of his travels with Sophie. Already they were receding into the distance and disappearing into the greenish-blue haze that was coming up the riverbed and rustling through the pampas grass and climbing uphill towards them. Already the sights and scenes of those journeys, Sophie's illness, the train, the baby – all were being swallowed up by the evening shadows. When a lapwing ran across the silvery sands below, crying its agitated query, 'Did-did-did you do it?' Matteo felt he was being addressed; he wanted to reply, 'No, no, I did not – I did nothing – nothing till now, here, here and now – '

Yet the words about the book had been spoken and there was a somewhat cynical twist to the Mother's voice, as if expressing her opinion of such work. 'I will tell you a story,' she said. 'It is about the Sufi Inayat Khan,' and the others hurried to catch up and be at her side to listen. 'He asked his follower, "Have you studied the book?" "Yes, murshid," the follower replied. The Sufi said, "It is not in the book." ' She chuckled with delight and the others chuckled too, appreciatively.

Patting Matteo's arm and then releasing it, she said, 'Come, I will show you something,' and threw the entire band of followers into consternation by turning away from the ashram wall and taking a new direction. Stumbling and bumping into each other like ants halted on a trail, they too turned and followed.

She led them onto a path that veered back towards the river but then brought them to a standstill in a grove above it. Here, under the trees where the birds were already quarrelling shrilly over their roosts for the night, there was a small shrine of the kind one might come across at the wayside anywhere – a small altar of bricks splashed with whitewash, a rounded stone daubed with red powder, some faded marigolds scattered around. Beside it, let into the earth, was a curious opening, as into a tunnel, covered with iron grating. There was nothing to explain it except an orange pennant fluttering on a stick nearby, showing it to be the abode of a yogi.

Matteo stared at the scene, feeling uneasily as if he had visited such a shrine before but not able to recall when or where. Then he heard the Mother chuckle, 'Baba-ji lives here. He has lived here for – how long?' she turned to ask her devotees, and one cried, 'Twenty years!' She laughed, 'How do you know? Baba-ji was here before we came. All the time I have been at the ashram, he has lived here above the river, in his cell. It may be for fifty years, or a hundred.'

'And does he never come out?' Matteo asked.

'Once a day, for half an hour. He fetches water from the river, and he goes into the bushes to do his business,' she giggled, 'and then he goes back. The cell is – oh, perhaps three feet by three feet? He has lived there all these years, in meditation.'

Matteo might have left without knowing if the old sage was actually there or merely a story told by the Mother, a fantasy, but just then the grating rattled slightly and moved aside as the aged yogi, who had perhaps heard their voices, came crawling out. The Mother called out a greeting and the old man, bent double, first blinked at her and then smiled a smile that spread slowly over his deeply wrinkled face, like a baby's when it sees its mother bend over its cot. He hobbled forward to touch her feet but she would not let him, she stooped to catch him by his bent shoulders, and stooping together, they both smiled and smiled. Then, as if he were a forest creature, uneasy amongst people, he hobbled away with his brass pot and the Mother said to her followers, 'Let us go away and leave him to do his business, eh?'

Matteo, before he turned away, glanced down the tunnel but could see nothing but darkness, feel nothing but darkness there, the close confined air of the cave coming out like an exhalation. He backed away in horror at a life lived within it: was that what it would mean to live a life of meditation and devotion? He did not think he could bear it – certainly not the darkness and the solitude and the being away from the Mother's radiant, golden presence. Was she showing him what it might be to live apart from her, locked away from her? Or was she telling him that devotion to her could mean closing himself into a state so grimly hermetic and ascetic? Was she showing him the rigours of a life of devotion to see if he was afraid? Yes, he was afraid.

The morning dispelled the fear. Matteo received a summons from the Mother to visit her in the house called the Abode of Bliss, where she lived.

This had once been the garden house, or retreat, of a devout and wealthy disciple of the Master's, and donated to the Mother so that it could form the nucleus of the ashram. Gradually the land around it had been bought, acre by acre, mostly wasteland, rock and scrub that was over the years transformed into the flowering estate now spread over them. The house was clearly the oldest one on the property, built in a more substantial style – that of a spacious bungalow, with a slightly sloping tiled roof under a gigantic banyan tree, deep verandas with pilasters of white stucco at regular intervals, wide steps lined with ranks of flower pots, and tall doors and narrow windows fitted with framed screens to keep out insects.

To approach it one had to pass through a grove of frangipani trees and bougainvillaea amidst which lay the *samadhi* of the Master, a plain block of stone painted white and decorated each morning with fresh flowers. These were heaped on it now: large livid hibiscus and canna flowers, handfuls of white jasmine, limp pink roses and garlands of marigold. For all the brilliant colours, the grove had a peaceful air: devotees came and went through gaps in the hedge, barefoot and silent, and there were always a few who sat crosslegged beside it, still as statues and eyes closed in deep meditation. Only a koel, hidden in the foliage of the banyan tree, dared to call out loud, 'Ku-hu? Ku-hu?'

Matteo went up the bricklined path as he had been

instructed, left his slippers at the foot of a flight of stairs leading to the veranda, and continued barefoot. The door stood open and he found the Mother seated on a pile of cushions on the carpeted floor under a gigantic painting of the Master that hung on the wall above her and was garlanded with roses carved out of sandalwood, lavishly perfuming the air. It depicted a bare-bodied figure, indigo in colour, seated upon a mountain top that was silhouetted, a deep violet, against a sky of rose pink. Around his massive head, a halo was tinted in the colours of a rainbow. In the midst of all this celebratory colour, the heavy, fleshy face seemed sombre, almost stern.

On a small, three-legged table of intricately carved walnut wood stood a photograph of the same figure, in a silver frame. Here he was shown upright and clothed and beside him was the Mother. It had been taken in the days of their prime, evidently, and both were smiling, resplendent in white silk robes and gold scarves, garlands of tinsel and blossom around their necks. It could have been a wedding photograph, and they a bridal pair – although of course Matteo knew it was not: if there was a marriage, then surely it was a spiritual one.

Incense swirled through the room from smouldering sticks in a small brass holder, and in its lavender haze the Mother reclined, wearing that day a robe of plum red with sleeves lined in pink. Caught up in its voluminous folds, she might have been a small aged idol had she not been in a state of constant motion.

Her mornings were clearly very busy: a fleet of secretaries attended her, kneeling to show her memos, standing with bowed heads to listen to advice, going in and out with ledgers and files, or seated to take dictation. She was at that moment giving instructions to Swami Kripa about a change of feed for the cows – cows! As if aware of Matteo's astonishment, she turned to him with a wonderfully girlish smile and, dismissing Swami Kripa, who hurried off busily, stretched out her arm and picked a banana from a tray of fruit before her.

'Please,' she cried, 'don't look so sad, so hungry. Come, eat this banana! The banana is a fruit that drives away sorrow and makes one as happy as a monkey!'

Matteo hoped she did not really mean that and took the fruit from her, knowing he was being teased, but she cried, 'Sit here, and eat. I want to see you eat!' To his great embarrassment, there was nothing for it but to peel the fruit and eat it, watched by the amused devotees who stood about the room. He felt its sticky substance bulge in his mouth, felt aware how his cheeks puffed out, how long his jaws took to masticate it, and then nearly choked when he tried to swallow. Laughing, she bent forward and plucked the peel out of his hands. 'There,' she said, 'that is better. I don't want anyone to starve. I want you to feel well, sat-is-fied – ' She pronounced the word slowly, dividing it into three, four syllables.

Wiping his mouth, Matteo gulped, 'I am, I am satisfied – '

'I want no one to starve. No one to feel pain,' she went on, straightening her back, looking more idol-like, the laughter retreating. 'We are here,' she said, 'to experience Bliss. There can be no bliss if you are thinking: I am hungry, I want food; I am sad, I want love. All that must go – ' she waved her long fingers and tossed away the banana peel – 'so Bliss can enter. Only on that should your mind focus.' Her face assumed a somewhat vague expression, as if her thoughts had drifted away.

Before she retreated altogether as she seemed likely to do, Matteo slipped in the question he felt he must ask. 'Mother,' he said, 'I have studied some Sanskrit. Please tell me what to read. I must learn.'

She opened her eyes very wide, as if stunned. Turning to the other devotees in the room, drawing them in to be witnesses to this phenomenon, she pronounced, 'Read nothing. Nothing. You have not come to a university. I am not giving out degrees. Mat-te-o of I-tal-y, Master of Mystical Ex-per-i-ence: will you take this degree and go out and show it to the world? Please, I beg you, close your books. Clear your mind. The way of *jnana* – the way of knowledge – is nothing compared to the way of *bhakti* – the way of love. Here we teach only Love.' Her eyes were sparkling within the rims of kohl that outlined them and made them so prominent in her gaunt face. She spoke with a fierceness, that of a younger woman. 'Here we dedicate ourselves to Love,' she pronounced, and her gaze rested on the framed photograph on the three-legged table that was placed so that she faced it, whereas the painting on the wall was behind her, framing her. 'What we do here, we do out of love,' she added. Then a smile began to tug at the corners of her mouth that had been so stern a moment before. 'We do very much, verry verrry much,' she drawled, and some of the devotees began to giggle. 'Ask them, they will tell you. I make them work. We all work. You too, Matteo, will work, no?'

'Oh yes,' he agreed ardently, thinking she would now disclose her plans to him, the plans whereby he would at last transform himself, leaving behind the old, sick, unhappy self, the self he despised and desired to get rid of, and assume the new one made wholly by her.

But she was not looking at him; she was twisting her head around, looking at the others in the room. 'What shall we assign him? Library? Accounts? Laundry? Dairy? Or – ' she rolled her eyes dramatically – 'kitchen?' The others doubled over with laughter as at a great joke. Matteo did not know what the joke was but squirmed, knowing himself to be the butt. Now she was smiling directly at him, a sweetly arch smile. 'No-o-o,' she cooed, 'let us not send him to the kitchen. He will be frightened. He may run away. N-n-o-,' she repeated and patted the cushion beside her. 'Mat-t-eo from It-a-ly, I will keep you here, by me. You can write my letters for me.'

It was more than Matteo could have hoped for, or anticipated. That it was also more than anyone else had expected for a total newcomer was evident from the murmur of surprise that arose, and the expressions of envious congratulation. Only known, trusted and dear devotees had been invited into such close proximity before, and Matteo could appreciate that, for what could be more intimate than her letters? Now he would enter not only into her physical presence – overwhelming enough, more powerful than anyone else's, including Sophie's – but into her mental presence, her intellectual world, of which only hints and glimpses had been vouchsafed till now. With that expectation, he hurried towards the Abode of Bliss in the early morning light.

Each day began so hopefully and propitiously – he never failed to pause and bow before the *samadhi* of the Master before proceeding through the grove to the house – but nevertheless each day dealt him a severe blow. The Mother's letters were not to swamis and yogis elsewhere on the finer points of theology or philosophy; they were not even letters to her devotees who appealed for help or clarification. They were her official correspondence with various departments of the town council about matters such as the clearing of garbage from the ashram grounds (which the council claimed lay outside their jurisdiction), the sale of a bumper crop of guavas that the ashram inmates could not alone harvest or devour, the building of more cattle sheds and the distribution of surplus milk in the town. Then there were the endless memos to the devotees who ran different enterprises – all remarkably detailed, precise and revealing a knowledge of housekeeping, animal husbandry, fruit and vegetable farming, health and hygiene and other specialised professions, stunning Matteo with their scope and profusion of detail.

She herself remained unflagging. 'Yes, yes, everyone is busy as a bee over here,' she said happily to Matteo. 'So many busy bees in my hive. I can see Matteo thinking – why? why? No, don't protest, I can see it, I can see it. He does not think so much of the little bee, eh? But is this hive to be empty and dry and useless? Or is it to be filled with honey, a store of good, sweet honey? And do not think I mean fruits and vegetables and milk, please. You must know I mean honey made from spiritual nectar, nectar to nourish your souls. All organisations are useless, Matteo, useless and dry and empty, if they do not contain the nectar of the spirit. I want it to be rich, rich, rich with this nectar.'

In deep shame and guilt, Matteo bent over his writing block and scribbled frantically, hardly able to keep up with her dictation and yet feverish with the need to do so. To be in her presence, involved in her work, and not worthy of it, not measuring up to it, would compound all the failures of his life and condemn him to an endless cycle of failure too terrible to contemplate. At times he wondered if she was putting him on trial to see if he could prove himself. He worked without pause, except for an hour in the afternoon when she let him go to eat with the other devotees and rest briefly before returning to her for further orders, further dictation.

When he flagged at the end of a particularly demanding and frustrating day in which messages regarding the publication of the Master's books by a small press in the city flew back and forth with countless misunderstandings and no resolution at the end to show for all the labour, he was devastated to hear her say, 'And what do you think, Matteo, of setting up our own printing press at the ashram? Would it not be better to take over from these in-comp-et-ent swindlers? Could we not run it much more eco-nom-ic-ally and pro-duct-ively our-selves? Hmmm?' She raised her eyebrows high and focused her great kohl-rimmed eyes upon him.

Matteo quailed as he thought of the mountain of work rising before him, obscuring – he feared – his true goal, that revelation for which he hungered and to which he knew he had come tantalisingly close. He had neither the time nor the strength to meditate any more, or to read, or even to think or reflect; his mind seemed stuffed and cluttered with the most minute details of the ashram's organisation and functioning. The regime – or the trial, if that was what it was – was taking its toll upon him and he trembled a little.

She saw that. Dipping her head to one side, she murmured, 'No, I see Matteo is not ready for that yet, hmmm? He must tell me when he is ready because I, I am ready. I am waiting for that day!'

What did she mean? Did she mean that day as one when she would accomplish some particular desire of hers, or one on which her mastery over Matteo would become complete and total? Matteo was utterly confused.

She leant across to him, her hand extended from a long sleeve of brilliant orange silk, her fingers nearly touching him but not. 'Poor boy, it is so hard,' she murmured. 'Hard, hard. Do I not know how hard? Do I not drive myself too? All for the sake of the Beloved? So the Beloved's life and work may con-tin-ue?'

This brought him so abruptly back to the true purpose of his labour that he hung his head in remorse at the egoism in the thought that he might figure in her plans and programme. She saw his change of expression and seemed pleased. Touching him on the wrist lightly, she spoke with that sweet lightness of tone that made her seem at times like a young girl. 'I must remember I should not drive you as I drive myself. You don't yet know that love that I have known, its pow-err, its forr-ce! You are young. You need laughter and play. Love is too, too hard.' Then she fell silent, began to adjust the folds of her robe, and her face became distant and remote.

She meant what she said, however, and that evening she had a neglected badminton court re-chalked and sent for a net and racquets and shuttlecocks from a sports goods shop in town, announced an hour of play and appeared herself in sports clothes – baggy white pyjamas, a long white muslin shirt exquisitely embroidered at the neck and wrists, and very large white canvas shoes – swinging a racquet and challenging the devotees to play.

From then on, every evening, no matter how hot it still was, and how the sun beat on the court, she insisted that they take turns at playing. Although the devotees, unused to playing games, found it heavy going and huffed and puffed through the games, they clapped with delight when the Mother herself played, marvelling at her agility, the speed with which she moved in order to chase the shuttlecock around, bringing to it that superlative will and concentration she brought to every-thing.

'Oh, see how beautifully Mother plays!' an elderly devotee exclaimed, nearly weeping with admiration as she came off the court, perspiration streaming from under the folds of her white turban down her cheeks. She tossed away the racquet lightly, saying, 'If you love the game, you can play. Love is what drives the player. Love *is* the game,' whereupon the elderly devotee gave a sob of joy.

Sophie, who was still confined to bed with a periodic slight bleeding that Dr Bishop needed to watch, listened to him describe these activities with an absent expression on her face; she was concentrating on knitting a baby garment – one of the nurses had shown her how – and wished him to see that his activities were of lesser importance.

Finally she said, 'It sounds like school, like a British boarding school.'

Irritated, he said, 'And in which British boarding school do they preach the doctrine of love?'

'Oh,' she said, giving the ball of wool a sharp tweak, 'is that what your ashram wishes to rectify?'

'Sophie, I am trying to tell you how different it is from all other ashrams. You will like it. You will be happy.'

Sophie put down her knitting. 'I wanted to go to the mountains,' she said to him bitterly. 'I hoped we would go to the mountains, by ourselves.'

'Later,' he promised, 'later. Now we must be together at the ashram. The doctor said you're well enough to leave.'

'I'm not! I'm not!' she cried, and grew so agitated that Dr Bishop, passing by, stopped to see what was the matter and sent Matteo away and stayed to pat and stroke and calm Sophie.

Matteo now had work that taught him how the organisation worked, and introduced him to the other devotees. Yet all of them brought him back to the centre again, to the Mother.

From Kripa, who ran the dairy, he learnt that the Mother had had to teach herself dairying and even veterinary science in order to run the place so impeccably. 'She knew nothing, of course, nothing,' Kripa smiled, fondling the pinkish dewlap of a placidly chewing cow. 'How could she have known anything about cows and milk and butter? But the Master had to have pure milk, pure butter, pure ghee, nothing adulterated, so she wouldn't buy from the market. She said, "We will keep cows at the ashram and make our own butter and curds and ghee. We will be the *gopis* who tended cows along with Krishna." When I am milking the cows,' Kripa said, fondling the cow who flicked her tail and went on chewing, 'I remember that.'

From Prema, who stood over the vats of boiling water in which everyone's pink robes bubbled and steamed, he learnt that the Mother was as fanatical about personal purity as about the purity of the heart. 'We can't just sit about, purifying our minds,' cried Prema through clouds of steam in the laundry room. 'We've got to go everywhere, see into everything, make sure there isn't a single germ left, not for miles!' She stood with her hands on her hips, her golden curls streaming down her damp cheeks, and made Matteo very aware of the dust and sweat of his own body.

Even the small children of the ashram grew up on such tenets of the Mother. Matteo, plodding from one end of the ashram to the other, carrying the Mother's messages, discovered that there was a large number of them living on the premises. Although the Indian devotees were mostly elderly, retired men or widows whose children and grandchildren occasionally came to visit them but did not stay, many of the foreign devotees had young families and were settling down into a life at once devotional and domestic. For such families there were separate cottages at the fringe of the ashram grounds, at the other end of the large vegetable garden. Many of the devotees who lived there were set to work in these fields, raising the tomatoes and spinach and carrots they needed for their children as well as the ashram. There was also a playground and a nursery school and crèche (at the furthest corner from the Abode of Bliss: the Mother was very prone to migraines, and noise could bring on an attack). Passing by their grounds, Matteo watched as their young teacher, Diya, held up a card with a picture of a bee and called out, 'Bee-ee!' Then she asked, 'What does the bee make?' and the children called back 'Hunn-ee!' 'And where do the bees live?' 'Ha-eev!' Then she beamed and raised her voice to call, 'We too are bees! We live in a hive! We make honey out of nectar! And what is nectar?' Then they threw their arms up in the air and yelled, 'Lo-ove!'

Walking away from the school building – painted all over with flowers and on its classroom wall a great photograph of the Mother smiling out of the frame – Matteo wondered if Sophie would be pleased with what she saw when he brought her here. He hoped she would be pleased; how could she not?

Reaching to hand her a sheaf of letters to sign, Matteo found the Mother smiling at him enigmatically. 'It is beginning, is it?' she murmured. 'Yes, yes, I see it. Mat-t-eo is planning to join us. Mat-t-eo is going to stay.'

He was touched by her quick insight, the welcome implicit in her voice, and it gave him the courage to say, 'And can I bring my wife to stay?'

She continued to gaze at him, her expression barely changing. He had not spoken of Sophie earlier but had assumed she knew of her. Now it appeared she did not and that she was adjusting to the idea. Finally she said, very smoothly, 'You must ask to be allotted a cottage. All families stay in cottages. And I would like you to start work on a kitchen shift.'

The day he brought Sophie to the ashram there was a thunderstorm, the kind that precedes the monsoon, breaking the terrific heat of the summer's zenith. They were together in a cycle rickshaw, pedalling along the road on which the dust blew in great yellow gusts, almost blinding them so they had to tie their bandanas over their mouths and noses, when the clouds broke and rain pelted down in large icy drops with a great roll of thunder.

Their hair and clothes plastered to their wet bodies, they climbed out of the rickshaw and ran, hand in hand, to the cottage they had been allotted in the family area called Love. Trees tossed on the wind, branches went flying through the air, the dust was sluiced away, rain ran in channels and beat upon the rooftops deafeningly, wide gardens turned into sheets of water where bushes and flowers were waterlogged and marooned. Instantly, the air cooled, became sweet and fresh.

Sophie, standing on their small veranda and listening to the downpour, saw a world washed and renewed. Grass and leaves glistened, the scent of wet earth was released. She herself, weak and reluctant as she had been to come, felt herself flower in the change of air. She turned to embrace Matteo. This place, paradisaical, had been given them, it would be their home, their child would be born here. She shook under his arm and he asked, 'Cold?' with such unaccustomed consideration and tenderness that she nodded and laid her head on his shoulder, allowing him to draw her close. She wondered if now their marriage would truly begin.

Then the worst stage of summer set in – those last weeks before the monsoon arrived, unbearably close and humid and still. The sun blazed again and beat upon the ashram roofs; under these roofs, the devotees lay, or sat, hardly able to lift themselves to their feet; each small action drained them. They worked slowly, and were exhausted.

In this heat Matteo started work in the kitchen. He tied his bandana about his head to keep the perspiration from running down his face and set to scrubbing the cauldrons in which the rice and lentils were cooked, washing up mountainous stacks of metal dishes after meals, keeping the fires of the enormous open hearth stoked with coal, scouring the ashes and grits off the floors and tabletops, carrying out buckets of steaming food to the dining halls, staying up at night after all the others were on the patio, listening to the Mother's discourse, clearing the kitchen for the day by sluicing it with buckets of water fetched from the pump outside.

He worked in silence, his face gaunt with the effort. The others on kitchen duty had been assigned to this work for much longer; they knew how to deal with it: they sang, and played jokes on each other and clearly knew each other very well. They tried to include him but he did not know how to join them; he worked with his jaw set, in silence, thinking only how the day had passed without seeing her, how he would not even see her on the patio at night.

Nor did he see much of Sophie. When he returned to the cottage, it was to fall, exhausted, to the floor, and sleep, too tired to bathe or change or climb into bed.

Sophie, bitterly disappointed at finding out how little she saw of Matteo, began to rail against the Mother. 'Would you work like this for your father if he asked you to join his business? No, you wouldn't, you'd refuse outright. So why do you do it for her? What do you get out of it?'

Matteo had woken and was preparing to return to work. With maddening patience, he said, 'That is the point. Father would make me work so I could become self-supporting, or so that I could take over the business from him. Father would expect me to want a big salary, a car, all that junk. But the Mother doesn't make me work for anything. She teaches us to work without desiring the fruit from that work. Isn't that a higher way of life?'

'Higher, lower – who cares? Work is work and *should* bear fruit. Or else, what is the point?' He could not make her see otherwise. 'If work doesn't bear fruit, it doesn't serve its purpose,' she insisted. 'Nothing would be done – no house built, no money earned, or spent – '

'You sound like your parents,' he interrupted, appalled. Then rushed out of the house, hands pressed to his ears, shouting, 'Money! I don't wish to hear that word, Sophie!'

She had overstepped: she should not have mentioned money. It was too strong a reminder that they were still dependent on her parents, who did the working and earning. She had not meant that: she stood with her fingers pressed to her lips, silenced.

• • •

Sophie was left to amuse herself. She had no books to read, and only one tape to listen to on her cassette player, of the Brandenburg Concertos. She would sit on the floor with it beside her, playing it over and over, listening to it with a moody intensity, chin cupped in her hand. When Matteo entered the house, she would be listening to it; when he lay down to sleep, she continued to listen. He said nothing and stubbornly she played it over and over as if she were wrapping herself in it, winding herself into a world separate from his.

Eventually the tape wore out; one day, snarled in the whirring interior of the cassette player, it was ripped to shreds. The music splintered and foundered in the dying whirr.

If Matteo felt like gloating, he bit his lip and said nothing to express his relief. Instead, he brought her a handful of tapes a devotee had left behind on departing. She looked through them with contempt. It was all music she despised – rock, pop – Matteo should have known that. The only piece of classical music in the collection was Beethoven's 'Moonlight Sonata'. 'The Moonlight Sonata – of course, naturally!'

The small house sank into a silent well of her disappointment.

Broodily, she sat on the veranda steps, listening to the great hum that seemed to emerge from a combination of sun and earth and leaf and sky. The Mother sent no summons for her; she was given no tasks, no diversion. Matteo had vanished into the heart of a world that remained shut to her. She had not thought she wished to enter it or explore it but Matteo's disappearance was so profound that her uneasiness grew. Yet she could not give up her conviction that she could draw him away and back to her, or the conviction that she must.

Eventually she got to her feet and ventured out of the cottage, walking along the hedged paths with her hands behind her back and her head bowed. When she saw the painted signs – *Love is Truth* and *Work is Joy* – her lips curled in contempt. Pink-robed figures flitting past her, barefoot or in

126

lightly flapping slippers, smiled and greeted her; the smile she returned was a sour one, determined not to be taken in by all this sunniness. The ashram as an earthly paradise, presided over by a benign deity – she knew better than to believe that. For her the Mother was a monster spider who had spun this web to catch these silly flies.

Unknown to Matteo, she did secretly go out one evening to observe the evening *darshan* at the end of a long, empty day out of which the desire to see the fabled Mother rose irrepressibly. But, in spite of the theatrical setting – the sky streaked pink and violet and saffron with sunset light, the great dark tree and the rustling birds with the devotees in attitudes of intense attentiveness like forest hermits in the presence of their guru – Sophie found herself disappointed to learn that the Mother was only a small shrunken creature with a throaty voice who made dramatic gestures and used those big abstract words that held no interest for her. Yawning unashamedly, she left before it was over.

At night, she told Matteo, 'She may be your Mother but I have one who is quite enough for me, I don't need *this* one.' She feigned a yawn and Matteo asked incredulously, 'You were *bored*?'

She did, however, have another encounter with the Mother, one she did not confess to having. She had grown tired of the ashram grounds, her walks along its neat paths through neat parks and gardens, and had scrambled out onto the hillside at the back of the ashram very early one morning before the sun began to beat upon the rocks and the sand in the river bed to give off its blinding glare. That brief hour of comparative coolness was quickly over; the sun was a white eye in the yellow sky, watching her as she made her way along a maze of goat tracks between the rocks. The dust that crept down her neck and between her toes proved defeating, and she turned back to the ashram. She found she had lost her way and, after stumbling about stones and bushes for a while, emerged on a slope directly above the Abode of Bliss where she knew the Mother lived. She could see its distinctive tiled roof in the shade of the gigantic banyan tree with its heart-shaped leaves and forest of aerial roots, and beyond it the intensely green grove in which the Master's *samadhi* made a single white mark.

Sophie, coming to a standstill with her hands upon her hips, found she could look right over the boundary wall into the backyard of the Abode of Bliss. To her astonishment and consternation, the Mother was seated there on a small cane stool in the shade of a tree with feathery leaves and large, livid red flowers. Under it, she looked very small and slight, not in the voluminous robes she usually wore but in a cotton shift, a rather faded and discoloured one. Nor had she her turban on: her hair grew in thin wisps, showing pink expanses of scalp. She was holding her hands on her knees in the classic yoga posture and she was very still, as if in meditation. But she was not: her eyes were narrowed in intense observation, and she was watching, or enticing, a flock of peacocks that were scrambling down the rocky hillside, fluttering over the wall and invading her garden. They were parading on the strip of gravel where she sat, up and down, the males spreading out their tails into enormous, weighty fans that thrummed like harps and that were made up of a thousand individual fans of brilliant bronze-like greens, blues and golds. They balanced on their toes and dipped and turned before the Mother, display-ing their glories with a preening expression of vanity. The smaller, drab peahens, brown and plain, with pathetically undeveloped and unsightly tails, scurried around awkwardly. The males paid them no attention: their eyes, so startlingly rimmed with white, and the hundreds of eyes upon their feathers, all seemed trained upon the Mother. They main-tained this display that was their tribute to her for long minutes, surreal to Sophie in this landscape of silence and solitude.

Then the Mother unclasped her hands, opened them to show they contained grain. It was the little peahens that noticed at once and darted forwards to peck at it, alert and greedy and cautious. The males seemed too proud to fold their fans and abandon their posturing, but they quivered, hesitated on their toes, feathers thrumming. With a laugh, the Mother flung grain towards them, calling to them with little vowel sounds deep in her throat: 'Aa-aa-aa-aa. *Piyari mor*, aa-aa-aa.' When the peacocks too folded up their gorgeous tails, dipped their heads and stretched their necks for the meal, she threw back her head to laugh a low, chuckling laugh.

As she did so, she saw Sophie standing on the rock, watching. The two women stared at each other, then simultaneously turned their heads aside, Sophie to scan the rocks for a path down, and the Mother to call to someone in the house. The flock of peacocks dissolved into the wilds, uttering their piercing, questing calls. One remained: it flew onto the roof with a violent beating of its wings and sat there, shrieking. It was the largest one, with a dazzling featherfall of blue and gold.

This encounter appeared to have two results. One was that Matteo was abruptly taken off kitchen duty and brought back to work in the Mother's office at the Abode of Bliss, for him a joyful prospect. He could not help thinking that there was a plan, a carefully considered plan in the way the Mother assigned duties and moved her devotees from one to another, and he felt that she had put him on trial in giving him the most menial of all work and was now rewarding him.

What he discovered was that she had decided to set up the printing press she had so often talked of, and wanted Matteo to involve himself in the publication of the Master's books, having taken them away from the publisher in the city through a long and complicated court case that had led to much publicised acrimony and rancour between the ashram and the townspeople who had hoped to turn the ashram to profit and now discovered the ashram intended to keep all its profits to itself.

After the initial joy at his appointment, Matteo became overwhelmed with self-doubt at undertaking a responsibility for which he had no training and no aptitude. It seemed to him that the Mother had chosen to place upon him the gravest responsibility of all: to present to the world the Master's teaching. The enormity of her expectations so overwhelmed him that they left him shaken and unsure.

There was a small reward for this monumental labour, a very precious one, however: at night, before the work was put away, Matteo was sent to fetch a tumbler of warm milk from the kitchen for the Mother before she retired. When he watched her drink it slowly, sip by sip, sighing with weariness and sleep as she did so, he resolved to tell her that he could not continue: the intimacy of the moment presented such an opportunity. Then, seeing her bend her head, reveal the frail back of her neck with its transparent skin and the knobs of her small bones, he felt that if he were driven too far, stretched to breaking point, then she shouldered burdens a hundred times greater than his, through no strength but that of her will and her great love. He felt that the role given to him was that of her protector, almost of parent, and she the child who caused such trouble, demanded so much, and yet was all that mattered to the parent, a cause and a reward in one. Instead of resigning his duties, he resolved to commit himself to more of them, to greater ones. He took the empty tumbler from her, bowing low before her, almost to the ground.

On Sophie that improbable, dream-like encounter with the Mother had an effect she was hardly able to articulate even to herself. There had been revealed to her both the mythical figure who could summon peacocks out of the wilds as she did devotees from the world over, and the aged, solitary woman with sparse hair and a faded nightdress. Against all her own expectations and intentions, the paradoxical, contradictory image stayed in her mind. She saw that the apparition was not one she could explain, let alone dismiss as she had so consistently done in her arguments with Matteo. She would not admit, even to herself, that she had had a glimpse of the spell such a being could cast on Matteo and the others, but she did tell herself that it was one that she needed to explore if she was ever going to arrive at the heart of it.

Her pursuit of it took her into all corners of the ashram and made her search out and establish links with the inmates that she had earlier shunned. She began to stop at the verandas of other cottages in the family quarters to talk to the women and the children there, or greet and converse with those she met on the paths, going about their work. Matteo was pleased to see her begin her own relationship with the ashram, and smiled in approval till she began to bring back bits of gossip or information to which she gave a twist of her own, and then he was disturbed.

'What is she anyway?' Sophie queried, putting on her brassiest tone to aggravate him. 'Looks Indian, sounds Indian, but not Indian. Well, what is she then?'

'You should never ask questions about a sadhu's past. They bury their past and are reborn when they take initiation.'

'Ah, so – she was born, or re-born, the Mother of the ashram, and that's all there is to it, is it?' Sophie mocked. 'But what if I told you what I've heard? What if I tell you she was once a dancer, that she first came to India with a dance troupe. The dance tour went to pieces – I suppose the manager ran off with the money instead of booking halls or printing posters, isn't that what they always do? So then there she was, on the lonesome, looking for a rich somebody to pick her up – '

'Sophie, don't!'

'Oh, don't look so shocked – you're not quite a monk, you must know something about the world.'

'I don't want to listen to you. I don't believe anyone in the ashram will have said such things about the Mother.'

Sophie laughed and reached out to ruffle his hair. 'You're right, no one did. They'd have been driven out, or lynched, if they did. No, what they said was that the Mother was a beautiful dancer who danced the role of Radha, pining for her lover Krishna. And behold, there was a blaze of light and there was Krishna. And they danced together – the divine lovers – '

In agitation, Matteo stammered, 'The Mother may have

been a dancer when she was young – I know that myself – but no one, no one has ever said the Master was one. I know because I am printing all the literature about him. I've read every word written about him and by him. He was a sadhu. He was taken as a child by his parents to a great guru and he lived in a hermitage as a monk. Later he travelled to a cave in the Himalayas where he meditated – '

'Oh, Matteo, no need to take this so seriously!'

'I am absolutely serious about this, Sophie. I will bring you books to read. You need to learn – '

He did bring her the books he was printing at the press, and Sophie gave them a cursory glance and made sarcastic comments about the garish covers, the pictures of pink lotuses and blue gods, but when Matteo was not there to see, she opened and read them. The clumsy language, the lurching from fact to fantasy, from the prosaic to the abstract frustrated her but it gave her further material to place before Matteo.

'Matteo! She was born in Egypt, did you know that?'

'Of course, Sophie. I published that book.'

'Why didn't you tell me?'

'I told you, the past is of no importance to a sadhu.'

'What rubbish, of course it is! To know that she is from Egypt makes one think of the Sphinx, and Cleopatra – '

'Enough nonsense, Sophie.'

'Is that nonsense, or a fact? Why isn't one allowed to discuss facts here?'

'We talk of nothing but the truth, all the time.'

'No, you don't. You talk of Truth with a capital T, not of the truth as in facts. Doesn't it interest any of you? Look, it says here that she studied in Paris. Very elite. But where, in the Sorbonne? And what? Not a word. Another uninteresting detail, I suppose. Then that she "studied dance in Venice". Now, that is not what you would expect to find in the biography of a sage! Are you not interested?'

'No, not in these unimportant details.' Then he said, tiredly, 'If you want to know about the Mother's past, you should talk to Montu-da, the ashram doctor. He is the oldest of her devotees, he has been with her longest.'

In the small white cell where he sat dividing his tiny homeopathic pills and powders into vials and spills, Montu-da looked at her through his gold-rimmed spectacles. 'You say you don't want pills, you want to talk about the Mother. My dear lady, that is the best pill – it is better than all my pills!' His broad face with its heavy, dark folds gleamed with pleasure. 'Please sit down, please let us talk. I too will share that sweetest pill with you, if I may.'

Diverted by his laugh, she drew up her chair; she had not heard anyone laugh in a long time. 'First you will have to tell me when you came to the ashram.'

He blushed a deep purple. 'Oh, why do you wish to hear about me? I was a boy when I came. My family wanted me to marry. They got hold of some poor girl and told me I had to marry her. How could I? My heart was filled with love of God only. I ran away from there and the poor girl was saved from marrying me.'

'And you came here?'

'No, no, this ashram did not exist then. It was to the ashram in Hardwar that I fled, up in the mountains, where the Master lived. I went to the Master to ask for *diksha*, initiation. I was studying there, learning from the Master, when the Mother came. Yes, yes, I was there when the Mother first came! The Master said to us, "The Mother has come amongst us. She is a manifestation of the Divine for which I have been preparing you. She has come to bring you enlightenment and through enlightenment you will receive the bliss you desire. You must all worship her as the Divine Mother. She has come to serve you, and you must serve and obey her. Then only can she reveal her full glory to you." And when he spoke those words, we prostrated ourselves before her. What joy we felt that she had come! We had a feast that day and sweets were given to everyone. I was so happy, I danced and sang and wept like a madman. You see, I had left my own mother, but now the Divine Mother had come to take her place.

133

'When the Mother first came – oh, she was so shy, so quiet, she would hide from us all. But the Master gave her courage, he gave her confidence by placing *his* confidence in her. Little by little he passed on his duties to her. He himself retired into meditation and study, and little by little the Mother took his place in the ashram.

'The Mother set about cleaning the ashram and bringing order to it. Before she came, the ashram was in such bad condition, I felt ashamed. The Master was absorbed in meditation and did not notice such things. But she could not bear that. If a tap was leaking, she had it fixed. If a lamp was broken she had it replaced. She served us in every way. She said the food is bad and she went to the kitchen and she showed the cooks how to bake bread, none of us had ever eaten anything so delicious. Yet it was plain bread! Some of the old disciples grumbled. They did not like her to change things, they criticised her for bringing luxury into the ashram. But they were wrong, completely wrong. She was making the ashram beautiful, a fit place for the Master to live in, and they did not appreciate that. They went to the Master and complained about her. They said she is a Muslim and a foreigner, she is polluting our ashram. The Master told them God is One and He is everywhere, in the temple and the mosque. He recited to us the verses written by Kabir – you know our great poet, Kabir? He was a simple weaver, of the Julaha caste, and of a Muslim family. But he lived in the holy city of Benares and he wrote songs to Rama. The Master made us learn these songs and sing them to purify our hearts of hatred and bad thoughts.

'But there were some people in the ashram who still said the Mother's influence is bad, she should go. What stories they made up – *toba*! You will not believe such things can be said in an ashram. Even if the Mother took me into her room to give me medicine or give me a glass of milk to drink, they would talk. They were like that, bad. I was not happy and I wept. I thought I had run away from all evil when I left my home where my family was always quarrelling, but *toba*, it was worse in the ashram!

'The Mother became very, very sad. She said, "I will go

away. I do not want to cause all this trouble in the ashram."
But the Master would not let her – he knew she was not evil!
One day he told the terrible story of the ashram to an old lady
who used to come on a pilgrimage every year from Calcutta.
She was a widow and very rich and she had land and a house in
the valley. She had given everything to the ashram – she
herself wore a white sari, no jewellery, she was a saint. The
Master told her about the sad things happening in the ashram,
he told her it was not a good place any longer. She herself
knew nothing, she was too saintly, she did not listen to gossip.
But she listened to the Master and she said, "Master, if you are
unhappy here, you must leave. I have a house in the valley,
please take it. It is all I have left but you must take it and start
another ashram. It is on the bank of a river. It was used as a
hunting lodge by my late husband and I have used it as a
retreat. No one lives there, it is in the jungle. Your presence
and the Mother's presence will make it a sacred place." That is
what she said, that saintly lady, and that is how we came here,
to this ashram.'

'When was that?'

'Oh, many, many years ago, my dear lady, before you were
even walking upon this earth, I am sure. Only the Master, the
Mother and I came – the three of us. But slowly, slowly other
disciples began to follow the Master – some from the ashram
up in Hardwar who had felt sad when we left, and new ones
who heard about this ashram. And we began again –
everything began here. The river was much closer then; now it
has receded. The Master and the Mother lived in the old
bungalow where she lives now; she had a garden laid out
around it, we all helped. That is the garden where the Master's
samadhi is now. Yes, she herself made it. She had only to say,
"I want this, do this," and we ran to do it. She brought in cows
to give us milk, birds to sing – she was fond of singing birds.
She herself cooked and served us food in those days. Even wild
animals would come out of the jungle to be fed by her –'

'What animals – tigers? Bears?'

But Montu-da was in full flood and went on without any

interruption. 'Each one of us was given duties, and she made us all work. She said we may have renounced the world but that did not mean we could renounce our duties. Work is good because it brings health and productivity. We had prayer and meditation periods, we lived a spiritual life still, but the Mother taught us the spiritual life must be full, that it should have variety and be rich, although there should be no luxury or excess comfort. And she worked harder than any of us, much harder! At four o'clock in the morning she was up to prepare our meals, to feed the animals – '

'She herself cooked?'

'She held her hands over the pots of food to bless them before the food was given to us. Her blessing gave it its goodness, its sweetness. The Mother brought the Divine Force into the ashram, you see. The Master told us she brought the Divine Force down to bless us.'

'But was he not the Divine One?'

'They were as one,' Montu-da said, and his face grew darker as it became pensive. 'They were not separate but two aspects of one divinity. He brought the Mother to us, and through our love for the Mother we could realise him. The Mother told us she could only exist because of him, but without her he would not have become manifest to us in the form of love.'

'Did they marry?'

Montu-da was shocked. 'What are you saying?' he cried in agitation. 'Please do not say such things in the ashram.' He got up from his seat, leaving pills and powders scattered across the counter. 'We are not speaking of – of ordinary beings, please. We are talking of supramental beings and the union of the divine.'

'There was a union?' Sophie persisted. 'Did they live as man and wife?'

Montu-da had been walking towards the door as if he wished to flee from her. Now he stopped to look at her in dismay.

'Didn't they?' Sophie asked more gently.

He repeated, 'They were one.'

'As man and wife – physically?'

Now he flushed purple again, and took out a large handkerchief to mop his face. Then he said, 'As body and soul are one, yes. Now please allow me – I must lock up the dispensary.'

Sophie got to her feet and followed him out, feeling somewhat repentant for causing him such discomfort but still driven by her urge to know. Had the Mother known love – ordinary, physical, mortal love? It was important to know. Montu-da's large hands were fumbling with the lock in his agitation. As they walked down the veranda steps, he said, 'When the Master died, the Mother gave us all courage. She told us, "He has not left – he is here, inside me, still living. He thinks through me, speaks through me and reaches you through me." That is what I mean,' he concluded, 'when I say they are one.'

Just when Sophie's search looked as if it might move in interesting directions, it came to an abrupt end with the birth of her child, several weeks earlier than expected.

It was to be a long time before she considered resuming it.

For the time being, she gave herself up wholly to the experience of motherhood, although when Dr Bishop delivered her and held up the child, saying 'A beautiful boy, just like a rose,' Sophie could only say, through dry lips, 'A rose?' She had never seen a person more like a rat, or monkey. She covered her eyes with her arm: Matteo was right, she saw too much, too well.

At the ashram she was told the Mother would choose a name for her son. Diya came running, with her pink sarong tucked up so she could hurry, to tell Sophie and Matteo that the Mother wished him to be named after the Master – Prem Krishna.

Matteo's face went white with incredulity and joy at hearing the message but Sophie said tersely, 'Tell the Mother I've already chosen the name. It is Giacomo,' and turning to Matteo, she challenged him. 'A family name, isn't it?'

Matteo went out into the dark. The monsoon had been active while Sophie was at the hospital giving birth, and the grounds were deep in water, the trees drooping with it and the foliage glistening. He walked till he saw the lights of the Abode of Bliss reflected on the wet leaves in the garden. He stood and looked into the lighted house, and it seemed to him that it was to that his heart reached, not to the house where he had left a woman and child.

The conviction was so powerful that he went up the steps to the room where the light shone and there he found the Mother still sitting up with her papers and work, large spectacles slipping down her nose. She looked up at his step and called to him in surprise.

He went in and knelt by her, his hands folded together. 'Tell me what to do, Mother. Living as I do, as a householder, with a family, can I continue to live here amongst sadhus? How can I be of your company now that I am a husband and father?' He stumbled over the words, bringing them out in a muddle through his great emotional confusion, but she seemed to understand.

Taking off her spectacles, she tapped him with them lightly. Her smile was amused and tolerant. 'You are not absorbed in family life, Matteo. I have only to look at your pure and shining face to know it is not so. No, Matteo. You are like the lotus that blooms in the ponds and lakes of India. Your roots may be in the mud but your petals are pure, the water does not touch them and the mud does not stain them. Be always like that lotus flower,' she murmured, 'clean and pure.'

Matteo, his heart thudding and bounding with joy at her words, knew enough not to repeat them to Sophie.

Not that Sophie any longer mocked him or questioned his beliefs; if she had any interest left in him it was to see him as a father. Her attention was given up to the child. 'Get a mosquito net for his cradle,' she ordered Matteo. 'This house is infested with mosquitoes. He may be bitten.'

'But we don't use mosquito nets ourselves, Sophie,' Matteo protested. 'They'll disappear after the rains anyway.'

'I won't wait till after the rains. Get one *now*,' she said.

She wrote to her mother for things for the child. Parcels arrived with what Matteo considered totally incongruous objects. Blue airmail letters lay about everywhere, bearing advice on child rearing. Matteo looked at them with the same loathing as Sophie regarded mosquitoes – as a source of disease.

If he had been spending more time at home, there would have been nothing but strife between them. As it was, Matteo found himself so deeply absorbed in the work of the press and the publication of the Master's work, there was little or no time left for family life.

Meals were eaten communally, and Matteo was strict about attending the evening *darshan* and setting aside time for meditation. Sophie did not try to break into his private time. She was like a lioness wholly involved with her cub, guarding it even against its father. If he came to her late at night, she hissed, 'Be *quiet* – you'll wake the baby.'

The monsoon meant that the baby's garments hung all over the house, dripping. Mildew grew visibly on the walls and woodwork, and damp insinuated itself into sheets and mattresses. Matteo was drenched on his way to work and spent the day in damp clothes. Many in the ashram fell ill: practically everyone suffered from 'flu and dysentery, and the mosquitoes that bred in the waterlogged pools brought malaria. Sophie found herself going to Montu-da's dispensary for pills and powders along with everyone else. 'Haven't you anything to keep the mosquitoes away?' she demanded.

He twinkled at her – his nose was swollen with a horrendous cold and his eyes were red – and he seemed to shine. 'This is the mosquitoes' season! You want to deprive them of it? My dear lady, this earth houses many creatures, not only us.'

She could see no reason for cheer. 'When will this monsoon of yours be over?'

'But madam, why do you want the monsoon to be over? It

is the season that made poets and painters and musicians rejoice. We have special ragas composed for the rainy season. Our painters have depicted the thunder clouds and the egrets that fly across them. Our great poet Kalidasa has written an epic about the monsoon clouds which you must read, dear madam. It tells the story of a lover who sends a cloud with a message to his beloved. It is so beautiful! Just like your great poet Goethe – '

If anyone in the ashram could make Sophie laugh, it was Montu-da. 'Oh, just give me the pills for the baby's colic for now,' she begged.

She was to find that her vigilance would not be at an end when the rains stopped and the baby grew old enough to be taken outdoors. Grimly, she set about guarding him from the greater world, so grimly that at times he cried.

'But, Sophie, what is the matter? He did nothing wrong.'

'Nothing wrong? But he nearly caught that ant, didn't you see?' or 'He would have put that chilli in his mouth if I hadn't pulled it away!' or 'Don't you know there are snakes about? That he could get sunstroke if he didn't wear his hat?'

'If we were meant to wear hats, we would be born with them,' Matteo grumbled.

The day that a parcel arrived from her parents and a sailor suit was unpacked from it, he protested, 'What is this? Can't he dress in a loincloth and sandals like the other children at the kindergarten?'

'He won't go to the kindergarten here. He will go to school in Europe,' Sophie said calmly. She had become much larger, more square-shouldered, and now adopted this ominous calm. She could defy him now, backed by her motherhood. 'We must leave now, Matteo. The time has come to go back.'

It was the time of their most bitter quarrels. There was no longer mockery, or sarcasm. Now they were locked into what both felt was a fight to the end, both desperate to save what they believed.

Matteo: 'You reject her because she is unlike anyone you know.'

Sophie: 'That is true. She is outside the society I know.'

Matteo: 'But can't you see that only extraordinary people, people who have lived extraordinary lives, are capable of taking us, the ordinary people, into their extraordinary worlds?'

Sophie: 'Why is the ordinary not enough for you? Home, family, a child? Why must you run after the extraordinary when you do not even understand what it is?'

Matteo: 'That is why, Sophie: in order to understand it. I see in her the one who can reveal the unknown to me.'

Sophie: 'Matteo, I can see she is a strange woman who has had an interesting life. But who knows who she really is? I see the glamour of that, how it intrigues. I am intrigued too, a little. But your love, and your devotion – why? And the love and devotion of all the others here – for what? Only a legend. Why do you give this legend your life?'

Matteo: 'Sophie, my love for her isn't the love one feels for a beautiful or glamorous or intriguing woman, a legend, as you say. You must see that! There is a difference between sacred and profane love. Listen, in her presence I feel I am more alive than I am in the presence of any other living creature. Her presence heightens and illuminates the experience of living as no one else's does. Why? Because she contains – she is the container of a power that *gives* the world this heightened and illuminated quality. When I leave her, I feel I am falling, down, down into darkness. No, not darkness but *greyness*, flatness, emptiness. When she appears, everything comes to life, it flowers, it brightens . . .'

Sophie: 'But isn't that what physical love does too, what you call profane love?'

Matteo: 'No, no, that obscures, Sophie, that *obscures*. It comes in the way – of enlightenment, clarity, peace – all that I need and want. The love that you and I share, that is mortal love. It exists but it won't exist for ever. The love I have for the Mother, that others have here for her, that is immortal. It does not depend on me, on them, or even on her. It will last when we are all gone.'

Sophie: 'What, like some ghost? A holy ghost flapping about in the air, this love?'

Matteo: 'Maybe that is the wrong word, a bad word. But whatever it is she gives us, it is immortal.'

Sophie: 'Yet you say it exists only when you are with her, in her presence, and fades when you leave her.'

Matteo: 'That is because *I* am mortal, *I* am limited! My *endeavour* is to make it lasting, so it exists even when I am away from her, when she is not there.'

Sophie: 'You mean, when she dies?'

Matteo: 'Sophie! How coldly you speak!'

Sophie: 'You see, Matteo – you fear death. You fear that she is mortal. Tell me, why do you fear the mortal? *We* are mortal.'

Matteo: 'But not love, not *her* love. That is the difference. If you and I know ecstasy for a second, the ecstasy of the Mother's love lasts and lasts, it has no end.'

Sophie: 'So you live in a state of ecstasy with the Mother?'

Matteo: 'Yes!'

Sophie: 'If that is so, if that is true – you would be burnt up. You would be reduced to ash. The human body and the human heart cannot stand so much ecstasy. They are built to survive only a few seconds of it. We are not made for ecstasy, or immortality.'

Matteo: 'Sophie, you are a destroyer. You will destroy me. That is what you are trying to do.'

Sophie: 'I am trying to save you! Take you away and *save* you.'

Matteo: 'No, you are trying to destroy me by destroying the only part that has any value. What you want to sustain is the part that has no value. The Mother's love sustains the valuable part. The Mother's love sustains!'

Sophie was silent.

Matteo: 'You see, that is the difference between sacred and profane love!'

Sophie: 'Maybe I read the wrong books. The books I was given to read told me they are one, the same.'

Matteo: 'They are one, Sophie, but not the *same*. The Absolute is *nirguna* – it has no form. It is *acintya* – it has no properties. How can our minds and bodies conceive of what is formless and without properties? So superior beings like the Mother are born, they provide the form within which we can see and recognise the Absolute.'

Sophie, covering up her ears and shouting: 'The Absolute, the Soul, the Supreme. Supra this and supra that. Don't use those words, I am sick of them. They are non-words.'

Matteo, bitterly: 'And what words do you like? Don't tell me, I can guess. Food. Bed. Baby. House. Are *those* your words?'

Sophie: 'Yes. Yes! They are good words and I like them. Say them again. I didn't know you knew them. I thought you had forgotten them.'

Worn by their battles through the night, and by the demanding work of the day, both were gaunt and exhausted. The ashram seemed to watch, in silence, to see who would win: they had witnessed such battles before. Couples had come, settled, had children, and then it had become evident that not both, not all, were equally committed to the ashram and the Mother. Other desires, other ambitions became evident. Sometimes they drew whole families away, at other times families were split and broken. None of it happened suddenly, dramatically. It took time. Years went by. The children grew, playing in the ashram gardens which were the only world they knew. To some it was everything; to others it was not.

Sophie, preoccupied as she was with Giacomo, was nonetheless aware, even if intermittently, of how the longer Matteo stayed the stronger grew his bonds with the Mother and the ashram and the life here. The arguments were turning into silences, and the silences were stretching and deepening. He was disappearing into them. She let him be, bitterly.

143

But when Diya came to sit with her on the veranda steps one evening and play with Giacomo, and said to her, 'Why don't you bring him to my school, Sophie? He is old enough to come to my school now,' Sophie was shocked. She had not noticed how much time had slipped by. She shook her head, refusing to answer Diya. The next day she began to pack their belongings, telling everyone she was taking Giacomo away to school.

It was at this moment that she learnt that she was once again pregnant.

The day she learnt this was the only time that Matteo saw her bewildered and vulnerable. She had concentrated with such intensity on taking over Giacomo's life and making it what she wished it to be that she had forgotten to protect herself, she had let an accident happen to her.

Matteo would have chuckled to see her, proud lioness, reduced to such a weak, stricken thing, had he not been so dismayed himself. He could not bring himself to give the news to the Mother when she asked after Sophie and Giacomo. She learnt of it from others, however, and said to him, 'The monk is becoming a family man, I hear,' but she spoke in an uncharacteristically flat, faded tone. She had lost much of her archness, her youthfulness. She seemed distracted.

The Mother was not quite herself. At the evening *darshan*, she spoke less, in a hoarse and difficult voice, and sometimes not at all, leaving Hariharan to sing his most beautiful bhajans in a voice that remained over the years impassioned and profound. She seemed to lose interest in the printing press and left it to Matteo to run. She referred to the time when the Master's work would all be under the imprint of the ashram 'and then my work will be complete here', leaving Matteo to wonder if his duties too would be terminated.

The truth was that her attention was elsewhere, drawn to a newcomer to the ashram, a beautiful child of fifteen who had been brought by his parents, devotees of many years' standing, and left in her care. The Mother had taken over the instruction of the boy in all aspects of yoga and meditation, and even in badminton. The other devotees gathered to watch the old woman play with the boy on the badminton court, summoning up reserves of energy and grace so that she seemed to float and drift about the court in her gauzy veils and robes, the boy to provide her with a youthful and robust foil.

Matteo did not watch. He hurried past the courts and in and out of the Abode of Bliss with his files and papers. 'Like a clerk, Mat-t-eo,' she teased once when she saw him. 'First a monk, and then a family man and now – a clerk. You are turning the cycle of life anti-clockwise,' she indicated how with a long finger.

It was the only cruelty committed by the Mother to which Matteo ever admitted.

Sophie, absorbed in her new process of gestation, said nothing. It was only when the child was born and she saw Matteo's face as he glanced at the child, expressionlessly, his thoughts elsewhere, that her old rage overcame her. She said to Diya who had come to help as she did with all small babies, 'Is this what the Mother does to her devotees when she's finished with them? Leave them with nothing?'

Diya was horrified. Her mouth opened wide in protest but she only said in a frightened whisper, 'Oh, why do you say such things, Sophie?' and looked to see if Matteo had heard.

He had, as he was meant to, but he merely turned his face away.

Sophie wished she could leave immediately. But the birth had been a difficult one and although the child seemed strong and determined to thrive, she herself was weakened and dispirited. The baby sucked at her breast day and night, screaming if separated from her, and Sophie felt not only her strength but her resolution draining away from her. She often wept with anger when alone but not when Matteo was there because then she saw herself through his eyes: strident, selfish. Diya came in the evenings to help but by then Sophie was too tired to talk and lay down and slept with the children as soon as they did, needing rest. Diya was worried enough to tell Montu-da, who sent pills which Sophie did not take. She thought of going to Dr Bishop but Dr Bishop seemed more occupied with the church than with the hospital now, leaving it to the younger doctors: she wrote Sophie notes on paper with quotations from the Bible, saying she was 'preparing to meet her Maker'.

Sophie watched to see if Matteo would notice her altered condition but he said nothing to indicate that he did. He was rarely at home during the hours that the children were awake; usually he returned after they were asleep.

When Isabel showed herself capable of walking and existing independently of Sophie's arms and lap, Sophie pulled out the boxes and cartons and began to pack. Matteo watched her in silence.

'Don't look like that,' Sophie said. 'I told you I'm taking them home. You won't even notice.'

At that moment his face was so agonised that she thought he might say, 'Stay' or 'Take me.' But what he said was, 'Sophie, she's ill. The Mother's very ill.'

Sophie paused in the folding and packing of baby clothes. 'Oh? What is wrong?'

'We don't know, but she is having tests. It could be cancer. Montu-da said –' but his voice choked and he slumped against the wall, shading his eyes with his hand.

Giacomo, on the floor, playing, said, 'He's crying, Sophie. Why is he crying?'

Then Sophie, marching across to Matteo and grasping him by his hair, tugged at it hard, hissing, 'And immortality, Matteo? What about immortality? Or is she only of our world after all?' Pushing him against the wall and jerking his head by his hair, she cried, 'Now find out – what is mortal and what is immortal, what is sacred and what is profane. Now find out.' She shook him and shook him by his hair till Giacomo began to cry for his father.

All day she went back and forth, emptying the house of its

146

belongings – they were hers and the children's, Matteo owned practically nothing – and putting them away in boxes. When she had finished at night, and put the children to bed, she went out on the veranda where Matteo was sitting in the dark, and leant against the balustrade.

Then Matteo began to speak to her, and he told her of his visit to the shrine a long time ago, and how he had seen a stone there. 'That was when I understood what had brought me to India, Sophie. It was only in India that a stone could have shown me the Infinite. Nowhere else, Sophie, nowhere else could a stone contain a glimpse of infinity. It was such – such perfection.'

'Perfection, in a stone?'

'No, no, not the stone at all – but the cosmic whole contained within the stone! Yes, that is why I stay here, Sophie, in this country where one sees the divine enclosed within the earthly.'

'Oh, the Mother. Once again, the Mother. Not the stone, not the shrine, Matteo, it is a woman who keeps you here. Call her what you like – the Cosmic, the Absolute – but she's a woman. Don't you see?' Sophie's breath was coming short and hard. She turned and went back into the darkened room. There was nothing left to say.

Apart from brief visits to the bazaar for milk powder or gripe water, Sophie had not left the ashram for so long that she was disconcerted to find she had lost the knack of manoeuvring her way about in the outer world. Paying off the rickshaw driver, purchasing tickets, standing guard over the luggage – all these exercises she had once performed competently now required prodigious concentration and effort. She frowned fiercely as she pushed her way through the crowds and found the railway carriage in which she had been allotted a berth. Settling onto it with the babies and the luggage, she became aware of the other passengers already in it, staring at her so acutely that she felt their eyes slithering across her body. She realised she had not been with strangers, with anyone other than the inmates of the ashram, in years. Then she had longed to be amongst 'normal' people again, by which she meant people outside the ashram; now, trying to hold them off by angry looks, she found herself hating their 'normality' if that was what it was. Then, she had thought the outer world contained the freedom she had lost; now, penned up with other travellers – a middle-aged man who changed from trousers into a dhoti before her eyes and lay back on his berth, waggling one foot over the other knee, a woman who was unpacking half a dozen containers of food from a basket and smacking her lips over some pungent pickles, a young man whose adam's apple bobbed up and down like a frog in a snake's throat as he stared at her fascinatedly – she felt herself caged in a zoo, or prison, forced into surrendering her freedom and privacy.

And she had thought it was the ashram that was the gaol from which she had to escape.

All through the journey she had to rouse herself to take care of such commonplace matters as ordering meals from the curry-stained waiter who went down the corridor collecting orders, reaching out through the window to buy tumblers of tea, bananas and packets of peanuts from urchins peddling them at wayside stations, and presenting her tickets for inspection. The sober, orderly routine of the ashram, the meals prepared and served them on shady verandas, all that she had thought of as so restricting now seemed to have provided a freedom in which she had lived without giving such matters a thought.

The outer world she had told herself was the 'real' one thrust itself at her like blows from its fists: people casually leaning out of the windows to spit, beggar children with the protruding bellies and strawy hair of the starving clamouring at the wayside stations where they briefly halted, animals that belonged to no one – wretched pai dogs and sad monkeys – scavenging for food, then a rotund merchant and his wife climbing into the carriage with great boxes and bags of luggage carried on the backs of coolies – all sights to which Sophie had developed an immunity on her earlier travels in

148

India, now struck her as being more brutal than she could bear.

Huddling on her berth with the sleeping children, she wondered if she would find the courage to make this escape from the ashram back into the world.

At the hotel in New Delhi where they stayed while Sophie arranged for airline tickets through a travel agent, she bathed and put the children to bed before having a shower and changing her clothes. Giacomo was awake, looking through a book she had bought him, and said she could go out, he would take care of Isabel. Earlier she had looked out of the window at the kidney-shaped swimming pool with its chemically blue water blazing in the sun and thought of going down to lie on one of the canvas chairs under a palm tree. She had also noted a pastry shop in the lobby with the kind of confections she had pined for at the ashram. Now that all this was available, she found herself drawing the curtain against the sight and walking past the enticing aromas on her way to the dining room where she told herself she would eat a Western meal of meat in order to mark her release from the ashram.

It was early and the waiters were setting tables. There was only one other customer there, a middle-aged and heavily built man who sat across from her and stared with unconcealed lust; under the table his legs were spread wide and he worked his knees rhythmically in and out. She tried to ignore him and cut up her meat and eat it but found it impossible to swallow when she was being watched so avidly. Finally, she admitted the taste of meat was sickening and, leaving the cutlet on the plate, she wiped her mouth on a napkin and asked for the bill.

The man rose and walked across to her table, holding his napkin in front of him. 'I'm in room forty-two,' he said in a slurred voice. 'Come up and I'll give you whisky.'

She sat as if she had been slapped. Her cheeks stung and turned red. She gripped the edge of the table, wondering:

should she throw it over, at him? Should she scream for the waiter, the manager, the police?

'Foreign whisky,' he said, twitching a finger with a gold ring.

'Get out – I'll –' what should she threaten him with that would be sufficient response to his vileness?

He protested 'You are alone. You want a man. All foreign women do.'

She leapt up and strode out of the room, then hurried up the corridor to the elevator, trying not to sob or scream. When she got to her room, she rolled onto the bed beside the sleeping children, gripping a pillow. Clutching it, she cried, 'Matteo! What about this, Matteo? What are you going to do?'

The phone rang and she picked it up hastily because the baby was beginning to whimper. She fumbled it to her ear and heard the man's voice say, 'Have you changed into your nightie? Is it see-through? Do you wear knickers –'

'I hate you,' she hissed at him. 'You filthy animal, I hate you,' and left the phone off the hook and lay back stiffly, prepared to hear him come and scratch at the door or even turn a key in the lock and enter. No one did, and she was alone with the children who sometimes slept and sometimes woke, needing to be patted and reassured, and gradually the voices talking loudly at the end of the corridor, the rattling of doors and the burble of television sets died away and there was a tattered, precarious silence, but still Sophie could not sleep for hate. If she had hated the ashram, the Mother, Matteo and their lives there, it was nothing, she now felt, compared to the hate she felt for the world outside. Matteo had spoilt it for her. Bitterly she thought how the standards he had set, of silence and intensity and purpose, had become the standards by which she would find herself judging all that followed in her life.

By the next night, when she had finally made her way through the queues and crowds and tumult of the airport, whey-faced at three o'clock in the morning, a sleeping child on each arm and a torn and bursting rucksack on her back, the sense of escape to freedom had entirely dissipated to be replaced by this bitter sense of loss and betrayal. Having laid the children side by side across two seats to sleep, she hunched over with her head in her hands, overwhelmed by despair.

An air hostess in the guise of a butterfly came fluttering up the aisle to ask solicitously, 'Are you okay? Are you okay?' She had to lift her face up to the little painted creature and dutifully nod – it was one of the duties one had in the world outside – and say 'Yes, okay.'

To begin with, she took the children to her parents' home in Frankfurt. Her mother had, after all, been a most concerned and conscientious grandmother ever since the children were born, and Sophie looked forward to sharing them with her now and having her help in rearing them. To have their help and support would surely transform the nightmare into the daylight of comfort and security, she felt. But she soon found she could not stand the sharing, or the being together with them in their home.

Her father held himself in the background, stepping forward only to bring the children chocolates, then stepping back again hastily before they started smearing the chocolates all over the white carpets and white furnishings of the elegant apartment, and it was his reticence Sophie resented. She noticed him wincing every time he came downstairs in the morning and saw the state of the breakfast table, and bending over his armchair to remove crumbs before he sat down on it. In her mother, it was the lack of reticence she found intolerable. At breakfast she would already be discussing what they would buy at the supermarket, what they would cook, what would be good for the babies. 'Oh, Mama, what does it matter? We will just pick up whatever there is!' Sophie cried in exasperation as the shopping list grew longer. When the mother insisted on taking them shopping for new clothes and went from one boutique to another in search of a party dress, a jacket, shoes, Sophie protested, 'Look, these children are used to just running around naked. You needn't overdo it, you know.'

Her mother wanted too much of the children, took them over so completely. Sophie found it difficult enough to have her choose what the chidren were to eat, what clothes they would wear to the playground, what medication was best for their coughs and colds, but when it came to demanding that they be baptised, and baptised in the same church that Sophie had been, then Sophie rebelled.

'No, I did not leave India and all its superstitions and rituals to come here and submit to the tribal rites of Europe,' she stormed. 'You talk of Indians as if they were barbarians because they cremate the dead and toss them in the river. But what about you? You believe a baby should be dumped in a basin of water by a priest and have some mumbo-jumbo said over its head or it won't go to heaven, eh?'

They were shocked. 'Where did she learn to speak like that?' they asked each other.

Holding hands as they lay in bed in the dark, Sophie's mother sighed 'We should never have permitted them to live in India, never supported them in that,' to which her father rumbled in reply, 'They would do that anyway. The young find ways to do what they wish.'

'What can you mean by that?'

'I mean drugs, guns, the Red Brigade –' at which she covered her mouth to stop herself from shrieking.

The next day she was especially patient and gentle with Sophie and the children, allowing herself only once to sigh, 'How you have changed, child! And we thought you would be happy to be back in Europe.'

'Yes, yes,' Sophie said crossly, 'but no one need think that by coming back to Europe I have come back to the church. I haven't. Oh, the hypocrisy!'

Quite soon she packed up and moved with the children to Matteo's home. Larger, warmer, in Italy, in the countryside, it would surely prove more relaxed, a place where they could live and breathe in spite of the old people's censure and disapproval. Sophie would not talk to them about India, or try to explain their years there; she was silent about that entire time, that past, and they were grateful to have her back and part of the family; Matteo would surely follow, they thought, and in the meanwhile they had the children.

Sophie, taking a straw hat, dark glasses and a book out into the garden, stretched herself on the grass and sunbathed through a broiling summer, only half-listening to the conversation of the children and the grandparents at the bottom of the grassy slope where the camellias indefatigably produced their coral pink blossoms.

In a way she felt she was convalescing and allowing the sweetness of the air to recuperate her. After so much tension and so much fighting, she now became torpid, a motionless lizard on a ledge. The more happily the children settled into the life of their grandparents' home, the more safe and secure and contented they became, the more she felt able to relax her fierce hold on them. It was as if the lioness who had guarded them so passionately earlier had now delivered them into a safe haven so that the need for that zealous protectiveness dwindled. Listening to their voices as they picked camellias off the grass and climbed over their grandparents' knees, she felt them recede from her.

Then it was Matteo who came surging back in a way she had not imagined would happen. To have left him behind in the ashram, with the Mother – that tormented her now. The Mother, the ashram – images of them rose to haunt her. She saw the ring of dancing peacocks, the old woman in their centre. She heard that memorable voice ring out in the dusk, under the great looming tree, and she saw the light in the eyes of her devotees as they listened, thirstily, Matteo amongst them.

Matteo. The thought of him made her turn her face to the grass and burrow into it to stop herself from moaning aloud, it hurt so shockingly. He had been the cause of pain all the years in India, and she believed to remove him would be to remove the pain. Now it seemed one half was ripped from her side, and she pressed her hand where it hurt so fiercely that it felt like a wound, a flow of blood.

153

Her face acquired a constantly preoccupied expression in place of the old watchful and suspicious one. She spoke little, she read and brooded but there was no stillness and no calm in her inactivity. In fact, she was consumed by restlessness.

Since she had made herself so irrelevant, no one objected when she started borrowing the car and driving off to Milan. She said she wanted to see Matteo's sister Caroline, do some shopping, listen to some music. It was not entirely untrue: she knew she must fill the huge emptiness of Matteo's absence and that this required some effort on her part. At one of the parties Caroline threw as part of her job in public relations, she met the young man Paolo who found this older woman quite fascinating; that she was wealthy, bore a distinguished name, dressed like a poor student, used no make-up, had a plain face and hair that she cut herself, and had lived in India, made her the opposite of all the young women he knew who were poor, with unknown names, dressed like mannequins, were deeply attached to the big cities of the West and wished only to travel to America. She was not particularly interested in him but took him as he was: he was like the young men she had known as a girl; he put her in touch with her pre-Matteo and pre-India days that had grown so dim and so distant: perhaps he could revive it. She imagined it coming to life again when she visited him in his small apartment on the avenue Ritter, mocking at its designer sparseness, its uncompromising black-and-white decor, but finding it pleasing, seeing it as an arena of possibility that had been offered to her before and that she had left unexplored.

She soon discovered why he was so fascinated by India: he connected it with the drugs he took. These proved not to be the ones she knew – though they did smoke marijuana together, he craved cocaine, heroin, the harder drugs she had herself never tried. She was not so young as to find this exciting in itself; she found the times when he was taking them very boring, very empty, and drove back to the lake, lay in the sun again with the babies crawling over her as if they were lizards, and she a stone, nothing more.

Before the summer was over she had had enough of Paolo. She found both his drug habit and his insistent questioning about India tiresome. When he tried to probe deeper into what she knew of India, wanting to hear about arcane practices of Hinduism and in particular Tantric Hinduism which he had heard involved acrobatic sex between trained yogis, she found herself hating him. Her life with Matteo had spoilt her for life with men like this Paolo; it was no longer possible. The day he suggested they travel together to India – 'We could visit your husband at the ashram, give him a surprise – think of it!' – she spat at him, 'You? You are not fit to even enter his presence. He – he is a god –' and got into her car, aghast at what she had blurted out, drove off and did not return.

Before she left Milan and drove towards Como, she stopped her car briefly on the Corso Garibaldi and quickly slipped into San Simpliciano. Walking under its brick arches and across the echoing emptiness of its chambers and the scatter of boxes and caskets, crosses and relics, she made her way to the great da Fassano fresco that soared up into the dome. Here a radiant rainbow arched over the benign head of God the Father, holding the white dove of the Holy Spirit in his breast, and blessing a Madonna who knelt at his feet while being crowned by another figure, perhaps God the Son. Around them hosts of angels hovered in all the hues that made up the rainbow glowing around and over them.

Sophie stood under it, craning her head to look up at the furthest reaches of the huge Romanesque dome and arches, as if searching in it for a glimpse of something she had left behind there, or remembered encountering there.

Then she turned abruptly and walked out, her heels sounding loudly on the bare brick floor.

She returned to the children. This was to be her life now: the villa, the lake and the children. She began teaching Giacomo and Isabel their lessons; she went down to the village to arrange for them to go to school. She took them to the mountains to teach them to ski; she took them to Frankfurt for Christmas. She wrote to the editor of the magazine she had once worked for, asking for assignments. The children watched her. They said nothing, not even to each other, but they held hands and watched, wondering: would she stay? Or would she go away again? She never spoke of India, although sometimes a letter arrived from one of the devotees at the ashram with news of the Mother who was now in great pain and sinking slowly, of the great sadness in the ashram, and sometimes small gifts to remind them of it – incense sticks or rose petals. Sometimes the grandparents broke out in anger and recrimination. She listened to their outbursts without replying. She might have put India behind her completely, but when the telegram arrived to say Matteo had been taken to the hospital, she grasped the news and reacted to it with such swiftness that it was clear her mind had been with Matteo all this time, her senses alert to receive any message from him. Now she packed her bag, bought her ticket and left with such speed it seemed nothing mattered to her but to be with him.

Death

To Isidoro de Blas

How hard they try!
How hard the horse tries
to become a dog!
How hard the dog tries to become a swallow!
How hard the swallow tries to become a bee!
How hard the bee tries to become a horse!
And the horse,
what a sharp arrow it yanks from the rose,
what a pale rose rising from its lips!
And the rose,
what a flock of lights and cries
knotted in the living sugar of its trunk!
And the sugar,
what daggers it dreams in its vigils!
And the daggers,
what a moon without stables, what nakedness,
eternal and blushing flesh they seek out!
And I, on the roof's edge,
what a burning angel I look for and am!
But the plaster arch,
how vast, how invisible, how minute,
without even trying!

Federico García Lorca

∽Chapter Three∾

Sophie's last conversation with Matteo in hospital began quietly. He had slept all afternoon while she sat up and read the small, badly written and cheaply printed booklet on the Mother that he had bought so long ago at a railway station on the way to her. When he stirred and she saw that he was awake, she went and sat by him and held his hand; it was so thin she felt she must be very gentle and not hurt it.

'Matteo,' she said, 'I have been reading again the life of the Mother.'

He sighed. 'Again. Why? What do you think you will find in her life?'

'I must find whatever there is to find. The book only gives you the legend. I want to go behind that, find out who she really is, how she came here, why. I want to know her. Then I can show you, too, who she really is.'

'But I know who she really is, it is you who do not. You cannot know her while you pursue these facts you love so much. I know her greatness and her power. It is not necessary that there is a connection between that and her life.'

'I think it is, Matteo,' Sophie insisted in a low voice. It was not to persuade only him that she spoke. 'I will make a connection between what you believe and what I know. It is the only way I will ever be able to understand you, what you have done to yourself.' She turned his hand over in hers; it seemed so fine it was almost transparent. The fingers were long and tapering, the veins blue.

He too spoke in nearly a whisper. 'I have given myself to her. Why do you want to keep me, Sophie, from pursuing my beliefs?'

'Because what you believe in is – nothing!' Involuntarily her hand rolled into a fist, squeezing his roughly.

He winced and withdrew it. His eyes moved from her face to some point beyond her, fixedly, and he clenched his jaw when she argued, refusing to answer.

'You have turned into a stone,' Sophie said at last, in despair. 'The power she has over you, it has turned you to stone.'

He sighed slightly, shaking his head on the pillow. His face was almost the same colour and texture as that washed and faded piece of cotton. He clutched at the sheet across his chest as if to shield himself from her anger. 'I will break that spell,' she went on, 'that stone – and I will make you see, *see* her, what she is – '

He turned his face slightly towards her, in a kind of appeal, but now Sophie could not stop, she went raging on. 'I am going to find out – I will write the true account – not all that nonsense you publish – but the truth, for you to read. I will have it published – circulated – and then you'll see, everyone will see – '

The moment for communication disappeared under the flood of her anger. She stopped only when she saw the light darkening in the doorway and heard the nurses clicking past the door, ordering their patients' visitors to leave for the night, and bringing in trays with medicines and meals.

One of them entered Matteo's room. Sophie rose, picked up her rucksack and swung out of the room without looking back at the still image on the bed.

As she walked down the veranda to the stairs at the end, she saw Matteo's doctor coming up for his evening round. He hesitated, ready to be questioned by her and to answer. But she merely raised her hand and walked past. He looked

160

slightly puzzled by her silence and turned to see her go down the stairs with her rucksack and make her way down the drive to the gate.

Cairo, rising out of the warm ochre sand, its buildings sand-coloured but vaguely Mediterranean, their flat façades marked with cornices and decorative flourishes, little balconies of wrought iron and long green shutters, and the palm-lined avenues grave and straight. But in the train to Alexandria, the flat grey landscape, the stands of date palms and orange groves, the fields of wheat and mustard interspersed with brick kilns and sand quarries, fill Sophie with the sense of being in India again, on another of those interminable train journeys, travelling on and on, dusty and tired, too tired to think or feel, all because of Matteo, that fool, that idiot Matteo . . .

She rises to her feet in a panic, her head swirling because she feels she has been turned around and is travelling backwards into India again, and the past. She must get off the train, she must not allow the journey to continue . . .

Then a man comes along the aisle with a trolley full of orange and lemon drinks, tea and coffee. He is smartly dressed and smiling. Other passengers buy from him and Sophie sees that two are large women in brilliant green and purple dresses who sit sprawled with beautifully dressed babies playing on their laps, and one is a man in a business suit who is scribbling on a pad of paper taken from his briefcase. They glance up at her. She rocks on her feet and feels the landscape trundle past – palm trees, buffaloes, a small village of brick and clay – and then sinks back into her seat, perspiring, reminding herself that this is precisely her intention: to travel back, back in time, although not her own time now but the Mother's.

It is dusk in Alexandria. The light is filtered through fine clay dust and sand. In Mazarita a little girl plays by herself. She wears a bright yellow dress with black velvet trimmings that are torn and she has left her sandals on the steps of an apartment building so that she can hop and skip freely on the sandy pavement. Her long hair hangs down to her waist and grows more and more wildly tumbled as she hops and skips and Sophie watches. Her eyes are like embers, charred and black but brilliant, on fire. There is a faint look of surprise on her face when she sees Sophie but she quickly turns around to play. She is conscious, though, of being watched, and she moves more lightly and gracefully than before.

The door at the top of the stairs opens and a woman comes out, holding a baby in one arm, shouts, 'Ferial! Get in, quick!'

The child flushes, glances again at Sophie, then recovers her poise and goes up the stairs with her head tossed back proudly.

؏

Alma was searching for her daughter. Everything was ready, the food in the oven, the table laid. The soup was hot, the bread warmed. It was evening, the sky had lost its light and out beyond the harbour bar the sea reflected its dullness. The child should not be out at this hour. What if Hamid came to know? Alma hit the side of her head with her fist. Should she call Hamid in for his supper? But what if he found the child was not back?

In agitation, she shuffled up the whole length of the curving passage that ran from end to end of the large apartment. She went out onto the balcony and looked up and down Mazarita. There were still children playing there, but they were all boys, rough loud boys kicking about a football. There were some office workers hurrying home. There was the seller of dates and nuts lighting up the lamp on his barrow. But Laila would have been visible amongst them all, in her bright clothes, with her vivid face and dancer's movements. Alma held her fists to her chin and moaned, 'Laila, Laila.'

Then she shuffled back into the apartment, making her way past the florid pieces of furniture that held the polished silver, the framed photographs, the shells and china vases that were the souvenirs of her and Hamid's families. She stopped at the front door, unlocked it and looked down the stairwell. The great spiral staircase was dark but at the bottom the concierge's family sat talking in the light from their small, suffocating room that stood open to catch the evening air; the heavy scent of incense they had lit billowed out in a cloud. The women were chattering as they passed an invisible baby from arm to arm, folded like a toffee in a pink wrapper. The children hopped on and off the steps like little lively goats. If Laila were there, her voice would be raised above all the others, bullying them, making herself heard and felt. She was not – it was too peaceful. 'Oh, Laila, Laila,' Alma mourned.

Out on the small terrace at the back she had made herself a garden – a fig tree in a pot that never grew very high, a grape vine on which grapes would not ripen because it was always in the shade of the other buildings, tubs of artemisia that the cat scratched up, and a jasmine that flowered and flowered as though it thought itself to be in paradise. Alma pottered there, searching for some herbs to put in the soup while Clio the cat, who had seen her from the ledge where she slept, leapt down and followed her about, crying for her supper. It was too dark to tell a blade of grass from a leaf of mint, and Alma went in with Clio.

Then Hamid came out of his study, blinking behind his spectacles, hungry, pitiful, wanting his supper. It could not be hidden from him: Laila was still out, had not returned, and it was dark. Where was she? he would ask.

But no, he came into the kitchen and sat down at the table with a sigh, holding his head in his hands while she ladled out a bowl of soup and set it before him. He needed only her attention, her care. 'Eat, Hamid,' she sighed, 'eat. Then the headache will go. Too much reading. Too many books.'

'Ech.' He did not like her to say that. He took up a long-handled spoon, dipped and ate. Her good lentil soup revived him. He tore off a piece of bread and gave her the most fleeting twinkle. 'And you?' he said. 'No books? No reading?'

'Mine is different,' she said, sitting down and putting her elbows on the table to watch him eat. Clio leapt onto her lap, digging her claws in through the cloth of her skirt, and made herself comfortable. 'Student papers. I go through them, like this –' She made a gesture of her thumb and finger to show how they rippled through her hands. Then she ran her fingers through Clio's fur, sighing: it was not student papers that weighed on her.

'Eat,' he told her, eating himself. 'Eat, Alma.'

Then she burst into a long wail. 'How can I – when the child is not home?'

Hamid put down his spoon, and the bread, and stared at her. It was dark, they had forgotten to turn on a light. The dark air was filled with their waiting.

Laila would come sprinting up the stairs at any hour at all. They would hear a commotion on the stairs as she called to the concierge, he yelled back, the children laughed. Laila would fly in, barefoot, her hair wildly tossed about, her bright dress dirty, even torn. She would swoop at the food waiting on the table, and cram it into her mouth with both hands hungrily. But she would not tell them where she had been, what she had done. Such a small child, so headstrong, so independent, it was dangerous, anyone could see that.

'Laila, you cannot do this. You do not know what bad things can happen on the street. And where do you go? We need to know. You must tell.'

She stared at them with eyes like coal, so black and so brilliant. 'I don't know myself,' she said so gravely that they could not accuse her of flippancy. 'I go down the street, I turn a corner – I don't know where I am.'

'Oh Laila,' Alma wailed, 'then tell us what you do.'

The child's mouth tightened. 'Do? I do nothing,' she retorted angrily. 'I walk, I play, I look. But I do nothing.' Her voice turned shrill.

'All right, all right,' the mother hushed her. 'Then go and bathe. Time for bed.'

Hamid, standing by the door, listening silently, said, 'And schoolwork? Has she done that, her schoolwork?'

Both parents – both teachers, both scholars – sighed. The house was filled with their sighing. Laila fled from it.

They could do nothing. He was in his study, making lists of the books that he believed had been in the Serapeum in Alexander's day; she was in the kitchen where she spread the students' French exercises on the table where she could look them over while she kneaded dough or shelled peas, now and then stopping to pick up a red pencil to mark them. Both kept their doors open and with one ear listened for the sound of their daughter returning.

As she grew older, she returned later and later. Often it was already night. Then to see her with her bare legs and a rent in her dress and flowers stuck in her hair – daisies, alyssum that she'd snatched up out of the dust – or with sand leaking out of the soles of her sandals, gritty with sea shells, frightened them so badly they wept, and that made her furious. When she was furious her face would contort and she would tear at her hair.

'You want me to be your prisoner,' she shouted. 'That is how I feel here – a prisoner.'

'Is this house a prison, my child?' the mother cried, and the father couldn't speak for sorrow.

'Yes, yes, it is, it is,' she shouted passionately, and with her hands she made as if to tear open her bosom. That was not a child's gesture. It was the gesture of a woman who knows what her breast contains. She had in her some of the rage, and the pride of a goddess. 'I want – I want – to dance,' she burst out, pushing at the air as if to clear a space for herself. 'Not sit here, reading, reading, reading –' she spat out – 'but out, dancing! Then I would be free –' and she made wide, sweeping gestures with her dancer's arms, swung them around and above her in a way that seemed to them wild and terrifying.

'Hamid, we cannot permit this,' Alma declared. 'This is enough.'

He was at his desk, studying. The ancient Serapeum of

Alexander was his obsession. It was painful for him to have intrusions made upon it. But he saw Alma had gone without sleep for nights, she was haggard. He took off his spectacles. 'Yes, my Alma,' he said.

'If we don't put a stop to this, who knows but she might pursue this mad idea of hers.'

He cringed at that: such things should not be put in words; it brings bad luck. At times his Alma was too blunt, too forthright, perhaps too French and Lyonnais. His own inclination was to the indirect, the circuitous and unspoken.

She was not satisfied. She stood in the doorway, loaded with her bag of books on the way to the girls' school where she taught French, although she had hardly enough strength to walk to the end of the road, let alone take a class, after a night of waiting up for Laila. She said sharply, 'That is not enough. Sitting here, waiting for her. More is needed. We must send her away.'

'Send her away?' he was amazed. He thought the entire intention was to keep her at home. 'Where? What will she do?'

'She must study. We must get her away from the streets. We must find what will interest her.'

Hamid knew that if his daughter had declared herself for dance then it was not books that would hold her. He had seen her take a black pen and slash lines across a page of print, or even rip a page out of a book, crumple it and fling it out of the window in defiance. That was what she thought of books and studies – she, the daughter of teachers, both her parents with university degrees, parents in the academic profession. Little made her so fierce as the idea of scholarship. It acted on her as the idea of home did – she had for it the scorn she felt for her mother's kitchen, her mother's terrace garden, the apartment filled with silverware and photographs and china dishes and statuettes. She had smashed some of them in her rage, seeing them as emblems of her imprisonment. She could have been born a gypsy child, a foundling they had adopted.

Alma could read her Hamid like a book. He did not need to say any of this to her: she saw his thoughts go through him as clear as lines of print. She said, 'I know what you think – this daughter of ours will not study. I know, I know. Listen, we must make it attractive to her. We must make it so she cannot resist. Let us tell her: go to Cairo. Study. If you study well, you might go to Paris.' Alma looked distraught. She spoke the names – Cairo, Paris – in a kind of despair. 'She might agree,' she explained, and unfolded her design: to send Laila to school in Cairo would prove their faith and trust to her; they would be treating her not like a prisoner or a delinquent but as a responsible adult; she would learn to be careful, to look after herself. Then, if she did well, they could send her to Paris, to the Sorbonne where both of them had studied (that was how they had met, Hamid having come to Paris to study). Alma's sister lived in Paris with her French husband and four French daughters; they would take in Laila, see to her education. If education were coupled with Cairo and Paris, Laila might be tempted.

She proved right: good Alma, good mother. Laila did not agree instantly – rebellion had become her stance, her habit – but she had hesitated. Alma saw that hesitation and moved quickly to take advantage of it. She had seen an ember of curiosity light in Laila's eye. She was not so stupid as to think the idea of study caused it, but perhaps it was Cairo, surely it was Paris. A part of Alma trembled to think of her daughter in those cities, alone. She thought of how Laila had lately taken to dressing in brocade vests, and ribbons and gold slippers, and using kohl to make her eyes larger and more brilliant. She thought of the morning they had found her curled up on the stairs, like a kitten, too tired to walk upstairs. But a drastic remedy was needed, and she took courage in her hands in order to apply it. She was rewarded by that hesitation in Laila's eyes. After that it was easy.

Laila had visited Cairo previously with her mother. When she was a child, it was the cakes and bonbons she was offered in the homes of her mother's French friends that made the city so sweetly agreeable; as a young girl, it was the great clamour of traffic, the sight of the Nile, the floating cafés, the lamps lit on them at night, the boulevards and the radio tower pricking the dark sky at night with red stars that made her heart beat faster. Now the *tantes* whose hats and dresses and cakes had seemed so beguiling when she was little turned out to be, in the eyes of the older girl, not quite as smart or elegant as she remembered them. True, Tante Mathilde had her bedroom all done in pink satin frills and yes, Tante Jeannette did take her to the Automobile Club for lunch and the ladies' room there was a marvel of mirrors and white fur rugs, but now Laila found her mother's friends less sophisticated, more matronly and boring than they had once seemed, talking of gall bladder and liver problems, doctors and treatments, the changes in the political atmosphere, the recent riots and demonstrations against the British, the huge strikes that demanded an end to the British Protectorate, the chances of Sa'ad Zaghlul and the Wafd of taking over power that should have come to them with the end of the World War and had not, the uncertainties of the future . . . Then there was the nuisance of being sent off with the children to walk in the Botanic Gardens or play tennis at the club. After she had made the first round of visits, eaten large, heavy lunches served by servants in white, and conveyed messages from her parents, she resolved to keep away from a society that seemed only a new Cairene version of provincialism.

At the American College for Girls in which her parents had decided to enrol her in preference to either a French convent or an Arabic language school, she quickly observed that there were two groups she might join, one of wealthy, Westernised girls in dresses and high-heeled shoes who learnt to play the piano and flickered their eyelashes at the young men who hung around the gates hopefully, and one of demure and serious students from the provinces who were there on scholarships, who took Arabic classes in addition to English and French, and carried their books with them everywhere. Laila could see that while the smart Westernised girls laid themselves open to observation quite candidly and there was no more to them than met the eye, the modest girls who kept their eyes lowered were the ones who had secrets, who had inner lives that might possibly prove to be intriguing.

As it happened, it was one of the latter group that first fell into step with her as they walked to their class, sat down at a table to study with her, and began to talk as if she, too, found the other intriguing. 'Shall we do our grammar together?' she suggested, and later, 'Shall we go and eat now?' Whenever Laila chose to study or to eat, Fatimah chose to come too, open her book or set down her plate, and assume a friendship that proved hard to deny: it was the first.

Fatimah even caught Laila's hand in hers, clutched at it fondly or turned it over and patted its soft pink cushions affectionately. 'You are not Egyptian, are you?' she asked one day, slyly. Laila did not like to confess her mother's French origins; in Alexandria she rarely had to, it was so well known, and she had hoped to avoid personal revelations in Cairo. 'Why do you think so?' she asked carefully. 'Oh, you look foreign,' Fatimah laughed. This made Laila put on a prim expression and say, 'But here I am, studying French – like you.' 'Yes, but you are so good at it – you don't seem to find it hard as I do.' 'Why are you learning French?' Laila turned the question on her and Fatimah fumbled, dropped her eyes and looked sullen. 'You know, my parents want me to. They think if I learn French, I will get a good husband. Good husband! They mean a rich man, a smart man,' she cried indignantly. 'I will never marry that kind of man. I will marry a good Muslim.'

Laila watched her closely, with a sharpened interest. What was this creature, a good Muslim? It had never ventured into her parents' agnostic, academic home. Fatimah's definitions were basic and naive but Laila paid them attention, flattering to the other girl. When Fatimah asked her to come with her to her Koran class, she agreed instantly, not unaware of what her parents would think of that. The two took permission to go out that evening and slipped away to a mosque below the Citadel walls where the mullah held a special class for girl students. The mosque was a clay-coloured ruin except for a few remaining tiles of turquoise and cobalt and indigo glaze in a Tree of Life pattern. In the dusty courtyard, by a gnarled and twisted pomegranate tree, some cotton rugs had been spread out and there the girls sat, each holding a copy of the Koran before her, swaying back and forth rhythmically as she read aloud. The mullah, a small, spare man with a chalky face against which his beard looked dramatically black, led them in a reedy, piping voice. For all her fear of seeming a stranger and out of place, Laila found the scene as intensely moving as the vivid and wonderful blue of the glazed tiles. Here were no giggles, no confusion, no blushes as there were in the French classes where the reading of a poem by Rimbaud or Baudelaire led the students to wink or catch each other's eyes or even the teacher's if they could. No one took such liberties with the mullah; the girls kept their eyes to the written page, their voices rose and fell, their bodies swayed and rocked as if fastened to the lines they read, and Laila saw a way of learning that had no opening to debate, discussion, doubt or argument as it had in her parents' home. Here was a book, a subject, a doctrine that did not allow questioning; that was powerful and authoritative in a strange and inexplicable way: it pleased her even as it puzzled. In any event, she applied herself to learning the verses with a fervour, hoping to catch up quickly with the others and not betray her ignorance.

When Fatimah praised her progress, Laila caught her hand and swung it, happy with the compliment. 'You should come to our meetings perhaps,' Fatimah ventured, looking oddly secretive.

Laila was confused: meetings other than those in the mosque?

'Oh yes, a students' meeting, started by students. I go there and we discuss different things – Egypt, the future. We talk of freedom.'

'Freedom?'

'From the British!' exclaimed Fatimah, astonished by her ignorance. 'Don't you believe we should be free?'

Laila hurried to assure her she did. Having invented a visiting uncle and aunt for the authorities in charge of their movements, she wrapped around her head the brown kerchief Fatimah lent her and followed her into the streets behind the Al Azhar University. There, at the end of a dusty lane where chickens and ducks squawked in their cages while a butcher sharpened his knife, and women sat stitching bright squares of cloth into rugs and hangings for sale, they entered a coffee shop where men were sitting on benches, bubbling at their shishas. Laila was taken aback at being taken to a male enclave by Fatimah, but Fatimah hurried her through it to a smoke-blackened room at the back. Here Laila pushed aside the kerchief from her face and saw to her surprise that the young men who sat around a wooden table greeted Fatimah as if she were a close friend. It made her look at Fatimah with a new curiosity but Fatimah pushed her towards a pair of chairs in a corner, and there they sat and listened to the young men read aloud from a news sheet they were planning to print. The words Laila heard them speak were utterly unfamiliar to her, as was the way Fatimah voiced her opinion with an ease of manner she did not display in class.

'We can make a beginning by handing this to the Principal,' one young man was saying. 'He is the first we must throw out of the country if he continues to insist we learn English and study British history. Let's start with him – '

'Don't waste your time,' another interrupted. 'It's the government that makes these policies we must attack. Why waste time on schoolteachers and such? They're just stooges.'

'Because it is educators who are weakening us instead of giving us strength. Unless we reform the educational system, we will not get a serious independence movement started.'

'That way you'll have to wait a few more generations. Reform? What has to be done is simply close it all down. Strike!'

That word led to such an uproar of enthusiasm that the proprietor came rushing in to silence them. It was his son who was leading this ring, and he got an earful of abuse from his father who warned him to take care or clear out. 'It is bad enough to have a son who won't lift a finger for the family business,' he stormed, 'must we have one who is headed for the prison?' 'Better to go to prison than live as slaves,' the boy shouted, excited by the presence of his friends. This made his father so angry that he landed a slap on the back of the boy's head whereupon his mother, who had been kneading dough at a table at the back, came up to scream at the father. Everything became very confused and the students who were torn between admiration for their leader and hilarity at his situation, decided to make themselves scarce on this occasion, and slipped away as discreetly as they could.

Laila was so excited that she forgot to pin her kerchief about her head on leaving the coffee shop, and had to be sternly reminded by Fatimah who added, 'And if you can't keep a secret, you had better let me know now. I can only bring you here if you promise not to let yourself be seen.' Laila made the promise fervently.

The news did, however, somehow filter out. The young women in the hostel were heard to say to each other, 'So, the girl from Alexandria has joined Fatimah's circle. How does Fatimah get her to be her tail, eh? Has she a handsome brother that any of you know of?' The parents in Alexandria received reports from those of Alma's friends that Laila had failed to visit regularly as promised but who remained – they pointed out to the parents – responsible and vigilant. This was the news that had come to them: Laila had joined a revolutionary student group and was in danger of being expelled from school, arrested by the police, imprisoned – who knew what, if she were not stopped.

'Hamid!' cried Alma, her voice rising in pitch with her terror, quite uncharacteristically. 'You must go! To Cairo! Bring her home.'

'Bring her home! Before she has received her diploma?'

'Yes, now, at once,' wept Alma. 'What diploma will she receive if she is sent to prison?'

'Ech, prison,' he scoffed, but rubbed his head thoughtfully.

'We must stop her, her foolishness. Hamid, you must bring her to her senses –'

'How can I?' he groaned.

Alma made the mistake of not instructing him: she saw him off on the train, handing him a parcel of cakes she had made for Laila, and warned him to be stern and frighten his daughter into mending her ways and abandoning all connections with dangerous revolutionary elements whether political or religious. Nodding miserably, Hamid accepted the parcel, got onto the train and opened up his notebook and fell to scribbling while the train travelled across the clay-coloured landscape to Cairo. At the hostel he requested a meeting with his daughter which was granted by the female supervisor but, after the first start of joy at seeing each other, he and his daughter were only able to redefine their old failures at communication. Laila sat primly in the official drawing room, her eyes cast down and her head neatly covered with a grey kerchief while Hamid, scratching his head in embarrassment, tried to convey all Alma's messages, managed not to, and broke down. 'Laila, if I may, I must go now to the library at Al Azhar to look up some manuscripts they have,' he pleaded, and Laila rose at once, in relief.

'She is studying hard. She looks a little pale, perhaps, but that may be because of her studies. Believe me, Alma, I saw this with my own eyes. She is preparing for the exams. Be calm, Alma, have faith,' he tried to assure his wife on his return, but she only accused him of running away from his duties and hurrying off to the library to indulge himself instead of seeking out Laila's friends and teachers and learning what he could about her.

'Sometimes I think Alexander and the Serapeum have gone too far,' she warned and, picking up Clio in her arms, retreated to the kitchen where she gave vent to her feelings by chopping up a mass of vegetables for soup.

Nevertheless Laila did remain in Cairo and gave no one any cause for complaint by carrying an armful of books with her everywhere and studying with all appearance of diligence. If Alma's friends observed that she still covered her head with a scarf, they could express their disapproval but not prohibit it. Because of her serious and studious demeanour they never suspected that Laila might have a secret life, a night life, any more than Fatimah knew of any existence other than what they shared at the college, the hostel, and the meetings they went to. It was true that the month before the examination was also the month of Ramadan and Muslim students could ask for special considerations for their hours of fasting and their prayers; few asked for them but Fatimah was one who did, and Laila imitated her. No one, not even Fatimah, was aware of the true attraction that Ramadan had for her, and her nightly escapes into the maze of lanes in the Khan-el-Khalili, as silent as those made by Clio across the rooftops of Alexandria. If she had earlier been drawn by the intensity of commitment at the Koran classes in the mosque's courtyard, and the students' meetings in the coffee shop, now it was by the celebrations that exploded on the streets when the cannon at the Citadel boomed to announce the end of the day's fast. What drew her would have been hard for anyone to tell at that stage – parents and friends would be equally uncertain and equally mistaken – for the truth was that she was drawn first in one direction, then another, wherever she saw passion taken to its extreme, whether celebratory or ascetic.

Her eyes took in the coloured, revolving lights with which the shops and restaurants were decorated, the red and yellow lanterns hanging on strings across the streets, the tables and benches set out where anyone could stop and eat the food heaped in generous basins, the mirrors and arrangements of grapes and sweets and butchered meats. She pushed past families strolling through the bazaars with their children, stopping to buy the baby new shoes or ribbons for the little girl's hair, paused to watch the street dancers swing and sway to the music of zither and flute, and made her way to the Café Fishawy with its cloudy mirrors and silvery lights where one could take one's seat upon one of the spindly bentwood chairs and observe the crowds by the hour amongst others who found that activity sufficient. Waiters hurried up and down with enamel pots of tea or glasses filled with coffee, and Laila too sat at a table, waiting to be served, a small smile on her lips.

She was not alone in doing so. Another woman sat there, night after night, established there with almost as much fixity as the fluted stucco pillars. She had been there much longer than Laila, perhaps longer even than the Café Fishawy. She was aged, ancient. She sat on a bench with her legs drawn up under her, her head swathed in a veil, showing only the pale triangle of her face in which her eyes were sunk deeply into their sockets, blackened with kohl. Sometimes she took a puff from a shisha that was being passed up and down, but mostly she sat immobile; her eyes alone could be said to move because they bored into the people who swarmed around her.

Laila noticed that the woman hardly spoke to anyone. Only when someone dared to push across the table to her a drained coffee cup did she glance down into it, then go into a kind of brooding trance so that the one who had dared began to squirm, wipe the back of his neck, murmur apologies and even rise to leave when she would suddenly push aside the cup and part her tightened lips to utter a few curt words. The person would listen, nod gravely, flee and she resume her silence and her staring.

Slowly Laila moved up to her, closer. From across the café to the same wall against which the hagdah sat. Four tables away, three tables away, then two and one day she was sitting on the bench beside her. There they sat, side by side, staring ahead. The men who also sat against the wall glanced at her – some seemed curious, others not, at the sight of the ancient crone in her swaddling of rusty cloaks and the young girl in her demure grey dress and kerchief: they made a striking pair, there was no doubt about that. Laila smiled if anyone spoke to her but said nothing; she fingered her small coffee cup: she had taken to drinking coffee.

Then there was the evening, towards the end of Ramadan,

when it was rising to the crescendo that would be the festival of Eid, and the whole café was filled with a throbbing music, almost unbearable in its mounting excitement, the waiters were running wild, trays of tea and shishas and even chairs held aloft as they wove through the crowds, and a young girl danced and clapped to the music at the back and peddlers circulated with watches, wallets and trinkets.

Under cover of the noise and confusion Laila suddenly put out her hand and pushed her cup across the table top so that it came to stand under the hagdah's nose. For a long time the hagdah pretended not to see it but stared ahead, her hands folded into her sleeves, staring into the crowds as if they were what held her interest. Laila did not squirm or wipe her face or murmur apologies. She just sat calmly, staring not at the crowds but at the small white cup she had proffered. Finally she reached out and touched it with a fingertip, rattling it lightly on its saucer, and said under her breath, 'Read it, please.'

The hagdah threw her a fierce look. Another would have wilted under that look, withered in its blaze. It was meant to wither but Laila stared back into her face. So the hagdah seized the cup between her hands and, without looking at it – perhaps she had already had a glance – parted her narrow, pale lips to say, 'In the north, a city stands in water. There god and goddess meet.'

Laila was only seventeen years old. The fact suddenly revealed itself as her face abandoned its well-made-up mask of sophisticated calm, and her eyes became troubled, her mouth opened, she wanted to blurt out questions: did the hagdah mean the city of Alexandria on the Mediterranean, and her parents, those good grey well-meaning elders? Could that be what the hagdah foretold – an ignominious return to her origins, to a future ordained by her parents? There was something still childish enough in Laila to be relieved at the thought – but she discarded that, throwing back her shoulders and raising her face to demand, 'And then? And then?'

'And then,' snapped the hagdah, jabbing one long finger, 'then eastwards to find a temple – ' did she say find or found?

– 'the temple of the Mother Goddess of the World.' Briefly she stared into Laila's face with her fantastically painted and enlarged eyes. Then her lids lowered over them, she tucked her hands back into her sleeves, and resumed her silent and unapproachable brooding.

Laila's mouth and eyes remained open. She sat still till the waiter came and snatched up her coffee cup and a group of young people pushed against the table urgently, eager for a chance to sit down in the rich ambience of the Café Fishawy on a night in Ramadan. Laila rose to leave. She stumbled as she went, her high heels wobbling under her feet, and if someone had come to take her hand and lead her away, she would have allowed herself to be led.

The examinations followed soon after. The results were unexpectedly good. The parents had now to keep to the next part of their promise: Hamid wrote to his friends at the Sorbonne ('She is my only daughter but it is not for that reason I detect in her an intelligence that might be channelled and trained . . .') and Alma to her sister in Paris ('It might persuade the child to give up the veil she has taken to wearing . . . '). Letters of acceptance arrived which they showed proudly to their daughter – was this not what they had hoped for and worked towards? But Laila, staring at the sheets of paper in their hands, frowned: Paris was not a city that stood in water nor was it the abode of gods and goddesses. This dampened and muted the mood of triumph her parents tried to create. Dissatisfied, Laila waited and watched for the signs to fall into place, and left it to her mother to pack a trunk for her with the clothes she had brought from France twenty years ago – 'good clothes always remain in fashion,' she said with pride, showing Laila the pleated tweed skirts, the blouses, the gloves. Laila gave a small shudder.

The parents accompanied her to the docks where the boat waited. It was a moment of triumph but also the onset of unease. This they ascribed to the fact that the War was only recently over in Europe; who knew how much it had changed the Europe they had known? In fact they realised they knew nothing of what was happening there now, what risks and dangers there might be for a young foreign woman alone and separated from home by the seas. They stood there, clutching hands like children smitten with terror of what they had themselves brought about, in the shadow of the white liner, and craned their necks to look at Laila who stood at the railing. She had worn her gloves for the occasion and waved a gloved hand. With a mighty blaring of its horn the boat was moving away from the shore, people were shouting and calling their farewells. The parents strained to catch a last glimpse of Laila and the flutter of her hand. Then, before their amazed eyes, they saw her unpin her kerchief, pull it off her head so that all her curls were revealed in a sunlit mass about her shoulders – they had not seen this sight since she had gone away to Cairo – and now she held it in her hands and fluttered it at them as if it were a handkerchief. She let it go – or the wind tugged it out of her hand – and it floated through the air that flooded in between the boat and the land, and descended lightly, tremulously upon the waves which dashed up, green and glassy, to receive it. Before a gull could swoop down and snatch at it, it sank and was gone.

~

The door has shut behind the little girl. Sophie goes up the steps and rings the bell. The door swings open and a man stands there; he is dark, he must be a Nubian, she thinks. Will he understand her? She asks after the el Messiri family – at least the name should be comprehensible. To her disappointment, it is not: the young man shakes his head and seems prepared to shut the door. She pleads in whatever French she can summon up: the family lived here once, have they moved? Is there someone who might know? The young man shakes his head again and begins to shut the door more purposefully.

Sophie glances up the spiral staircase to see if she can glimpse the little girl in the bright yellow dress in the gloom.

Hanging over the banister, at the very top, she sees the face gazing at her, its pretty mouth pouting and long hair falling forwards. They stare at each other a moment before the mother's voice rings out again: 'Ferial!' Then the door closes on her. She walks down the steps onto the pavement. It is dark now and the date and nut vendor's acetylene lamp flares garishly on his barrow. Out at sea, the lights of the ships dip and rock with the waves.

Sophie sinks onto a bench under the plane trees, stretches out her legs to ease her feet, and half closes her eyes against the sunlight that pours onto the stretch of cobblestones, the stone basin of the fountain in the square, the blinding white sail of the boat a small boy in white knickers is pushing across the pool with a long cane, the gluttonous pigeons that hobble about amongst the crumbs, the façade of a tall house across the square with its blinds lowered against the sun, the stretch of the stone stairs up to the Saint-Sulpice that stands at the other end with its doors closed, containing its darkness. She thinks of getting up and climbing up those stairs to go and sit in the darkness, knowing it will be cooler there; her head is throbbing from the light and her own tension.

She does not get up. Her eye is caught by the swing of silk pleats and feet in narrow shoes going past her. She follows their passage across the square, for a few moments lit by the sun as by fire, the bright buckles threatening to ignite, then passing into the shade of the plane trees where the girl stands hesitating before she chooses a seat on a bench and sinks onto it. She sits there, not in Sophie's ungainly sprawl, but with her legs crossed, her skirt falling in graceful folds about her, her face lifted alertly to the scene. Sophie cannot make out her features, she is too far away and the glare is strong, but she feels the girl is smiling at her, or at the small boy sailing his boat, or at the pigeons that come waddling towards this new visitor to the square. Then her hands unfold a paper napkin on her lap, and she lifts a sandwich to her mouth. Sophie is forced to look away; it would not do to watch anyone in the act of eating. She tries to concentrate on the pigeons, on the trickle of water falling from the fountain to the pool. She feels a twitch in the corner of her eye that she tries to suppress, that compels her to look again in the direction of the girl, but now the pigeons are swarming around her, forming a shifting screen, a feathery curtain in their grey and tinted frenzy.

~

In the house on the rue des Bernardins all the rooms were curtained against the street and the light. At all hours the glass was screened with lace curtains and these were never drawn aside – the street and the light were considered too harsh to be borne. In addition there were heavier drapes of velvet, or satin, and these were drawn carefully before any lamp was lit indoors. The velvet had both width and girth – its folds were so capacious – the windows were truly blanketed. Above them hung tassels, or fringes, of green and bronze, or blue and gold, or rose and silver, drooping and pendant with their own weight.

Laila had not known before that windows were objects to be dressed as opulently and lavishly as rich women might be dressed. She eyed them with hostility and loathing. When no one else was in the room, her hands flickered forwards and she grasped and drew aside some of that concealing lace and velvet. But either her Aunt Françoise would become aware of the light flooding in and scream, 'What are you doing? The carpets will fade!' or one of the cousins would call out in warning, 'Oh look, she is at the window again!'

Of course opening a window was totally out of the question; they remained shut, sealed even.

Shelves and tables, too, Laila learnt, had to be dressed. They wore skirts, long or short, often with gilt borders, or else ruffles, and the clothes were of rich damask that fell in heavy folds. Moreover, they were weighed down with a great quantity of objects – boxes of embossed silver or rosewood inlaid with ivory or enamel painted with bright birds or dark foliage, vases of porcelain and silver and crystal, photographs of whiskered men, roseate children and pallid women, all framed in silver or in gilded wood. In addition, there were bowls that held potpourri, candlesticks either tall and straight or twisting and branching, boxes of cigars and boxes of matches – all objects of value that might have had price labels or museum notes attached to them, they appeared so self-conscious. They seemed to dare Laila to touch them or shift them. Her fingers fidgeted and flew out to do just that but instantly the children took up the warning, 'Look, Laila is touching the china figurines!' and then Aunt Françoise screamed, 'You'll break them!'

How could such objects break? They could only fall upon the thick deep piled carpets in which forests of vine and foliage grew horizontally in spreading pools of blue, green and grey; or they might slip into the crevices of the sofas and couches and come to rest between cushions of rose and mustard-yellow damask. But they could not lose themselves – they were so established, so prominent, like rings that had been placed on fingers with ancient, binding vows.

Laila despaired of dislodging a single one. But she could not stop herself from disturbing them; that happened almost without her willing it.

She retreated to the bedroom that she shared with her two older cousins – Yvette and Claudette. Although here too the windows were swathed in white muslin and pink silk, the dressing table with lace and the beds with a profusion of thick and downy layers, there was more scope for disturbance. It was not permitted to open windows or draw aside curtains or alter the position of the silver powder box or the china soap dish or the hair brushes arranged on the embroidered runners, but Laila could always contrive to have her blue silk coverlet slip off her bed and drag on the floor, to leave her shoes flung across the sheepskin rug, to throw her dresses into the cupboards instead of hanging them on the quilted satin hangers, and bring in a damp bath towel and drop it onto a velvet seat.

Yvette and Claudette were horror-struck, their eyes widened at this disregard for the rules of the house. They reproached Laila, they reprimanded her, they picked up her things and showed her how the coverlet should be stretched over the bed, the dresses hung, the shoes placed. She smiled mockingly in silence as she watched them tidy the room, then carelessly combed the hair out of her brush and left it trailing over the lace runners.

The bathroom, after Laila had visited it, was in even greater turmoil – the amount of damp and steam and stains and puddles and smears and wastage of soap, shampoo, pastes and powders that she accomplished when locked inside it, often for the better part of an hour while Yvette, Claudette, Ninette and Babette stood complaining in the corridor outside, was stupendous, nothing less.

'Now look, my girl,' Aunt Françoise said to her, opening up a cupboard and taking out all the instruments of hygiene and cleanliness – mop and broom, duster and dustpan, cleaning fluids and powders – 'if you wish to make such a disgusting mess in the house, then you must be taught to clean it,' and she gave Laila a bravura performance as a lesson, whirling about the bathroom till it shone and dazzled, mirrors and tiles and porcelain all of blinding brightness.

It lasted only a day and then Laila had turned it into a washroom again, hanging dripping stockings on the rail, leaving pools of water on the floor, hair in the bathtub, grime in the sink, the soap melting in a tray of water, the shampoo trickling out of an open, fallen bottle and the towels, rugs and nighties all in a soaking heap on the floor.

Aunt Françoise, rolling her eyes heavenwards, cried, 'What has that sister of mine been doing? Can she have forgotten entirely the ways of the civilised world? She has brought up a savage!'

Now the cousins had a word for what had left them speechless before: savage. 'Sauvage,' they whispered and mocked, and kept out of Laila's way when she returned from her classes, covered their ears when she talked, and watched her eat with the wonder of children at the zoo watching the beasts devour their meals. It was true that Laila could not be bothered with the array of silverware beside her plate and preferred to pick up bits of bread or cheese or fruit to eat with her hands, sitting sideways at the table, her legs crossed, her feet carelessly waving, pretending to ignore her aunt's harangues: 'Babette, elbows *off* the table, elbows *close* to the side, please! Ninette, is that the way to eat your peas? It is abominable! And the napkin, please, the napkin!' She restricted herself to throwing fierce looks in Laila's direction at the table as if she could not tackle such barbarity at this ritual of civilised behaviour. Also, perhaps, she did not like to draw the attention of Uncle Bertrand to her savage niece too much or too often: it would upset his delicate nerves upon which his digestion depended, and Aunt Françoise was very concerned about Uncle Bertrand's digestion; it was of importance equal to that of her daughters' manners and upbringing, and the two preoccupations together caught her face up in a nest of wrinkles that the heaviest powdering and pinkest rouge could not efface.

'Bertrand, my dear, did you find the chop tender? I bought the very best piece I saw at the butcher's, but I don't know . . . I did think of telling Edith to grill it fifteen minutes longer, but sometimes that has the effect of drying up the juices, and I know how much you like gravy with your meat . . .' she went on nervously while Uncle Bertrand ate stolidly, paying the closest attention to his plate and avoiding any involvement in the twitching, sighing, muttering, murmuring world of females around him.

He was able to pursue this path only till the day when Laila, breaking and stuffing bread into her mouth in the coarse way she had adopted since entering this household, held up her plate of meat to Edith to be taken away uneaten.

'Now, what is this?' her aunt enquired, the nest of wrinkles drawing closer. 'The meat that is so expensive and good enough for the rest of us – it is not good enough for you, a girl from Egypt?'

'I hate it,' Laila told her, 'and will not eat it.'

This penetrated even Uncle Bertrand's hearing, preoccupied as he may have seemed with the sounds of digestion deep inside him, ominously loud and alarming, and he too put down his knife and fork to stare at the girl who sat there with such an attitude of careless indifference amongst his daughters, each one so erect and obedient at table.

'Do you hear that?' the aunt cried, and the girls all nodded solemnly. 'Did you hear her call the steak hateful? A steak so succulent, so excellently done as she can never have had, in Egypt?'

'Oh, it is not the cooking,' Laila assured her lazily, 'it is the meat itself. It is disgusting to eat meat, and from now on I shall eat only bread, fruit and vegetables. And,' she added, slyly looking around at her awestruck cousins from under her black brows, 'chocolate if I get *very* hungry.'

The girls opened their mouths to exclaim 'O-oh' in unison, and Aunt Françoise and Uncle Bertrand exchanged stunned looks. Laila smiled as if pleased with the effect of her words, and picked up a small spoon and slid it into the crème caramel Edith had placed before her in the glass dish. '*This* is delicious,' she told them after tasting it, 'and does not run with blood or expose bones.'

Aunt Françoise rose from her seat and marched down the length of the table to where Laila was seated to snatch up the glass dish from under her chin. 'No sweet for whoever does not first finish the meat,' she declared and carried away the dish to the kitchen where she was heard to pour out her outraged feelings to Edith. Uncle Bertrand, who had never witnessed such a scene at his table before, did not seem to understand what had happened: he frowned, he muttered, he looked about him – it was all inexplicable.

However, it was only the first in a series of such confrontations over the table. Meat was cooked and cut and placed before Laila as before everyone else every night, and every night she refused adamantly to touch it, carefully picking the carrots and potatoes away from the slab of pink flesh lying in its pool of dark gravy, and instead ate a basketful of bread hungrily and untidily. Aunt Françoise refused to let Edith serve her any sweet because she must be punished for not eating the meat, and Laila looked across at her aunt and her cousins with eyes that grew ever stonier.

She told her cousins, 'I am a vegetarian. No one will make me eat the flesh of slaughtered animals. Do you know what you are eating? Have you been into a butcher's shop to see it when it is raw? Or into an abattoir to see how they slaughter the bulls and the calves and lambs and pigs and rabbits and ducks and chickens and all else that you eat?'

They covered their ears and shrieked, 'Don't, don't!' and no longer ate their meals with such neat expressions of satisfaction or obedience. Instead, they pinched their mouths, set their jaws, cut the meat into the smallest shreds and bit into them as if they expected to be bitten back. Laila looked and watched, pleased. Aunt Françoise was nearly in tears.

'Look what you have done! You have spoilt our meals for us all, the meals Edith has prepared and I have planned with such effort. See how the girls have taken to wasting it,' she lamented as Edith carried away the unfinished platefuls.

Goaded beyond endurance by these laments one evening, Laila electrified them by suddenly picking up her knife and fork and attacking the meat with such ferocity that gobs and strips of it flew around, spotting the snowy table linen with bloodied gravy.

'What are you doing, you mad, wild beast?' cried her aunt.

'Killing the ox, killing the ox!' Laila shouted back, then flung down her knife and fork and put her hands to her face which was hot and flushed and tear-streaked.

'If you were not such a big girl, I would send you to sit in a corner until you came around to behaving yourself,' her aunt scolded, getting up to clear the table.

'If you did that, I should tell my father and mother who have never punished me once in my life,' Laila replied, 'and would not believe that punishments are carried out in civilised homes.'

Then Aunt Françoise reached her own breaking point and screamed, 'Bertrand, did you hear? Do you hear how my own sister's daughter speaks to me?'

Uncle Bertrand put his hand up to his head. It was a completely bald head, pink and shining as if polished, between two tufts of soft brown hair like a pair of brushes. He closed his eyes behind his spectacles and said 'Françoise, bring me some digestive powders. I really cannot endure this nightly fracas.'

The aunt immediately recovered herself and scurried away to do as she was bid, but Laila said calmly, 'And have you thought of what the animal endures under the knife?'

No truce seemed possible and Laila revealed a certain prudence, or instinct for self-defence, in keeping away from the house as much as possible and avoiding aggravation of the situation by constant proximity and friction.

Her classes, in French, were few and she could not extend them, nor did she wish to: they were taught to unhappy lots of foreigners by teachers bored by going over elementary lessons in classrooms devoid of any cheer or hospitality. Even if Baudelaire, Rimbaud and Musset had invited them into this world once, the invitation had lost its warmth, leaving nothing, not even a scrap. Anxious to avoid each other's homesickness and melancholy, the students separated at the door after classes and drifted in different directions, following their own odysseys of exile. Laila found she had hours to spend alone, wandering through museums, browsing at book stalls, walking down stony streets in the heat of early summer that was already grey with dust and the foliage yellow in the parks. She wore holes through the thin soles of her sandals that she insisted on wearing, having refused, with scorn, her aunt's offers to choose her a pair of 'good shoes'. Nor would she touch the clothes the cousins offered her, stubbornly sticking to those bits and pieces she had brought from Egypt – her brocade waistcoat and a cap with sequins and gold embroidery that she either wore on her head or held clutched in her hands as if it were the insignia of a separate existence and her allegiance to another land.

Drifting through the alien city, she stopped once to let pass a bevy of young girls who stepped out of a large silvery automobile and slipped through a doorway, short white muslin tunics fluttering about their legs. That was an unusual form of dress, and she looked to see where they went. A signboard informed her it was *L'Institut d'Eurythmie à E. Dalcroze* and underneath, in small letters, was the name Mme Beaunier. As Laila stood studying it, she heard a piano played somewhere upstairs, behind closed doors, but whenever the doors were opened the music intensified and floated down like a voice addressed to her. She did not go up or in that day but walked past the door several times. One day she took with her a bag containing a veil and a tambourine she had brought with her from Egypt, and that day she climbed the stairs and went in. She had waited till the students had left, streaming past her in their short skirts and long cloaks, and then slipped in before the doors were locked, to place herself in front of a woman she took to be the instructress, a large, heavily built and pale woman in a grey dress who still sat at the piano with a look of exhaustion.

Laila made her speech, holding her hands clutched before her in appeal. The woman did not seem very interested but agreed tiredly to play a little piece to which she asked Laila to dance. She did open her eyes wide when she saw Laila draw out of a bag a gaudy veil stitched with sequins that she draped about her head, and nearly protested when Laila whipped out the tambourine, but then turned to the piano to play a few bars while Laila, throwing back her head and raising the tambourine in the air, struck a pose she had seen dancers assume in the streets of Cairo and Alexandria. Then, totally ignoring the music being played for her, she began to leap and twirl about the room. Madame Beaunier brought her hands down on the keyboard with a crash, crying, 'No, no, no! Oh, do you not hear the music? Can you not feel the music? It is the music you must express – the music!'

Laila stopped and stood panting, holding the tambourine against her skirt. 'Show me how,' she ordered the woman, and there was in her voice that tone of complete authority that few who heard it ever resisted. Whether it was that tone, or the proselytiser's zeal that moved Madame Beaunier it is hard to tell, but she rose from her seat to seize Laila's arms, manipulate her stance, force her into assuming the first position and then instruct her to listen to the music she would now play.

Perhaps she saw promise in the exotic figure of the girl from the East, or she decided to civilise the savage with Dalcroze's theories of marrying rhythmic movement to musical elements, but she did not send Laila away.

Nothing was said about it in the house on the rue des Bernardins; Laila was aware of how the news that she had abandoned her French studies for eurhythmic exercises would be received there, and how it would carry across the Mediterranean to her parents. She obtained the money from her father by means of a plea for funds for extra books and clothing, and kept the secret to herself. Only her cousins saw her swaying and twirling in her nightgown in the bedroom and thought it further proof of her craziness. 'That's not dance!' they cried. 'Ooh, you should come with us to our dancing classes!' and they linked arms and showed Laila the steps they learnt there, giggling. Laila threw them looks of scorn.

For some months she persuaded herself that she was at last doing what she wished most to do. It was not easy to maintain that conviction in the face of Madame Beaunier's almost military system of drill – separating the elements of music into tempo, dynamics, metrical patterns and pitch, then putting the girls through exercises to go with each. The repetitiveness of these exercises, and the sight of the young girls marching, stamping, running, skipping, bending and bowing in unison, began to bore her so much that she ached. Very soon she started to defy Madame Beaunier and her young assistants, refusing to obey the music. This was a sin that could not be overlooked. 'Use your body to translate into movement the rhythm, the melody and the harmony you hear!' was Madame

Beaunier's dictum, and it became clear that this was not dance to Laila.

Coming to a standstill, her hands on her hips, while everyone else continued to run, tiptoe, skip, walk and march to the piano, she demanded to know, 'But why? *Why* must we do this?' Madame Beaunier's hands came to halt on the keyboard. She swung slowly around to stare at Laila. 'You ask why? And what do you mean by this *why*?' The girls had all come to a stop like puppets whose strings had been cut, abruptly. 'Yes, why?' Laila called out. 'What is the purpose? What is the meaning of these movements? Why do we perform them? For what reason? What cause?' and everyone began to titter or whisper or exclaim till Madame Beaunier banged down the lid of the piano and rose, towering above them. 'And what is it you wish to express, mademoiselle?' she asked crisply.

'Whatever it is the music expresses,' Laila replied, crossing her arms over her chest, 'and that is sometimes joy, sometimes grief, sometimes desire –' and here everyone burst openly into laughter, and Laila flushed. 'It is not about *nothing* – not just to make us jump and skip. It has some meaning surely? It must be about something?'

'Perhaps you can enlighten us then, mademoiselle,' Madame Beaunier responded with great dignity. 'Pray interpret this piece of music for us that I will play,' she requested and seated herself at the piano and began to play a piece of music that Laila, who had no musical education, could not identify. She stood listening, her arms folded about her and her head bowed, and the music seemed to her a puzzle that was being worked out on the keys, a problem that was set and then worked through and solved. She could not find in her body any response to it; it was cerebral and devoid of emotion. Her arms remained folded, her feet remained still. The students watched, holding their breaths, but she could do nothing to meet their expectations. It appeared that she met Madame Beaunier's, however, for that woman threw her a triumphant look at the end of the piece that she came to with great precision and certainty. 'So,' she challenged her rebellious pupil, 'and will you now enlighten us as to what this music expresses? Does it perhaps tell a story? If so, would you like to interpret it to us? A la Isadora Duncan, perhaps?'

This was the cue for everyone to start laughing which they did, with great relief, and Laila turned to leave the room, pack up her sequinned veil and put on her sandals. In the streets, she found her eyes blurred not with humiliation but with anger and frustration, so that she nearly ran into a bus.

It was a defeat but Laila was stubborn; she returned to the studio, and worked at submitting her body to the precepts set before her, partly because she needed to show Madame Beaunier that it was something she could do and partly because she had not found something that might replace such a method. That she was the most lithe and graceful student in the class helped her to retain her place in it, but she felt herself isolated, the only one who had questions and felt the need for something else, different. She prepared herself to be the one who was misunderstood, who would be solitary.

In this manner she drifted through the Jardin des Plantes, seeking the shade of great trees along the narrow gravel paths on which children rolled their hoops and balls and maids and mothers pushed perambulators. She avoided looking into the cages; it distressed her to see cockatoos dropping onto leafless branches, baboons squatting desolately on squares of concrete, scratching at their sore red patches and rummaging through empty peanut shells, and her nose wrinkled in revulsion at the reek of urine, faeces and decayed food in the rabbit houses. The loops of a somnolent python sent shudders through her and she reared away from it as much as from the crowds that gathered around it, trying to prod it into wakefulness.

In trying to get as far away as possible, she found herself one day brought up short at the cage of an animal altogether different.

Instead of sinking with the others into late summer torpor,

and the lassitude of the watched beast, the black panther still prowled the jungles of its memory, still inhabited an unpopulated wilderness of the past that it paced and paced with a kind of restrained frenzy, demanding of the barred square of concrete some reminder of freedom, or danger, or challenge, or beauty that it would not yield. Refusing to be refused, it paced and paced – its great paws treading into the unyielding surface, its senses alert to pick up the faintest response should it come.

At last it found what it searched for – or at least a fleeting, ephemeral glimpse of it: Laila's bright, sequinned cap that she stood holding at her side and twirling and twirling upon her finger. That flashing saucer caught the panther's eye and might have seemed a forest butterfly or fluttering bird; at least, it paused in its furious ambulations, and the paws faltered to a halt for just an instant before it turned its eyes away and went relentlessly, restlessly on. But when it came round again, its slant eyes fastened on the bright beads, the winking sequins, and again it paused – a little longer this time. Laila, noticing, stopped spinning the cap and held still. This made the panther veer away and race on, intent on its pursuit. She stared in wonder at the muscles that flowed like water under the sheen of black skin, the frantic eyes that would not meet hers but glanced away as if in wild rejection.

Unconsciously she began to twirl the cap again and this brought the panther to a stop directly before her at last. Reaching out one of its gigantic paws, it dangled it before her, quite gently, as if inviting her to shake hands. She held her breath, overcome by its size, its closeness, the hot, steaming wildness of the beast, and the cap twirled more slowly now. When it came to a halt, the panther's paw flashed out between the bars, caught it on a nail and, drawing it into the cage, set about worrying it as if it were a toy or a kitten.

Laila had gone white with shock as the cap was ripped from her hand; now she watched the panther toss it in the air, send it skimming across the floor of the cage, pounce on it, bury its muzzle into it, toss it up again, make of it a skimming, shining, dazzling thing that seemed to light its eyes by its reflection. She began to smile, then laugh, as one might laugh at the play of a child, merging into its delight in a moment of unconsciousness, a moment when time either pauses or even moves back instead of forwards.

A huddle of boys on the other side of the cage stood pale and scandalised: it went against everything they believed in or found acceptable – a young girl and a black wild beast sharing a game; it went against nature, it excluded them, it filled them with agitation and outrage.

Both panther and girl were oblivious. They were the only two that existed in that enclosed world they had made. When Laila moved, the panther rose and moved beside her. She walked the length of the cage and the panther kept pace beside her, docile and calm, with just a hint of playfulness in its eyes. When she turned and walked back, it too turned, as a stream turns, with a rushing, rippling motion, and walked with her. She circled the cage, and the panther circled too, making the boys retreat in a shambles. They ambulated together, panther and girl, keeping pace, sending out messages of mutual admiration, building a web between them of delicious complicity.

So the game might have continued had it not begun to draw so many onlookers: Laila had not thought of her complicity with the panther as a public performance. It was a relationship to her, and when the boys who stood watching began to boo and catcall or urge her on as if she were a circus trainer and the beast her victim, she threw them looks of withering contempt. What did they know of such relationships, such communion?

'Where'd you go?' Yvette and Claudette interrogated her; they were already bathed and in their dressing gowns, smelling of soap and powder in a room lighted with pink lamps.

'To meet a friend,' Laila told them with a twist of her lips that could not be described precisely as a smile.

'Oh? Who? Where?'

'In the Jardin des Plantes,' Laila said, and now she did smile, broadly and openly into their shocked faces. Lying back on her bed, she let her dusty sandals fall onto the rug. She was utterly, deliberately infuriating.

'Oh, we'll tell Mama,' they threatened in retaliation.

'Tell,' she challenged them airily, 'tell.'

Laila returned to the gardens, to her new friend. But she could never find a time when she might be alone with the panther. She needed her communication with it to be private, even secret, convinced that its depth and intensity depended on that. If her tormentors were already there, hoping for some further entertainment, she would turn away, knowing they would distract her and distract the panther, making what passed between them, so electrically, an impossibility. In a way it was a repetition of the experience in the eurhythmics class: the exercises came in the way of her communion with the music, and that was what she wanted of it.

Darkness fell earlier, the gates of the park closed in the twilight, and soon she ceased to go there altogether and wondered how long she would continue with the eurhythmics, and what would replace these in her life which appeared to grow steadily narrower and bleaker.

Now she walked up and down the long straight avenues of the Luxembourg Gardens – what was this passion the French had for long straight lines? she wondered – under trees so vigorously pruned and pollarded as hardly to appear trees any more but more like bunches of fingers, or fists, at the end of long arms. Laila walked, listening to her feet on the gravel, and ignored the boys who followed, whistling, as she ignored the old man on a bench with a drop hanging from the end of his nose, who sat with his bottle in a brown paper bag and his toes protruding, green with mildew, from his cracked shoes.

Out by the round pond the scene was brighter but for her equally charmless – the beds with stridently coloured flowers, the boys in sailor suits sailing their boats, the lovers on the benches, inextricably clasped. Then she came upon the

Fontaine de Médicis and found the plane trees closely clustered on either side still heavy with dark foliage, and between them chrysanthemums in rich saffron and golden shades strung as garlands from trunk to trunk and reflected in the black water of the pool. She thought they might rise up and break through the surface of the water and flower for her, like golden lotuses on a lake. As she waited for that magical happening, the words of the hagdah swam back into her memory, opening out their petals for her: 'In the north, a city stands in water. There, god and goddess meet . . .' But with darkness the words faded, the reflections faded, and it was not only night but it was cold. Russet leaves fell from the trees into the water, small empty boats staying afloat.

In that dark autumn, Laila found herself driven down the streets, along with the jostling crowds simply for warmth and light.

She hovered about the shopfronts, standing close to the lighted windows for comfort, staring at objects, whether bowls of flowers or painted china or hats fashioned out of ribbons and feathers. Every time the shop door opened and someone went in with a dripping umbrella or came out with an armful of parcels, there was an accompanying waft of warm moist air and excruciatingly brief as it was, it went through Laila like a physical experience of the heat she had known in Alexandria and Cairo. She knew better than to go in without any money to spend – a special hostility was reserved for a woman who was not only dark and foreign but also penniless.

In the Métro, pressing through the damp, steaming crowds without knowing where she was going, she heard a voice sing out as if it were a banner, flaring out above their heads with strident colours. She looked and saw it was a dark man, perhaps from Africa, perhaps from the Caribbean, selling pineapples which he had sliced and held up by their green tops, one half in each hand, running with juice, while he sang, 'From far to near, from away to here – ' and when he caught her eye, he gave her a wink, as if in recognition.

• • •

It seemed she was being edged, little by little, almost imperceptibly, down the rue Descartes to be brought up short by a shop window in which a strange statue of some dark metal struck a dancer's pose within a circle of flames. Stopping to decipher its expression, pose and gesture – one that said, so authoritatively, 'Stop! Look! Pay heed!' – she saw piled around it untidy heaps of books, all with titles referring to l'Orient or l'Inde. They were books of travel, art, philosophy and religion, and after gazing at them for a long time, trying to read some of the unfamiliar words – *Rig Veda, Samhita, Ratnavali, La Kama Sutra, Brhadanayaka Upanishad, La Bhagavad Gita, The Sacred Books of the East* – she straightened the bag slung over her shoulder and went in. Partly it was curiosity that made her take the step and partly it was the feeling that this shabby, hidden place would not reject her: perhaps there was more that she could not, or did not, analyse. The regally calm expression on the face of the exotic statue conveyed a sense of welcome and greeting that she could not define and did not stop to.

A ringing ping of the bell announced her entry a bit disconcertingly and in the small poorly lit room crowded with tall bookshelves there was a faint stir behind the counter, against the dark green wallpaper, where a woman, with her grey hair cut very short like a man's under a thick and unshapely felt cap, coughed and looked up from under heavy black brows that were startling in a face so pale and grey. It was all the more curious seen as it was under brightly tinted oleographs that hung on the wall, displaying a pot-bellied elephant dancing on two delicate feet, a blue-bodied shepherd playing a flute under a flowering tree, a dark ascetic seated upon a tiger skin with a serpent poised above his forehead, and other such startling scenes in rainbow hues. These were lit by a lamp that shone on the counter, leaving the rest of the room even more shadowy by contrast.

A little unnerved, yet by no means frightened, Laila turned into one of the aisles, laid with worn coir matting, and began to browse her way through the books on the tall shelves that made it clear she had come to an Orientalist bookshop, and more specifically, an Indological one. She slid a great heavy volume off the shelf, the *Aitreya Brahmanan* of the *Rig Veda*, and read:

There is no happiness for him who does not travel, Rohita! Thus we have heard. Living in the society of man, the best man becomes a sinner . . . Therefore, wander!

The feet of the wanderer are like the flowers, his soul is growing and reaping the fruit; and all his sins are destroyed by his fatigues in wandering. Therefore, wander!

The fortune of him who is sitting, sits; it rises when he rises; it sleeps when he sleeps; it moves when he moves. Therefore, wander!

Once again, for the second time that autumn, the words of the hagdah rose in Laila's mind. She browsed on for an hour that day, for two hours the next, and for the whole of Saturday morning thereafter. The grey-haired woman never stirred from behind the counter, merely coughing slightly to indicate she noticed Laila's arrival and departure. The only other movement was of the steady upward drifting of thick cigar smoke from her corner. It drifted through the small, over-heated shop and lay in clouds amongst the books that also smelt of tobacco as a result. Laila found herself developing a small, sympathetic cough.

Of course, other customers entered the shop. Most were young men in large, long coats, and Laila noticed from the corner of her eye that the book most frequently placed on the counter for the old woman to make up a parcel was the *Kama Sutra* which they surreptitiously slipped into their coat pockets. After leafing through a volume, she decided against making the same purchase herself, although the idea of smuggling it into the pink-and-white bedroom of her aunt's house did titillate her for a moment. Instead, she made an occasional purchase of a postcard from the Musée Guimet collection, or a small volume of verse, Tagore's or Toru Dutt's, that were second-hand and damaged and therefore reduced in price. She bought them partly to justify the long hours spent in the bookshop for which she could find no satisfactory explanation even for herself, and partly to have some communication with the hagdah-like figure at the counter, even if only commercial, which was ridiculous when one considered what an intimacy there was between them, thickening like the cigar smoke in the closed and ill-ventilated room.

Glancing at a tattered copy of Edwin Arnold's *Light of Asia* that Laila brought to her, the woman reduced the price still further, pointing out its loose pages and battered binding. Laila gave her a smile. She had to speak. 'Are these Egyptian cigars?' she asked without thought, confirming that it was the familiarity of the odour that drew her to the shop.

In reply, the woman turned to the shelf behind her, untidy with papers and envelopes, and picked up a narrow wooden box and placed it on the counter. She pointed at the words – Tiruchanapally, S. India – stamped on the pale wood in violet ink.

'People who go to India bring me back things,' she explained in a voice hoarse with smoking and from disuse, and half-turning on her seat, jabbed a finger at the oleograph that hung on the wall behind her, so surreally bright. 'Cigars, prints,' she said vaguely.

'India,' Laila noted politely. 'Do you smoke Egyptian ones too?'

The woman gave a shrug, turning down her lips. 'Never,' she said.

'I can get you some. I come from Cairo, and my father smokes them,' Laila said, feeling foolishly ingratiating. That evening she wrote to her father and requested a box.

When it arrived, she hurried to deliver it. The woman said nothing but opened the box, lifted out a cigar and sniffed it with the critical appraisal of a connoisseur. 'Mmm,' she finally murmured, and put the box away on the shelf beside the Indian one.

Her visit was noticed by a group of students from Laila's language class who were sitting in the window of the café next door and when she went for one of her rare cups of coffee that evening, they called her over to their table and laughed, 'You've become a regular at Madame Lacan's, eh?'

'You know her?' Laila's eyes widened, looking at them: they had not seemed to her particularly interesting young men or women, being as aimless and adrift as she in Paris.

'Ah, who does not go to Madame Lacan for a copy of the *Kama Sutra*?' chortled one of them in a way she found distasteful.

'But who is Madame Lacan really?' asked Laila.

One of them told her, 'Her father was some kind of civil servant – employed in the post office, I believe – who in his youth found a book on yoga and was so fascinated by it that he set off for India to find himself a guru – you know, a teacher – and returned filled with enthusiasm for the mysterrr-i-ous East – ' he rolled his *rs* drolly, being himself from Turkey – 'and started this funny little bookshop and had dreams of starting a yoga school here in Paris. Then he took against trade and commerce and wanted only one thing – to return to India. Finally he did – like the Buddha, abandoned his wife and child and disappeared in the East. So, the child had to take over the bookshop in order to survive and support the mother till she died, and there she sits, trapped.'

'Oh, non, non, non!' another of the students cried. 'What a boring, what a bourgeois interpretation that is, Ahmet! You have no imaginative bone in your whole body. The story is, I assure you, much more romantic than that. Madame Lacan fell in love with a young man from India, don't you know. He taught yoga, I believe. She thought he would take her back to India with him when he left, but all he did was send her letters and books. Books, books, books, and the message she was to stay and instruct the West on Eastern mysticism and spirituality. So there she sits, poor thing, carrying out his wishes and waiting, waiting for the call that does not come, oh!'

'Banal, banal – only a woman could think such banality romantic,' Ahmet retorted.

Clearly they were all embroidering on a few fragments of known facts, and Laila was free to do the same. She would observe Madame Lacan from over the top of a book she had taken off the shelves to study, and add to what she had been told. The most fruitful area for observation and interpretation was Madame Lacan's reaction to Indians who came to the shop; Laila noted her attitude towards them – it seemed to her especially brusque, and at the same time especially attentive, as if they represented what she most feared and distrusted and at the same time what she felt most fascinating. Surely it had to be so, or why was she here, running this obsessive, obsessed little bookshop and sheltering within it such commercially unpromising curiosities?

What Laila did not admit to herself, possibly because she barely noticed or understood it, was that this fascination was proving as infectious as Madame Lacan's smoke-fed cough in that tobacco-saturated atmosphere.

She did notice it, admit it and understand it the day she came to the bookshop and saw, pinned to the door, a poster. In large letters at the top, it advertised: 'DANSES ET MUSIQUE HINDOUES PAR KRISHNA RAJA ET SA TROUPE'. Beneath it was a picture of two figures – one indigo blue, the other a pale gold – beneath a flowering tree. Their feet were bare and on their ankles were rings of bells. They gazed at each other with the elongated eyes of desire. The caption for the picture was

Krishna Lila

The words caught at Laila with a snare so sharp that she almost cried out. Krishna, and Lila. The words, together and separately, were what struck her so sharply between the eyes. Krishna Lila. Krishna. Lila. Each seemed to point a finger at her, and she drew herself up, stood very upright, a little open mouthed, gazing back as if in recognition. Later she was to say that at that moment she was confronted by her true self, that she at that moment discovered it. Laila, Lila. Laila, Lila. Krishna Krishna. Krishna Lila.

Pushing the door open, she went directly to Madame Lacan at the counter. 'Who has put up that poster?' she demanded.

Madame Lacan seemed faintly taken aback by the tone: up till then, the girl had been mostly ingratiating, and deferential, but now she sounded demanding. 'Some Indians who are, I believe, sponsoring the dance troupe.'

'And the dancers? Do you know them?'

Madame Lacan leant backwards, away from the girl's demands – she did not care for such persistent questioning. 'You want to meet them? Why not go to their performance? I can sell you a ticket, I have them here.'

There was something feverish about the way the girl opened her purse and spilled out all the coins. Together they did not amount to the price of a single ticket, but Madame Lacan swept them up and gave her one anyway.

Laila barely thanked her. She went instantly to the book-shelves and began to comb them in search of a book on dance in India. Impatiently she went through the books on temples, on Hinduism, on wild life and jungles, travels and philosophy, and then came upon a large, heavy, cloth-bound volume that had on its cover – providentially, she was certain – a small print of exactly the same painting she had seen reproduced on the poster, and bearing the same words: *Krishna Lila*. Tearing it open, she found it was a volume of miniature paintings from India, and sank down on a step to leaf through its pages. The paintings, each sheltered beneath a sheet of fine tissue paper, blazed up in the shadows with primal colours – purple skies in which cranes flew in streaks of blinding white, lawns of veridian green in which flowers clustered in groups of pinks and yellows, walls and roofs painted ochre and vermilion, arched gateways through which caparisoned elephants paraded in gold finery and palanquins passed in flowered drapes, trees in which green parrots fed on saffron mangoes and beneath which women with jet hair and fish-shaped eyes danced in gauzy robes or sat smoking hookahs with silver mouthpieces or lay in the laps of turbaned lovers under a night sky with a sickle moon. In many of them the lover had a body of indigo blue and wore about his waist a cloth of saffron yellow while his head was crowned with peacocks' feathers.

Usually he stood beneath a tree, playing upon a flute, and around him danced either a single or a whole ring of ecstatic women in gold and silver blouses and skirts of gauze or brocade; in one, they had stripped off their garments, strewn them on a bank and plunged into a river from which pink lotuses sprang. In others, storm clouds were pierced by lightning, or serpents reared and towered over small cities and fleeing rivers, but it was to the paintings of the blue god and the dancing maiden that Laila returned again and again, watched from a dark corner by the perturbed and silent Madame Lacan.

In the small, shabby auditorium, poorly heated and smelling of the damp clothing of the sparse audience, these paintings revealed themselves on the stage and sprang to life.

A maid in a saffron costume edged with gold plucked flowers from invisible trees in an enchanted grove, strung them into garlands with her long, exquisite, ringed fingers, lifted them to drape them on the god she awaited, circling the stage in search.

The god appeared, in a loincloth of celestial blue, wearing on his head a crown of dazzling peacock feathers, holding an invisible flute to his lips and half-closing his eyes as he played a piping music almost too sweet to bear.

A ring of damsels in rainbow colours – colours Laila had only seen before in the parakeet house of the Jardin des Plantes – came holding hands and were joined by the maiden with the garland and all together performed a dance vibrantly rhythmic and angular as well as graceful and swaying.

The music that welled out of a flute and some drums that were being beaten in one corner of the stage where incense had been lit in a censer, and cymbals that were being struck by a singer seated crosslegged and singing in a voice at once harsh and pellucid, appeared to surge through those dancing bodies in their sweeping, leaping, elegant, ecstatic, joyous, anguished, effortless poses and postures, and Laila found herself knotted in agony upon her seat, so intense was her desire to leap up and perform to that music. This, she knew, was what she had sought so long and missed.

Now the ring ceased to circle. Now it broke and dissolved and the maidens disappeared with a suggestive tinkling of their anklets, leaving only the one with the god. Now they performed their final rite of union, and the union was that of the worshipped and the worshipper, the god and the devotee, and the music rose to its climax, so piercing, so ecstatic, that it seemed to Laila the very roof would lift and fly into the sky.

'I must see them, Madame Lacan,' she cried in the bookshop next day, 'with my own eyes I must see them. I can't believe they are real – and yet they are more real than you and I, far more – '

'Ah,' said Madame Lacan with a caustic smile that was just a twist of her grey lips. She was doing her accounts, had not removed her spectacles from her nose, and was ostentatiously keeping her pen going, dipping it into the ink well and scratching with it loudly while the cigar grew its knob of ash in a bowl nearby. 'You are not real? And I am not real? I did not realise.'

'Not in the way *they* are,' Laila assured her, pressing on the counter with both hands in her eagerness. '*We* don't dress like that in Paris, or dance like that, or move or sing like that – '

'And have you been to the opera? Or the ballet here in Paris?'

Laila made a dismissive sound, quite rude; the urge to express herself was now bursting out in the most unseemly way.

Madame Lacan, too, could be rude. 'You have not? So what have you seen of Paris, or France?' She took off her spectacles and glared at Laila. 'Without finding out what exists here, you want to go running after those heathens from the East – '

'Yes,' Laila agreed, 'I want to run, run and catch them,' and her teeth gleamed in a smile, and her eyes half closed with delight as she mimicked her words with the extravagance she had witnessed on the stage of a shabby, gloomy hall for people who coughed and sneezed and shifted on their seats and yawned. She had felt a certainty then that she belonged to those on the stage, not to the audience. Could Madame Lacan not see that? What she did not tell Madame Lacan was her certainty that she had once been one of them, possessed what they had, lost it but now saw she must grasp and recover it – for surely that was why she had come to Paris.

Madame Lacan only shook her head to indicate her lack of both interest and understanding, and Laila dashed out of the shop and went to wait at the theatre for a glimpse of her celestial god and goddesses. She did not have the money to go in but she watched them arrive – bundled in their unsightly Western coats and scarves – and leave. She stared with a painful jealousy at the audience that filed in and noticed that it had dwindled down to a few Indians, poor students to judge by their appearance, and a few French friends they had brought along.

At their last performance, desperation made her push past some sleepy, yawning ushers, find backdoors that could be unlocked, and make her way up steep, clanking iron stairs and long dimly lit corridors with ragged, dusty carpeting, to a dressing room where there was light, a smell of food and oil and heat, and the sound of voices, and there she found them – not the butterfly creatures of the stage to be sure, in gauzy draped costumes and glittering jewellery, but seated around a small gas stove on which tea with a spicy odour was being brewed in a kettle while they sat with their bare feet tucked up on the chairs, swaddled in shawls, their faces still encased in stage make-up like grotesque masks.

Yet Laila recognised them instantly as objects of her ardent desire, even though the male dancer who had danced Krishna had removed his crown of peacock feathers, draped his bare torso with a thick shawl, tucked his feet under him and was holding a saucer to his lips and loudly sucking up the sweet, spicy tea. But his face was the one she had seen on the stage – celestially calm, powerfully noble, the eyes half closed and dreamily smiling. It was the face she had first seen in the miniature painting in the bookshop – the same playfully glinting eyes, the same teasing half-smile, the same large calm brow and skin so dark it made her think of cinnamon and peppercorns. Or perhaps it was the scent of the tea that led her to think of them.

She became confused and unsure now, standing in the doorway in her aunt's purple cloak that was too big for her and that she had to hold about her shoulders like an Indian shawl. Dressed in that oversized cloak, staring with her frightened eyes, she looked to them like an alarmed child, and it made them turn to her and smile.

'You are wanting – ?' one of them asked, a woman whose pink make-up was heavily streaked with perspiration.

'Yes?' queried the god-like dancer, who stared at her the hardest.

'I want,' she said, knotting the cloak in her hands, 'I want to dance. I want to dance Lila, to be Lila.'

They all laughed then, including Laila, uncertainly, but the woman with the liquefying pink and red face beckoned her to come in with an arm on which a gold armlet was pushed up above the elbow and fingers weighted with rings. She wore a diamond in her nose that she touched frequently. 'Lila is the dance, not the dancer,' she instructed Laila. 'The dancer is Radha, beloved of Krishna.'

'I will learn!'

'But we are gypsies,' the god-dancer smiled at her. 'We will go away, like gypsies.'

'I will come with you,' Laila said to him, and stepped away from the woman and closer to him. 'Please take me, and teach me.'

'Teach you? Teach you?' His dancer's brows rose mockingly in arcs, and his painted smile became mocking too, as if he were miming surprise, alarm and amusement.

The women dancers turned to each other and began to chatter, and Laila was reminded of the parakeet house again, this time for the sounds and not the colours. She tried to decipher from their tones how her proposal was taken, but the male dancer was not joining in the talk, he was smiling at her from over the saucer that he held upon his fingertips, delicately.

'Are you a dancer?' he asked, and she nodded rapidly, blinking. 'Oui, oui.'

The women were speaking to him, addressing him, in loud tones. She could not make out if they spoke so loudly out of enthusiasm or out of anger and warning. So she continued to gaze at him, addressing her plea entirely to him, and at the same time exposing her eagerness to his frank, probing appraisal. The gift of acceptance had to come from the god, she knew. But he turned away, and spoke to the women. They all talked together, no one waited for one to finish before the other began. The noise rose. Laila might have been at an auction, herself on the auction block. When would she learn their decision? She stood trembling with the tension of waiting.

Then the door banged open rudely and the stage manager – or someone with some authority – entered and threw up his hands on seeing them still seated at the stove with their tea, and began to shout at them in French to wind up, pack, leave.

Laila looked around in horror to see if they understood his French. They were laughing again, and getting to their feet with a ringing of bells. They began to collect their boxes of make-up and jewellery, their stage props and shawls, and stuff them into large cartons that stood around the mirrored dressing table. Some of the women handed her a bundle and pointed at one of the boxes, clearly asking her to help. When she had filled the box with the objects she had been given, she lifted it in her arms and watched to see the dancers leaving. One of them turned and called, 'Come, come,' and she hurried after them.

The four cousins turned their faces to her. Their mother did not. She kept hers scrupulously turned away as Laila entered, bending over a very small circle of embroidery held taut in a brass ring, stabbing at it rapidly with her needle.

Laila kicked off her shoes at the door and wandered in barefoot over the carpet. The cousins looked down at her bare

205

feet. The mother looked at her embroidery, stitching and stitching at the circle of silk. When the thread was so short that she could stitch no more, she bent and bit the thread in two. Everyone's teeth were set on edge by the sound of that bite.

Then Aunt Françoise looked at Laila at last and said, 'Did you take the purple silk cloak out of my closet, Laila?' and the cousins' faces turned pale, almost transparent, as foreboding enveloped them.

Laila had stopped by one of the gilt-legged tables. She had picked up a small onyx ball that her mother had once sent her aunt. She caressed its chilly silken surface playfully and said, 'Yes.'

'Why,' asked her aunt, through lips that still seemed to feel the bitter thread between them, 'did you take what does not belong to you without asking?'

Laila tossed the onyx egg in the air with a laugh and caught it as it plummeted. 'Because you were not at home and I needed it.'

'Needed it,' repeated her aunt. 'For what?'

'I was going to a dance.'

Now the cousins let out the sounds they had held back so long, in one spurt. The younger ones pressed their hands to their mouths and sputtered through their fingers. The older ones threw back their heads and laughed with derision. They had seen Laila's muddy shoes at the door, and her grimy feet. How could she have been at a dance?

'A dance?' enquired the aunt. 'Can you tell us more about this – affair?'

'Not an affair,' Laila said, shaking her head emphatically. 'It was a dance of the gods,' she added and then withdrew abruptly and hurried to the bedroom, eager to be alone.

The cousins exchanged looks. Some smirked, and one put her finger to her head and rotated it like a screw. Their mother gave them a severe look and her lips were so tightly set and her face so drawn, they subsided with only a murmur.

Over a pot of stew, a fine rich stew in which herbs simmered and onions bubbled and meat made thick and solid, Aunt Françoise glanced at Laila who sat with her roll of bread and reminded her, 'Tomorrow morning we will all go together to church.'

Laila raised her heavy brows to meet her aunt's eyes. Crumbling the roll between her fingers, she said, 'But I told you, Tante Françoise, I do not go to church.'

Uncle Bertrand, lowering his head and settling into the plateful of stew he had been handed, muttered something about Moslems and mosques that made Aunt Françoise throw him a pained look.

Laila too had heard him. 'I am a seeker after truth and have given up *all* orthodox religions,' she said, looking around the table to see the effect of her words on her cousins' faces. 'I find them the repositories of ignorance and suppression – '

'That will be enough, Laila,' her aunt's voice rang out, and to emphasise the strength of her feeling, she rapped a silver spoon against the pot of stew in front of her. 'May I remind you, we are Christians here at this table.'

'So perhaps I should leave it,' Laila replied, and rose.

She stood between his knees, placing her hands on his shoulders, and rubbing them slowly over his skin.

'Shall I come?' she asked in a barely audible voice. 'Do you want me to come?'

He put his hands around her waist, as if it were a wand. He smiled a sleepy smile, heavy-lidded both with sleep and kohl. Beneath the lids, the eyes seemed both mysterious and mischievous, playful and elusive as fishes in a pond. She traced his eyebrows with a fingertip and repeated, 'Do you?'

He pushed her slightly away from him although his knees still held her. 'And what will your family say if I take you away?'

'They are not here. My parents live in Egypt.'

'Egypt,' he said, taking the word from her as if it were a curious fruit, one he had not tasted before. Then he smiled, enjoying its flavour. 'That is what the others said, that you are Muslim. But why are you here, alone?'

'I came to study. But what good is it to study what does not interest one?' She gripped his shoulders more urgently, saying, 'I will not be a European dancer. I want to be an Indian dancer.' She swayed in his grasp, urging him to respond.

He drew her close again. 'An Indian dancer,' he murmured against her waist. 'So white. So small. Muslim. Egyptian. How can you be an Indian dancer?'

'I will, if *you* teach me. If you take me and teach me, I *will*.'

He drew her down beside him on the ege of the bed, its iron rail cold under their knees. 'I cannot, without the permission of your family. You don't know, but in India we have a special ceremony when the parents bring a new student to a guru. They come with gifts on a tray – a piece of silk, a coconut, some betel leaves. They make an offering and ask the guru to take their child and give it the training. The training is his gift, you see.'

She laid her hand on his knee, gripping it. 'Then give it to me,' she said with a fierceness that made her narrow-eyed and white-lipped.

He lay back on the mattress, folding his arms under his head so that his long hair fell over them in a fold. His face had a brooding expression on it; he was not looking at her any more but at an inner picture. It made her wild to think of this picture to which she had no access and in which she played no part. It was not only him that she wanted but his whole world. A great deal, perhaps, but she wanted it intensely and passionately.

'Why can't you?' she broke out, and then felt chagrined to hear herself wail like a small child. 'Why? I will make a good dancer. I know it. I have never been so sure or wanted anything so much – '

'It is not for you to want,' he said in a lordly way, silencing her. 'It is for your family, your parents. I cannot take you. They must come to me, and offer you to me. Only then can I say yes.' He mimed this with his eyes and hands – their pleading, his acceptance.

She stared at him in a kind of rage. His indolent attitude upon the bed infuriated her now. She wanted him to rise and strike the pose, perform the gesture, assume the expression that would transform him from a heavy-set young man in his underwear in a cheap hotel room into a god of grace and authority, visiting from another realm. She could have fallen upon him with her fists, or her nails and teeth, pounded and clawed him and drawn from him the divinity she desired. But a part of her remained controlled, calculating, even cold, and she found herself saying, 'I can't bring them to you. But I can take you to my aunt. She will speak to you.'

'Yes?' he raised his eyebrows languidly, only half interested. 'And she is – your guardian?'

Madame Lacan was knitting. Laila had never seen her knit before, but on that afternoon of pouring winter rain, she sat in a tailored suit of black-and-white stripes, a red wool scarf tied raffishly around her neck, its bow under one ear, slightly askew, and in her hands were the knitting needles that she worked assiduously, click-click-clack. She gave him the most fleeting glance when he entered, in his own black-and-white suit, Western style, with an astrakhan cap on his head, also slightly askew.

Laila made the introductions, her hands fluttering about agitatedly, damp with nervousness. How did she know how to behave in this servile, humble, even abject way? It was not her way at all but it came to her now out of the air and she assumed it most naturally. Madame Lacan merely nodded and as for him, the dancer, he was looking at the poster of his dance performance, smiling at it in a pleased way as if looking into a mirror.

'Ah, you came to my dance?'

'Non,' Madame Lacan told him, 'but Laila did.'

'Ah,' he said and laid his hat on the counter. 'She told you?'

Madame Lacan gave a nod. She was never talkative but, Laila thought, could she not pretend to be just for once? So angrily did her eyes glare that Madame Lacan could not ignore them. Slipping stitches over the smooth knitting needles, she asked, 'You are leaving Paris?'

'Yes, we are going on a tour – to Marseilles, Lyon . . . One month we will tour. Then we will go to Venice. My friend there is giving us her house for practice. I will choreograph a new ballet for our American tour. She is a great admirer of India, of Gandhi and Tagore and Indian art and philosophy. She says, "Come to Venice, it will be an honour to have you. Come and stay in my house and practise there." So we are going.' Now, to Laila's instant and intense joy, his eyes met hers in smiling complicity.

Madame Lacan seemed aware of it even without looking. 'Hmm,' she said, 'and then – America, you say?'

'And then – America,' he smiled. His smile was still directed at Laila who leant against the counter to still her trembling. 'Your niece wishes to come with us and study dance in Venice.'

Madame Lacan went on with her knitting. Laila was about to seize it from her hands and throw it on the floor when she said at last, 'Laila can study dance here in Paris. Paris is the centre of the dance world. We have the ballet here, the opera, also the modern dance movements. Do you advise her to give up such fine possibilities and take up *Indian* dance instead?' She pronounced the words with superb disdain.

There was a moment of total silence while the dancer turned away from Laila to regard Madame Lacan, fully aware of the disdain. In that moment, the balance of things, till then hovering in the air in a tentative manner, with an almost audible sound of grinding and turning, reared about and established an entirely new balance. This one, unlike the old, was not tentative at all. It rang in the air as clearly as a bell.

Taking his arm, and his fur cap, off the counter, the dancer stood before Madame Lacan and said, 'I have seen ballet in Paris. I have been to the opera also. It is entertainment only. Not spiritual like Indian dance. No spiritual side at all.' He was putting his cap on his head now, straightening it, and his face looked dark beneath it. 'If Laila wishes to develop the spiritual side of dancing, she must learn Indian dance, not French ballet and opera and all that.'

Madame Lacan put her knitting down where his cap had been earlier. She was staring at him with a kind of interest now, even regard, really staring and really taking his measure. She even seemed to be smiling, an almost indecipherable smile under her grey moustache.

But as soon as she saw that Laila was watching her, she picked up her knitting again. 'So,' she said, 'you think Laila should accompany you on your tour?'

'No,' he said, 'she should come to Venice where I will hold classes, where she can learn. It is essential,' he said, 'for her spiritual development,' and now he threw Laila a look that was not only authoritative and proprietorial but also, to her intense gratification, nakedly covetous.

He was about to sweep out of the bookshop when Madame Lacan, remembering what Laila had told her, suddenly called out, 'Please have a cigar.'

He turned at the door and said to her, 'Madame, in India a man who teaches dance is a guru, and a guru is not only a teacher, he is a spiritual teacher. I do not smoke or touch alcohol.'

Afterwards Madame Lacan was in a thoroughly bad temper. Laila remained to hover around, to talk, longing to confide and be confided in, but Madame Lacan only snapped at her, threw away her knitting, held her head in her hands, said she had a headache, said she had to go home and rest, she was tired, tired of it all, she had seen everything, gone through everything before, what was the point of going on any more?

Laila found it prudent to stay away for a few days, fearing Madame Lacan might regret the role she had played at Laila's request and withdraw her acquiescence to their plan, their plot. But once Krishna and his troupe had left on their tour, she could not bear to be anywhere else but in the bookshop, sitting on a step, reading and studying. The female dancer's laughing exposure of her ignorance about Radha, the beloved of the blue god Krishna, and about Lila which was the dance, the play of the gods, made her confront the vast area of her ignorance about the art and the country she was about to embrace. Now, instead of looking at beautiful pictures that might give her beautiful dreams, she read Edwin Arnold's *Light of Asia*, Pierre Loti's *L'Inde*, Kalidasa's *Sakuntala*, went through *Great Religions of the World*, Max Müller's *Sacred Books of the East*, Vivekananda's *Raja Yoga*, the *Bhagavad Gita*, Tagore's *The Gardener* and *Gitanjali* – pouncing on every reference to Krishna, to Radha, seeing in their romance the model of her own affair, and yet clinging, secretly, to the name she had first chosen: Lila of Krishna Lila, because that contained the first impulse, the one that led the way.

Returning to the house with an armful of books Madame Lacan had loaned her, her eyes tired with the strain of reading by dim light, Laila looked so worn by her studies that no one in the family could suspect her of neglecting them. They noted however that, tired as she seemed, she slept badly. Of this the two older cousins were of course the most aware, being the victims of Laila's nocturnal restlessness. They would beg her to turn off the light, to go to sleep, only to have her sit crosslegged on her bed, her sleeplessness almost audible in the silence of the dark.

She was already up when they awoke, again sitting on her bed, wild haired, and when they looked at her inquisitively, she laughed. 'Oh I have had such a dream – it woke me up! Shall I tell you what I dreamt?' and she would launch upon a story that they later described to their mother as being crazed, weird, even frightening.

'She told us the story of a woman who gave birth to a serpent – '

'And a serpent who had a ruby in the middle of its forehead and lived in a dark cave and attacked anyone who came to steal it – '

'And a holy man who meditated night and day for three years and then turned into a tiger – '

'And a witch who had her feet turned the wrong way and lived in a tree over the road where travellers would pass –'

'And a princess who married a lion – '

Aunt Françoise hushed them fiercely. 'Let us not have such

talk in this house,' she cried, covering her ears. 'Not a word. Silence!'

Silenced, Laila turned even stranger. The cousins would wake to strange sounds in the night and see her, in the pale light filtering through the curtains, performing the most outlandish movements and gestures in the middle of the room, striking poses and weaving her arms about her head. When they hissed at her in fright, she jumped into her bed and pulled the covers over her head. Next morning she claimed to have no memory of the incident. 'I must have been sleepwalking,' she told the cousins, terrifying them out of their wits.

In early spring Laila walked along the Seine where the willow trees were strung with the glass beads of their new leaves and the shopkeepers on the bank were unpacking boxes of books, rolling out racks of clothes and setting up gilt-framed pictures, but the air still blew chill as ice. In the Luxembourg Gardens she watched the gardeners carefully unwrapping straw from around the young, tender saplings; the plane trees were still bare, stark as amputated limbs in the transparent light that was another aspect of ice. On the tennis courts figures in white were already running about and the ping of balls on racquet strings were like cracks appearing in that ice.

She wandered down to the Fontaine de Médicis and sat there on the ledge; there were no garlands and no lotuses in that icy light, but when she leaned over the glassy blackness of the water she could see the reflection of her own face float in it like a pallid fish. She sat staring at it as if it were a face she might not see again and ought to memorise. Then she could leave it behind, in the Fontaine de Médicis, and go in search of a new one.

On Sunday mornings in spring, Aunt Françoise's exertions rose to their pitch. Since daybreak she would be flying in and out of her daughters' rooms, exhorting them, watching over them as they washed and powdered themselves and dressed and had their hair done. The Sunday breakfast was no meal of

213

repose or leisure. Instead, mother and daughters sat in partial undress, on the edges of their chairs, some in tears, all in a state of tense endeavour. Rolls crumbled and coffee half drunk, they went through the ultimate stages of their toilet till summoned to the front door by the father, in his grey coat and hat, a furled umbrella in his hand. He looked more melancholy than ever – perhaps he would have preferred to linger over breakfast and the newspapers but he was taking his family to church. Aunt Françoise appeared at her most painstakingly elegant, her hair pinned upon her head in curls, and topping them a frivolous hat, all bits of feathered net and berried twigs, a vision of soft and gleaming surfaces and textures, even her face an unnaturally floral pink and violet. She had a little smile of triumph upon her lips, a sense of her own achievement as she looked over her four daughters – Claudette and Yvette in pink, with white gloves and white hats and white shoes, and Ninette and Babette in sailor suits with straw hats, snowy stockings and jet patent-leather boots. All assembled, they were ready to march to church.

Before they exited, however, Aunt Françoise sighed. 'Now, where is she? Where is that one gone, that Laila?'

The girls tittered as they informed her, 'She's out, she said not to wait.'

Aunt and uncle exchanged looks of mutual helplessness, outrage and offence, then they set off and, once outdoors, Sunday shone upon their heads like blessings upon the good.

What was unforgivable, what was really not to be endured, was that when they came out of church, there was Laila sitting quite calmly in the spring sunshine in place Saint-Sulpice itself – she had not thought of taking herself elsewhere so they would not come upon her. No, she was sprawled out on a bench, holding a paper bag on her lap and her legs stretched out before her. Her head was tilted up to the trees with their fine new greenery, lit by the sun to a pale yellow sheen, her eyes half closed to their dazzle. She held a croissant to her mouth and was nibbling at it slowly, clearly enjoying every crumb.

While the family stood transfixed on the flight of stone steps, staring, the entire flock of pigeons that inhabited the square swooped down on Laila, and in a moment she was covered by pullulating feathers and pecking beaks and grasping pink claws. Laila's arms flailed, scattering them, but they were Parisian pigeons, a tough and not too timid breed, and they only rose a little in the air and then descended again onto her head, her shoulders, and the bench. Finally, with a shout of exasperation – making the family on the steps start – she flung the remaining croissant half across the square, and sent the pigeons swooping and seething and hustling after it like a mad mob of rainbow-tinted grey harpies. She was revealed upon the bench again, in the spring sun, defiant.

⁓

The pigeons have risen in a cloud, the girl is revealed in the sun, and now stands up, brushing the crumbs from her silk shirt. Sophie watches her as she slowly crosses the square, stops by the fountain where the small boy is trying to get back the sailing boat that has moved beyond his reach, and then looks up, across the square directly at Sophie. Between them the sun is blazing with its summer violence, stones and walls and water are all lit to incandescence. Sophie is dazzled. She raises her hand to shield her eyes and as if the girl were an apparition, or made of drops of water, she evaporates.

Sophie has drawn her chair under the striped canvas awning of the café on the Zattere, her eyes shaded by huge dark glasses, her cup of cappuccino and her Venice guide on the table beside her.

Up and down the length of the Zattere young people lie as though they were on a beach, and the sun is pouring out of the cloudless sky onto them to further the illusion. Pale blond hair, tender pink flesh, all stretched out and exposed as in some pagan salutation to the sun.

The milky green water, a pale opalescent jade, of the canal is

215

churned up by the water traffic – the traghetti, the vaporetti, the gondole, the cargo boats ply it continuously, and in the distance there is some indication of larger ships on larger waters, belonging to the world of trade and enterprise that is here rendered obsolescent by art.

Across the lagoon looms the marvellously geometric mass of San Giorgio in a pink solidity magically rendered into an abstraction of lines and globes, and the houses that line the Giudecca in their own simpler, smaller perfection of ochre, sepia, burnt siena and terracotta rose.

Sophie, her head tilted back and her legs stretched out before her, drinks in the liquid colours of the scene as if she were drinking sweet, syrupy sherbets. She feels within her a suffusing warmth. It is enough to lull one first into a dream, and then sleep.

But she twitches herself into wakefulness, pays for the cappuccino, collects her guide book, feels in her purse to make sure she has her address- and her notebook, and then strolls past San Gesuati which is shut, with people sitting in contented indolence on its steps, awash in sunlight, and then turns away from the lagoon, down a lane which is shadowed and silent and where she becomes aware of the sound of her sandals on the stones, into a stony campo that is chill with shadows.

There she stands and opens her guide and studies it alternately with the scene. The door in front of her is heavy, ancient and shut.

~

Signora Durante stood at the head of the great flight of stairs that curved up in two semicircles from the stone courtyard, a single camellia tree in bloom between them. As the gondola arrived, she let out a cry and spread out her arms in welcome to the little band of Indians slowly and with difficulty disembarking onto the stones that were lapped by the water of the narrow canal at high tide. The gondolier was gallant, offered the ladies a crooked arm, but they ignored it and struggled out, clutching at the saris and shawls that dipped into the rising water. Signora Durante gave cries of warning and advice and eventually they managed to lift themselves free of the gondola and the water and into the courtyard. Lifting up their hems, heavy with water, they came up the steps, gazing up at her and the façade of the great house behind her, and for a moment Signora Durante was able to imagine her home in the time of her ancestors, for so they must have looked, in silk gowns and embroidered shawls, arriving in Venice at the end of a voyage.

Alas, she had no troop of servants to rush down and help them with their luggage. There were only she and faithful Gianni in the whole echoing palazzo. But she flung open her arms and let out a deep and throaty cry of 'Kr-rish-naa!' that stopped the small band in its approach and made them stare at her as she stood, her hair wrapped in a tall turban of green silk stitched with gold, wearing pyjamas of purple silk and her feet bare on the stones with a gold chain looped over one ankle. Behind her were the tall shuttered windows, the sagging doors, the carved balconies and the waterlogged silence.

They smiled tentatively and she came rushing down the stairs to meet them halfway, fleet as a girl in her delight, laughter bubbling up in her throat. She drew herself short of embracing Krishna. In fact, she seemed overcome with uncertainty over whether to embrace him or fall at his feet, and so collapsed in an attitude that suggested both and accomplished neither. It was an attitude expressive of the shyness of a young girl in the presence of the adored. Her lined and heavy face blushed as pink as a rose or a peony.

He, not shy, not embarrassed, put out one hand to touch her in blessing, but she was taller than he, and he touched only her shoulder and said, 'See, we have come. I have brought everyone.'

She tore her eyes away from his face on which she had been feasting, and looked at the others. She knew them and greeted them by name: 'Ah, Vijaya. And Sonali. Ah, I am so happy –' and then she noticed Laila standing on the bottom step, hanging back, looking away in embarrassment, her hair in a long black pigtail down her back. There was a little silence and then Signora Durante asked, 'And this – this little one? A new one, my Krishna?' and her voice seemed to have a crack in it. Out of curiosity, then, Laila looked up at her.

Signora Durante had been hostess to Krishna's dance troupe in Rome, in Paris, in Lausanne. They had already visited the various outposts of her family's empire; they remembered the apartment in Rome, its immense shuttered windows opening onto tiled roofs where cats prowled and quarrelled at night and the nearby river gave off a muddy effusion; the apartment in Paris with the equally immense but glassier windows that looked onto the Eiffel Tower piercing the sky in its theatrical fashion; and the house in Lausanne where they held aside the curtains to see purple crocuses emerge from the snow and there had been goosedown quilts and a prevailing smell of freshly ground coffee. In each she had appeared in a suitable costume – chic black suits and feathered hats, flowing Fortuny gowns, embroidered dirndl skirts – and fabricated an enthusiastic welcome and maintained her generous hospitality, throwing parties at which she might introduce Krishna to likely impresarios or supporters of Oriental art and mysticism, without allowing him or his troupe a glimpse of the tensions and tantrums that lay behind the graceful façade – the fights with her children, the arguments with lawyers, the warnings of friends, the spiteful gossip of neighbours and the complicated dealings with bankers and tradesmen . . .

But now, in Venice, these were beginning to show. Making sly, mocking appearances in the cracks and rents in the old, decrepit house in unguarded corners and moments, they began to intrude in a way the guests could scarcely fail to notice. If they had been guests, that is, and not a dance troupe that had come to perform and establish itself even though others might have told them that Italy after the War was hardly a dance stage; their leader might not have listened even then, he could not conceive of anything hindering such a divine aspiration.

While they draped themselves across the sofas and couches after a practice session in the grand salon upstairs with its painted ceiling and its long tapestries, exhausted and hungry and unable to see why they were not being served their dinner, only Laila was aware that at the moment Signora Durante was scuttling about the kitchen downstairs, her silk pyjamas stained with grease and badly inflamed burn marks on her wrists and arms, crying to Gianni, 'Gianni, Gianni, the eggplants are burnt! Oh, how could you let them burn, Gianni? My God, do you know what I did to obtain them, Gianni?' and Gianni, phlegmatically stirring a huge pot of soup that he had sprinkled liberally with cayenne pepper, was saying, 'Calm yourself, my dear, calm yourself. If they are hungry enough, and you say they are very hungry, they will eat burnt eggplants and even burnt shoeleather.' 'Ah, Gianni, how can you say such things? Don't you know they are Brahmins, Indians of the highest caste, from Benares, the holiest city in India? You are not to mention shoeleather to them, Gianni.' Signora Durante wailed and wrung her hands so that Gianni was left to carry the dishes up to the dining room and set them out on the long oak table under the chandeliers, then light tall blue candles in the pewter stands, bring chairs down from the salon to make up the necessary number, and finally bang at the gong to announce the meal. He wiped his brow with a corner of his apron: he had worked for this moment since daybreak, only to save Signora Durante from shame.

'Signor! Signorina!' he called down the stairs, and when they entered made an expressive gesture of his hands and only Laila saw the mockery and sarcasm.

Only she noticed the consternation on his face and Signora Durante's when they realised that the musicians for whom there was not room at the palazzo and for whom rooms had been found at a more modest establishment whose patron did the washing for Signora Durante, nevertheless intended to stay for dinner. Their appetites were already notorious, as were their eating habits.

Still, after a glance at the Signora's stricken face, Gianni obligingly dashed off to the kitchen and returned, bearing on one hand an immense oval silver tray on which he balanced a small bunch of grapes and a few oranges which were multiplied by reflection, and in the other a lute which he proceeded to strum once he had placed the fruit before the musicians. Almost as if he were enjoying himself, he began to prance around the table in an improvised dance and to make up a song that sounded so full and rich in tone that it made the carved rafters ring and Signora Durante turn rosy with gratitude and pleasure as she stood ready to serve her guests. What was more, Gianni's dance distracted them from the burnt eggplants, the less than sufficient soup. Clapping their hands in rhythm to his tune, they began to laugh and Signora Durante was able to feel, for a moment or two, the gratification of a great hostess who has given pleasure, has somehow contrived to give pleasure to her guests. In an excess of emotion, she caught Gianni by his sleeve and, linking arms, kicked up her slippered feet and did a little impromptu dance with him.

Only Laila noticed how Krishna looked away, embarrassed: obviously, in his country white-haired ladies did not cavort to music. The musicians exchanged contemptuous looks with each other.

Laila noticed because she belonged to neither one party nor the other, only watched and watched to see where she might go.

Laila slept in a long narrow room that ran like a passage outside the larger, square room shared by Sonali, the leading female dancer of the troupe, and old Vijaya who sang the songs to which the dances were danced. Sonali might have been her daughter, more likely her younger sister, or possibly a distant relative, or no relation at all – Laila could never make out. What she clearly saw was the deep intimacy between the two who spoke to each other in low, cryptic tones and passed a silver box of betel nuts and spices back and forth between them, sharing its mysterious ingredients. Old Vijaya would help Sonali tie on her anklets, fuss over her costume, tie the blouse strings at the back and comb out her hair with long, loving strokes of a large, clumsy comb, then twist and wind it about in intricate chignons held in place with ornate pins. Their relationship seemed almost animal in its comfortable silences, its mutual attentions, its undertones of an invisible and complicated liaison.

In the long narrow room with its uncurtained windows, Laila slept beside the two younger dancers of the troupe, Chandra and Shanta. They were quite clearly sisters but not because of any such intimacy or familiarity in their behaviour. On the contrary, their impatience with each other and the quick tempers with which they responded to each other were what gave away their family relationship. When they spoke, they seemed to quarrel, their voices were so high-pitched and agitated. Although they did help each other dress and would paint each other's hands with henna patterns and feet with red *alta* and would comb and braid each other's hair, there was a perfunctoriness about their actions, and often open animosity. They reminded Laila of her cousins in Paris.

All of them moved together in a web; only Laila was outside it.

The older women woke first and came to the young girls' bedroom before daybreak, in the dark, calling them to practice. There was scarcely time for a toilette; the drummer was already tuning his drums in the salon, and Krishna was seated on the parquet floor in the lotus position, beneath the unlit chandelier, his eyes closed and his hands placed precisely on his knees, palms upturned, in the meditative pose, having already performed his salutation to the sun and his repertoire of yoga exercises.

Hurriedly tucking the end of her practice sari in at her waist, and bending to strap on the heavy anklets, Laila would take up her position beside the other dancers. When old Vijaya beat her wooden *thatakalli* upon the floor and burst into a wailing song, Krishna rose and called out the *tala* to which they first moved their eyes, then their heads and necks, finally their hands and feet till their bodies were moving in unison, and the dance began to throb in them, faster and more inviting with every beat. Now Laila began to feel she was at last doing what she was meant to do, had come here to do, had been called upon to do. Throwing back her head, and then her shoulders, her feet were now performing what was asked of them by the music, her face what was asked of it by Krishna.

In the small room to which the Signora had moved, giving up her own to Krishna, Gianni sat up on the bed and struck his head with his fists. 'Crazy!' he shouted. 'Crazy! This house has gone mad – dancing at night when the whole of Venice lies asleep!'

The Signora made soothing, placating sounds with her lips, patting the warm pillow beside her with a begging hand, but her head, too, ached. Once she had even ventured to ask if Krishna could not postpone the lesson by an hour or so.

He had gone quite mad then. His eyes had flashed and his teeth ground in a pantomime of rage – only a dancer could express rage so, and the Signora, trembling, had to admit it was quite spectacular. He had swept out of the room and in his anger begun to fling his belongings into a leather trunk, crashing each one in with maximum effect. While the Signora stood wringing her hands, he had shouted 'Why should I stay? How can I stay where my art is not understood, not even tolerated? Where my music is thought of as *noise*, my dance a *nuisance* to the royal highness asleep in her bed? Do you know what I and my dancers create while you sleep? Do you have any idea who you are housing under your roof? But we will not stay another day – another minute – ' and in went the shoes, the fine Venetian leather shoes she had bought him only the other day, and the handsome fur hat he had picked for his American tour, and the silk scarf, and the bottle of perfume, of talc, of oil – she screamed when it broke and threw herself on the floor to save his feet from the shards. Deliberately, he trod on them so they might be cut. 'See, see!' he howled at her.

In Paris, Sonali had danced the leading role – Radha to Krishna's Krishna, Sita to his Rama, Parvati to his Shiva. From the way they performed together it was clear they had danced these roles over and over till they seemed two limbs of one body. In Venice, too, in the big salon during the practice sessions, Krishna performed these dances with Sonali and Laila watched, watched intently, copied, copied exactly, every gesture she saw, standing aside alone, without a partner. Then, quite casually leaving Sonali's side one day, he beckoned Laila forwards and instructed Sonali to guide her through these roles. Standing to one side, he beat the *tala* with his hands, calling out the rhythm, and watched Laila obey with a look of approval, of pleasure and satisfaction that spread across his face in a slow, wide smile. Sonali's face settled into the stillness of carved stone but her limbs continued to move with precision, with accuracy, and now and then she called out an instruction of her own, harshly.

Then Krishna stepped forward and began to perform with Laila what he had previously performed with Sonali. Now behind her, now beside her, he enfolded her in his arms, helping her to feel what was required of her by the music and the song. The others fell away, moved to the walls where they leant, watching, one foot resting against the other, while Sonali stood beating the *tala*, Vijaya sat singing of love and ardour, and Krishna danced the divine cowherd, the godly flute-player, the darling trickster, and Laila was the lover and devotee, plucking lotuses to weave into a garland for him, adorning herself to please him, or weeping and pining for him under a tree.

Finally Krishna tore his eyes away from her to call 'Come, all of you, form a ring around Laila, dance with her.'

Signora Durante, coming in from the market, or the laundry, or the kitchen, stopped in the doorway to watch. A bag of vegetables, or a stack of sheets in her arms, she stood by a great mirror with a convoluted gilt frame, and watched the dancers assume the poses of shepherds and dairy maids, pounding the parquet floor with bare feet made heavy with rows of bells on their anklets, twisting and turning around each other in the attitudes of pursuit, escape, desire and possession. Incense was lit in the tall silver holder, the air misty with its smoke, and combined with the watery sunlight of Venice outside, her salon was transformed into a musky Oriental grove. Signora Durante breathed in the air deeply, her chest rising and falling, but then the music stopped, the dancers, abandoned by its rhythm, stood still. Only Krishna continued to dance around Laila, demanding that she continue too, and now the two danced alone, in silence, and it was clear Krishna could not bear to have her stop, that he danced for the sake of seeing Laila dance, that he could not have enough of her dancing limbs and her intense face and the charming gestures she had been taught and that he now watched and guided, drawing them from her as earlier the music had done.

At last Signora Durante could bear it no longer. Setting down her parcels, she began to clap and cry 'Bravo! Bravo!' as loudly as she could. But her voice was not steady, and she bent to retrieve her parcels and hurry off with them, not able to bear the sight of Laila with her long black hair in a sinuous pigtail down her straight back, Laila's tiny blouse no more than a scrap of gold brocade with a silk sari caught between her legs and draped low on her breast where a gold pin held it. Even worse, the passion that glinted and shifted about in Krishna's eyes as he struck the pose of the divine flautist and had her circle him once more, gloating to see her in his spell.

Making her sit on the kitchen stool and bringing a napkin out for her face, Gianni said to her, 'You could ask them to leave, my love. It is your own house, after all, and they are here only because you are so good, so good – '

'How could I ask them to leave if I am so good?' the Signora cried. 'You are so foolish, my Gianni. Can one be good and also unkind at the same time?'

'You can manage it, Gabriella, if anyone can!' Gianni declared, trying to brush her hair away from her wet eyes, and she was obliged to push his hand away, he was so silly.

He had served her with exactly that tenderness as a waiter in Florian's where her eyes had first been caught by his deft hands, the flourish with which he twirled his tray and set dishes before her. Her eyes and her sapphires had all flashed their appreciation at him.

She already knew Krishna then. She told Gianni about her visit to India, her enchantment with the city of Benares, the music and dance with which she had been entertained in her friend Rani Chunni's palace. She showed Gianni the silks and shawls she had brought back with her. Lovingly she draped him in first a mango-green silk, then a saffron yellow one with a purple and gold border, and clapped her hands as he swept about, wearing them as cloaks or as skirts. 'Like Krishna himself!' she cried. 'My little Venetian Krishna!' He had had no idea what she meant then.

Now she pushed his hand away, and the wet napkin, then blurted, 'How can I bear it?'

She beckoned to Laila as Laila walked past the kitchen door, barefoot but with her anklets ringing. Laila stopped and looked in at her and Gianni sitting by the kitchen table. She placed her hands on her hips and stood in a dancer's stance. Her face still streamed with the perspiration of her exertions, but she stood quite calmly, almost regally before them.

It was the Signora who flushed and began to pull at a thread in her sleeve, nervously.

The silence went on for too long: something had to be said.

'You come from India?' the Signora asked at length, both her face and her hands twisting in embarrassment.

Laila gave her head a shake. 'No. From Paris.'

'Ah, you are French?'

Laila shook her head again.

'No? But you live in France?'

Again, Laila shook her head.

'Then?'

Laila stared at the woman, wondering what she wanted of her. What was she being told? Why had she been called? There must have been something hostile in her expression for Gianni rose and came to stand by the Signora, protectively. He was much smaller than she however, a small man dressed entirely in black, his pale triangular face ending in a small, trimmed beard. He ran his fingers over his beard now and Laila saw the light of a diamond ring travel back and forth as he stroked it. She had seen the ring on the Signora's hand the other day. The two of them, they make a pair. What did they want of her?

The Signora pulled now at a pink and orange scarf around her neck. Her face too was pink and orange, pulpy and fruity.

'You will go on tour with them?' she asked at last, miserably.

Laila swung away from them. Her hip jutted out in that faintly insolent way they had noted in the Indian dancers; now this girl had learnt their tricks. She swung her hip as she walked away, saying, 'If Krishna wants.'

'And – Sonali?' the Signora cried after her.

Sonali followed the instructions given her by Krishna, to teach Laila. Taking a place beside Vijaya on the rug, she sat crosslegged and called out the *tala*, interrupting herself now and then with a piece of advice on a stance, a pose, a beat. But she did so perfunctorily, without any interest in how her instructions were carried out. She watched, but with a face as expressionless as wood. Sometimes she fell silent altogether, leaving the dancer to perform to the music without any instruction at all. She huddled inside her shawl and crouched by Vijaya, growing more and more impassive.

To begin with, Krishna did not seem to notice. He was on his feet, moving from one end of the salon to the other, guiding the dancers, dancing first with one and then the other, and mostly with Laila. Eventually all the others became observers, he and Laila and their dance a private affair between them, and most certainly the centrepiece.

•   •   •

Laila in love, in the old, dark house with its heavy oak furniture, its faded tapestries, its unlit chandeliers, and the water lapping at its walls. The house and the lagoon seemed to sigh, to grumble and watch with foreboding. Laila was aware of that hostility – it was directed at her from every face, every mirror, every corner and window. Yet she could barely restrain herself, when walking down a shadowy whispering corridor or waiting in a solitary corner, from leaping in the air, performing a swirling dance of joy. Her skin tingled with the recognition of Krishna's love, with her awareness of it. He looked towards her continually. When that look was directed at her, or when she stepped into the circle of his arms that urged her to move in time with him, and felt his hand cover her arm, or waist, she felt encircled by his adoration. His eyes went liquid with love, his touch transformed her into his princess, his beloved, his goddess, whatever role she was dancing. She could hardly tell them apart. Dance and love, they came to be one in this old dark house in Venice. She could not tell one from the other: they were twined together and shimmered the way the light shimmered upon the Canalezzo, on the swooping gulls, the gliding boats, and she was being woven into that fine, silken, precious weave.

She could not have described her love, nor did she have any words for Krishna. Slightly giddy, slightly faint, it seemed to her that he, the dancer, the male physical presence, was also the figure she had first seen in a volume of paintings in Madame Lacan's shadowy bookshop. He was also the god she had studied in the books she drew off the shelves there. He was also the country and the art and the religion that had become her obsession there. When she danced with him, she wondered if she was not already transported to it.

Had there been someone who knew how to question her, she might have explained, 'Krishna is my country and my religion.'

One day Krishna said, 'This afternoon we will have a dress rehearsal. Come in your costumes. Sonali, give Laila the jewellery. Paint her hands and her feet for her. I want every detail exactly as it will be on stage. Quickly. Go and prepare. Sonali, help Laila.'

And Sonali lifted her costume out of her trunk and brought it to Laila. She helped her dress. She fastened her necklace around Laila's neck and put the earrings into her ear lobes, and pinned a pendant to her hair. She went through all these motions without a word, but when she felt Laila trembling at her touch, her mouth twisted wryly.

'Your turn has come,' she said.

After the rehearsal Laila was in her room, removing the jewellery, carefully unpinning and unfastening it, when Chandra came in, dishevelled from the dance, and said, 'Vijaya wants you.' In answer to Laila's questioning look, she tossed her head in the direction of the older woman's room. Laila took up the jewellery, thinking that was what was wanted, and went in.

Both the women were seated on the bed, wrapped in their shawls. They were looking down at their laps and did not glance at Laila when she entered. It seemed that they had called her to look upon their bitterness and hostility: these were posed and presented as in a tableau.

Laila was still breathing heavily from her dancing. She was also heated from it in a way that made her bold. She thrust out the jewellery at them, returning it.

But that was not what was wanted from her. Vijaya gave her a look and said with both authority and bitterness, 'You think you are Indian dancer now. No. Indian dancer must practise from childhood. Must have training. Must know our language, understand our music. Not everybody can be Indian dancer.'

Laila stood with her hands placed to one side of her waist, listening intently in order to catch all the nuances buried in those few harshly spoken words. She heard the resentment and the jealousy as well as the hate. She stood with her eyes lowered but her toe traced a fanciful pattern on the floor. As if to herself, in a low voice, she said, 'Krishna-ji himself has trained me.'

228

'Trained you! In just one, two months you can be trained?' Vijaya laughed derisively. 'We – Sonali and myself – we have trained for twenty, thirty years – '

Mischievously, Laila glanced up at them, not quite suppressing a smile. It was clear what she thought of their age.

Infuriated, the woman cried, 'And you think you are ready to perform?' Laila nodded, smiling openly now. 'And he is taking you to America also?'

Laila nodded. She could not have known how enormous her eyes were within their painted outlines, and how brilliant.

'He asked you?' the old woman pursued.

Laila nodded again, still more affirmatively, even proudly.

That made the old woman explode. Suddenly she spat out the words, 'Go home. Go back home.'

Laila was so startled that she gave a gasp that became a laugh. Looking at the old woman from whose mouth spit had sprayed and was now hanging on her lips, and whose eyes were as if they had been smudged with coal, and whose teeth were old and discoloured, and on whose head the hairs were thin and few so that bare patches showed, Laila could not refrain from laughing. Jealousy from such as her? 'No,' she said very clearly, 'I will go with Krishna-ji,' and turned around to leave them, shaking a bit with her own bravado, and cruelty.

Krishna declared he had choreographed a solo dance for Laila. It was called *The Peacock*. He urged Signora Durante to design the costume. When Laila hesitated, fluttering, murmuring that she had never seen a peacock, he gazed upon her with the radiance of his love, assuring her, 'The bird is beautiful, as beautiful as you, rani.' He called her rani, queen.

The tale that he had invented was that a raja's favourite dancing girl was cursed by his wife and doomed to dwell in the body of a peacock. 'The peacock is always calling, "Peeo, Peeo," – beloved, beloved,' he explained to Laila, and taught her the Hindi word for a peacock – *mohr*.

The Signora, rushing all over Venice for the components,

designed a costume for her made up of a headdress of plumes, a brief bodice of gold brocade, and a skirt of green lamé with a jewelled train. 'It is not bright enough,' he complained, and swore he would have an aquamarine spotlight trained on her when she danced, and he himself searched through all the jewellers' shops in Venice for stones that would glitter in such lighting.

Having helped her into the splendid costume, the Signora clasped her hands on seeing the effect. 'An Indian peacock in Venice!' she exclaimed, awed by the strange combination that had come about in the floating city and in which they, all three, had taken part. Surely that had some meaning?

She ordered a gondola to take them down the Grand Canal. Gianni himself handed her in, smiling a small tight smile that gave her a pang and made her squeeze his hand in appeal before lowering herself onto the seat. He stood aside as Krishna followed her into the gondola. Krishna was heavy, unused to boats or water, and it dipped and rocked under him. The gondolier whistled sharply, sprang about to set the balance right, then plunged his pole into the glassy depths of the water and the boat shot forwards, with Gianni standing on the stone steps to watch it go.

When he turned and went back into the courtyard, he saw Laila whirling around in the doorway and vanishing up the stairs – she was the only one of the dancers who was so slim and moved so swiftly. 'You think I would follow?' he snarled, and went into the kitchen to start work on the dinner. For some reason, the troupe had not taken it over as they had been doing in recent weeks, insisting on cooking their own meals, complaining they could not eat what he had prepared, they could not be sure it was not tainted by meat. He had been furious to begin with – at their insinuation that he was unclean, as well as the sight of his kitchen turned upside down and spattered with oil and spices which to him stank rankly. But the Signora had soothed him and placated him – her gifts so lavish, her generosity so great – he had retreated sulkily to the pantry to make himself the meals he liked, pacified by the thought she would share his meals, not theirs, as much as by her gifts. Today he found the vast kitchen empty – they had all disappeared into their rooms as if making a space for Krishna and the Signora to have their idyll together.

For the Signora the dream had been to be seated beside her Krishna in a gondola that glided out of the shadows of the narrow canals between tall houses into the sunlit Grand Canal where the water turned to an opaque jade, a colour fresh and young, with herself and Krishna reclining on black and scarlet cushions while she feasted her eyes upon his golden skin and undulant black hair and the hugely enlarged and elongated eyes that shifted with such subtlety. Krishna's delight lay openly in the scene itself: after a cursory smile thrown at her sideways, he abandoned himself to the pleasure of lying back upon the cushions and smiling past the gondolier who bent and twisted at the waist, threw up his arms and manoeuvred the pole with a wonderful athleticism and theatricality. In the background, the palazzi slipped by, a little sombre when in the shadows but in the sunlight transformed into fantasies of gold and rose and ivory that the reflections of the water stroked and set to rippling and trembling like silk tapestries. Then there were all the other gondole out in the spring sunshine, and the passengers who celebrated the beginning of summer. Krishna turned to watch a young couple, pale with intensity, locked together on the seat of a boat under the benign guardianship of the gondolier obligingly singing a Verdi aria. His smile and look made them start and tremble as if a god had passed and blessed them. Then there was the old Contessa Daniella whom all Venice knew, taken out in her shawls and capes and hats and scarves like a doll lifted out of its box in the attic for an airing; Krishna waved to her blithely and saw her, too, start and then respond with a smile that displayed her ageing features altering miraculously to their earliest youth.

Timidly, the Signora tapped him on his knee. 'Krishna,' she said, reminding him of her presence, 'you are so well known in Venice!' As if to corroborate her words, voices rang out from yet another gondola speeding by on its way to the Lido, crying 'Krishna! Krishna!' in youthfully ringing voices.

'Ah, the Mazzinis and their friends from Rome,' he acknowledged, graciously waving. 'So friendly! They love me,' he added, settling the silk folds of his shawl about him complacently.

'They do,' she sighed and looked down at her feet in their sandals beside his. 'You could stay here, in Venice, my Krishna, and dine out every night.'

He threw back his head, for a moment glancing up to see a gull swoop low over the waves, but then craning around to see who it was that fluttered a piece of pink and purple silk in a gondola quickly slipping by. Thinking he knew the owner, he waved, and said carelessly to the Signora, 'True, true. But that is not the life of a dancer, Gabriella. For these ballet dancers you have here, maybe – drinking and parties and all that. But in India, you know, dance is worship, it belongs to the temple . . .'

At another time he might have gone on, inspired by his lofty vision. She had often heard him on the subject: devotion to the gods, discipline, respect for the guru, the waking before dawn, the long hours of exercise, the fatigue, exhaustion, dedication, bliss . . . but today his mind was not on it. Venice caught at it, distracted him, and the day was exquisite, so exquisite.

The Signora, suddenly remembering a line from some-where in her Austrian heritage, blurted out: 'Verweile doch, du bist so schön!'

'Hmm?' he enquired, but immediately turned away from her to yet another gorgeous aspect floating by.

She recalled herself. Settling the folds of her silk dress – she had put it on especially for this outing, a new one of taupe silk, soft as moleskin, and stamped all over with gold triangles, knowing how fond Krishna was of the colour gold – she could not keep the pleading out of her voice as she spoke the rehearsed words: 'Then why not stay, my Krishna? Why not make Venice the base for your company? You have friends here, and I – '

He seemed scarcely to stop scanning the lively scene for a moment – they were out in the open water before the Salute now, steamships loomed, barges floated, making everything tilt and rock. 'No, no,' he said quite impatiently, brushing aside the suggestion. 'It is time for the tour now. We must begin.'

'Why, Krishna? You know Italy will once again be the home of music and dance. The War is over, it will prosper again – '

But he seemed uninterested in her arguments.

Perhaps it was the sight of a steamship, all white and gleaming with brass and paint, its passengers lined up on the top deck, looking out on the city they were leaving, crying out their farewells, that made Krishna brush aside the suggestion of staying on, and say, 'Ah, but think of America, they had no war there at all and Mrs du Best will arrange our tour. We will visit New York, Chicago, San Francisco – '

It was true what he said – America had not suffered as Europe had, and there were riches to be won that she could not provide. Still she said, miserably, 'I don't know.'

He gave her a strangely cold look before glancing away. 'I told you we would leave as soon as we finished rehearsing and Mrs du Best sent for us.'

'And have you? And has she?'

But the gondola was turning around now in an arc, against the pressure of the waves and the turbulence created by the water traffic at San Marco, and Krishna's face was turned to the new scene, all its rushing, fluid lights and changes. He was not going to pay attention to tiresome details now.

They were making their way back to the Grand Canal and were once more in the shadow of the palazzi. They would soon be at the Casa Rosa again, her time with him would be over. Signora Durante doubled over as if in pain. 'And the little one,' she asked, 'that little Laila, you are taking her?'

'Of course,' he replied. 'She will be the leading dancer on this tour.'

'Ahh!' the Signora cried out. 'And Sonali? What will Sonali – '

'Sonali is returning to India.'

'To India?' the Signora repeated. She had known Sonali for so long now – in Paris, Rome, Lausanne – aware that Sonali did not care for her, but accepting the long acquaintance. 'So,' she said sombrely, and then something quite unrehearsed, something she knew she ought not to say: 'Why not take me with you, my Krishna? You know, I can – can help, I can do things for you – '

'No, no,' he said at once, smoothly, giving her a small smile that was the merest movement of his lip muscles. 'Not in America. What can you do for me in America? Mrs du Best will take care of us there, don't worry.' His eyes travelled down to her dress, and as the gondola bumped against the stone steps of the Casa Rosa, he said, 'Why grey, Gabriella? Why not pink, red, orange – the colours of the sun? The colours of India? You know, I do not like this grey.'

Laila, slipping into the kitchen as she grew hungry, and finding Gianni there alone, was just giving him the same information that Krishna had given the Signora.

The soup was simmering in a pot, making his face glisten. 'You are eating all the peas raw,' he accused her. 'They are meant for the soup. But you will be gone soon, eh?'

She laughed, tossing peas into her mouth, and nodded.

'America? All of you?' he shook his head, marvelling: America; he would not mind that himself. He had heard of its glories: jazz, black musicians, the foxtrot, the Charleston . . . while over here the people seemed unable to shake off their experience of war and their fears. Some said Mussolini would surely put all in order again, was already undertaking great reforms, but others spoke of the reprisals and atrocities carried out by his blackshirts. Anyone who doubted or dissented simply disappeared, or so it was said. And it was true, his friend Dino had fled over the border to France rather than to submit to their rule, and now lived in exile. Exile would not be so bad if only he could find himself another patron. He brooded, watching Laila, who seemed to have no such worries.

She, munching peas meanwhile, was saying, 'No, not all. Madame Sonali, she is going back to India.'

'Eh?' Gianni turned to her again. 'That one?' He imitated the wooden-faced one whose jaws worked perpetually on a small hard nut she fished out of a pouch.

Laila laughed. 'Yes. She is too old.'

'Heh, too old for what?' Gianni exploded. 'Eh, for what?'

'For dancing,' Laila replied coolly, opening her eyes very wide as she stared back at him. 'A dancer must be – young.'

'And when they get old – then?'

'Then,' she shrugged, 'retire.'

'So,' he said, 'the old retire, eh?' He looked at her perching on the edge of the table, scraping peas out of the pods, quite composed. 'Good news for the young, eh? But not so good for the old, no.'

Laila shrugged. 'Have you bread?' she asked. 'I will not eat that.' She wrinkled her nose at the rich soup bubbling.

He seized a loaf, broke off a piece and tossed it at her. 'For the Principessa Laila,' he mocked.

Then the bell at the great door in the courtyard rang and they both leapt to their feet.

Now that the word had gone out about their readiness to leave, the Signora's efforts as their hostess and benefactress reached their peak. She could not do enough for them. She had been placed in charge of getting the costumes ready long ago, along with Vijaya and Sonali, and she rushed about to tailors and seamstresses, buying materials, having models copied, going back tirelessly to see if they were done and the least mistake corrected. In addition she helped her guests with little attentions – getting their trunks mended, buying them medicines for possible aches or colds, choosing gifts for each, urging Gianni to bake cakes and ice pastries to please them, light more candles at table, play music while they ate – as if she wished to pour upon them every last drop of her hospitality and generosity. Yet her face was drawn, her hair straggled, her eyes watered, and she seemed never to have time to change her silk pyjamas or brush her hair or even find a camellia to pin to her blouse any more.

Then – a final, extravagant gesture – she threw a party for them. 'So Venice can bid you *buon viaggio*!' she declared expansively, and did not add what else was on her mind: that it was a farewell to the past, to the Italy they knew, which she felt would never be the same again.

Gianni dressed in black dancer's tights and one of Signora Durante's shawls, a piece of orange silk with gold thread woven through it, tied about his middle in a great bow, as if he were a parcel, or a gift. In that festive costume, he received the guests who stepped out of their gondole onto the water-logged steps and led them into the courtyard that he had lit earlier that evening with torches. These flared in the dusk, driving away the stars, and lit up his gold and orange trimmings. He glittered with welcome and led them up the stairs at the top of which the Signora stood in a purple Fortuny gown that she had inherited from her mother and the sapphires that had been her mother-in-law's, and her face was tinted pink with powder so that on that day it bloomed again like a rose or a camellia.

Under the great bronze chandelier in the salon Krishna stood in his finest white silk dhoti, wrapped in a shawl of Pashmina wool from Kashmir, and on his feet were pointed gold slippers with curling ends. He stood with his arms folded, bronzed and statuesque, and when the dowagers came to him, crying out, 'Oh, you are not leaving Venice? Gabriella says you will go to America but please say it is not true,' he smiled at them with the triumph of one who knows he will be missed but has no intention of changing his plans to suit them.

The dancers and musicians of the troupe played a different role. Seizing the platters of hors d'oeuvres, they circulated amongst the guests and offered them, although Gianni, now stripped of his butterfly bow and wearing a chef's hat instead, gnashed his teeth and cried, 'They will drop them, my little canapés. Why can they not leave them on the table where I arranged them around the pineapples and grapes? That was my design!' The Signora murmured, 'Ah, what does it matter, my Gianni, when it makes them look so beautiful? See Signora Celli take one from Shanta – how pretty!'

'Now she has spilt her champagne, poor thing, over her saffron gown,' Gianni pointed out.

'Never mind, never mind,' cried the Signora, darting up to the scene of the mishap with a napkin extended. 'Oh, Magdalena, Magdalena, your dress! Come, let me wash it out for you – '

The good-tempered Signora Celli merely patted the hand that held out the napkin. Her mouth was full of crumbs and through them she murmured, 'Lovely, lovely, Gabriella. How splendid he looks, like an Oriental prince. I see him pass on his way down the Canalezzo in a gondola, a wonderful shawl thrown about his shoulders, lounging there on the cushions like a Prince de l'Inde. Yes, a Prince de l'Inde!'

'A raja, a raja,' the Signora laughed back, delighted. 'That is what he is, is he not?'

'And where did you find him, in a palazzo, in India?'

'Oh no, Magdalena. It was I who was staying in a palazzo, with my friends the Raja and Rani of Begumpura; they arranged a tiger hunt for my Gaetano, you know, in the days when poor Gaetano was up to such things. And Krishna came to a party they gave in their palazzo for us. That is how I met him. He himself lived in a poor, poor quarter of the city of Benares – you will not believe how poor, not even a bed or a table, just the bare floor on which they slept and ate. But when he came to the palazzo to dance, bearing himself like a prince, he was much more a prince than my poor Gaetano or the Raja of Begumpura who was only this high and not too beautiful.'

Signora Celli gave Gabriella a little tap with her fan which she carried about in her plump pink hand as if she were still a young belle of another century. 'Then ask him to dance for us as he did for you. Let us all see him dance.'

The Signora looked alarmed. 'I don't know,' she said hurriedly. 'I don't know if he wishes to do that. He is so sensitive, you know, to people, and the atmosphere – but if he wishes, he will, Magdalena,' and she darted sideways to receive another guest. 'Dear Ambrose! Here is Ambrose!' she cried, opening her arms to a small dapper man in black who stood by the door with his eyebrows raised quizzically at the scene. 'My oldest friend,' she burbled, perhaps not tactfully, planting a kiss on his cheek. 'And always the perfect English gentleman,' she added, surveying the perfection of his dress and toilette while he fingered his cravat and began to play the role asked of him in Venice of the English dilletante, a painter of watercolours, instructor of dozens of hopeful English watercolourists who filled the city in the spring and summer, and above all that of a perfect guest at all the best Venetian homes.

Trusting him to perform that, she led him up to be introduced to Krishna, but the meeting turned out to be cool, quite noticeably chilly in fact. The Englishman did not seem to find the Indian dancer quite so wonderfully exotic as the Venetians did, and the Indian dancer seemed no more enthusiastic at meeting the Englishman. They turned away from each other quite soon, and Ambrose was heard crying 'Gianni, my dear fellow, have you one of those lovely little fishes from the lagoon for me to try? I'm feeling peckish, you know,' when one of his former pupils suddenly appeared and greeted him effusively: 'Ah, you are still here! I'm so relieved! Everyone is leaving Italy in droves, I was so afraid you, too – ' 'Leave Italy? leave Venice? Why, what nonsense!' he replied.

The party might have swirled around in a circle without a centre but Krishna now clapped his hands, imperiously, and with a glint in his eyes announced he would present to them a new dancer and a new dance especially choreographed for her here at the Casa Rosa itself. He even threw a generous look in the direction of the Signora as if offering it to her, and she leant back against the wall, crimson and damp with delight.

At his signal, Laila stepped forward, and she was in the costume the Signora had designed for her, the peacock's costume of green lamé and gold feathers and blue lapis lazuli jewellery. Her appearance was so striking that silence fell even before the drums began to beat or the cymbals to ring. Then, with Krishna calling out the *tala*, she took up her stance under the chandelier and began to move first her eyes, then her neck, then the arms and shoulders and hands, till finally her feet took up the beat and moved to his command.

The guests formed a ring, watching, and as she shimmered and sparkled before their eyes like some creature of the tropical forests and exotic lands, they could not be sure if what they marvelled at was this human creature transforming herself into an inhuman apparition, or at her assuming a wholly Indian art and culture and making it uncannily her own, or at something altogether inexplicable and subtle for which they had no words, only applause.

Krishna too stood watching, clapping, and now and then casting a look around to see the effect on the audience, when Signora Celli cried out, 'You, too, beautiful prince, you too must dance,' whereupon he stepped forward, slipped into the rhythm of the music and began to dance with Laila under the chandelier, lifting his arms till he encircled her, turning back his head as if basking in her glory.

The performance, although brief, brought forth such a storm of applause that it drowned out Ambrose's voice, saying plaintively 'Oh not that tired old peacock dance again! They can scarcely pass that off as classical, can they? Why, it's what street performers put on in India.' The others were crying 'Bravo! Bravo!' and if there had been roses around, they would have certainly rained them upon the dancers.

Instead Gianni doffed his chef's hat and crying 'Olé!' leapt into their midst. He had fetched his guitar from the kitchen where it always hung by the onions and the peppers, and tied a red napkin around his neck, and now he struck it loudly, stamped his feet and standing before Laila, called 'Dance! Dance!' The Signora's hands flew to her mouth in horror, and she looked to see how Krishna took this intrusion. As she feared, his face darkened, a storm cloud settled low on his brow, but the irrepressible Gianni had seized Laila around the waist and the girl did not break away from his grasp. Instead, she gave a light laugh, stamped her feet in their anklets a few times in keeping with his, but within a minute she had danced out of the circle the younger guests now formed, responding to the Spanish music Gianni beat upon his guitar. Signora Celli's daughter Dora was stamping her high-heeled shoes and clapping her bangled hands while her friend Pietro, a clown of a man, rotund and bald and gold-toothed, began to swing and prance too. The salon was beginning to swirl with dancers; everyone was turning into a dancer.

The Signora, transfixed with horror, watched Krishna fold his arms about him and turn into a stone statue, even the bronze glint faded from him. How was she to distract him from this mood? She hurried away, thinking in her desperation of dear old Tatiana Bronowska, where was she? Tatiana went to every dance performance in Venice, entertained every dance troupe in her splendid salon, and knew Krishna; she would help, with all her enchanting gossip about Diaghilev, about Nijinsky and Pavlova . . . As the Signora searched for her, she heard voices around her she had been able earlier to ignore.

'Say what you like, my dear, but a man like Mussolini is needed if we are to recover, and as for the squadristi, why should you fear them? They are here to protect us, and have they not brought the strikes to an end? Do you remember what one went through? But they have things under control now. Without them, we should be taken over by the Bolsheviks – '

'Oh, what fantasies! Are we not a democracy? have we not elections?'

'You wish to leave such matters to the populace? What gives you such confidence?'

The Signora raised her hands to her ears; she could not bear such talk in the midst of what was to have been a celebration, a festival of beauty. She looked guiltily towards Krishna to see if he had heard them too, and then saw Laila, stepping forwards from the dancing swirl, holding a small glass of orange juice in her hand and offering it to Krishna as prettily as if it were a flower, smiling in that way both flirtatious and serene that the Signora found so breathtaking. It was a totally Indian gesture and Indian expression, and yet Laila was not Indian: what was she? The Signora stared and watched as she coaxed Krishna into accepting the glass, into smiling even, caressingly, in a way that perfectly complemented hers.

The following morning she sent for Laila – Gianni brought the message to her as she sat on the parquet floor of the salon, untying her anklets after an hour of solitary exercises amidst the debris of the party. The Signora waited for her up in the small room on the top floor. She was seated on the bed, holding in her lap a little box. She looked at Laila with the face of a child trying very hard to be brave and not cry. She must have been crying earlier: her face was pinker than ever.

'Oh, thank you for coming, my dear,' she said to Laila, 'thank you. You are so sweet. What will I do when you all leave – ' She began to search for a handkerchief but she did not want to release the box and so was not successful. Her face seemed to dissolve.

Laila stood at the foot of the bed, holding the anklets in her hand, waiting. She shifted on her bare feet, she hoped not too evidently with impatience: if only the leavetakings were done with and they could go.

The Signora did not miss the impatience. She opened the box hurriedly and held out something that shone on the palm of her hand. 'It is an opal. The setting is Venetian, in silver. I wanted – I tried to give it to Krishna-ji, but he would not take it from me. He said he could not. Why? I wanted him so much to have it. It belonged to my family – to my grandmother – and is what you call an heirloom.' She turned it over and over with trembling fingers. 'It really belongs here, in the Casa Rosa. But I thought it would be, for Krishna-ji, a nice – a nice memento.' She looked at Laila in appeal for understanding but Laila's face betrayed no feeling whatever. 'No, Krishna-ji will not take it from me. So please, my dear, will you let me give it to you? And I will ask you please, when you have left Venice, to give it to him. He will not be able to return it to me then, you see,' she explained when Laila frowned, puzzled by the Signora's plan. 'I want him to have a memento of his time in the Casa Rosa. Perhaps he will wear it sometimes? On his hand, you know, the opal will look – ah, bellissimo!' she ended and began to cry, holding out the ring so piteously that Laila stepped forward, plucked the ring from her hand and marched out, wanting only to bring the curtain down on the scene.

That night Laila was woken by a dream so vivid that it broke through her sleep. She saw Krishna lying in the water of the canal, a few feet below the surface, his silk shawl and his long hair spread out around him, floating with the weeds. She was stooping over him in terror when a long black gondola sped up and slid right over him, its whole black length like a hearse covering him. When it had passed, there was no sign left of Krishna but a great trail of bright red blood instead, flowing river-like through the canal between the palazzi.

She shot up in bed with the horror of that bright blood washing against the stones, lapping even at her bare feet. She sat clutching her knees to her and panting for a normal, waking breath and saw, at the window, the moon so bright that it must have been that that woke her.

The Signora came down the steps to see them into the gondola although it was so early that the dim light tinged everyone's faces green and made tempers short. She was sending Gianni along to see them onto the train at the station; she would not come herself: it was not clear if Krishna had forbidden her to and she was obeying orders, or if she was staying back to see to Sonali who was to be sent on her way to India later in the day; the Signora had booked a passage for her. 'You must not worry about her,' the Signora assured them as Gianni helped them onto their seats. 'I will take such good care of her, she will be safe, and when you reach India – there she will be, waiting – '

'Yes, yes, yes,' Krishna snapped in annoyance, wrapping his shawl about him against the damp of early morning. 'She will be safe, you will be safe, all will be safe. But now we must leave or we will miss our train and then we will not be so safe.'

The Signora stepped back as if slapped. For a moment shock wiped every expression off her face so that it seemed a part of the stones of the wall behind her.

The gondolier was bending at the waist to exert every effort upon the pole and cast off from the steps. The water swirled as the boat veered about and Gianni's voice rang out in the silence like a gull's: 'Damn! I have water in my shoe!' Shanta and Chandra tittered behind their hands. Laila craned to see the early sun light up the gulls that swooped along the length of the canal, crying, and the tops of the palazzi, bits of gold pricked out in the grey and beginning to gleam. Krishna touched her hand and said, 'My princess, my rani.'

While the others watched the scene slide by, bemused by the light and the silence, she opened the box she held in her hand and took out the Signora's ring. It looked pretty, even moon-like in the half light. She held it out to Krishna. 'The Signora gave me this,' she said, 'to give you. She wanted you to wear it.'

He was looking at her hand, at the delicacy and slimness of her fingers, and their pallor. He only glanced at the ring and it seemed to fill him with disgust. 'That? That is only silver, and an opal. How can I wear such a thing?' He gestured it away. Laila was left with the ring in the palm of her hand.

༄

Sophie arrives at the courtyard by way of a small wooden door in the lane at the back of the house. This is not a grand entrance, in fact it is mean, but the courtyard is the same that can be entered through a great doorway that opens onto a flight of stone stairs that leads down to the canal. For such an entrance, however, a gondola would be necessary and Sophie has not engaged one. The courtyard is cobbled but there is one camellia tree, not in bloom, and in the corners some tall uncut grass, quick movements and rustling to indicate a family of felines that lives there invisibly, but there are none of the torches, or the sudden and striking exits and entrances that might be imagined as within the history of such a house and of which she knows only one slight chapter.

She has written ahead to announce her visit – or, rather, to request it, and she is expected, so she climbs the stairs to where she thinks is the salon where Laila first danced in public, the Venetian public, if such a word can be used for that galaxy of Italian society as had once been guests here.

But the white-haired but still upright woman who meets her at the top of the stairs takes her down a narrow hall to a small room that carpets, chairs, framed photographs, boxes and a tea tray contrive to make even smaller. Box-like, it is clearly a compartment of a larger room that has been divided, as great houses so often are. A glance upwards shows the mouldings on the ceiling disappear behind a wooden partition to spread elsewhere.

Sophie feels disappointed but she is asked, 'You will have tea?' with perfect politeness, if with the chill of caution, or suspicion even.

She feels tea can only help, not hinder, the questioning she must embark on, and accepts. She tries not to be too open in her searching of the woman's face, dress, hair, hands. Although she has found photographs of the Signora, she has never seen any of her daughter or the rest of the family. What strikes her now is the total absence of silks, jewels, flamboyance and colour that she has naively expected. Here is only plainness, economy, sobriety; not poverty, but not wealth either: the shoes are square and brown, the stockings cotton, the dress no designer's.

'Will you mind,' she asks when the silence is first broken into by the tinkling and clattering of tea things and then is empty again, 'if I ask you a little about your mother's friendship with the Indian dancer Krishna and the time he spent here in this house?'

As she had feared, the woman shrinks back a visible inch or two and her face is clenched with dislike. There is a yellow tinge to her skin, unhealthy. She holds her hands on her knees, tightly. How could the laughing, loving, rich and colourful Signora have mothered this daughter? But it was often so, the daughter recoiling from the mother even in the matter of physical resemblance. Doubtlessly she herself has a daughter who loves party frocks and trinkets –

'Is it necessary?' the woman queries with distaste.

'For a book I am writing,' Sophie apologises, drawing out a yellow notepad in an effort to look professional. The tea stays undrunk.

'And the book is about – ?'

'Ah, I see – so many characters. No, it is not about the dancer Krishna. Nor about your mother,' Sophie assures her. 'It is about a young girl who was with him – she was called Laila then.'

'Oh! And what is she called now?' asks the woman, raising her eyebrows very high.

Sophie laughs: the sarcasm is unexpected, and welcome. She settles back in the old leather of the chair, more at ease. 'She lives in India,' she informs the woman. 'She has become famous there. She is known as the Mother.'

'And whose mother is she?' the woman queries.

Again Sophie finds herself laughing at the tone, so sharply sarcastic. 'No one's! She has, I believe, no children. Perhaps no husband either. But she is the Mother in – in the religious sense.'

'A Mother of God?'

Sophie explodes into a giggle: she is enjoying this. 'A Mother in an ashram in India. Mother to the devotees there – ' she tries to explain, and finds she must explain on and on. The clock against the wall strikes five with a loud, ringing whirr and much clatter, making her stop short. 'It's already five! And I had wanted to ask you – do you remember her?'

'I never saw this Mother,' the woman replies promptly and emphatically, 'and no one like her. As a child I saw the dancer Krishna often in our house. That was enough.'

'Do you have any letters of your mother's regarding this person? Or photographs that I might see?'

For a moment it seems that Sophie has gone too far, intruding too much. The woman seems to withdraw again, hold herself in tightly, as if checked. But she undoes her fist, gets to her feet and goes to the desk that stands under the clock and, opening a drawer, brings out a box. 'When you wrote you were coming,' she says, 'I brought these down from my mother's room. For you to see.'

Sophie is on her feet too, her hands eager to receive. 'Oh, how kind. Thank you. You can't imagine what this means – '

'It is nothing,' the woman says shortly. 'They are just old photos. They mean nothing to me. Those dancers – they were an obsession of my mother's, unfortunately. An expensive one. You can look through them if you like. I can't promise what you are looking for.' Spilling them out of the box onto the sofa, she leaves the room with the tea tray.

Sophie thinks she is alone now with the photographs but something she had taken for a lump, a piece of knitting or a cushion, heaves up on a corner of the sofa and leaps to the ground to follow the woman out of the room as though the photographs are the final insult.

Sophie walks slowly back to the Campo San Barnabas to catch the last of the evening light before returning to the hotel which will be, she knows, dark and damp and unwelcoming. Here the flat white façade of the church still catches the light and shines, and in the campo a priest in his black frock kicks a football lustily into a cluster of boys who, with yells, scatter to pursue it and kick it back. Sophie presses against the sunlit wall, feeling the warmth of the sun, watching the game as it disappears towards the far end of the campo.

Her bags are packed, she is waiting for the bellboy to carry them down into the lobby. As she stands smoking a last cigarette, looking out onto a narrow strip of a canal below her window where a cat is delicately performing its toilette in the bow of a gently rocking gondola, it occurs to her that there is still time to telephone the children once more before she leaves, and she turns to the telephone, begins to dial.

She had visited them briefly, between her visits to Paris and Venice, to reassure herself, and them. Had she been reassured? Certainly they had been as well and happy in that house on the lake as she could have hoped. But it had troubled her to see the degree to which it had become their home, as if they had no other. It was to their grandparents they talked of their day at school or their play in the garden and although they had been patient and polite in their response to Sophie's fumbling questions and caresses, it had been clear they no longer needed her. This should have been a relief to her, but it also hurt.

Now their voices seemed to travel across a great distance to reach her. They have been called in from the garden and there is still some rough play going on between them that she can hear in their giggles, in their panting. 'I will be back soon and we will go rowing together,' she tries to tell them but they are not listening. She winds up with a forlorn admonishment: 'Now be good. Listen to Nonna and Nonno. Don't give them any trouble – ' and puts the phone down and stands listening to the silence that follows with a great sense of desolation falling upon her like the fine mist of Venice.

It comes to her that in her search for the Mother she is abandoning them much as Matteo has abandoned her in his search, and that in following her she is entering an area of the chill, bleak bitterness of renunciation. Matteo has his belief, but she has – nothing. She feels fear beginning to creep over her and when the bellboy enters the room with his trolley and his hearty, 'Buon giorno,' he finds her standing with her arms wrapped around herself and a stricken look on her face.

Sophie picks her way through dog turds and litter on the pavement, looking up at the brownstones on either side of the street that block out the sunlight and cast everything into shadow. The number she searches for is at the end of the street, almost obscured by tall laurels and a heavy iron lantern. There is no signboard. She climbs the steps and puts her finger on the bell. She can hear it ring inside the closed, silent mansion. No one replies, and she is left shifting from one foot to the other, and peering in through the window. No one appears.

~

If in Venice there had been a surfeit of sights and scenes and textures and colours, then here in New York their world seemed stripped of them or, at least, concealed from the troupe of Indian dancers that entered Mrs du Best's mansion. Everything was covered with dust sheets that were themselves the colour of dust; the carpets had been rolled up against the walls; the chandeliers hung in bags and could not be lit. Their slippered feet made dispirited, lamenting sounds in the big, bare rooms as they followed Mrs du Best's secretary through them and down the hall, glancing covetously into the rooms they passed in the hope of finding some glimpse of comfort and hospitality.

At the very end of the hall some smaller rooms were found for them which the secretary informed them would be put in order; the manner in which he gave them this information made it clear that he was most reluctant to perform this service and would have preferred not to; he was not to be persuaded that this would have been Mrs du Best's wish.

Once more an incredulous Krishna said to him, 'And she did not tell you? She did not say anything about our coming?'

He had asked too often; the young man's very pale eyes flashed behind his spectacles and his 'No!' was explosive under the small bristle of a ginger moustache. 'Mrs du Best has many, many things on her hands at this moment, many new projects that she has. If you did not have her letter to show me, sir, I would not have admitted you at all.'

Krishna, seeing that the letter was the one card he could

play, opened it once more under the young man's nose, rustling the sheet of paper as loudly as he could. 'Yes, you have read it now. You can see we are invited, and are expected. She promised us – '

The young man tried to brush it away. 'I can say nothing about that till I have spoken to her.'

'You will be speaking to her? When?'

'I shall be telephoning her regarding your arrival, of course.'

'Then let me have a word also,' Krishna said at once, and followed him back down the hall, clutching the letter.

The others stayed back, hoping the telephone call would correct the mistake and turn back the clock and allow them to re-enter the house in the manner they had expected.

However, that was not so: Krishna was cryptic in his report on the telephone call when he returned; it had clearly not gone as well as they had hoped. 'Now she is telling me her husband's business is in trouble because of Prohibition,' he informed them, clearly flustered. 'She is with him in Pittsburgh, or somewhere where they had their breweries. She has to stay there and cannot come.'

'Then?' asked the women fearfully, huddling together in one of the small rooms.

'Then? Then what? We will stay here and practise and prepare our performance so when she comes back she can book a hall for us and arrange the publicity as she promised.'

'Ah!' they exclaimed with some relief; then added, 'When?'

'When? I can't tell you when, she did not say when,' he grumbled and, picking up his bag, went in search of a room of the kind to which he had become accustomed. There was martyrdom in his posture – his stooping back and handling of the heavy bag without their help which he insisted on waving away.

One of the maids appeared, however, sent by the secretary, it seemed, and taking the bag out of his hands said crisply, 'Follow me, sir.'

From then on they were in the hands of the staff. It had been invisible and, for a large part of the time, remained so. Clearly, the cavernous mansion had a subterranean region in which it was housed, but its presence was sternly disciplinary and could not be ignored. There was no possibility of going into the kitchen and cooking for themselves the familiar things they longed for; meals were served on the dot of time, at a glass-topped table under one of the bundled-up chandeliers, to be eaten by the etiolated light of the bulbs fixed to the dark green walls, and the meals were what the staff chose to present regardless of whether the guests found them edible or not. Krishna pleaded in vain for rice and vegetables and curds, and for the removal of offending pieces of meat, but the secretary shrugged his shoulders and said it was not a matter he dealt with and therefore he could make no change. 'Mrs du Best gives the orders,' he said.

'Mrs du Best can never give such orders!' Krishna retorted, but this made the secretary turn quite pale with anger, and his voice rose as he replied, 'Are you suggesting, sir, that I am guilty of an untruth?'

Even the small narrow rooms they had been assigned remained cheerless, in an area of the house devoid of carpets or curtains and clearly deemed second-rate by the owner and the decorators. Even if they threw their shawls and sandals about, these were instantly picked up and cleared out of sight so the rooms would continue to look, as far as possible, unoccupied.

The women huddled on the dust-cover-laid sofas in the grey living room; the musicians stood at the windows and stared through the long oblongs of glass at worlds of grey – grey concrete, grey stone, grey streets, a lead-coloured sky. In the leaden light that entered the room the dancers in their coloured silks, drooping on the dust-shrouded furniture, might have been trapped insects, doomed and despairing.

The first to venture out was Laila. Murmuring something about needing a cake of soap or some other essential article, she slipped past the secretary's room which stood open beside the front entrance, and shut the door as quietly as possible behind her.

Then she made the discovery that at the end of their own lifeless street was an avenue so crowded, so busy, so raucous that she was at once overpowered by the contrast as well as its similarity to something she had known in an earlier existence – the streets of Alexandria and Cairo. The discordant yelling of the vendors, the barrows of food spoiling in the sun, the smell of rotten fruit and vegetables lying in the gutters, the dusty window displays, the garish signboards, a wide leer here, a sly gesture there, the sense of hurry, of crowding, of overtaking and invasion – the memory of them overwhelmed her in a great wave and then receded, leaving her shaken and wondering where it was that she had arrived. Nevertheless, she was determined to set out and explore, determined not to return to the tomb-like house and its atmosphere of funereal despondency.

Here summer had not halted life. Bakers were delivering racks of bread, coalmen dumping sacks of coal down chutes on the sidewalks, butchers heaving great sides of stiff white meat out of carts and onto their backs to deliver, and when a water wagon went by, spraying the street, the odours of horse dung and gasoline stirred up out of the mud. Children were jumping in the spray from a water hydrant, pushing at each other and screaming with the joy of it.

Laila looked up at the window cleaners dizzyingly at work in the sunlit spheres above and then down into the shop windows to study arrangements of coloured candy in one, fish lying on slabs of ice in another, and brushed past the suits and flowered frocks hanging from racks and awning bars.

By evening she was in Central Park with its trampled grass and drooping trees in full summer leaf, slow horse carriages drawn by great blinkered horses, people on benches, slumped forwards or tipped backwards. As dusk fell a band struck up – she could hear the cornets and tubas and drums pounding and bleating somewhere. Her feet turned in their direction, drawn to the expectation of music and dance, but she became aware of darkness falling and the need to return.

As she walked back – and by now her feet were swollen, red

and burning – electric lights were coming on all along Broadway with a profligacy she had never imagined, lighted headlines running around the Times building in Times Square, the theatres all lit up, advertising *The Best Show in Town, The Dancin' Devils, Black and White Minstrel Show, Worth's Family Theatre, Vaudeville Show Tonight, The Casino Roof Theatre* – against a sky that flickered and filled with these ranting screams for attention.

Although the dance troupe had been beside itself with anxiety during her absence, and explosive in their reprimands when she returned, her daring did have an effect upon the fear and disappointment into which they had retreated and in which they had been living. The truth was that they were admiring of her, even envious, and now some of them determined to emulate her. The musicians, in particular, began to find excuses to go out, and stayed away for longer and longer periods. The strict discipline and sense of corporate endeavour they had maintained till now threatened to come apart in the lazy dissipated atmosphere of high summer.

As if aware that if he allowed this to go on he would be left without a troupe or a tour, Krishna announced he would set out himself in search of a promoter, see the managers of some theatres where they might perform, discuss the arrangements for their performances. If Mrs du Best was not there to do this for them, he would. The women all looked at him dubiously; they smiled and nodded but their eyes were hooded and they glanced at each other. That spurred him into making even grander promises to arrange a season of performances here in New York to be followed by a tour in the autumn.

'Do you know anyone in New York?' Laila ventured to ask. 'Managers, agents?'

He took it for insolence. How could she have doubts about his abilities? 'No, I don't know any,' he replied heatedly, 'but they know me. Have I not performed here before? Before you joined our group? Sonali, Vijaya – they know, they were with me. I have reviews, press cuttings, from American papers, I can show them – '

Laila began to play with the end of her pigtail. It was the most innocuous gesture she could make. The rest were silent.

They had forgotten, in this period of discouragement and uncertainty, that Krishna had indeed performed in America previously, although not in New York – and they were unaware that made a difference. He had performed as a boy in San Francisco and Los Angeles in 1910 when people still remembered the figure of Swami Vivekananda in his orange robes and stately turban, lecturing at the Congress of Religions, and the thrill of his voice 'resounding out of the distant caves of the East', as one reporter had written. In any case, on that coast there was a large Oriental population and a climate in which mysticism and the exotic could thrive. The San Francisco papers had carried columns of advertisements placed by clairvoyants and spiritualists, and the variety theatres presented Greek dances, Mexican dances, Chinese gymnasts and acrobats – anything foreign and from far away. And in that heady atmosphere the sublime Pavlova herself had proclaimed an interest in Indian dance and chosen their compatriot Uday Shankar to partner her on a tour sponsored by the great Sol Hurok which was even now having a glittering success.

Did they know that? Krishna demanded of them. And Uday Shankar was not the only Indian dancer to perform in the West. Here he flourished the programmes of the troupe with which he had performed the dances of Shiva and Parvati, of Radha and Krishna, with the very young Sonali as leading dancer – billed as Sonali Devi. 'Exquisite, charming, mysterious,' the reviews read – he pointed out the line with a threatening finger – 'A living world of indescribable grace', 'Eastern magic', 'Entertainment extraordinary . . .'

The dancers were chastened and became respectful. Only Mrs du Best, when reached by telephone, voiced scepticism. 'Krishna, a tour of the kind you plan is a costly thing. And I have explained how my husband's business is ruined by Prohibition. We are trying to start all over again and it's not easy.'

Taking up his big folder of cuttings, he slammed out of the house with more determination than ever.

To their astonishment, he did eventually secure an engagement (he told no one the number of managers' offices he had visited – even forced his way into – clutching the pink folder, or how many rebuffs and even hoots of derision he had met with). Modestly – he could afford to be modest now – he admitted, 'We will not be putting on a performance by ourselves – Mr Herbert Moody says no one in America will listen to Indian music or watch Indian dance one whole evening, but we will be able to perform two, three dances in between other performances – '

'What performances?' they asked, bewildered.

He was evasive. 'Other Oriental dances and music. Some from China, some from Japan, Egypt . . . an Oriental evening, that is Mr Moody's idea.' He refused to be more specific, pleading ignorance. Also, the lack of time and the urgency to prepare.

In spite of the secretary's furious protests, he insisted on rolling the furniture in the drawing room into corners and against the walls, clearing space on the parquet floor for their rehearsals. As in Venice, they woke up before dawn now to make their salutations to the sun, and perform yogic exercises that he insisted on as a necessary discipline, and then begin, to the sound of drums and cymbals, to practise the dances he intended to present. Using American ignorance and impatience as a reason, he cut down the lengthy ballet he had choreographed in Signora Durante's hospitable salon, to brief five- and ten-minute sketches. No longer did he speak of the artistic purity of dance, or the spiritual quality at its heart; instead, he added to the dance of Radha and Krishna a sketch called 'Hindu Wedding' that showed Laila as a coy bride, and another called 'Eastern Bazaar' in which Chandra and Shanta were transformed into flower girls. Even the musicians were to join in the last by abandoning their instruments – no need for strings, percussion alone was necessary and that was provided by a grim Vijaya – and tying coloured turbans around their heads and rising to their feet to stamp and swirl alternately. 'This is America,' Krishna reminded them. 'We too must become children like them. Play, please, *play*,' he begged as they stood around uncertainly and awkwardly. When Laila was taught how to undulate her arms and imitate the rippling motion of a snake, Shanta and Chandra exploded into giggles and old Vijaya's lips plunged downwards in harsh disapproval. Laila became stiff with self-consciousness, understanding that this dance had nothing to do with any religious belief or spiritual exercise, Indian or otherwise. But he, perspiring profusely in the sweltering heat of a summer morning, wiped his brow and wheedled, cajoled, and manoeuvred till they did his bidding.

Now it was time to design the costumes and props. Here was no kindly Signora Durante to undertake these tasks for them – much of what she had sent with them proved useless now, and in any case new stuff was required, but on the telephone Mrs du Best only hummed her long hmms and cautioned Krishna, 'Please, no extravagance, my friend. You know how Prohibition has ruined everything – '

'Prohibition? What has Prohibition to do with our dance? People will forget everything when they see our dance,' he replied, leading her into another doubting, 'Hmmm. You are very lucky, you know, to get an engagement at short notice in the summer – hardly the season.'

Exasperated, he decided to go ahead without her, and by riffling through the telephone book, made a glorious find – the Asia Bazaar on Fifth Avenue, whose owners, a wealthy family from Bombay, not only opened up to them a virtual treasure-house of silks and brocades, shawls and trinkets, and all the brassware and incense they required, but proved magnani-mous in their patronage, claiming to be proud to be of service and offering not only discounts and special rates but more help than even Krishna had counted on mobilising. The joy of it went to his head: he took the women shopping in the aisles of the Asia Bazaar, delightedly drawing off the shelves treasures to make their eyes, and his, gleam.

Then he moved his troupe into the theatre for rehearsals. The time allotted them was between three and five in the afternoons when, unfortunately, in their Indian way, they were most overcome by heat and lassitude and barely able to stay awake. But he himself was galvanised into activity; gone was his magisterial dignity, his godlike aloofness, as he rushed about the stage, directing them, exhorting them, in a kind of frenzy of will and energy. It was his first experience of stage organisation, of having to play not only director but producer and agent as well: the New World imposed its tricks on him, and dire need created the impulse to accept them.

Returning from their exhausting rehearsals, when the others retired to their rooms to rest, Laila withdrew onto a fire escape she found leading out of the bedroom into a small square fenced backyard, nothing more than a square of gravel and rubble over which neighbourhood cats prowled amongst the cans and bottles tossed in by residents. The sky was still brassy with afternoon light, and she sat with her arms about her knees, her head hanging low as she pondered this phase in the journey, one which she had not expected or prepared for or wanted.

At night she sat at the foot of his bed, looking out of the open window at the street now lit by lamps that peered in intrusively. The headlights of cars flickered over the walls and travelled across the floor and the bed, lighting them up and keeping her awake.

'Go to sleep, Laila,' he muttered on waking and seeing her, then turned over to indicate his own intention to sleep, but she continued to sit there, would not even lie down. So much was unsaid in her mind that clamoured by night when others were silent, so much rose up in the dark that would not subside. Like the lights of New York, that was when they blazed most fiercely.

When he was breathing evenly in his sleep, even snoring a little, she said in a low, level voice, 'This is wrong. It is not right, Krishna. I will not do it. I will leave you. I promise.'

If he had woken then, he would have seen the expression on her face in that nocturnal light, and paid attention.

Nevertheless Herbert Moody's show, *Oriental Nights*, opened on a steamy summer night as advertised, and the curtains parted on a pyramid of cages filled with lions over which a moustachioed gentleman in scarlet tights, and whose name, according to the programme, was Signor Furioso, cracked his whip in an effort to draw roars out of the somnolent beasts. All they emitted was the stench of sick animal flesh that filled the backstage dressing rooms with its heavy, nauseating presence. The dancers went barefoot down the narrow passage, past open toilets and fiercely lit cells where other performers desperately painted their faces pink and purple, teased their hair into forests of tinsel or caps of brilliantine, and either donned or tore off footwear of a dozen ethnic origins.

Their turn was billed *Hindu Temple Dances from East India,* and prominent beside Krishna's name was that of the leading dancer Lila Devi. (It was the first official appearance of the name Lila, the one Laila assumed and retained thereafter.) Krishna had devised a cardboard construct of a South Indian temple; the incense that drifted out of two tall burners on either side and the shadows cast by the flickering light of a lamp in one corner where the musicians were seated, turned it into sand and stone for the audience. Vijaya had set up her brass statue of the Nataraja, the Dancing Shiva, and although no marigolds were to be had, or the chrysanthemums that might have imitated them, a handful of sunflowers had been found and thrust into a brass vase before it while the Bhambanis of Asia Bazaar had arranged for a garland of roses.

This Laila held in her hands as she appeared out of the portals of the temple (the audience did not question why Radha the Shepherdess should emerge from a South Indian temple rather than a grove upon a northern river bank). The flute piped up its sweet lament and to its tune the Divine Lover appeared from the shadows, garbed in blue body paint, gold jewellery and peacock feathers and only a brief saffron

257

loincloth. He performed his dance, Radha garlanded him, and the themes of love and worship blended into each other without anyone noticing.

In some confusion, the audience stirred and clapped, yawned and sighed, then sat up for the next item, the livelier spectacle of a Turkish dervish dance. A great many waiters had been rounded up from around the city, as well as sailors from ships at the docks that were held up for one reason or another; now they were dressed in white robes, topped with tarbooshes and set whirling in giddy circles. Laila appeared once more, and, to everyone's relief, not in a sepulchral temple courtyard but in the gaiety and colour of an eastern bazaar. For this Krishna's good friend and patron, Jal Bhambani, had been entirely responsible: the carpets strewn about so lavishly, the baskets heaped with bananas and oranges, even watermelons split into halves and quarters upon brass trays, garlands of paper flowers drenched in rose and jasmine water, and a multitude of brass pots and vessels everywhere. Shanta and Chandra wandered through this maze of merchandise, baskets of fruit and flowers held on their heads or at their waists, and Krishna had transformed some of the clerks from Asia Bazaar by dressing them in gold vests and bright turbans into rich customers who engaged them in banter. Krishna himself was seated centre stage, dressed in rustic rags of ochre and russet, a disreputable turban askew on his head, bending and swaying vigorously as he played his pipe above a flat basket before him. He leant forward to remove the lid from the basket, and the rings on his fingers with huge green glass jewels soldered onto them gave a sinister glitter. It was at this point that Laila sidled onto the stage in a flesh-coloured body suit striped here and there with black. Her eyes had been painted with kohl into long, large spheres, and her hands covered by Vijaya with intricate henna patterns, making them positively like snake skin. She lifted her arms and began to ripple them with a sinuous, boneless motion, then wrapped them around herself, her fingers too beginning to ripple, while her feet slithered over the floor as she mimed a dancing cobra. The itinerant hawkers and customers stopped to watch, Krishna's pipe played and played till at last it arrived at a long hiss and Laila, as cobra, subsided to the ground and vanished beneath the ochre shawl that he flung over her as a lid.

The audience had gasped to begin with; some had even whistled, but after the rippling and slithering had gone on for a while, a certain restlessness set in, and in subsequent performances Krishna elaborated the minimal roles of Chandra and Shanta to add to the movement on the stage, much to their delight.

'They will not detract any attention from your central role,' he assured Laila who replied in a low voice, 'If you ask me to leave the stage altogether, I shall not mind a bit.'

There was no question of that and after an Egyptian belly dancer had displayed her delectably roly-poly skills, and a Japanese dance that confused Madame Butterfly with a dancing insect rather than the tragic heroine of an opera, Laila returned to the stage for the final dance concocted by Krishna to woo the New York audience: a Hindu wedding for which she was dressed in a sari of scarlet sprinkled with gold spangles and edged with tiny bells. She played the modest, the shy, the flirtatious and eventually ecstatic bride, to begin with seated and her sari drawn veil-like over her face, then, in response to Krishna's questing look and pleading gestures, raising it to reveal herself and meet his eyes, finally rising to dance with him while Shanta and Chandra showered them with rose petals and Vijaya, clashing her cymbals, sang full-throatedly of love's sweet madness.

Dripping and exhausted, Laila was assisted off the stage by a Krishna whose solicitude lasted only till they were out of sight of the audience, and then there was a rush to disrobe and to pack their belongings and move out to make way for a Cambodian dance duo and the Chinese acrobats who were already whirling cups and plates in the air and drawing paper umbrellas out of ice cream cones.

Out in the foyer of the theatre, decorated kiosks had been set up to serve Oriental food instead of the usual cigarettes and ice cream. The Indian kiosk, installed by the Bhambanis, served spicy sweet tea and vegetable fritters; their shop clerks, now dressed as waiters, grand turbans on their heads, went around offering glasses and platefuls on brass trays. They had even been induced to salaam the audience that was streaming out at the interval and was reduced to giggles by this unusual experience. Everyone sweated in that enclosed heat and many were heard to exclaim, 'It could be India!'

'Sixth Avenue Darkies in Bells and Turbans bring India to Broadway!'
   'Temple Rituals by Hindu Dancers Mystify!'
   'Southern Tribe of American Indians in Gold Paint and Mosquito Netting!'
   'Lila is one of the most lyrical dancers on the stage, posing and floating in her golden veils.'
   'Krishna is an Indian magician who produces dancers like snakes out of a snake charmer's basket and makes the audience swoon.'

Mr Herbert Moody was more plainspoken and less flowery in his reaction. 'That music you folks play – it just drives everyone right out of the theatre,' he said flatly. 'Sounds like every one of your instruments is out of tune. I'm just telling you what everyone *says*. No one's going to put up with that, or pay good money for it. Do something about it.'
   'About the music of my country? You are asking me to create a music for American ears instead? To throw away my own heritage?'
   'Yeah, at least while you're dancing for us,' Mr Moody said, without a bit of sympathy.
   Krishna's brow lowered and darkened like a thundercloud but Mr Moody had already turned to the Japanese dancer and was saying, 'Speed it up a bit, will ya? It's just too damn slow for New Yorkers. This ain't corn country, you know, where folks are willing to sit and watch the corn grow – '
   He paid no more attention to Krishna. The problem was

something he would have to work out with the musicians. To his amazement, they were not nearly as perturbed or offended as he had feared. In fact, it turned out they had their own plans and did not intend to go on tour with *Oriental Nights* at all: they had been offered jobs in an Indian restaurant, the Taj Palace, where they were to prepare the vegetarian curries.

'You will work as cooks?' Krishna was incredulous, and the women speechless with dismay.

The musicians, however, seemed to feel no such compunction – they had been offered better pay, and intended to enjoy New York. They packed their belongings cheerfully and moved into lodgings on Lexington Avenue, near the restaurant. Krishna was left with the problem of devising music for his dances. A frantic appeal was telephoned to the absent patron, and Mrs du Best was begged for advice. She generously got in touch with the Progressive Stage Society and located an Orientalist who came over to the house with an armful of records and information regarding the music of Debussy and Delibes that they might use. The opera *Lakmé* yielded exactly what was needed for the bazaar scene.

Another decision forced upon Krishna by the outspoken Mr Moody was to cut down the number of nuptials celebrated on stage: the duet of Radha and Krishna was exchanged for Laila's peacock dance which proved, luckily, a spectacular success.

'Indian ballerina – Bird or Reptile?' screamed the newspapers.

The young Jal Bhambani who had bought a seat in the front row for the opening night was so enthralled that he bought one for every other night of the show, and the night on which Laila first performed as a peacock in her glittering lamé skirt with an aquamarine light illuminating her jewelled train, he stood waiting at the stage door for the dance troupe and urged them to allow him to drive them home in his car. They were not enthusiastic – tired as they were, they looked forward to walking back so they could stop at the food barrows and buy nuts and fruit and bread since Mrs du Best's staff claimed they

261

had no instructions to offer food to guests who came home later than six o'clock in the evening – but found it hard not to give in to Jal's importuning. However, Krishna turned down very firmly his invitation to dinner at a restaurant: none could be trusted, in New York, to offer them vegetarian fare untainted by meat.

The newspapers reported the exotic, outlandish adventures of the Oriental dancers in their midst:

'Court Musicians of India Leave to Cook Curry on Lexington Avenue!'

'Nautch Dancers Seen Leaving Theatre in Black Chevy – Whose?'

'Peacock Finds Perch in New York!'

Krishna, studying the headlines, seemed not to know whether to be pleased by the attention or dismayed by the content; his face was a study in conflicting emotions.

The stage and the nightly performance gave Laila a raging headache, making it impossible for her to sleep, exhausted as she was. She remained upright on a sofa, while her colleagues brought her wet cloths to lay on her forehead and occasionally stayed to massage her neck or her feet in an effort to ease her distress. Tears sometimes ran down her cheeks because the pain was so acute, and she cried to them, 'No, no, you can't help me. No one can help me –' in a way that made them stand back and shake their heads in gloomy foreboding. Jal Bhambani was beside himself with concern and brought her all kinds of goods from his father's store that he thought might ease her pain – giant bottles of eau-de-Cologne and rose water, salves and ointments – but none did. Krishna would toss them aside, saying with grim satisfaction, 'I knew they would not.'

He himself was brusque when he addressed her in the presence of others, and seemed least concerned about her agony, anxious only that she be well by morning for practice sessions and rehearsals. She usually managed to be, although pale and strained after the night's ordeal. He would always smile with relief and gratitude when she appeared for the morning session, and once, after she had run through all the exercises without a word of protest or complaint, drew her to him when the others had left and told her, with his old tenderness and warmth, 'When we go to India, I will take you to my old *hakim*; he has cures no one in the West has even heard of – he will cure you.' She looked at him, large-eyed with hope, and he said, in a low murmur, 'Don't worry, I *will* take you to India.'

The contract, however, had to be fulfilled: the theatre had been booked for three weeks; that had seemed short to Krishna when he had been offered it, but proved long to live through. The summer heat was rising, and the audience dwindled, clearly preferring to stroll in the park and listen to the band to buying tickets to be crowded into an airless theatre. In the second week the numbers dropped from five hundred to one hundred or so, and the decline continued.

Mr Moody devised other plans: he pared down the acts, allowing each of the Oriental troupes one turn on stage, no more, and hired reliable and durable American entertainers to fill the gaps between them – a trained poodle, a ventriloquist, an 'aerial ballet' performed by dancers on pulleys bathed in coloured lights, a 'danseuse gymnastique' in Greek robes, a 'kaleidoscopic bicycle dance' and a sword swallower (dressed in a Chinese hat and curled slippers to indicate Oriental connections for the sake of the title) – and booked them on a tour of the eastern states, through small towns that could do, he said, with some entertainment in the summer months.

It was not the kind of tour Krishna had been on previously when his patrons had been not hard-headed theatre managers and avaricious businessmen but artistic and wealthy ladies like Mrs du Best. Nonetheless, he urged his troupe, reduced as it was by the defection of the musicians, to pack their belongings and prepare for the tour.

New Jersey Advocate: 'Sensational Dances by Barefoot Dancers from Himalayas in New Jersey.'

Hartford Courier: 'Eastern Bazaar on Connecticut Stage.'

New Haven Independent: 'Fiery Curry of Eastern Dances Sets Stage on Fire.'

Springfield Bulletin: 'Snakes and Peacocks from East Arrive.'

Whenever Laila came near Krishna, sometimes at the centre of the stage, bathed by the rosy or the azure lights of the cyclorama, miming a bee and a lotus, or a hunter and a deer, and sometimes when they passed each other in the dim-lit hall of a boarding house, she said to him in a low voice no one else could overhear, 'Krishna, I will leave. I will not go on.' He had a particular expression he assumed at these moments, even under his stage make-up: it was indulgent, it was benign, but at the corner of his mouth there was a tightening to be seen as he answered, also under his breath, 'A little longer. Then we leave – together – for India.' He also told her, when not constrained by public view, to colour her pale cheeks and white lips. 'You are looking ill,' he said with disapproval. 'People are saying to me, this dancer seems ill. You must try to look healthy.'

'But I *am* ill,' Laila replied. 'Ill, ill, ill.'

He looked both shocked and disbelieving. 'What is wrong?' he asked, coldly and cautiously.

'You know the thing that is wrong. These headaches – I cannot sleep.'

'Oh,' he said, his voice lightening with relief. 'That will get all right.'

When he saw one of the Chinese acrobats pass her a little tin and watched her dip her finger into it and apply the contents to her temples, he came over to snatch it from her. 'What is this? Tiger balm? It is rubbish. These things won't help.'

Laila flushed, the Chinese acrobat took his tin back and left, and she said to Krishna with a sharpness not heard before in her voice, 'Only one thing will help. That I stop performing. That I stop this tour.'

He stood before her and took her hands in his, casting his eyes down sadly. 'Laila,' he said, 'if you do this, you will ruin

264

your Krishna who has given his word to Mr Moody to complete the tour and must make enough money so that you, and Vijaya, and Shanta and Chandra, can eat. Will you do that to me, your Krishna?'

On that day, in the middle of her dance, dressed in her peacock costume, she came to a standstill on the stage, her hands clasped to her face, and began to cry. At first the audience was not aware that this was not part of the dance she was performing, but they soon became uneasy, and Krishna hissed from behind the curtains, 'Laila, dance! Dance, Laila!' Slowly her hands resumed their pose, she began to sway again and later it was said that the lovelorn peacock's dance had never been so poignantly danced as on that night.

In Springfield they staggered out of the railway station in search of lodgings. Krishna led them, carrying his walking stick, and the four women followed him, carrying his bag for him along with their own.

As it grew darker, the women began to falter, hold back, reluctant to go further into the sinister unknown. 'Look,' Krishna urged them, pointing with his walking stick, 'see the light there – that must be the city centre. Come, we will find a hotel.'

They did: it was Miller's Family Hotel, A Strictly Temperance House, where the landlady, having served them bread and boiled vegetables at a long table lined with silent boarders, folded her hands to thank the Lord, and added, 'And may our visitors from the dark lands see the light and give up their pagan ways to follow Thy path, O Lord,' to which all breathed a husky, 'Amen.'

At Holyoke, silk and paper mills along the black and foetid canals, stares from curious passersby and suspicious landladies. The ramshackle wooden house where they boarded was no worse than its equivalent elsewhere, and a kind of resignation settled on them as they moved into it. Laila found herself sharing a room with Vijaya at the end of a narrow passage across from the common lavatory; it had a chipped enamel bowl in the corner to wash in and its single window looked out onto the kitchen window of the house next door so that the torn blind had to be kept lowered for privacy, resulting in an instant and early darkness falling across the brown wallpaper, the yellow linoleum and the fly-flecked poster of a winsome girl advertising a brand of soap.

They were the only guests at the landlady's table. Handing out plates of cabbage soup, she told them, 'Time was when folks lived off the land. Now they're all in the mills. Ain't no living to be made off the land any more, eh?' She handed them bread, dry and hard, and went on gloomily, 'So farmhands are what I get now, in my own house.' She seemed to think they were darkies off the cotton fields and there seemed no point in enlightening her.

It took their appetite away, they hardly ate. When she said grace, it was said grimly as if accusing the Lord rather than thanking him. They retired early so as to rest before the next day's show at the Victory Theatre.

The following night Laila told the other dancers that she would not eat dinner and would stay in her room to nurse her headache. When she heard the sound of spoon on plate and glass on wood, she quickly changed from her Indian clothes into a dress she had last worn in Paris and that had been folded at the bottom of her cardboard case, creased and crumpled. Hastily collecting her toilet articles and putting them all in the case, she left the room, leaving the door open rather than click it shut, and went silently down the back stairs into the alley that ran along the tall sooty brick houses. Keeping her head low as she went by the fence, she hurried down the alley past the row of ashcans, and out onto the street where they caught the bus to the theatre every evening. She turned the other way and began to walk towards the railway station.

She did not know when she would be able to get a train. She did not even have a very good idea of where the railway station was located. Once she turned into a road where the red and blue lights of a diner indicated public habitation, but it only led down to one of the dark canals that oozed through the city. A phrase she had heard for the city in one of the boarding houses – 'the Venice of the North' – entered her mind like a sliver of cold iron.

Eventually she came to a corner store, a pawn shop, a laundry. All were closed but there were people sitting on the stoops of the stone houses across the road, listless in the summer night with nothing to do, and she asked the way to the station. They pointed it out to her, showing no curiosity now that she was no longer in Indian dress, and she hurried along in fear that Krishna might arrive before the train did. Then she reminded herself that he would be preparing for the evening performance, leaving for the theatre so as to be on time with his troupe, and would not be able to search for her till later. She was right and no one came for her as she stood under the railway bridge, looking up and down the dark street, then climbed the iron stairs to the platform where she bought a ticket for New York from a man sitting in a booth and reading a paper in the light of a lamp that spread over his counter like a pool of oil. He stared into her face as he handed it to her and said, 'That's the last train tonight.' She could hear it approach, whistling and grinding its great wheels to a halt.

'You must help me,' she informed Jal Bhambani, pressing the palms of her hands together in eloquent appeal. 'Give me work. Find me work.'

His face had gone waxen with fright. 'What work can I give you? You are a dancer, an artist.'

She shook her head violently. 'No,' she told him. 'No dancer, no artist. I am alone. I need work.'

'What work can I let you do?'

'Let me work in your shop,' she told him. That was why she had come to him in his small office at the back of the store, at his desk amongst the packing cases and crates that smelt of tea and incense.

He got up and began to pull on his jacket and hat. 'We'll go out. We'll talk outside,' he told her hurriedly, fearful that she might make a scene here, in front of his father and the shop assistants. Scenes should be kept in the theatre, he thought, flushing at the thought, and stood aside, holding open the door, showing her the way out, then leading her across the street and around the corner to a cafeteria.

Here he seated her at a marble-topped table in a corner, away from the plate glass window, and ordered tea. When the waitress had brought the tray and left it for them, he leaned across it – pale, tinged with a little yellow even – and explained, 'You can't be a shop girl in my father's store, Lila. I have too much respect for you.'

She was in tears of disappointment and humiliation, and sat crumpling a paper napkin in her hand, leaving the tea untouched although she had had nothing to eat or drink since she had arrived in New York: Mrs du Best's secretary, annoyed at her reappearance, had offered her nothing. She said something under her breath about his respect for her being of little help.

'Help, of course I will help,' he cried, 'but not – not in that way.'

'What way then?' she demanded. 'What way is there for me?'

As soon as they had exchanged those words, the idea of what the way might be entered their heads simultaneously, and along with it their revulsion from it. He had broken out in beads of perspiration at which he wiped constantly and surreptitiously, and she stood up, pushing her chair aside, and began to make her way out of the cafeteria, urgent in her need to leave. He rose, too, crying, 'Lila! Listen – wait, Lila!'

The waitress at the counter who had been moodily staring out over the row of salt and pepper shakers and vinegar cruets into the street outside, turned her gaze upon them. A man reading a newspaper lowered it to glance furtively at this cafeteria drama: the ashen-faced young man in a suit too tight and warm for this hot summer morning, the pale girl in an old-fashioned long black dress trying to push past him, averting her face.

Jal, choking in order to keep his voice down, repeated, 'Listen. I will take you to a friend of mine. He may help. He is a painter, he may let you model – '

She stopped to regard this suggestion, and her expression changed slowly into one of attentiveness. She turned around to question him.

Jal had returned to their table. He held her chair out for her so she could rejoin him. The waitress and the reader of the newspaper watched to see how it would go. She did return. As she did, he breathed, 'You are so – beautiful, Lila. Artists will paint you – '

'Will they pay?' she asked tersely. 'Will your friend pay?'

Jal stared down at the table and the untouched tea things. He could not bear to speak of payment, or money, to Laila. He thought of her as the shimmering creature from some tropical forest who had dazzled him on the stage, moving like a sylph to music that he coud still feel playing inside him. 'Please,' he said, 'drink your tea. Then I will take you to see him. Please have something to eat – a cake? An ice cream?'

Laila began to smile. She had not been asked that since she was a child; no one since then had imagined it might be what pleased her. She nodded. 'Both,' she said.

The waitress and the man with the paper saw her nod, smile. They sighed, returned to their familiar occupations, yawning slightly: the drama was over.

When Jal brought her back to the house on 174th Street, the secretary was in the hall, waiting. 'He is here,' he told her, grimly nodding towards the drawing room.

Krishna was standing against the curtained window. In the subdued light that filtered through, his face looked grey, the shadows under his eyes deep. His head was bowed, and his shoulders drooped. Instead of looking at her, he stared at the floor.

Seeing him so, Jal detached himself from Laila's side and began a curious crab-like motion that propelled him away from her, but unobtrusively, towards the door. She did not even notice his departure. After hesitating for a minute, she hurried forwards, faltering, 'Krishna-ji.' He still refused to look at her, only sighed. She came close to him, her face and hands contorted with distress, but still he refused to look at her. His eyes remained hooded and his head sank as he told her, 'The tour is over, Laila.'

She was agitated, not knowing whether to fall at his feet, or clasp him to her. Then he looked up and she saw in his eyes an unfamiliar emptiness: the glitter, the glint was gone. He said dully, 'We will go to India, as you wish.'

Laila did give a sob then, Krishna did relent, and they embraced. Thereupon they both began to talk volubly – he accused her of wrecking the tour and the troupe, she begged his forgiveness and pleaded for understanding. There was all the drama anyone could wish for, although sadly there was no audience, and all that stirred in that dim room were motes of dust circling in the air that they agitated.

Late that night they emerged from it, Krishna supporting a Laila close to collapse with exhaustion, but he himself erect now, recovered and with a regal stance to his head and shoulders and measured step. When the secretary looked up from his open door to see them pass, Krishna did not let go of his hold upon her waist. He even halted so the secretary would see them thus, and said, 'Please inform Mrs du Best we will be leaving soon, for India.'

'That,' said the young man, 'was what she suggested you do in the telegram I forwarded to Holyoke for you.'

Laila swayed a bit in Krishna's grasp, but she was not so exhausted that she did not hear. She tilted her head to regard Krishna. 'A telegram?' she questioned.

'Yes, the telegram I forwarded to Holyoke yesterday,' the secretary replied for him.

Krishna gave a nod, nonchalantly. 'Yes, she has very good news. She has been able to get us passage on a ship.'

'Yes, and she suggests you take it since it is free,' the secretary added, a trifle too loudly. 'You may not get such an offer later.'

'Oh,' said Laila, staring, 'then that is why you came away, Krishna.'

He had let his hand slip away from her waist and was walking down the hall to his room. Hearing her tone, he turned and said angrily, 'I came to take you to India. Didn't you say you wanted to go to India?'

'Yes,' she found herself crying, 'yes, Krishna.'

Mrs du Best did make an appearance, at the very end. She came on board the ship just before they sailed, looking about her from under the brim of her small hat and through its spotted veil at the second-class deck as if she had never seen anything so inferior. 'I would have brought champagne,' she said, 'but since you do not drink, here is my gift,' and she thrust bunches of red roses at them. Over their extravagant profusion, she stared at Laila, her face so intent that it was pinched, like a rodent's. 'So,' she said, tucking her sharp little chin into the collar of her silk blouse, 'you are going to India – where I have always meant to go – and have never been.'

Laila gave her a faint smile and dropped her eyes, not knowing if the words were spoken in envy or resentment.

Krishna, glowing with pleasure at Mrs du Best's presence, looking about him to make sure everyone saw and noticed, chuckled, 'You told me you had not the courage to go to India, Mrs du Best. But you see, Laila has the courage.'

'Courage?' said the old lady. 'Is that it? Perhaps it is. But, you know, I felt I already had the India of my books and friends and art treasures. Perhaps I didn't really care to have another India, the real India.'

Laila regarded her over the bunch of red roses with curiosity. The India of books and art treasures and the real India – were they not the same? She turned to Krishna for an answer.

But Krishna was in the high spirits of someone embarking on a journey. He laughed loudly. 'You were afraid, Mrs du Best, you were afraid. But see Laila – she is not afraid.'

'Hmm,' she continued to peer at Laila as if uncertain of what she saw. 'And are you sure you wish to go on this long journey, my dear? Why not go home to your family instead?'

Krishna smiled upon both of them with magnanimity. 'But I am taking her home, Mrs du Best. I am taking her home to India.'

'Oh, my dear Krishna-ji, you know it is not that to the poor girl even if it is to you – '

'You are wrong,' he laughed, 'India has always been her home. She has never been there, you are right, but it is where her soul was born. Her soul is waiting for her in India!'

'Ah, Krishna,' Mrs du Best exclaimed, 'you make India sound like a form of death!'

Simultaneously with her exclamation, the ship's horn gave its raw, harsh howl. There was an increased bustle of activity on the decks, and she turned to leave before the gangplank was raised and the sooty, dark vessel turned seawards and thrust into the black waves.

When she reached the pier and turned to wave at them, she saw them at the railing, Krishna's face golden and benign with smiles, Laila's pale and frowning with earnest thought.

⌐

Amtrak turns Sophie out at Springfield where a thin drizzle is falling from a heavy sky; passengers flee, clattering down the stairs into a railway station where a man is punching the coffee machine, a woman with orange hair is waiting for someone with her hands on her hips and a fierce look, and the plastic bucket seats are askew on their rail. She walks down the road and under a low bridge that suggests crime and danger, and then into the bus station. She waits here for the bus to Holyoke, watching a man with grey frizzled hair and a beard talking into a telephone, laughing violently as he does so; it is clear that there is no one at the other end and eventually he hangs up and limps away in shoes without laces.

She rides the bus to Holyoke and looks about her uneasily as she gets off; it is later than she would like and although the rain has stopped, the light is sooty. She walks past Joe's Shoe Repair shop, Sunshine Cleaners 24 Hours Service and Nu To U that has a show window filled with faded cloth, broken glass and felt hats. All three are shut and look as if they have been for a long time. The mills had all closed down, or moved south, and the mill workers moved away. Eventually she comes to a place that is open; it advertises, in red letters, *Subs. Pizzas. Coffee*. Its owner is wiping glasses, talking to a man smoking at a table.

'Railway station?' he stares at her. 'Ain't no railway station. Why, the trains stopped coming here in – hey, where you from? You been in Holyoke before?'

Shaking her head, she leaves.

᪥Chapter Four᪥

The address given Sophie is in a suburb of Bombay and, although it is not far from the sea or the festivities of Juhu beach, it has no relation at all to that holiday world. Instead, it is staunchly, oppressively dour, related to the cotton mills of the area and the life related to the mills. The housing is drab, in grey blocks of concrete that ooze green slime and are marked by the rust from leaking drainpipes. Although the more substantial flats have balconies attached to them, the balconies are used as adjunct rooms, most often as stores for tin trunks, broken furniture and ruined appliances, but also as laundries with strings and strings of heavy, sagging washing. In fact, the washing of one flat tends to drip onto the washing of the flat below, so that the sides of the building are curtained with long strips of saris, *dhotis* and underwear, not colourful and bright but faded and stained with over-use.

Sophie locates the building she wants and enters a hall painted a murky blue and lit by a single light bulb coated with dust so that the names of the tenants written on a wooden board are hard to decipher. She finds the one she wants, however, and begins to climb the stairs which are ancient and rotten. The higher she goes the stronger the cooking smells grow – pungent, oily, spicy. Different noises issue forth and mingle: music on a radio or a television drama at top volume, children screaming and voices raised in argument. Sometimes a door is flung open and someone comes hurtling out and into her, nearly throwing her down the stairs in the rush to get to the shops, the cinema, the streets, the night shift at the mill. Mostly they look back in curiosity: not many foreigners enter such buildings, not even shabby and tattered ones like Sophie. Some even call back, asking her where she is going. Then they wave her further up and she mounts the stairs slowly, reluctant to touch the banisters because they are black with grease and the dust of years, but beginning to wonder if she can manage without their help. The heat that has accumulated in the centre of the building is as weighty and oppressive as the smells and sounds.

The door to the flat is no different from the others: it, too, has a smudged and faded pattern of rice powder drawn on its threshold and a string of dried marigolds hangs across the door. Only a small wooden sign indicates it is the end of Sophie's search: *Krishna School of Dance* it says.

The door is slightly ajar, and Sophie stands looking in. The flat seems empty, the room is entirely bare. But the red terrazzo floor is worn with use and Sophie can tell that dancers' feet have trodden it for years. The room beyond it seems to be the domestic heart of the house as sounds of cooking emerge from it. Everything seems strangely familiar. There is a sudden hiss of a pressure cooker, the equally sudden switching off of steam, and then, in answer to Sophie's call, there is a rustle of garments and a woman appears.

She is middle-aged, thick-set and heavily built. She seems to have no waist and her curving bosom is covered with a purple cotton sari that swathes her whole. Her face is square too, and blank of expression. The only decorative or frivolous touches are the vermilion dot on her forehead and a small diamond in her nose.

Staring at Sophie, the woman assumes a dancer's pose – both hands placed to one side of her waist, and the hip slightly jutting. Her face, too, takes on an expression of query that is exaggerated in the way a dancer exaggerates expression.

'Does Krishna-ji live here?' Sophie asks. 'I wrote – I am Sophie.'

The woman maintains the pose for a long moment, regarding her.

Then a man's voice calls from another room, querulously, and the woman comes to life, nods and beckons Sophie to follow her, holding aside a curtain of striped cotton in the doorway to let her in.

There, in a room painted green and lit with a blue fluorescent tube, on a mattress spread with a white sheet upon the floor, sits Krishna. Sophie recognises him although there is little resemblance to the photographs she has seen of the young dancer in Paris, Venice and Lausanne. These tumble through her mind now in the stark black and white of xeroxed copies that so highlight smiles and grimaces. When they recede from her mind, she is able to take in the figure that has replaced them: a shrunken creature whose grey skin hangs in folds from his spare form. He has propped himself up on one bony arm, and from the way his jaw droops onto his chest, Sophie sees that he is toothless. Yet there is still an elegance about the way his sparse white fair falls onto his shoulders, and something both languid and commanding about the way his eyes shift under the heavy lids. But his face is as blank as the woman's, and Sophie cannot tell if he welcomes her visit or even if he can see her.

There are no chairs and, after a moment or two of standing awkwardly before him so that he can see nothing but her legs, she lowers herself onto the floor. At least now she is in the direct line of his vision. The woman has vanished behind another striped cotton curtain into the area that is evidently the kitchen, for it is lively with the clatter and clink of pots and pans and spoons.

The old man suddenly calls out in a very loud, harsh voice, 'Bring the visitor tea, will you?'

Sophie murmurs that it is not necessary, that she has only come to see –

'To see? Yes?' he urges her when she hesitates.

'To see – you,' Sophie admits.

'You are interested in my dance?' he questions immediately, with a certain eagerness.

Sophie flushes. It is not what she is prepared for although she sees now that she should have been. What else would the old man still be interested in if not dance, and particularly his own? It is a moment when it would have been a relief to lie. Sophie regrets, not for the first or the only time, not having the skill.

She had hoped to lead up to the subject while she should have foreseen that the old have no time to waste, nor large areas of interest. If their world has shrunk, so should it for others.

This gives her a clue and she snatches at it. 'In your European tour,' she tells him. 'In your time in Europe.'

'Ahh,' he sighs, as if with relish, and relaxes. His bony upright arm folds up on his lap and he gives his knees a waggle, settling into a space he knows, that is familiar. His mouth twists in a smile. Yes, he is toothless. 'The nineteen twenties, that is when I toured Europe. Between the wars you understand. My time in Europe was – was –' His voice founders, his eyes swivel under the heavy lids that droop lower, and Sophie fears she has lost him. He appears to be looking inwards, brooding upon whatever he sees there.

'Paris?' she prompts him softly. 'Venice?'

'Ah-ah,' he cries, his jaws seizing upon these morsels, and finding them feasts. The contortions of his face and the sounds he utters become so frantic that Sophie is clutched by remorse and fear. She wonders if she should stop what she has set in motion when the woman appears from the bright and noisy room beyond, bearing a small tin tray on which are balanced two glasses of tea. Seeing his state, she hurries forward and, setting down the tray, bends over the old man. It is not clear what she does to calm him and compose him but when she rises it can be seen that she had handed him his dentures and fitted them in his mouth, given him his glass of tea and helped him sip some. Then, instead of leaving, she settles down on the floor, crosslegged, to keep watch.

Now the old man begins to talk in a rush, in spasmodic outbursts, repeating words and sentences over and over again, spraying them out over the glass of tea and the thin mattress in Sophie's direction. She feels them squirted at her, like gobbets of spit – she is inundated, she struggles to catch a straw here and there.

'Paris. Paris. The Théâtre des Champs-Elysées in – in nineteen twenty? Twenty-one? Twenty-two! The programme. Where is the programme? I have it somewhere. What did it say? What? Do you know? "Danses Hindoues par Krishna et sa troupe" – yes! Yes, that was my troupe, my dance. It was like magic to them, like paradise.'

The woman coughs.

He hears, half turning his head, and laughs. 'Yes. To them I was a Hindu god, they had never seen one before. "Bronze Shiva" they called me. Our ancient dance –'

He might wheeze and stammer on without stop. Sophie tries to interrupt and ask, 'And the dancers? Who were they?'

'Ah, my dancers. Radha, Parvati, Durga – all the goddesses. Our religious art –' he goes on, and his eyes glitter like fishes under the dark lids, the hands twist and twine in elaborate gestures, miming the grace and beauty of the creature he tries to recreate for Sophie, his fingers clustering together, then opening like the petals of a lotus, one hand poised in mid-air like a deer leaping, arms rippling like a banner in the breeze, his face coming awake with delight.

Sophie, embarrassed, looks down at the floor: she does not want to watch an old man miming a beautiful and bewitching dancer. How to stop him?

The doorbell rings. Providentially. The woman gets to her feet and goes out, calling something over her shoulder in Marathi. Sophie hopes this will stem the flood and save her from the falling debris of the dancer's past, but he does not seem to have noticed, although he had waved one hand vaguely in the woman's direction; he continues to babble.

Sophie decides she must dare. She interrupts, firmly. 'And Laila – or Lila – was one of them?'

He babbles on, 'In Paris, they called them goddesses from India. Yes, the press – the press –' and then he pauses, and stops, giving her a blindly unfocused look. He falls silent and his hands come to rest on his knees.

'Lila?' Sophie repeats softly, 'or Laila? From Egypt – or France? Was she one – ?'

He has clenched his teeth together tightly, setting his jaw. Now he snaps them apart with a click and barks, 'Why are you wanting to know? Who is sending you here? She has sent you?'

'Oh no,' Sophie assures him with obvious sincerity. 'She does not know I am here. She would not want me to come, or send me.'

'Then – ?'

'I am trying to learn something about her. She is very famous. She is called the Mother. People come from all over the world to her ashram. I would like to learn about her life, her past.'

He has closed his eyes. Now he tilts his head back, far back, so that it rests against the wall, and then opens his mouth, and out of it comes a series of laughs, so dry, so unpractised, they are like coughs, rasping through his throat.

Sophie stops explaining. She watches and listens to him, not certain if he is coughing or sneezing or choking or actually laughing. If he is laughing, why is he doing so? No one has expressed amusement about the Mother, ever. 'You have heard about her?' she asks. 'The Mother?'

He is shaking his head from side to side, as if uncontrollably. 'Too good, too good,' he cackles, and tears seem to glisten in the corners of his eyes. 'That Lila – I trained her. She was a child, she came to me for training. I taught her Indian dance. She had never seen Indian dance before. The first time she saw me, she said, "Teach me." I was like a father to her. I took her everywhere – to Paris, Venice, New York – everywhere. But here in India – when I brought her to India –'

'Yes?' Sophie leans forward so as not to miss anything. 'Over here – ?' she prompts.

'Here she began running after gurus. She said dancing was not for her, she wanted to live a spiritual life. What is dancing, I asked her, if not spiritual? But she was mad! The Mother! Oh, too good, too good,' he begins to hawk and cough again, incoherently. His face is distorted by a grimace – of laughter, or of derision; whatever it is, it is laced with spite and malice and rage, Sophie is sure of that – he looks so like a grinning gargoyle.

She had not wanted anything so emotional, so excessive.

Just information, photographs, proof, corroboration – solid, substantial things, not emotion, and certainly not such a tangle of emotions. She reminds him, 'I am doing research, I plan to write a book. Can you give me photographs, press releases, reviews, anything to do with Lila – the Mother?'

He stops laughing to stare at Sophie. 'I have everything,' he states flatly. 'Everything – photos, reviews. Why do you want them? There is nothing there. Nothing. But what I have of Lila, that no one else has, no one else knows!' He has raised his voice, his excitement is once again rising.

This brings the woman back from the front room. She parts the curtain and looks at them questioningly. He tries to wave her away, impatiently, but she says, 'I am talking to my new student. The student has come with her parents –' Sophie catches the word student, student repeated – then she turns away, the curtain falling into place behind her.

'What?' Sophie asks urgently. 'What?'

He beckons to her. 'Listen. Go to that box there, in the corner. Open it. It is full of papers – photos, reviews, posters. Many, many, many. But look underneath. At the bottom you will find a notebook. Red. Bring it to me.'

Sophie had thought the room is bare – that is the impression it had made on her. Now she realises that there is a tin trunk in one corner, so old and battered it has the air of being a part of the room itself, like a shelf or a hole. It is covered with some sheets of newspaper and a variety of objects – scattered bills, some tins of talcum powder, small bronze images of gods and goddesses. She removes them in order to lift the lid. It creaks rustily; it is clearly not opened often. Inside, as he has said, there are stacks of yellowing papers, some wrapped in cloth or paper folders and tied with bits of string, others in loose sheets. She sifts through them, wishing there could be time to sort them and go through them. She might be able to find them in libraries or archives but being possessions of Krishna gives them special value. But there is clearly little time to waste and so she plunges in her arms and feels around the bottom of the trunk till she comes up against something hard-edged and thick. She draws it out and sees it is a notebook with many loose sheets interleaved with its pages, a cover of red paper peeling back to the cardboard underneath.

She brings it to Krishna who snatches it from her roughly. 'See?' he hisses. 'See? Her book. She wrote it. This is what she wrote here in India. Then she went away – to that guru, to that ashram. She did not want the discipline, the struggle, the *sadhna* of being a dancer, she ran away. You will read here –' he turns the pages, fumbling through them – 'how she went mad. She began to think she was holy – she was the Mother. Oh, what lies, what lies, what lies,' he cackles, thrusting the book at Sophie. 'This diary she sent me from the ashram. "Read this," she wrote to me, "this is the truth. Read the truth about me. It is here." He pushes it into Sophie's hands but will not relinquish his hold on it – in fact he tugs at it when he finds Sophie holding it. 'Read,' he spits through his teeth. 'You will see she was mad. She ran away to that guru. Was *I* not her true guru?'

The curtains are swept aside again, and now not only the woman re-enters but with her is her new student, and the student's parents, all dressed for a special occasion – silk saris for the women, fine cotton *dhoti* and shawl for the man, and all coming towards Krishna in a group with their hands folded in respectful namaskars, and their heads bowed. Gold glints, anklets tinkle, the scent of jasmine garlands swirls headily around.

The woman announces, 'They want to pay their respects,' and she gives the young student a little push so that the girl goes down on her knees before the old man with greater precipitation than planned. She touches his feet with her hands, then her forehead. He draws back, confused, making little sounds of refusal, but then he relaxes, he smiles in a distraught way, and the student's mother comes forward with a tray on which they have placed their gifts – squares of silk neatly folded, a green coconut, some sweets, some flowers. She bows, offering them, while the father and the woman stand back, watching proudly.

Sophie creeps backwards, thrusts the notebook into her bag, and slips away while they are so occupied, only to hear the old dancer's voice raised querulously, 'But the other student, the foreigner? Where is she? I will initiate her too, I will initiate both –'

Sophie's feet, in slippers, clatter down the stairs at a run.

Only when she reaches the bottom does she realise why the flat had seemed so familiar when she first entered it: it had been so like that flat where she and Matteo had visited the first holy person they had met when they arrived in Bombay, many years ago.

Standing on the railway platform, waiting for the train north, Sophie straddles her old, patched, filthy backpack that contains the notebook, and wishes, when she realises that the train is late, and that she will be here under the ringing iron roof and rafters in the cruel heat of afternoon for several hours, in the press of coolies and passengers, baggage trolleys and luggage, flies and pai dogs, that she had arranged to stay a day longer. It would have meant putting up with a filthy hotel room for a night, but it would have given her time to go out into the suburbs of the city she remembers, revisit that flat and see the holy person who created perfumes in honour of God. What god? she would ask. And why? Tell me, she would beg, explain – why?

In the urgency and anxiety she feels, Sophie sweeps her hair off her neck and shoulders and shakes her head angrily, ordering herself to be calm, to be controlled, not to give way to panic. She places her hands on her hips, keeping her feet on either side of the denim backpack, and guards it with such ferocity that the young men who have been eyeing her speculatively over the bottles of soft drinks they are sipping, drop their eyes and simulate boredom instead.

She waits for the train that will take her north. It will be a long journey, and she will be able to read through Lila's diary.

~

On Board the Kaga Maru

The great boat rides the waves of subconscient darkness. We travel this vast distance in order to arrive at the borderland where the light will rise above the eastern horizon and the great truth will be revealed.

Now I am still trapped in its dark hold, and all around me are the ignorant and the unenlightened. I see their cattle bodies and their cattle faces as they troop past on their way to 'Sunday service'. I hear their cattle voices lowing the mournful words of a hymn. The captain and his officers stand showing their glittering medals. I cover my eyes to shield myself from the sight of such idiocy. I cover my ears so I may not be invaded by the sounds of their ignorance.

I know that what I am travelling towards is not the world of this ship's passengers – the meals, the laughter, the flirtations, the deck games, the Sunday services and the pompous authority of those in charge of it. All these I shall leave behind – oh, deep at the bottom of the great, green ocean! I am travelling away from them, I am travelling eastwards to meet the great sun, the great light. I must prepare my soul for the sweet union.

We are in the harbour at Bombay. The boat has docked and at dawn we will disembark. The night air is a heavy purple cloak wrapped about me. There are lighted lamps on the mainland and on the islands, and invisible people awake, moving and talking.

O mysterious India, I can feel you stirring in the dark. The morning sun will reveal your face to me, just as the hagdah in the coffee shop in Cairo predicted you would, so long ago. I know it, I know it for a certainty now.

I am excited, my body is trembling with eagerness to rise and meet this ancient world. India! I am come. When the sun rises, I shall set foot on Indian soil, the land of Shiva and Parvati, of Radha and Krishna, of the Buddha, the Light of Asia. When the sun rises, I will step off the boat and be amongst them at last. May this vision be shown me. May the Light shine on me. I tremble. I bow to it in worship.

In Bombay

I do not know where I am. Krishna led me and I came. This house is no temple where I may worship. It is dark and filled with noise and stench. Outside black crows are fighting and screaming. A woman in a ragged sari comes out and throws a bucket of refuse to them. They swoop upon it and tear it from each other's beaks with screams. They frighten me so, I stay indoors. But this is no refuge and I have no peace. The women I travelled with and came to know have become as strangers; no longer silent and subdued, they now shriek and laugh and chatter, and not a word can I understand. My Krishna is gone from me, I do not know where. Outside I hear the trams in the street and blind beggars wailing.

Where is the river, the scented grove, the jasmine garlands? Where is the music of flutes and the sound of the conch?

I beg to be taken to a temple that I might see the face of my Lord and make my obeisance. Krishna has no time for worship but the women of the house take me. There is a temple of pink stone in a street of commerce. It is filled with men of business. Its walls are plastered with bank notes, stuck there with the prayers of merchants and brokers. The reek of money is everywhere.

Yet outside are beggars with running sores and fevered eyes, stretching out their hands and begging for alms. Pilgrims pass them by, dropping a coin here and there without seeing, without knowing, without learning.

Barefooted, I follow the women over a wet floor, bearing in my hands a basket with a green coconut, a garland, some bananas. I am taken to a silver shrine and there, draped in pink gauze and crowned with tinsel, sits the smiling doll, the Goddess of Wealth. A priest stands by with a tray of red powder and a pot of holy Ganges water with which to anoint me. But when I look upon the pink, smiling face of the goddess doll, my heart fails me. This is not where I will worship. I cannot be made to worship what I do not believe. The truth is elsewhere. My search is not over, I must continue it. O where is my Lord whose calm face shines only with the pure light of truth?

The world is as much with me here as in New York, or Venice or Paris. I thought we had left it behind when we sailed from America and that once on Indian soil we would dwell in a temple of devotion. But it is not so. Krishna runs from theatre to theatre and manager to manager and is concerned only with tours and performances. Sonali has reappeared and sits with Vijaya, stitching clothes, haggling with cloth merchants and jewellers, and no longer are they silent and withdrawn; their voices ring out, they talk without ceasing, they give orders and shout, and it is as if their true selves are released by the heat and the light of the Indian scene. When I say to them, 'I did not come here to perform; I came to worship at the feet of the Lord,' Krishna replies, 'Is not dance prayer? Is not dance worship? Have I not taught you even so much?'

No, it is not what you taught me or showed me, Krishna. You have shown me devotion to worldly success, to financial gain, to fame – not to the true light for which I came.

Rehearsals all day in this dark house that looks onto tram lines and railway yards and is full of cooking smells that sicken me. I long for a silent cell where I may meditate in peace but everywhere I hear the beggars wailing in the street, Vijaya playing the harmonium and the dancers ringing their anklets. Once I was one of them and danced, believing I danced in worship of the Lord. But now my head pains and I am sick both in body and in soul. How can Radha dance when she no longer sees Krishna? She can only weep.

Is it for this that I risked the long voyage from America on that ship of horror? Is it for this that I left Venice and Paris and Cairo where beauty dwelt and flowered? Have I been banished to a desert waste to die?

I said to Krishna, 'Take me to the mountains. There, in a temple, I may find my Lord. I came to India to find my Lord.'

He said, laughing, 'Do you think the Lord is dancing on top of the Himalayas? Do you think the Lord reveals Himself only on a mountaintop? Not here on earth? Open your eyes and look. See, the Lord is here before you,' and he held the peacock crown upon his head and laughed at me. That is to me a travesty and a mockery. His dancer's paint and costume is a mask behind which is an evil joker who mocks me. I know now that if I were to rip away the mask of the Blue God, I would see Krishna the dancer – no other.

• • •

Today we were to perform in a theatre – I Radha, he Krishna – with a new troupe of gopis. But by the afternoon the pain was so bad, not only in my head but also deep in the pit of my belly, that I lay upon the floor and cried for help. A doctor was fetched – a man who looked filthy and evil, and I would not let him touch me. Krishna angry, Sonali and Vijaya frightened, the girls in the doorway, staring. I screamed, 'Don't touch me, you –' and Sonali and Vijaya said 'Hush, the neighbours may hear. They will think you are being killed.' Thereupon I screamed, 'I am being killed, help me!' Then they changed their ways and became kind and gentle. Vijaya tried to press my feet and Sonali wanted to press my head, but I screamed at them not to come near. I wanted everyone to hear me. Then Krishna came and sat on the floor with his head beside my pillow and he cried – he pretended to cry. He said, 'Oh, Lila, I have made you ill. It is all my fault for bringing you here. Forgive me, forgive me.' But I did not wish to forgive him. So I turned away and looked at the wall, saying, 'Leave me,' and after some time he left, and then I did sleep.

The room was dark when I woke and there was no one there. I listened but heard no sound. Whatever sounds there were, were outside – in the streets and in the nearby houses, but not near me. I found the pain in my head and my belly less. I got up and walked into the kitchen and the other rooms and there was no one. It was night and dark except for the street lamps outside. I was glad to be alone and to have silence and I knew this was meant to be.

When they returned from the theatre, I went and lay on my bed and pretended to be asleep. Only this morning I opened my eyes and allowed Krishna and Sonali and Vijaya to come near me. I took the tea they brought me but I said, 'I am ill, I cannot dance,' and Krishna said, 'Please do not worry. Menaka will dance Radha from now on. She is from Madurai. She has trained from childhood. She performed very well last night. Everyone said she was perfect. I am very happy. You need have no worry.'

Now they leave me alone. I hear them rehearsing in the morning. Every day the sounds of the drums and anklets, of Vijaya singing and the crows on the balcony wake me. No one comes to ask me how

I am or what I need. They dance till midday. Then Krishna comes, bathed in perspiration, only to say, 'Please rest, please do not worry. Menaka is dancing brilliantly. I am very happy.'

He brought her to the door so I might see her. She came, her anklets ringing, and stood there with her head bent and her eyes lowered like a bride's. She was dressed in pink and had flowers in her hair: they smelt so sweet they sickened me. She seemed to be fourteen or fifteen. I stared at her but she would not look at me. Then Krishna smiled and said, 'Here she is, my new Radha. How do you like her?' and then she looked up and smiled too.

There is no reason now for me to rise from this bed. I have been lying here for days, in this small room that is used as a store room, with trunks piled on top of each other, rolls of bedding lifted onto them and baskets hanging above, so that I fear they will all fall and bury me beneath them. I lie still but the webbing of the bed cuts into my body which is thin and weak and I feel it could cut right through me. They brought me another doctor and said, 'This is a good doctor, Lila, please let him take a blood test so we may know your illness and medicines may be prescribed.' I tried to fight them but I was too weak and they held down my arm so the doctor could take blood out of my veins, and I wanted to scream and struggle but I could not and was silent.

I am in the hospital. I have been here for some days. Today the nurse made me sit up although I did not wish to, and then she brought me the pen I requested so I could write in my diary, so I forgave her. Her name is Mary and she is a kind girl. When I asked her, 'How long have I been here?' she said, 'Why do you worry? Stay here and let us make you well. Why do you want to go away so soon?' and she laughed at me as if she were my friend. I told her, 'No, I don't want to go back.' But when I added, 'I will die here,' she laughed again and told me, 'Many people in Bombay get hepatitis and also amoebic dysentery, and they get well. Why will you die?' So I pushed away my pillow and lay down and said, 'I wish to die.' Now she brings me small presents and says, 'I am your sister. I will make you get well.'

Krishna and Vijaya have been here to see me. They brought me oranges. Krishna said, 'We are rehearsing for the tour. I am choreographing a new ballet which I will première in Madras.' He started to tell me about this ballet which is about an ascetic who is meditating in the forest when the courtesan Menaka appears and seduces him. He talked and talked and I listened. He did not ask me how I was or about the hospital or my treatment, only talked of this ballet and the courtesan Menaka. I said to him, 'How lucky you have the dancer Menaka to dance the role of the courtesan Menaka. It will be so life-like except for your not being an ascetic sadhu. But she can seduce you anyway.' I was surprised to hear these words from my mouth, I had not planned to say them, it was as if someone else spoke them, they were so filled with hate and anger. He looked at me with his great black eyes and said, 'Oh Lila, I know you wanted to dance with me and be the leading dancer. Why did you fall ill instead?' I turned away from him and closed my eyes and did not speak again. The words that I had spoken left the taste of dust in my mouth and the words that he had spoken struck my ears like stones.

Today Mary brought me a piece of cloth on which she had embroidered a pink flower. She is so sweet and when I said to her, 'When I get well where will I go?' she replied, 'Come and live in my house. I live with my grandmother but you can live with us.' But of course she began to look troubled and I said to her, 'I can't live with you, Mary, you and your grandmother can't have me to stay,' and she became very sad and asked 'Won't you go back to your friends' house? They came to bring you fruit. Won't they look after you?'

Then I thought that I can never go back to them, there is no place for me beside Krishna any more, and I began to cry. Mary wiped my eyes with the little piece of cloth with a pink flower in the corner and she cried too. The Sister in charge of the ward noticed that and came and sent her away. She said to me, 'You had better think of getting up, you are quite well and you can go home now.' So I cried more. Where is my home? I left my home so long ago and so far behind that I cannot return to it. Yet I have not found the Lord's dwelling that I came to India to find. I am lost. In which direction can I go now? O Lord what have I done that I am cast out without refuge or haven? Am I to perish alone in the darkness? Why this punishment, Lord?

I have looked about me now that they have removed the green cloth screen from around my bed, and I have seen the people who are in the ward with me – a young woman with a baby she never looks at and that she seems to hate, a very old woman with a hump who is looked after by three women who may be her daughters but talk to each other as though she did not exist, another woman who is completely bandaged from head to foot so I cannot tell if she is young or old, a little girl who is so thin and wasted she might be a rag doll, and another who is so bloated that she cannot look out of her eyes – and I think, where do they live? Have they homes to which they can return? If they do, I know they will be homes where no beauty dwells, and no joy or hope. Are we all condemned to live in a world devoid of them?

I cannot believe that this is so, and that the dreams and hopes that propelled me on my travels and brought me to India had no Truth and no Power and were merely delusions. Somewhere there must be One who is mighty and wise, who will open up to me the Cosmic Infinity where I may dwell in peace and make my search for Eternal Knowledge and the Supreme Light. Somewhere there must be One who is tranquil and patient and comprehends all things and conquers all forces and against whom no evil can prevail. Somewhere there must be One who can show me the luminous wisdom I know exists, the vision that I crave, the answer to my questions that will assuage my hunger and thirst with love and joy.

Somewhere my Master must exist. All my life I have known of His existence and seen the signs He sent me. Yet I have been misled because of my weakness and ignorance that made me mistake what is only human for what is Supreme and Almighty.

Forgive my ignorance, Master. Remove the blindfold from my eyes and give me a vision of the Truth so I may dedicate myself to it.

If I cannot, I will sink into darkness and sink so low that I die. Till I find the Supreme Being, my own being remains unfulfilled and incomplete. I need a vision of the Supreme that I may enter into harmony with the Spirit. Then only will my body and mind come together, thought and action, the world and the spirit. In my dance I sought this harmony but because I had a false master found only disharmony. Lead me out of the world of such sorrow and delusion into the world of light and clarity. Lead me out of the world of the ugly, the coarse and the sordid, into the world of beauty and grace. Lead me out of the hell of hate into the paradise of love.

There is still, in my innermost soul, a last faint shred that is alive and pines and yearns. Answer it, O Master, answer it.

Mary came to me with my medicines on a tray and a glass of water, and when she had given them to me, she reached into the pocket of her white uniform and took out a gift for me that she pressed into my hand. When I opened my hand, I saw she had given me a crucifix. It was a small thing made of black tin and it hung on a chain of black beads. It was so ugly that I threw it on the ground, crying, 'Do not give me that, Mary. Never give me what is so ugly and so sad. Do you think I need to have an image of sin and suffering? Take it away. I want joy and beauty and love.' I cried so loudly that Sister Philomena appeared before Mary could pick up the crucifix from the floor and she saw it and she said, 'What have you done, you wicked girl – thrown Christ's cross upon the floor?' She began to scream and cross herself, and everyone stared at the sight. But I did not repent. They say I hurt their feelings, but what did they do to mine? They assaulted them, they crucified them. They have sinned. I am no sinner. My dwelling place is not in sin and suffering but in truth and beauty.

Sister Philomena has moved Mary to another ward and I am attended only by an ayah, a woman who chews betel nuts all the while and spits out the juice in a corner of the ward in a red splash, and talks loudly to the ward boys and smells of cheap cigarettes. She is filthy and low and ugly. I am being punished because I am the daughter of beauty and joy and these are hated here.

At night when everyone is asleep – not quietly but with all the groans and cries of their unhappy souls ringing out in their sleep – I look up at the blue light on the wall that keeps darkness away and prevents all these horrible sights from disappearing for a few merciful hours. I try to fix my mind upon that light and see it as a symbol of the eternal. But somebody in the ward cries out in pain, another screams for the nurse and I see that the light is not the Eternal One but only a nightlight to keep us awake and punish us by exposing all that is ugly and sorrowful on earth. Then I feel myself truly separated from the Eternal Truth, and I know it is this separation that makes me ill. O Master, come. Come and reveal yourself to me that I may rise and dance for you in joy. That dance will not be the depraved dance of the peacock and the courtesan that I was led into by my false master, but the divine dance of joyful prayer that I crave to perform for you and you alone, O Master.

Krishna came, saying, 'I have come to take you home,' and he brought me back to this ugly house that stands between the tram lines and the railway yard so that I feel myself caught in a vice. Home? This is a prison in which he has placed me – this airless hole where I lie amongst boxes with no single object of beauty to look upon. If I go out on the balcony to see the sun set in the orange sky that flames over this black city, crows come and settle on the rail and caw at me, and down in the street a beggar rolls by on his cart because he has no legs, and raises his tin to me, crying, 'Maa, O Maa!' Then I return to my room to hide.

He said to me, 'Put on your anklets, Lila, and dance. Soon we are going on a tour of the South. The South is full of temples I want to show you and where you must dance.' For the sake of the temples I rose and put on the heavy anklets although my head spun and I felt sick and weak when I bent to fasten them. I went into the classroom where Vijaya was singing and playing and the new dancers were rehearsing. Then he said, 'Now you must show them how you danced Radha. I want you to teach Menaka how to dance Radha,' and once again this girl stepped forward, her hands on her hips, to stand before me, smiling and shining with pride. She was dressed in red like a bride and glittered with gold jewellery and never thought to look down in shame or modesty.

I turned and went back to the hole in which I dwell, this black hole which is indeed become my home.

He is angry at me. He says, 'But we are leaving for the South. If you are not strong enough, and you are still sick as you say, you cannot come. I will leave you behind.'

I said to him, 'If you leave me behind, I will die. You will come back and find my dead body lying on this floor.'

I thought that if he had a heart, he would repent now and ask me to forgive him, and take me in his arms and promise me his protection. If he was my Master, that is what he would do.

Instead, he shouted, 'You want to keep me sitting here beside you like a woman. You are trying to prevent me from dancing and taking my troupe on tour and making it known in India. You want to destroy my career. You want to destroy me.'

I said to him, 'I did not know it was your career we came to make in India. I thought we came here to find the Eternal Truth. You told me it existed only in India and that we would together search for it and find it.'

Then he turned into a madman, stamping about the room, laughing and mocking my words, then tearing at his hair and shouting at me. I saw the others come to the door and stare. I knew everyone was listening, but I did not care because I had spoken the truth and he had lied.

Why do you punish me, Master? Why do you still hide from me and keep me in darkness? Have I done wrong to search for you through dance? Have I done wrong to come to India in search of you? Answer me, Master, show me the path to travel in order to reach you. In this darkness, I can see nothing, not even You.

This morning Vijaya took pity on me. She came and told me she knows of an ashram in the Himalayas; when she was younger, she used to go there on pilgrimage. She says some of her family will be going there on their annual pilgrimage and will take me with them. She says in the mountains I may recover my health. She says the ashram will let me have a room and food and rest. She says there is a river and forests and meadows. She says she will tell her family to buy a ticket for me on the train and then escort me into the mountains. She says she has told Krishna of this plan.

'And what did he say?' I asked her because I had to know.

She replied, 'He said it was a very good plan.'

I will not see him again. He is preparing for the journey to the South. The whole house is filled with the business of packing and departing. I can hear them and sometimes they come to my room and take out boxes and trunks. I sit crosslegged on the bed and stare in front of me and concentrate my mind not on the world outside but on the vision I have of a temple by a river in the Himalayan mountains to the north.

It is over, the Journey. The Journey I was intended to make.

When I was on the train with Vijaya's family, sitting in the little space allotted me on a crowded bunk and looking through the grey and grimy window at the passing landscape of India, I knew this to be the final stretch of my journey.

Certainly I could not have undertaken another. My strength was seeping out of me, my body was wasting rapidly, my eyes becoming blurred so that I saw everything before me indistinctly: the barren earth littered with the bones of animals expired from thirst and starvation, mean dwelling places like earthen burrows, lonely telegraph poles, dusty isolated palm trees, cattle-drawn ploughs tilling the soil just as they do in my own distant, long-forgotten land, peasants bowed under the weight of the great brassy sky . . . I wanted to weep for it all, weep. It seemed to me that this earth was forsaken by the Great Spirit. The Great Spirit had departed from it in despair and left it as it was – caught in the nightmare of death and desolation. In the grip of that nightmare, I do not know how I passed the night, whether asleep or awake. I am only aware that I felt the great iron wheels of the railway hurtling through my very bones, and whether I opened or shut my eyes, I still saw that same sad land to which I had come in search of beauty, truth and wisdom only to find them fled. How those prophetic words came back to me: 'India is a form of death!'

What was it I had thought to find? Groves of flowering trees in which fabulous birds sang and fruit glowed? Maidens in robes of gauze and princesses wearing jewelled crowns? Processions of magnificent beasts bearing the great and the good of the land? Was I so simple, so naive? I will not put a name to my expectations except to say that what I wanted of India was the outward manifestation of what already existed inside me, what had been growing inside me like a flower grown from a seed I had discovered in a Paris bookshop of my past. And it was the death and burial of this flower of hope that crushed me through that long and dreadful night. It had been a foolish and perilous thing to pursue that secret dream to the very ends of the earth, and I was paying for my error, oh horribly!

Yet morning came, as morning must, and the train stopped at a small station along the way. I was stiff from the cramped corner of the carriage that I was crowded into by Vijaya's family and the other passengers, all giving off the sour odours of poverty and squalor, and so I stepped out to exercise my aching limbs a little. The sun had only just risen but already the sky was on fire and I felt its heat strike me like the sun in the land of my birth, an eastern sun, white-hot and purifying like a holy furnace — not kind, no, but drastic. Men were selling fruit in baskets that they carried on their heads. I bought oranges, and bananas. Others were carrying kettles of tea and glasses and pouring out for the passengers who called to them from the carriage windows. Small children were begging and I gave them the fruit I had bought. Then a monkey leapt from a tree and scampered up to me to beg for some and I laughed to see the funny little fellow reach out its lined pink hands to receive it from me. As it swung itself up into a tree to eat there in peace, I saw that it was a great spreading tree of the kind I had read of — the holy banyan, with its massive branches, hoary with age, letting down fine air roots to the earth that had taken root and sprouted into yet other trees — a tree eternally dying and eternally giving birth, the Tree of Eternity.

In its shade sat a holy man. I was certain he was a holy man, although no different from a beggar in appearance: he wore no more than a rag round his waist, his body and legs and feet bare, his hair dusty and matted. He sat on the beaten earth with a begging bowl beside him, but he did not beg. He sat crosslegged, his hands resting upon his knees, and his gaze fixed upon the soul within him. It was clear he saw neither the station nor the train nor the passengers; he cared not for the commerce and the hubbub of the world; he dwelt in another realm, and for him time and space had a meaning other than we could comprehend who travelled bodily but without escape from ourselves.

I stood and gazed upon the holy man's serene visage, and there stirred in my sick, starved body the great desire I had always had ever since I was a child, to be free of this world and escape into another, a better and brighter. I believe I cried out to him, in appeal for his help, and before my eyes the great banyan tree burst into light, and I saw light travelling, pouring through the veins in its leaves, its twigs and branches and the very trunk itself so that it was transformed into an earthly sun and fire revolved through it as blood revolved – once more! – through my body. I was on fire, the tree was on fire, light blazed and the whole sky was illuminated. I cried out and covered my face with my hands.

My fellow passengers were hard put to recall me by shouting my name and even so one had to come out and drag me by my arm and push me back into the railway carriage before the train drew out and continued its journey. I sat by the window with my knees hunched and my sorrow at leaving behind me the vision I had had of Eternal Light was so great that I wept openly. My fellow passengers showed kind concern for me and I was sufficiently aware and moved by it to make answer at last and they continued to treat me with care.

So for the rest of the way – and it was a troubled way – I had the vision to sustain me, and it helped me through the dreadful city where we dismounted from the train into a scene from Hell. Had I not had the vision, it would have destroyed me. It seemed that all the dirt, the disease and hideousness of the earth had collected there to assault my vision.

Yet somehow we found our way to a cart hired for us that was to make its way slowly and painfully out of the city and along stretches of dusty road through parched fields and sand and miserable towns populated by emaciated folk and whipped and beaten beasts till at last it was travelling through rock and scrub into low hills and the mountains appeared upon the horizon and since then I have had the Mountain before my eyes. Higher and higher we climbed and sweeter and fresher became the air, so that my heart lifted and soared and when I raised my eyes, there in the north stood the Himalayan peaks, white and pure and shining as in my dreams.

The town we have come to is only another heap of hovels clinging to the hillside. It is true that there is a river racing through the gorge below, and if it were in the wilderness it would be beautiful but, as it is, the whole town gathers there to bathe, wash clothes, to fetch water, as well as dispose of garbage so that it is almost a public sewer. The temples that line its banks seem only to add to its horrors.

The ashram to which Vijaya's family has brought me is fortunately above the main bazaar. It is ugly enough – in the way that the town is ugly. The rooms open onto long verandas and I share one with an aged aunt and a young niece who is a cripple and has to be carried about on the backs of her relatives. It consists only of a bare floor on which we unroll our mats to sleep. I do not mind the austerity of it. But I look over the rooftops all of corrugated iron which has rusted and on which people have piled old crates and baskets and other unwanted rubbish, to the narrow streets of the bazaar from which rises the confused noise of traffic and commerce interrupted by the loud clanging of bells in the temples along the river. The view would be no different from what I had in the city if it were not for a strip of the river below, dashing against the rocks and swirling around them in white foam and green pools. Then, on the other bank, the hills drop away to the plains in folds and one sees only a village here and there, with smoke rising from their hearths by day and lamps glowing at night.

Night. Night is when I have a glimpse once more of the eternal. Then the sky spreads its blue velvet cloak over us and the stars are gems that shine upon it. I walk up and down the long veranda, looking out at the stars, and they call to me. They seem to say, 'Higher, climb higher.' I am too weak to go climbing. The night air is cold. My shawl is thin and provides little warmth. This gives me a feeling of frailty. I need strength and courage, and then I will set out, and I will climb, and I will go up the mountain into the heights. For this, I came to India.

I have climbed the mountain and I have reached the peak.

A little path led me, winding through low bushes and under the branches of conifer trees. No one passed me but an old woman carrying a load of wood on her back. She greeted me without lifting her face. I thought: Now I will leave behind me all such faceless ones, now I will go where I shall see the Face I came to see. I climbed on till I reached a grassy slope and saw there was nothing left to climb but great rocks that rose sheer into the sky now tinted rose by the setting sun. I had reached the mountain peak at that magic hour between day and night – entre chien et loup, they would say in France – and I asked myself: What will I meet here? Will Day come to meet my Night?

I wished so passionately for this meeting, for this union, that I knelt in the grass and prayed, even wept, and all the while my heart beat so I knew it was the hour of my fate.

The wind blew about me, and there was music in it as it played upon the harps and lyres of the trees around me. Other than that, there was silence. Out of that silence, a cry. A long, piercing cry that went through my breast like a sword. A great eagle soared forth out of an invisible crevice in the rocks, spreading its wings and floating out into space, launching itself into the unknown to search. With it, my soul too set out in quest.

At that moment the evening star appeared in the heavens and shone out from the deep blue of infinity. Was that not a promise? An augury? I knew it was, and rising to my feet, I began to dance in ecstasy, the ecstasy of knowing my time had come.

> My body danced,
> In prayer, in Joy
> And ardent expectation.
> I danced my love, my ardour,
> My yearning and my pain.
> I danced the dance of the milkmaid
> Pining for the Shepherd,
> And my swelling heart called:
> I wait! O come!

> Behold, He came!
> By the light of the evening star,
> At the sight of the rising moon,
> My Master appeared,
> On the dark hilltop
> Beneath a stately tree
> He stood, watching me.

298

Upon his golden face
The sweet calm
Of One who has waited
Many years, many aeons,
For me to come to Him.

And when my dance was done
And I stood with my hands
Pressed to my heart
My Master's voice rang out:
Who art Thou,
O beauteous dancing maid?
Standing still as a statue
I beheld Him and replied:
I am Lila, thy Devotee.

Thou art Shakti, he pronounced,
Supreme Power.
Thou art Durga,
Mother of us all.
Thou art Kali,
The Divine Force,
And Parvati,
Sweet Goddess of the Mountain.

And all at once
The Heavens burst into light and music
Of joyous celebration.
The stars sang their jubilee
The Moon its blessing gave.
Fresh Himalayan winds blew
From the Abode of Snow.

The Master stepped forth and
placing on my shoulders
A shawl of ochre silk,
Maiden, said He,
Come follow me,
And henceforth my home
Thy Haven shall be.

That night, when I returned to my small and crowded room, I
packed my belongings and as the sun rose I was already hurrying
down the hill and through the narrow streets to the temple by the
river. My heart beat with joy as I went and although the sun had
not yet touched the rooftops and few people were about, it seemed to

me the whole pilgrim town rejoiced for me that I had found my Master. I smiled at every old man I saw shivering upon his doorstep in the early sun; I smiled at the mangy dogs that foraged in the dust, and even the crows that morning seemed to sing, not scream. At the bottom of the valley the river ran and there were people already bathing in its icy waters, standing upon the rocks in their thin ragged clothes, lifting their brass pots above their heads so the sun caught the flash of water as it fell and blessed them. I stopped and, stepping close to the river, I let it splash my feet as I bent and filled my cupped hands, then lifted them to the sky and let the water fall upon me. It was as ice but I laughed and nearly cried out: I too bathe today in the waters of divine love! The river flows and carries my past away and leaves me pure and joyous as the new-born, fit to meet with the divine.

In such spirits I entered the temple precincts. Pilgrims were streaming in for the morning prayers, and the bells were rung again and again, their sound clear and sweet in the mountain air. At the gate I stopped and bought a basket of fruit as an offering. With it, I climbed the stairs and went through the doorway into a courtyard. There a priest stood before the sanctum, holding his tray with red powder and a pot of holy water with which to anoint our foreheads. But, seeing the idol within the sanctum, an object of stone or metal albeit decked with gold and gems, I declined to bow before it. Although the pilgrims stared to see me, and the priest called, 'Stop! Who are you?' I continued on my way, into the second courtyard.

There I beheld the Great Sage seated upon a carpet amidst pots of basil and garlands of marigold, preparing to give his discourse. To him I went with my little basket and at his feet I laid it. He held out his hand and blessed me and bade me be seated. I obeyed my Lord and sat before him, gazing my fill of the Divine Visage. He spoke and his voice was sweeter than the ringing of bells, sweeter than the song of birds; it had the power and the force of the river itself. He spoke of Divine Love and love filled my every limb with its nectar and I was Radha who beheld, at last, the true Krishna.

> I travel the River
> That had its Source
> In a far country.
> Long have I wandered
> The face of the earth,

Struggling through desert wastes,
Knowing hunger, thirst and fear.
I have been shunned and derided,
Mocked in the market-place.
I have been shown great wealth,
Fine possessions
In the world's courts.
Yet none could soothe my thirst,
In none ended my quest.
False priests misled me,
With promises and gifts.
Villains imprisoned me
In barbarous cells.
Devils, I cried, I am not yours,
I will be free
And seek the Divine.
Voices mocked me, saying:
Divine? Are we not that?
Faces leered at me, smiling:
Are we not fine enough for you?
From somewhere strength came to me
And I repelled them,
Knowing it better to die
Fighting Evil
Than to live without His Grace.

Arriving at last in the green valley,
My feet quickened their pace,
My Lord's voice in my ear, beckoning.
I know now my Journey's ended,
I see now that Mountain peak
That had been my true home
From which I was kept
And is now shown me
In a vision so radiant
I cry out in Joy:
Love, I am come.
The Sun pours upon the Abode of Snow
It dazzles my eyes —
Everywhere is Brightness.

All day I remained in that courtyard, even after He withdrew. His
presence lingered as a scent upon the air. His voice continued to
ring in my ears even as a lion's roar. To all else I was oblivious.
Priests and pilgrims came to rouse me, to urge me to eat or rest, or

else leave. I did not stir. Only late in the evening, when the sun had withdrawn from the heavens and the purple hues of night tinged the deep valleys, did I begin to shiver and stir as though I had woken in the night to find my lover gone. Then I permitted them to help me to my feet and when they asked where I lived, I began to weep: 'Here, only here. Let me stay, I beg you, do not send me away.' They took pity on me and found me a room within the ashram. It was a small place, dark and without furnishings, but they brought me food and a blanket and shut the door on me, and I remained, weeping both with the joy of being within the temple of which I had dreamt and at the pain of being separated thus from him.

The heavens heard my prayers. In the night, they rumbled and thundered with the rage I felt in my own heart at this cruel separation. The very temple shook upon the hillside. Daggers of lightning stabbed at it from the sky and it was as if they plunged into my breast. The pain was so intense, I shrieked aloud. The heavens burst and the rains poured down. Poured and poured, tumbling out of the black sky, down the mountains into the valleys. Poured onto the temple, onto its roofs and courtyards, the cell of my sorrow becoming flooded thereby. I stood in the water, wailing, my clothes drenched and my wet hair streaming about my shivering body. Am I to drown in sorrow? I wailed. Have I come so far only to die?

He heard me, my Lord and my Beloved. The door was flung wide and He stood there in his saffron robes, bearing in his hand a lantern that gilded his face with gold. He stood there in the light of that lantern of love, golden as a rose, golden as a lotus. Seeing Him, I cried: O, you have come to save me!

He said no word but placed his arm about my shoulders and, drawing me to him, led me out. The lantern waved in the storm, the waters rose to engulf us, but as we stepped into the deluge the rains ceased, the clouds parted, the moon appeared and the storm was stilled. Peace reigned, complete and utter peace. He spoke. 'You will come and live with me within my ashram,' and by the light of the washed and silver moon, we crossed the courtyard and entered his Abode.

Here I dwell now where I was always meant to dwell and where I resolve to live, never leaving His side, His true Devotee and Lover.

❧Epilogue❧

Matteo has left. He is not at the hospital, he has been gone for some time and no one can tell Sophie where he went. She stands confused in the corridor. The urgency to see Matteo, to tell and reveal, had so overtaken her, she had not thought that for Matteo, too, the wheel had turned.

In silence she returns to the rickshaw and makes the journey to the ashram where she had not thought she would need to go again. She finds herself fighting panic as she approaches it, walks through the gates and down the paths that lead through the gardens. She realises she had hoped she would not have to confront Matteo here, on his own territory, but very quickly she sees that here too is a scene of endings and departures.

As she walks through the gate, which is standing open, and down the garden paths, she senses abandonment and loss in the air; everything is left hanging loosely, no longer held together and cared for. There are flowers in the beds still, but wilted, unwatered, and fruit on the trees, but unpicked, left to rot. Many of the cottages seem to be deserted: there is no washing hanging around them, no children playing.

Sophie finds she does not want to go into the hut where she lived once with Matteo and the children. Instead she makes her way slowly to the dispensary in the hope of finding Montu-da there, busy with his pills and powders. But already from a distance she can tell it is shut – no one is waiting on the veranda for their medicines.

So she must go to the Abode of Bliss after all. And it is here that she finds others, sitting crosslegged in the shade of the trees, meditating by the *samadhi* on which flowers are still placed. Their faces are intent and concentrated.

Seeing her appear between the hedges, Diya gets to her feet and, raising her hands to her eyes as if she cannot believe what she sees, comes hurrying to Sophie and puts her arms around her. 'Sophie, Sophie,' she cries, 'oh, Sophie, you have come. But the Mother is dead and Matteo has left, Sophie. He was here but he is gone.'

They sink down onto the ground by the hedge together, holding each other closely. Diya tells Sophie how the Mother died, how Matteo received the news in hospital, how he came back to the ashram and spent days and nights lying on the gravel by her *samadhi* – there it was, freshly whitewashed and garlanded, beside the Master's.

'We thought he would die, Sophie. He wouldn't eat, or drink, and he wept so much. We didn't know what to do. No one knew. Then he just got up one day and told us he would travel north to the mountains where the Mother received enlightenment, and he left. No one could stop him. We didn't think we should stop him. Perhaps over there he will find peace.' She strokes Sophie's hair as Sophie sits with her head bent over her knees, grey-faced with fatigue.

After a while Diya persuades Sophie to come with her to her hut. She starts to cook food for her – no one eats communally any more, those who remain look after themselves. They sit making a pretence of eating, and then Diya spreads some bedding on the floor and urges Sophie to lie down and sleep. Diya has always been good to Sophie and Matteo, and she has loved their children – she still sends them cards on which she pastes coloured chocolate paper and small photographs of the Mother which they greatly prize.

Turning out the light, she stretches herself beside Sophie. The room swelters with the day's accumulated heat; they are pressed down by it as by a thick and heavy cover that makes it difficult to breathe.

After a while Diya asks, 'Where did you go, Sophie? We tried to send you news but no one knew where you were.'

Sophie is staring into the dark. Through dry lips she tells Diya, 'I went on a long journey. I went to find out the truth about the Mother.'

'What did you find?' whispers Diya.

'Nothing much.'

'It doesn't matter,' Diya comforts her. 'Not a bit.'

'I suppose not.'

They are both silent for such a long time, they might have fallen asleep. But then Diya is heard whispering again. 'What will you do now, Sophie?' she asks. 'Will you follow him?'

Sophie is lying as still as a stone, with an arm across her eyes, thinking in the dark of that first pilgrimage she went on in India that had ended in the death of a child. Now she knows why the mother went on that pilgrimage, why anyone goes on a pilgrimage, and why she must go too. She says in a flat voice, 'I'll have to,' and adds, 'what else?'

~

Grandfather is sitting on his chair under the lamp, half asleep, but not able to go up to bed till the clock on the stairs has struck ten. His eyelids droop low and he has so far given up the pretence of reading as to take off his spectacles and sit with his fingers pinched to the bridge of his nose with an expression of agonised weariness.

Everyone knows he must wait for the deep, harsh hum to start up in the heart of the clock till it finally gathers enough momentum to spit out the hours in short, rasping coughs – and then he will be free.

Ten o'clock, but outside there is still light, the trees and shrubs float like bluish daubs, accretions of shadow, without substance, in its opalescent pallor. Low over the grass a late swallow skims lightly, cutting through the blueness, and disappears. In the distance an owl is calling, in such a deep voice as if it means to frighten small children and send them running home to bed.

Then Giacomo enters the room, his face white as the petunia in a pot outside the door. He is breathing heavily as he does when he has an asthma attack coming on, and it makes Grandfather drop his hand and stare at him.

'Are you not in bed, Giacomo?' he asks, surprised at this breach of routine. He looks around to see if Grandmother is not there to re-establish it.

Giacomo does not answer. He walks towards his grandfather and stands very stiffly at his knee, staring into his face as if about to make a confession. The old man puts out a freckled hand to stroke the boy's head and that makes Giacomo crumple. He sinks onto the floor at his grandfather's feet and bends over his slippers, his head on his knee.

'Is it not time for bed, Giacomo?' Grandfather repeats, and now the clock is striking – both its harsh whirring and its tinny coughs proceeding out of the stiff upright clock on the stairs like the voice of authority asserting itself.

Giacomo answers by pressing his face into his grandfather's trousered leg. He sits in the attitude of a frightened animal, and Grandfather can feel how tense he is.

'What is it, my boy?' he asks.

'I saw my father,' Giacomo says at last, into the flannelled trouser.

Grandfather was about to stroke his head but now his hand is halted in mid-air, uncertainly.

'I saw my father,' the boy repeats.

'Where?'

'In the garden.'

'Where in the garden?'

'He came out of the hedge as I was going up the hill to look at the owl's nest.'

'And – how – what?'

'He stepped out and stood there, waiting for me.'

'And?'

'And I went to him. He was very thin. He was wearing no clothes, Nonno.'

Grandfather is gripping Giacomo by his shoulders now. He shakes him angrily. 'What are you saying? You are talking rubbish, you know.'

'No, he was wearing just a white cloth, tied like an apron. No shoes. Nothing else.'

'Nothing else? Don't be a fool, boy. That wasn't your father.'

'Then who was he?' Giacomo wails, raising to his grandfather a face blurred with tears. 'He smiled at me. He said Giacomo, Giacomo –'

'You heard him?'

'Yes, Nonno. He said Giacomo –'

Grandfather gives his shoulder another shake. 'Rubbish, boy, rubbish. Do you take him for a parrot?'

'Then he said – but I don't know what he said,' Giacomo wails. The clock has stopped striking, the house is filled with silence into which falls the sound of someone thumping down the stairs.

Grandfather gives him a little push. 'It's all rubbish,' he says angrily. 'You've learnt to make up stories like a girl. A fine thing. Inventing all these lies. Your grandmother needs to give you a good smacking.'

Giacomo is crying into his knees. 'I don't know what he *said*,' he repeats. 'He talks – like a foreigner.'

Grandmother hurries in, tightening the cord around her dressing gown and looking grey with sleep and suspicion at the same time. 'What's the boy doing here? What are you crying for, Giacomo? Why aren't you in bed?'

Grandfather answers for him. 'He's come to me with a pack of lies. Spends all his time inventing stories.'

'What's this? What's this?' Grandmother pulls Giamono to his feet. 'What's he saying?'

'He says he saw his father.'

Nonna stares fiercely into Grandfather's face and then into Giacomo's. 'No, you did not.'

Giacomo nods and tears fly off his cheeks. 'I did, Nonna. In the garden. He called me and he said – but he talks like a foreigner and I couldn't understand, Nonna.'

'And then?'

'And then he went away.'

'Where?'

'I don't know,' Giacomo cries, and flings himself at his grandmother's soft woollen middle. 'I don't know.'

She pushes him away. 'Get to bed, boy. Get to bed at once.'

Isabel emerges from under the duvet at the sound of the door opening. It is dark now but against the white wall by the door, she sees Giacomo standing.

She draws up her knees to her chest and lies against the pillow, looking at him. 'If Nonna hears you –' she warns.

Giacomo tiptoes up to her, setting the floorboards creaking. He stands then, not looking at her lying against her pillows but at the window behind her bed, as if looking at someone in the silent garden.

She reaches out her hand and pulls at him till he sits down on the edge of her bed. 'Now tell me, where did you go?' she asks, and her voice sounds very like her grandmother's, it is so prim and censorious.

When he does not reply but continues to stare, she gives his wrist a pinch.

It makes him talk. 'I went up the hill to look for the owl,' he says. 'You know, it lives in the wall by the pine tree –'

'And did you see it?' Isabel asks in her grown-up voice, not really interested.

'No,' says Giacomo, 'but I saw Father.'

Isabel flings away his hand in contempt. 'You are a liar, Giacomo.'

'I am not lying. I saw Father.'

'Oh, so you saw Father,' she mimics in a mocking tone. 'And what did he do – give you chocolate, I suppose?'

'No. He had nothing. Not even shoes. He was barefoot. And –'

'And?'

'He had no clothes.'

Isabel gives a whoop and slaps his knee playfully. This is

play after all, not serious. Her legs unfold, bare under the duvet. She grins at Giacomo's joke. 'And – what did you see?'

'Nothing. He had a white cloth tied around his waist, like an apron,' Giacomo tells her, 'and he was very thin.'

'Yes, Father *is* thin,' Isabel agrees, wanting to join in the joke. 'And what did he do?'

'I said – Father, and I went to him, and he said, Giacomo, Giacomo –'

'Oh, like that?' Isabel mocks. 'Like an owl? Perhaps it *was* the owl.'

Giacomo looks down at her at last. 'He spoke to me but I couldn't understand him.'

'Father mumbles,' Isabel agrees. She likes to pretend she remembers him.

'No, he didn't mumble. He spoke very clearly – but in a foreign language.'

Isabel's eyes look blurred. 'Father can speak many languages,' she says, bored.

'But I couldn't understand. Then he went away – and *I don't know what he said*,' he wails in spite of himself.

'Don't be a baby,' Isabel says serenely.

'I'm not –'

'You are. You're crying like a baby.' She grasps his arm and tugs. 'Lie down here and be quiet, you baby,' she orders him, and shifts to make room.

He unfolds himself upon her sheets but will not come under her duvet which she holds up invitingly. He lies stretched out straight, his hands folded on his chest. 'Father has a beard,' he remembers. 'He looked like the painting of Jesus in church.'

Isabel edges close to him, her knees hunched, touching him with them. 'Perhaps it *was* Jesus,' she teases.

'Perhaps,' he sighs sadly, and suddenly yawns.

She does not want him to sleep. She puts out her finger, digging him in the ribs, and sets about tickling him till he laughs.

ACKNOWLEDGEMENTS

I wish to acknowledge my debt to the following books for much of the material of my novel:

The Mother by Wilfried, Sri Aurobindo Society, Pondicherry, 1988; *Mother's Chronicles* (I – *Mirra*; II – *Mirra the Artist*; III – *Mirra the Occultist*) by Sujata Nahar, Institut de Recherches Evolutives, Paris, 1985; *Divine Dancer, Ruth St Denis* by Suzanne Shelton, Doubleday & Company Inc, 1981; *An Unfinished Life*, Ruth St Denis, Harper & Brothers, 1936.

I have also drawn upon the following for information and instruction:

Iravati Karve's essay 'On the Road' in *The Experience of Hinduism*, ed. Eleanor Zelliott & Maxine Berntsen, State University of New York Press, Albany, New York, 1988; *Autobiography of a Yogi* by Paramahansa Yogananda, Jaico Publishing House, Bombay, 1985; *Hidden Journey* by Andrew Harvey, Henry Holt & Co, New York, 1991; *The Thousand-Petalled Lotus* by Maha Sthavira Sangharakshita (aka D.P.E. Lingwood), Heinemann, London, 1976; *My Guru and His Disciple* by Christopher Isherwood, Eyre Methuen, London, 1980; *The Ochre Robe* by Swami Agehananda Bharati (aka Leopold Fischer), Allen & Unwin, London, 1961; *Confessions of a Sannyasi* by Mukunda, Atlantic Publishers & Distributors, New Delhi, 1988; *Flowers of Emptiness* by Sally Belfrage, The

Dial Press, New York, 1981; *Siddhartha* and *The Journey to the East* by Hermann Hesse, translated by Hilda Rosner, Peter Owen Ltd, 1954, 1956; *Flight of the Swan* by Andre Oliveroff, E.P. Dutton & Co, Inc, New York, 1932; *Inayat Khan* by Elisabeth de Jong-Keesing, East-West Publications, The Hague, 1974; *The Mystics, Ascetics, and Saints of India* by John Campbell-Oman, T. Fisher-Unwin, London, 1903; *The Gospel of Sri Ramakrishna*, translated into English by Swami Nikhilananda, Ramakrishna-Vivekananda Center, New York, 1977; *The Other Mind* by Beryl de Zoete, Victor Gollancz, London, 1953; *Indian Dancing* by Ram Gopal & Serozh Dadachanji, Phoenix House Ltd, London, 1951; *Dances of the Golden Hall* by Ashok Chatterjee, Indian Council for Cultural Relations, New Delhi, 1979; *Forbidden Journey, the Life of Alexandra David-Neel* by Barbara and Michael Foster, Harper & Row, San Francisco, 1987; *A Mystic Link with India, Life Story of Two Pilgrim Painters of Hungary* by R.K. Raju, Allied Publishers Ltd, New Delhi, 1991; articles by Joan L. Erdman in *Bansuri, The Drama Review, Selected Reports in Ethnomusicology* and the collection *Arts Patronage in India: Methods, Motives and Markets*, edited by her and published by Manohar Publications, New Delhi, 1992; the paintings of Nicholas and Svetoslav Roerich, Elisabeth Brunner and Edward Hopper; and information on education in Egypt provided by Carolyn Berkey.

Special thanks to the Rockefeller Foundation Center in Bellagio, Italy, where I started work on this book in March 1992.

Anita Desai

A NOTE ON THE TYPE

The text of this book was set in Bembo, a facsimile of a typeface cut by Francesco Griffo for Aldus Manutius, the celebrated Venetian printer, in 1495. The face was named for Pietro Cardinal Bembo, the author of the small treatise entitled *De Ætna* in which it first appeared. Through the research of Stanley Morison, it is now generally acknowledged that all oldstyle type designs up to the time of William Caslon can be traced to the Bembo cut.

The present-day version of Bembo was introduced by the Monotype Corporation of London in 1929. Sturdy, well balanced, and finely proportioned, Bembo is a face of rare beauty and great legibility in all of its sizes.

FOR THE BEST IN PAPERBACKS, LOOK FOR THE

In every corner of the world, on every subject under the sun, Penguin represents quality and variety—the very best in publishing today.

For complete information about books available from Penguin—including Puffins, Penguin Classics, and Arkana—and how to order them, write to us at the appropriate address below. Please note that for copyright reasons the selection of books varies from country to country.

In the United Kingdom: Please write to *Dept. JC, Penguin Books Ltd, FREEPOST, West Drayton, Middlesex UB7 0BR.*

If you have any difficulty in obtaining a title, please send your order with the correct money, plus ten percent for postage and packaging, to *P.O. Box No. 11, West Drayton, Middlesex UB7 0BR*

In the United States: Please write to *Consumer Sales, Penguin USA, P.O. Box 999, Dept. 17109, Bergenfield, New Jersey 07621-0120.* VISA and MasterCard holders call 1-800-253-6476 to order all Penguin titles

In Canada: Please write to *Penguin Books Canada Ltd, 10 Alcorn Avenue, Suite 300, Toronto, Ontario M4V 3B2*

In Australia: Please write to *Penguin Books Australia Ltd, P.O. Box 257, Ringwood, Victoria 3134*

In New Zealand: Please write to *Penguin Books (NZ) Ltd, Private Bag 102902, North Shore Mail Centre, Auckland 10*

In India: Please write to *Penguin Books India Pvt Ltd, 706 Eros Apartments, 56 Nehru Place, New Delhi 110 019*

In the Netherlands: Please write to *Penguin Books Netherlands bv, Postbus 3507, NL-1001 AH Amsterdam*

In Germany: Please write to *Penguin Books Deutschland GmbH, Metzlerstrasse 26, 60594 Frankfurt am Main*

In Spain: Please write to *Penguin Books S. A., Bravo Murillo 19, 1° B, 28015 Madrid*

In Italy: Please write to *Penguin Italia s.r.l., Via Felice Casati 20, I-20124 Milano*

In France: Please write to *Penguin France S. A., 17 rue Lejeune, F–31000 Toulouse*

In Japan: Please write to *Penguin Books Japan, Ishikiribashi Building, 2–5–4, Suido, Bunkyo-ku, Tokyo 112*

In Greece: Please write to *Penguin Hellas Ltd, Dimocritou 3, GR–106 71 Athens*

In South Africa: Please write to *Longman Penguin Southern Africa (Pty) Ltd, Private Bag X08, Bertsham 2013*